FORTRESS FALLING

A Moon Brothers WWII Adventure
By
William Peter Grasso

Novels by William Peter Grasso:

Jock Miles-Moon Brothers Korean War Story
Combat Ineffective, *Book 1*
Combat Reckoning, *Book 2*

Moon Brothers WWII Adventure Series
Moon Above, Moon Below, *Book 1*
Fortress Falling, *Book 2*
Our Ally, Our Enemy, *Book 3*
This Fog of Peace, *Book 4*

Jock Miles WW2 Adventure Series
Long Walk to the Sun, *Book 1*
Operation Long Jump, *Book 2*
Operation Easy Street, *Book 3*
Operation Blind Spot, *Book 4*
Operation Fishwrapper, *Book 5*

Unpunished

East Wind Returns

Cover design by Alyson Aversa

Fortress Falling is a work of historical fiction. Events that are
common historical knowledge may not occur at their actual point in
time or may not occur at all. Apart from the well-known actual
people, events, and locales that figure in the narrative, all names,
characters, places, and incidents are products of the author's
imagination and are used fictitiously. Any resemblance to current
events or locales or to living persons is purely coincidental.

Author's Note

This is a fictional work of alternative history, not a history textbook. Deviations from commonly accepted historical facts are intentional and provided only for the purposes of entertainment and stimulating the reader's imagination.

The fortress city of Metz was, in actual history, a roadblock to the progress of Patton's 3rd Army from September through December of 1944. Fort Driant, an amazingly well-fortified artillery base, became the linchpin in the efforts to stop the Americans' rapid advance. Built in 1902 for a very different type of warfare and seemingly obsolete, it nonetheless denied Patton avenues of access to the city and prevented his army from crossing the Moselle River in force. The fort itself was never taken by direct military action. Instead, its small garrison finally surrendered once it was isolated and its situation made hopeless.

Operation Aphrodite was, in actual history, a US Army Air Forces attempt to use the new technologies of television and radio control to crash unmanned bombers laden with enormous amounts of explosives into targets of strategic significance. From summer of 1944 through early 1945, the Air Force flew thirteen Aphrodite missions. None hit their targets; technical faults, anti-aircraft fire, and operator error were to blame. The US Navy conducted two missions as part of an associated effort known as Project Anvil. Neither of these missions were successful, either, the first causing the death of Lt. Joe Kennedy, Jr. and his co-pilot when their aircraft exploded shortly after takeoff.

Note: in actual history, an Operation Aphrodite flying bomb was not used in conjunction with the Metz campaign.

The designation of military units may be actual or fictitious.

In no way are the fictional accounts intended to denigrate the hardships, suffering, and courage of those who served.

Contact the Author Online
Email: *wpgrasso@cox.net*

Connect with the Author on Facebook:
https://www.facebook.com/AuthorWilliamPeterGrasso

Follow the Author on Amazon:
https://amazon.com/author/williampetergrasso

Dedication

To those who scale the walls others choose to build.

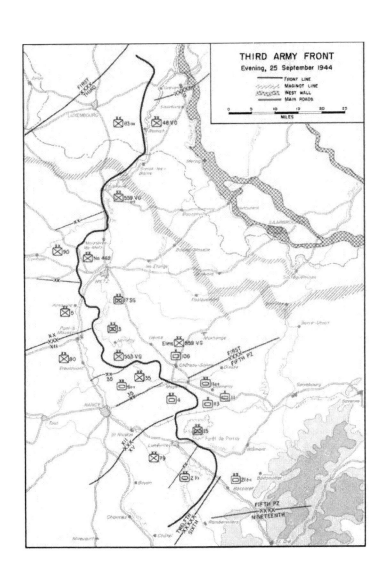

THIRD ARMY FRONT
Evening, 25 September 1944

FRONT LINE
MAGINOT LINE
WEST WALL
MAIN ROADS

0   5   10   15   20   25
MILES

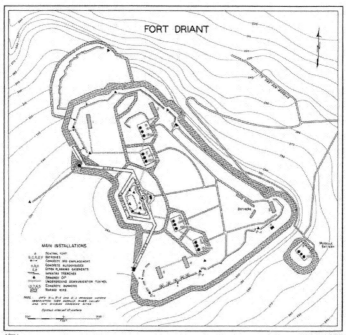

FORT DRIANT

MAP NO. XXIII

Chapter One

12 August 1944

1730 hours

"You really think she's gonna fly, Mr. Kennedy?" the mechanic asked. "She's awful heavy for a *war-weary* bird."

The question put a smile on the face of Lieutenant Joe Kennedy, Jr., USN. "She'll fly just fine," he replied. "It's where she lands that's going to matter." His broad Bostonian *a* in *matter* made it sound like another word entirely: *maaada*.

The mathematics of flying or not flying was on Joe Kennedy's side. He'd flown plenty of PB4Y-1 patrol bombers—the Navy's designation for the Army's B-24 *Liberator* heavy bomber—just like this one on those seemingly endless antisubmarine patrols from Great Britain over the Atlantic. Those four-engined monsters, laden with ordnance and full of fuel for missions that could take up to ten hours, had takeoff weights just as heavy as this machine. And being *war-weary* didn't mean she couldn't fly, just that she no longer met all the stringent standards for a combat plane and it would cost too much to make her so. *Uneconomical to repair*, in government lingo.

But Kennedy knew the cause of the mechanic's concern: it was *how* this plane had come to achieve that takeoff weight. On a standard patrol, three-quarters of the useful load—almost 15,000 pounds—was fuel;

bombs and depth charges made up the remaining 5,000 pounds. The *baby* Kennedy and his co-pilot were about to take up, however, was carrying 21,170 pounds of the highly potent Torpex explosive for her payload. To permit the weight of all this destructive power, she'd been stripped of her defensive armament and non-essential equipment and would carry only two pilots as crew, not the usual ten-man complement. The pilots would only be on board long enough to get her off the ground, fly her to 2,000 feet, confirm the remote control was functioning properly, and arm the explosives. Then they'd bail out over the English countryside. There was a minimal fuel load in her tanks since she didn't have to fly very far, just across the English Channel into coastal France.

The *baby* wouldn't be coming back. This would be a one-way mission. Her final one. The reason: she wasn't a B-24 or PB4Y anymore. Her new designation was BQ-8: a radio-controlled bomb.

"You know, Mr. Kennedy," the mechanic said, "it would be really something if this remote-control stuff was good enough to do the takeoff, too."

"Wouldn't that be great?" the lieutenant replied, genuine in his agreement. "But we'd have to evacuate half of Norfolk to be on the safe side. *Project Anvil* still has a way to go on that score, I'm afraid. In the meantime, the least dangerous way to do this is to have a human pilot get her up in the air."

They looked up to the sound of aircraft engines overhead. Three twin-engined planes were doing lazy orbits over the airfield. Two of them—Navy PV-1 Ventura *motherships*—carried the radio-control transmitters and their operators. The third—an F-8

Mosquito photo recon ship from 8th Air Force—would film the mission and provide damage assessment of the flying bomb's strike.

"Looks like they're ready to rendezvous," Kennedy said as he ducked to enter the open bomb bay. "I'd better get the star of the show up there with them."

He climbed up to the cockpit. It was swirling with furious activity as three bickering civilian engineers struggled with one of the television cameras installed in the BQ-8. The co-pilot—another Navy lieutenant named John Williams—was already in the right-hand seat, trying to ignore the chaos in the cramped space around him and focus on the pre-start checklist.

The camera, one of two on board, was the one that relayed the flight instrument data to the motherships. The other was mounted in the glazed nose and provided a view forward of the aircraft. When she was in her terminal descent, that camera would—hopefully—be painting a clear image of the target on the motherships' monitors.

"You lads almost done?" Kennedy asked the engineers. The impatience in his voice was impossible to ignore.

"The video was all washed out," the lead engineer replied. "We had to bring the gain up and—"

A second engineer interrupted him. "I'm telling you, Frank, the gain's up too damn far. The contrast on the ground image when she's upstairs will be so strong the controllers won't be able to make out any target details at all."

The third engineer chimed in. "We need to change out the camera. This'll never—"

Joe Kennedy had had enough. "Hold it, gentlemen,"

he said. "This isn't a debate club. Is your system ready to go or not?"

All three engineers began to talk at once, a jumble of impassioned but disparate opinions. Kennedy broke in: "Let's just hear from the boss, okay?"

The lead engineer replied, "It's ready, Lieutenant. We'll get out of your way."

"That's good to hear," Kennedy replied, "because we're running out of daylight. If we don't get her in the air soon, it'll be too dark over France for your camera to see a blessed thing, anyway."

He slid into the left-hand seat as the engineers gathered their tools and co-pilot Williams waited for the *clear to start engines* signal from the ramp.

"It'll be another minute or two before we're clear," Kennedy said. "There are still a lot of vehicles around the ship." He tapped the fuel quantity gauges with his fingertips, trying to make sure their pointers weren't stuck. He'd never before taken off with so little fuel on board. Thinking you had fuel you didn't could result in running a tank dry and losing one or more of your engines, a *crash and burn* mistake of epic proportions. She'd never take off, climb, or even hold altitude on anything less than all four engines.

Williams asked, "You did watch them stick the tanks, didn't you?"

"Yeah, I did. But like the crew chief said, *it's hard to get an accurate reading with a dipstick when the tank's nowhere near full to begin with*."

"So those gauges are right, Joe?"

"They'd better be."

The thought occurred to Kennedy that neither he nor Williams needed to be in this cockpit. They were both

4

highly experienced pilots and had already chalked up enough combat missions to go home. But both had volunteered to stay on for *Project Anvil*, the US Navy's contribution to *Operation Aphrodite*, the American attempt to match the explosive power of the British six-ton *blockbusters* dropped from Lancaster bombers. Lacking an aircraft capable of lifting such a bomb load, the only American solution seemed to be turning war-weary heavy bombers into radio-controlled missiles. They were just going to be scrapped, anyway. Even though the radio-control technology was far from perfected yet, why not *scrap* those planes while they were destroying some key German targets in the process? There was no way either of these pilots would miss the chance to crew this flight—*Anvil's* inaugural mission—which would target a suspected launch site in occupied France for German missiles falling on Britain.

Joe Kennedy, Jr. not only didn't need to be in this cockpit, he didn't need to be in this uniform. The scion of one of America's wealthiest and influential families, his father had brashly predicted that Joe Junior would one day be the first Irish-Catholic President of the United States. There were any number of ways politically connected young men like him and his younger brother Jack could've stayed in safe, cushy desk jobs or avoided military service entirely. But both had taken commissions in the US Navy and volunteered for combat duty.

In a world where the term usually meant you were unlucky enough to have been within sight of someone looking for men to do undesirable jobs, Joe Kennedy and John Williams were true volunteers. They were in that cockpit of their own free will.

They got the *clear to start* signal. As each engine rumbled to life in turn, a voice over the radio—one of the pilots of a mothership loitering overhead—said, "C'mon, already, you guys. We're burning gas like crazy up here...and we're gonna lose the sun pretty damn soon."

"Tell them to keep their drawers on," Kennedy said to Williams as the taxi-out began. "The *baby's* on her way."

Turning onto the runway, they noticed every vehicle on the airfield hurrying to get as far from the BQ-8's takeoff run as they could. "They aren't dumb," Kennedy quipped. "They know what'll happen if we fuck up this takeoff."

Even with the throttles to the stops, it seemed to take forever for the lumbering beast to get up a head of steam. "Halfway mark," Williams said, his voice tense as they roared past the point beyond which aborting the takeoff was no longer possible. They *had* to fly now.

But the ship didn't seem convinced of that necessity. Kennedy's eyes were fixed on the trees at the runway's end. They loomed larger with each passing second, like a wall his ship lacked the energy to scale.

Precious yards of runway slipped beneath her wheels, but she still wasn't at flying speed. "One-ten," Williams called out, his eyes dancing from the airspeed indicator to the runway's end. It didn't take much estimating to realize that at their sluggish rate of acceleration, they'd probably never reach the 120 miles per hour needed to lift off before hitting the trees.

They were down to the last thousand feet of runway. "One-twelve...no, one-thirteen," Williams said.

"Never mind," Kennedy said, "I've got no damned

choice." He pulled back hard on the yoke, the heavy control forces fighting him every inch of the way.

Her nose reluctantly pitched up, freeing the nose wheel from the grip of the runway. But the rumble and jostling of the takeoff roll continued—her main wheels were still firmly stuck to the ground.

Williams grabbed his control yoke and pulled back with Kennedy, as if the urgings of two men on the controls might coax her into the air. But it made little difference.

C'mon, you son of a bitch...

It was no use. She wouldn't fly; they were sure of it now. The ten tons of explosives on board would very shortly be obliterating them and the Norfolk woods, not a German missile site.

They were already bracing themselves for the inevitable impact with the trees—one hand still pulling back on the yoke, the other outstretched against the glareshield—when the miracle of physics happened.

The rumble and jostling of the takeoff roll stopped. She was slipping through the air as if held up by the angels. She wasn't climbing very quickly, but at least she was flying.

"Unbelievable," was all Joe Kennedy could say. "Probably got a branch or two stuck in the undercarriage, for sure."

It wouldn't matter, though, because she'd never land on her wheels again.

After ten minutes of a tortuously slow climb, they reached 2,000 feet. Kennedy gingerly removed his hands from the yoke and throttles as a controller in the lead mothership attempted to take control. He and Williams breathed a sigh of relief as the *baby* held her attitude and heading.

The controller put the BQ-8 through a gentle turn, which went without a hitch. Then he pitched her down a few degrees, letting the speed build a little before advancing the throttles for the climb back to 2,000 feet.

"Looks like we've got a winner here," Williams radioed to the mothership. "We're moving on to Phase Two."

Phase Two: arming the explosives. There really wasn't much to it; just operate several switches. The triggering circuit for the Torpex would then be active.

Joe Kennedy hesitated for just a moment. An impassioned plea from one of the ordnance technicians flashed through his mind. *I don't think that system's safe, Mr. Kennedy*, the tech had said. *There's just too many ways for it to glitch. A short circuit, a little leakage in a fusing mechanism, radio interference...*

With all due respect, Mr. Kennedy, you're crazy to want to fly that thing. Too much room for error. Waaaay too much room.

He shrugged it off. The tech had a reputation in the squadron as a habitual worrywart, a *Chicken Little* who thought the sky was always falling.

If you listened to people like that, Kennedy told himself, *you'd never accomplish anything in this life.*

He threw the first switch.

One of the mothership pilots finally broke the moments of stunned silence: "What the fuck just happened?"

Joe Kennedy's plane had vaporized in a blinding

flash. There was nothing left of her but a huge cloud of smoke that rained smoldering fragments of what had once been the BQ-8 on the English countryside below.

Frantic controllers on the motherships, though still not quite believing what had happened, checked their equipment again and again as if it—or perhaps *they*—had somehow caused the explosion.

When the radio report was made to mission headquarters, it was met with the typically ridiculous questions offered by those who could not—or would not—grasp the severity of the incident.

The first ridiculous question: "Is the baby still flying?"

"Negative. Repeat—negative. The baby has disintegrated."

The second question: "Are there any parachutes?"

"Negative. Not possible. No chutes."

It finally dawned on Headquarters that they had a disaster on their hands. Their first instinct was exactly what GIs of all ranks had come to expect from the brass: obscure the truth for as long as possible. All personnel were ordered to maintain radio silence regarding the incident.

But they couldn't hide the obvious for very long: Project Anvil was off to a disastrous start.

Chapter Two

30 September 1944

0800 hours

Lieutenant Tommy "Half" Moon was running out of time. He banked his P-47 Thunderbolt hard left, trying to get a better view over his wing of the French terrain 8,000 feet below. But the low, broken cloud deck was making it difficult to find his target. If he didn't locate Fort Driant and attack it in the next five minutes, the four-plane section he led would have to clear the airspace; it would then be the artillery's turn to pummel the fort. The Thunderbolts—*jugs* in US Army slang— would have to find someplace else to dispose of the napalm beneath their wings...

And the ground-pounders will think we're letting them down again, Tommy thought. *True, we haven't been much help the last couple of weeks, but it's been the damn weather's fault, not ours.*

Or maybe they'd rather we bomb them by accident because we couldn't see shit? Like that hasn't happened a thousand times before.

At least I'm back in the cockpit again, where I belong. That six weeks I was grounded with a broken arm was a real pain in my ass.

He checked the clock on his ship's instrument panel. It had clicked off another thirty seconds since the last time he looked.

Cutting it real close...

The only landmark he could see clearly through the clouds was a bend in the Moselle River. But it was so easy to mistake one bend in a river for another and be miles from where you thought you were. Fort Driant was just west of the river and about two and a half miles southwest of the city of Metz.

But I can't see the damn city right now, either. Nothing but clouds. It's got to be to my north...or am I looking the wrong way?

Tommy still found it hard to accept that now, in the middle of the twentieth century, the US Army was attacking nineteenth century forts—and failing miserably at it. Two rings of forts protected the ancient city of Metz and the frontier of Germany beyond, and the mutually supporting fire from the turret guns of those forts had stopped Patton's 3rd Army in its tracks.

Tommy Moon's squadron—the 301st—had been attacking the forts of Metz for the past few days with high-explosive bombs to no apparent effect.

It was like the sons of bitches bounced right off all that thick concrete and steel. Maybe if we can get this napalm on target and some of it runs down the ventilation shafts into the heart of the fort, we can burn the Krauts out. The intel people say Fort Driant's the key: if we can knock her out, we can steamroll past the other ones.

Another thirty seconds had ticked off the clock before Tommy got the break he needed. Through a hole in the clouds, he could see Fort Driant, its outline like a misshapen gray bell in a greenish-brown sea, an anachronism of concrete and steel burrowed into commanding terrain. Tommy's four *jugs—Blue Flight—* would have just enough time for one dive-bombing run before the artillery barrage began.

"*Blue Leader* to *Blue Flight*," Tommy said over the radio, "target identified. We get one shot. Drop it all. On me, out of the north. Escape heading is one-eight-zero. Here we go."

He rolled his plane—named *Eclipse of the Hun II*—on her back and started the steep dive. As he did, the voices of his three pilots acknowledged in sequence, each with a simple *Roger*.

It took hardly a minute for *Eclipse* to plummet from 8,000 feet to the release point at 3,000 feet. The pullout from the dive took her down to 1,500 feet before she sprinted away in level flight, clear of the incoming artillery rounds.

At least there's been no serious flak around here, Tommy told himself, *so it'd be a damn shame to get knocked down by your own artillery.*

He wasn't sure why they were bothering to bombard the fort with artillery at all. They'd been doing it for days and, just like the Air Force's bombing, hadn't hurt the Metz forts much, if at all. But Tommy had a theory: *They're probably just doing it so the Krauts will keep their heads down while our infantry's moving in.*

Blue Flight was re-forming a few miles to the south as the last plane to drop its napalm—*Blue Four*—reported, "It's burning like a son of a bitch, y'all. Great drop."

There was no doubt he was right. It *had* to be burning *like a son of a bitch*, because that's all napalm did: it burned, and burned ferociously. The question was whether or not the flaming jellied gasoline had worked its way down into the bowels of the fort. If it hadn't, the raging fire on Fort Driant's roof was nothing more than a spectacular but ineffective sideshow. If it had, the fort's vast underground chambers were being transformed into crematories, with the fires sucking the oxygen from the enclosed corridors, forcing those not already incinerated to the surface.

Whether dead or alive, the Germans inside the fort already knew the answer to that question. The next ones to know would be the American infantrymen who'd try and attack the fort shortly.

The napalm fires had burned themselves out, leaving behind a cloud of acrid black smoke that hung over Fort Driant like a shroud. The American artillery still rained down on the fort with great accuracy, pinpointing the infantry trenches and machine gun bunkers protecting its perimeter. Most of the rounds were fused for airbursts, intended to keep any German defenders not killed outright ducking for cover, just as Tommy Moon had suspected when he was hurrying to get his aircraft out of the artillery's way.

A battalion of American infantry from 5th Division—2nd Battalion of 2nd Infantry Regiment—was converging on the fort from the north and south. It had been relatively easy going so far; casualties had been light—only one man killed and a few wounded by machine guns which, once located, were silenced, at least temporarily, when an artillery forward observer shifted a volley onto the gunners' heads.

If an airman like Tommy Moon was having trouble accepting the idea of a fortress siege in the age of mobile warfare, it was nothing compared to the fear and incomprehension of the riflemen who actually had to conduct that siege. As they advanced slowly up the towering hill, they could see the thick belt of barbed wire encircling the fort at its peak like a crown of thorns. They wondered what was in store for them once the artillery clearing the way had to cease fire so they could set foot on the objective.

"What're they gonna do?" a GI wondered as he trudged reluctantly uphill. "Pour boiling oil down on us, like in them Errol Flynn movies?"

"I'm betting it'll be archers...with crossbows, maybe," another soldier wisecracked.

"Shut the hell up, both of you," their squad leader said. "This ain't no medieval castle. They're gonna shoot your ass with rifles and MGs, just like they've been doing since we set foot in this fucking country."

Still another GI asked, "At least the artillery's gonna slice that barbed wire up for us like cutting spaghetti, right, Sarge?"

"We'd better fucking hope so," the squad leader replied.

A platoon of GIs managed to sneak through the wire right in front of Fort Driant's central fortification, a diamond-shaped bastion hundreds of feet long. Its armored OPs were surrounded by a ditch wide and deep enough to swallow a tank. At the corners of the ditch, machine guns in concrete bunkers were laid to cut down anything trying to cross it.

If the GIs were going to get into the fort this way, they'd have to cross that deadly ditch. A bazooka rocket was launched against a machine gun bunker; it splattered against the structure with a feeble *thud*, dislodging nothing more than a tiny chip of concrete.

"Shit," the platoon leader said. "They sure as hell know we're here now. We'd better pull back and bring up the engineers. Maybe they can blow those things sky high."

But crossing the ditch would have to wait. At first the GIs thought the American artillery—which should have stopped firing—had accidentally been shifted onto them. "TURN IT OFF," a company commander screamed at his FO as he watched his men being cut down left and right.

The FO screamed back, "IT'S NOT OURS. IT'S THE KRAUTS."

The howitzers of Fort Driant couldn't touch the GIs; perched on the hill, they couldn't lower their barrels enough to put fire on the Americans. But her sister forts—*Verdun* two and a half miles to the southeast; *Jeanne d'Arc* three miles to the north—had no such problem. The Americans were learning the hard way just how mutually supporting the ring of forts around Metz truly were. Attack one fort, get clobbered by the cannon of a few others. The Germans inside Driant had no problems being shelled by their comrades; the forts, carved into hilltops, with their retractable steel gun turrets, hardened concrete blockhouses, and subterranean corridors, withstood German artillery just as easily as American.

The battalion commander's order for his men to withdraw wasn't really necessary. It merely put a legitimate face on what was already happening across his command. He tried to tell himself his GIs were making an orderly withdrawal.

But there was very little *order* in their retreat. It had the look and smell of a rout.

★★★★

There was no happy face to put on the end-of-mission debrief at 301st Fighter Squadron, either. The 3rd Army liaison officer—an arrogant major from Armor who probably thought *prop wash* was something that came in a fifty-five-gallon drum—had blunt words for the assembled pilots:

"General Patton is most unhappy with your ineffective attacks on Fort Driant, gentlemen," the major began. "The fort appears completely unimpaired. Its turret guns were firing on 5th Division positions less than a half hour after your napalm attack. You failed to get any napalm into the ventilation system, which was clearly identified in photo recon—"

Colonel Pruitt, commander of the 301st, interrupted. "Just a minute, Major. Nothing—I repeat, *nothing*—was clearly identified in those photos except the gun turrets and the above-ground structures. We dropped the napalm precisely where intel *thought* the ventilators *might* be. The mission footage will back me up on that." He gestured toward the large aerial photo of the fort hanging on the wall. "Now, if the general has someplace else on the premises he'd like us to drop the stuff, we're all ears."

"Please don't shoot the messenger, sir," the major replied, his tone less cocky than it was a minute ago but—typical of Patton's staffers—by no means apologetic. "I'm only here to relay the general's directive."

"Fine," Pruitt replied. "Get to the directive and spare the reprimand, Major. You haven't got enough shiny stuff on your collar to be chewing me and my men out."

Chastened, the major stepped up to the aerial photo of the fort. "Very well, Colonel. As I was trying to say, General Patton continues to believe the fort is very vulnerable, as are all static installations."

Tommy Moon found himself grumbling along with the rest of his fellow pilots. *Vulnerable, my ass*, he thought. *Hell, eighty-eight millimeter anti-aircraft guns are static installations, and they'll knock the living shit out of a jug. I guess this tanker forgot those same static eighty-eights can turn his tanks inside out, too.*

Ignoring the dissension in the room, the major pointed to Fort Driant's southernmost battery and said, "The ops order for tomorrow's missions will specify the following: the 301st Fighter Squadron will attack this one battery—designated *E* for *Easy*—with napalm. The G3 believes that if a fire can be started in the chambers below the turrets, the cook-off of the one hundred-fifty-millimeter ammunition in those chambers will devastate the fort's southern defenses as well as the bunkers connected to the battery by underground tunnels. That should allow our infantry an easy foothold within Driant's perimeter."

Tommy asked himself, *Ain't that convenient? The fort's got five batteries, labeled A through E, and we get the one called E for Easy. Is that some kind of sick joke?*

But he had a different question to ask out loud. "Sir, this squadron's been hitting Driant's turrets for days now with five hundred pounders, and the artillery's been doing the same with everything they've got. It hasn't hurt those turrets one bit. They just retract into the ground and seal up tighter than a drum. What makes Third Army think another dose of napalm's going to make any difference? All we're going to do is leave more scorch marks on the roof."

The two dozen assembled pilots murmured their agreement.

The major tried to fix Tommy in an intimidating gaze as he replied, "Lieutenant, you know how napalm is—it flows like oil but sticks like glue. We won't need to get much of it inside the fort—with all that ammo stored in those underground bunkers—to blow the top of that hill it's on right off."

His gaze hadn't intimidated Tommy or anyone else. His logic was equally unpersuasive.

Colonel Pruitt took back control of the debrief. "All right, gentlemen…get a good night's sleep, all of you. Briefing is at 0500. Be there, bright-eyed and bushy-tailed."

As the pilots filed out of the room, Pruitt motioned for Tommy to join him.

"How's the arm doing, *Half*?" the colonel asked.

Half: the nickname that would never leave a short man with a last name like Moon. He'd been called that his whole young life, way back to the streets of Canarsie in Brooklyn, and he'd long since come to the rationalization that it was better than so many other things he could be called. Like *Shorty* or *Tiny* or *PeeWee*. His fortuitous surname even made *Half Pint* a waste of words. *Half*—all by itself—fit the bill perfectly.

"The arm's swell, sir," Tommy replied. "Not giving me a bit of trouble."

"Very fine," Pruitt said. "I was worried you and the doc were rushing it a little…but I do need you up there. Tuttle gave it his best as *Blue Flight* leader while you were down, but I missed your—"

He hesitated for a moment, searching for just the right word, before concluding, "Let's just say I missed your good judgment."

Chapter Three

Blue Flight's number two pilot, Lieutenant Jimmy Tuttle, was in fresh khakis, ready for a night on the town, however short an 0500 briefing would force it to be. He asked Tommy, "Are you coming into Nancy with us, Half?"

"Nah, I think I'll stay here, catch up with the maintenance guys and study the charts for this area."

"You ain't still pining for that little French girl back at Alençon, are you?"

"I guess you could say I am, Jimmy," Tommy replied. "I'd rather be back there with her than touring the bars of Nancy any day."

"Suit yourself," Tuttle replied. "But I'm telling you, Half...this town's a whole lot hotter than Alençon ever was. Things have really been jumpin' since your brother's outfit blasted through here like a bat out of hell."

His brother: Staff Sergeant Sean Moon. Tank platoon sergeant in 4th Armored Division's 37th Tank Battalion, part of Patton's 3rd Army. A few years older than Tommy, a lot taller—

And still a whole lot tougher than me, Tommy told himself.

It had been only a matter of weeks since they were reunited at a field hospital. Tommy had fractured his arm when he hit the stabilizer bailing out of his shot-up plane, the original *Eclipse of the Hun*. Sean had survived his tank being blown up by a Luftwaffe bomb, an attack that killed two of his four crewmen. But it would take more than a concussion, sprains, and bruises to keep the veteran tanker away from the fight. Two days after they'd found each other at the hospital, Sean had given the doctors the slip and went right back into combat with the 37th. Tommy had only seen him once since, when he'd hitched a ride on a supply convoy headed to 4th Armored.

He'd gotten plenty of time with *the little French girl at Alençon*—Sylvie Bergerac—while his arm was mending and the squadron was still based there. But 3rd Army had moved steadily eastward, pushing the Germans across the battlefields of the last war toward the Fatherland, and XIX Tactical Air Command needed to stay close behind the ground forces on the tip of Patton's spear. Fuel had become precious as Allied bases and supply lines stretched almost completely across France; tactical support squadrons like the 301st couldn't be wasting it by having to fly their gas-guzzling aircraft hundreds of miles to get to the front lines.

So, two weeks ago, the 301st had closed up shop at Alençon and moved three hundred miles to a just-captured airfield at Toul, a few miles west of Nancy and only thirty miles southwest of Metz. And though this new airfield—called A-90 by the USAAF—would keep Tommy Moon far from Sylvie, at least he was only miles from his brother's unit.

And if he keeps managing to not get himself killed, Tommy thought, *maybe I'll get to see him now and then.*

✯✯✯✯

Sergeant Sean Moon was perched on the hatch ring of his M4 Sherman tank, listening in the quiet of this moonless night for the sound of German engines. The other three tanks of his platoon were dispersed and concealed on a tree-covered rise. It offered excellent fields of fire over the gentle terrain any German counterattack would have to cross. The dark shapes of the other Shermans had disappeared into the night a half hour ago.

"I don't like this shit," Sean's gunner Fabiano said. "We're stuck out here in the fucking dark with the Krauts on three sides of us. I think Colonel Abrams has lost his fucking mind."

"I beg to differ," Sean replied, his Brooklyn accent making this attempt at the *King's English* sound comical. "In case you haven't noticed, Fab, us guys of 37th Tank have been kicking Kraut ass left and right for the last two weeks. The colonel's had us in the right place at the right time just about every damn time. Did you forget the fight at Arracourt already? You ever shot up so many Kraut tanks since we set foot in France? It's like they forgot how to do this *panzer* shit. And they wrote the fucking book, remember?"

"All I know is we're way out in front of the whole damn division—*again*—just sitting here and waiting to get our asses sliced up when the Krauts cut in behind us. We ain't even got enough gas to get back across the Moselle River, either."

Fabiano had a point. Fourth Armored Division's advance had been so relentless the past few weeks it would be days before their supply trains caught up. Fuel was life to an armor unit and right now, life was precious.

But Sean had a point, too: this didn't seem like the same German Army they'd been fighting the last four months. It was like their adversaries had all these fancy top-of-the-line tanks but absolutely no idea how to employ them anymore. A Sherman up against a Panther or Tiger tank—or even the latest, improved model of the old Panzer IV—was at a big disadvantage in firepower. The only chance to kill one was to get first shot at their sides or rear, and you still had to be pretty close. Too damned close. Your odds of flanking or getting behind one were slim; their powerful main guns could take you apart from any angle at a far greater range. And your chance of burning to death in an instant was still pretty good, even with the improved armor and water-jacketed ammo storage of the newer models of Sherman tank.

In the eyes of the American tankers, they were still *Zippos*—as easy to bring to flame as the cigarette lighters of the same name the GIs carried.

Yet, the tankers of 4th Armored had been killing German tanks of all types in record numbers since pushing across the Moselle and Meurthe Rivers near Nancy. Lieutenant Colonel Creighton Abrams, commander of the 37th, had a theory: *These are the most inexperienced German soldiers we've ever encountered. It's like they're being sacrificed just to slow us down.*

But Abrams knew better than any of his tankers that the German high command needn't have bothered sacrificing anyone—even rookies—because his battalion, along with the rest of 4th Armored, would have to halt their eastward advance whether German resistance was present or not. The Americans' success was their undoing; 4th Armored's fifteen-mile-deep salient on 3rd Army's right flank invited a counterattack at its base that could sever Patton's line, isolate and encircle individual divisions, and invite those divisions' piecemeal destruction. A straight, cohesive front line could preempt such a disaster. Third Army's stalled progress at Metz was the anchor curving that line, pulling it back to the west, well behind the present position of 4th Armored.

Fabiano pulled his lightweight tanker's jacket tight across his chest. "And it's getting cold, too. I almost froze to death last night…and it ain't looking any warmer tonight."

"Ah, shut the hell up, Fab. It ain't that cold."

"Oh, yeah? Give it a week or two. I bet it'll be snowing in this fucking place by then. And we ain't got no winter gear. The brass said we weren't gonna need it, remember? We were supposed to be home before winter. And with no gas, we can't even run the fucking engine to keep warm."

Fabiano scanned the night sky warily, as if it were possible to see airplanes in the darkness. "Maybe the next one that drops a bomb on us will do us a favor and just kill us outright…like the one that got Hogan and Linz."

"Give that shit a rest, Fab," Sean replied. "There's a lot more panzers out there to worry about than Kraut airplanes."

They didn't have to wait more than a few minutes for Sean's words to be proven true. The tinny growl of Maybach engines drifted through the night air, growing louder as the panzers grew closer. Fabiano slid back inside the turret to man his gunsight.

"How many you figure, Sarge?" he asked Sean, who was still perched in the hatch, scanning the darkness with binoculars for any glimpse of light the Germans might show. Hopefully, that first glimpse wouldn't be a muzzle flash.

"There's more than two out there, that's for damn

sure. They gotta be on the road. We'll probably see their exhaust flare once they come out of that dip. We'll hear them a lot better, too."

"You want to get the artillery to light them up with *illum*?"

"Hell, no," Sean replied. "Let 'em get closer. If they stay on the road it'll be another broadside turkey shoot."

"But what if there's a whole company behind them? Or a battalion?"

"There ain't, Fab. Don't let your ears go berserk on you."

Kowalski, the Sherman's driver, asked, "You want me to crank her up, Sarge?"

"Not yet, dammit. Like I said, let 'em get closer."

The night can play tricks on you. Sounds can seem to change direction. Or even seem to come from several directions at once. Without visual clues, your mind tries to fill in the void however it can, even if it's based on nothing more than hope or fear.

But as much as Sean wanted to believe the German tanks would stay on the road, displaying their vulnerable flanks to his platoon of Shermans, the sound of their invisible approach was painting a very different picture.

He radioed his platoon, "All *Papa Gray* units, this is *Papa Gray 2-6*. Looks like they're coming straight at us. Crank 'em up, hold your position, and cover your sector."

Coming straight at us: the worst possible scenario. All the firepower and armor protection favored the panzers in a frontal fight.

"Son of a bitch," Fabiano said. "I'll bet those bastards know we're here."

"Negative," Sean replied. "If they knew where we

were, they'd be shooting already. They've got the range. Let 'em get a little closer."

He knew he was gambling, but it was the lesser of two evils. To pull back now—in the dark—would lead to confusion and open a gap for the panzers to exploit. The only thing more chaotic than fighting in the dark was having to fight *and move* in the dark; any semblance of order a unit might have would break down immediately. When order broke down, men died for nothing.

They couldn't hear the German engines now, not over the rumble of their own. But the panzers were still coming—Sean could *feel* them out there, somewhere. Close enough to kill, probably. But not close enough to see.

But where exactly is somewhere? I still can't make out shit. It'd be like shooting blindfolded. We miss, we give ourselves away. And we're dead.

Only one thought kept him from pulling his platoon back: *I'm right about one thing, at least—they don't know we're here. If they did, they would've fired already. You can bet your life on that.*

Hell...I am betting my life on that.

Then he saw it.

Didn't even need binoculars.

A dim red glint...no, *two* red glints. Close together. Bouncing up and down like a tank would over the contours of the ground.

But it wasn't the glow of exhausts. Before the binoculars even got to his eyes, he registered what he was seeing:

They ain't buttoned up. The tank commander and the driver got their heads out...and I'm seeing the reflection of the red interior lighting off their goggles. It's lighting their faces up like skulls in the funhouse at Coney Island.

These morons don't even know how to drive blacked-out. Don't they realize even a little light travels forever when it's this fucking dark?

He called to his gunner, "Fab, target tank ten degrees left, range four hundred yards. Further identified by red light through the hatches."

He radioed the other tanks in his platoon not to fire until they'd actually laid eyes on a target in their sector.

The turret of Sean's Sherman traversed slightly left as the main gun's tube inched downward.

"Got it," Fabiano said. "Corrected range three-six-zero yards. *On the way.*"

He fired. The Sherman shuddered with the shot's recoil.

Hardly a second had passed before the German tank erupted in a brilliant ball of flame. The two tanks trailing her in a ragged wedge were suddenly visible, exposed in the unforgiving light.

Look at that, Sean told himself. *Just like rats in the cellar. You can only hear them skittering around...until you turn on the lights.*

The two Shermans to Sean's left fired a split second apart. Their shots turned the remaining German tanks into blazing hulks, just like their leader.

Then came what passed for calm after a fight: the rumble of your tank's engine; the pops and crackles from the beaten tanks, their ammo cooking off as they burned; the pounding of your racing heart.

Fabiano poked his head from the turret for a wider view of their victory. He whistled softly—the sound of

27

relief, perhaps. Or maybe he was mimicking the sound of a shell in flight. "I guess you were right, Sarge," he said. "They really didn't know we were here, did they?"

"Looks that way."

"Stupid bastards," Fabiano added. "They must be pretty damn green. That ain't no way to probe in the dark."

"You ain't complaining, are you?"

"No way, Sarge. No fucking way."

Chapter Four

Advanced Landing Field A-90 came alive as the sun rose, providing an eerie backlight for the thickening ground fog. The engines of the 301st's P-47s thundered to life, as if defying the poor visibility that threatened to keep them from flying. Their propellers churned the fog into a swirling white mist like something out of a ghost story. Each of the twelve planes was laden with three napalm canisters for the attack on Fort Driant's southern turrets.

In his cockpit, Tommy Moon watched the gauges as *Eclipse's* engine settled into a smooth idle. Tech Sergeant McNulty, Tommy's crew chief, leaned into the cockpit to shout over the mechanical din into his pilot's ear. "Maybe I don't understand *hypodermical* situations so well, Lieutenant, but why the hell can't Patton just bypass them forts?"

Tommy shrugged. He had no doubt *hypodermical* meant *hypothetical*. If he'd learned anything in the past year, it was how to make sense of McNulty's strange grasp of English. Maybe it helped they both came from Brooklyn and shared that same sense of urban subtext. But even with the translation in place, he still couldn't answer the question.

"Don't know, Sarge," he replied, tapping the shiny silver bar on his collar. "*First louies* aren't high enough in the food chain to understand the big picture, I guess."

"Well, sir, if this soup don't burn off real soon, the big picture ain't gonna matter, because you guys won't be going nowhere."

Wishful thinking, Tommy thought. *By the time we*

all taxi out to the end of the runway, the fog will thin out enough to take off, at least. And maybe with a little luck, it'll be nice and clear by the time we're over Fort Driant.

McNulty began the final check on Tommy's seat belt and shoulder harness. "I'm telling you, Lieutenant, if I was you, I woulda said the hell with it and flown straight to Switzerland a long time ago. I ain't shitting you."

The look on the sergeant's face gave no indication he was joking, either.

"You'd really do that, Sarge? Take a perfectly good airplane to a neutral country and sit out the war on your ass?"

"Who's gonna know it was a perfectly good airplane, sir? Maybe she got all shot up and could only fly south. It'd be your word against nobody's."

"I'd know, Sergeant. I'd know."

McNulty gave one last tug on a shoulder strap. His look of righteous certainty had faded to something that looked more like regret—or maybe even shame—for speaking those words.

"Yeah, maybe you're right, sir. Forget I ever said anything, okay?"

"Forget what, Sarge? You say something? I can't hear you over all this noise." A wink and a smile went along with the words.

Tommy had been right about the fog. Once all twelve jugs were lined up, ready to take the runway, it had thinned enough to allow single-plane takeoffs at a lengthened interval. Usually, planes would roar into the air fifteen seconds apart—often two at a time—when visibility was unrestricted. Today, with the initial climbout in this pea soup, they'd spread themselves so as not to blindly collide with each other. It would take longer for the three flights of four planes each to form up once airborne, but at least they'd all be there.

This morning's mission on Fort Driant would be a dive-bombing attack, the best way to ensure an accurate delivery of the napalm. With the fort only thirty miles away to the north, the ten-minute flight to the target would be a continuous climb to 8,000 feet, the standard altitude to begin the run. Plummeting down at a steep angle, they'd release the napalm canisters at 3,000 feet and pull out of the dive, screaming down to 1,500 feet before finally leveling off and making their escape. The squadron's pilots had done it so many times before. All they needed was a good enough view of the ground to find the target.

To Tommy's surprise, their view of the ground around the target was excellent. No fog, just a few patchy clouds. Driant's distinctive bell shape stood out clearly, a gray imprint on an earthen background. *Blue Flight* would go first, followed by *Red Flight* and *Green Flight.*

Looking pretty good so far, Tommy told himself as he led his flight to the IP—the *initial point,* the start of the bomb run—over the Moselle River, a few miles east of the fort. *Clear skies, no flak, no Luftwaffe. Just pray no trigger-happy GIs start shooting at us.*

Down they went, *Blue, Red,* and then *Green.* Twelve ships in all, thirty-six napalm canisters.

All dead on target: Fort Driant's southern turrets. *Easy Battery.*

One hour later, after the napalm fires had burned themselves out and the American artillery had swept the ground ahead of them, infantrymen of 5th Division attacked Fort Driant once again.

As they trudged up that towering hill, they couldn't help but notice that the fort at its peak hadn't suffered the internal explosions they'd been promised. It seemed every bit as impregnable as the last time.

And like the last time, their attack was repulsed.

As they retreated, the three big howitzers of *Easy Battery* added insult to injury by firing on their assembly areas. The napalm fires might have blackened the domes of their turrets, but that was the extent of the damage. They were still fully operational.

Chapter Five

George Patton wasn't thrilled to see the jeep of General Omar Bradley—his boss, the 12th Army Group Commander—pull into the courtyard of 3rd Army Headquarters. Since the failed attack on Fort Driant earlier that morning, Patton was more in the mood to fire a division commander or two than entertain his superior. He knew Bradley wasn't stopping by just to say hello, either.

Bradley got right to the point. "I don't need you getting tied up in some medieval siege of a fortress city. Please tell me you've come to your senses and decided to isolate Metz rather than decimate half your divisions trying to take the damn place."

"I don't fight wars of attrition, Brad," Patton replied. "You know that."

"All too well, George. All too well. That's why I want this one stopped immediately."

"Dammit, Brad, if Ike would give me the gas I need I could be across the Saar in two weeks. Fourth Armored is already—"

Bradley cut him off. "I know damned well where Fourth Armored is. It's got its neck stuck out way too far. You need to pull them back right away. Your army is all over the place, just asking to get sliced up, enveloped, and destroyed."

"Just get me the fucking gas, Brad, and we'll be in Germany before—"

"You know that's not going to happen, George. Ike's made up his mind. The gas is going to the northern flank for now."

"To fucking Montgomery, you mean."

"Yes, to fucking Montgomery," Bradley replied. "You're going to have to recognize that sooner or later."

For a moment, Patton's demeanor was unlike anything Bradley had ever seen before. He was striking a most *unpatton-like* pose, as if quietly accepting he was on the short end of the supply train. There was no sign he was going to rant and rave, as he usually would. He seemed almost *reasonable*.

"I'll tell you what, Brad. If Ike can do the Brits a favor and give them my gas, then maybe he can get them to do me one in return."

Bradley's eyes narrowed skeptically. *Reasonable, my ass,* he thought. *This is just another one of his little games.*

Patton continued, "The RAF has those *blockbuster* bombs, right? Twelve thousand pounds of TNT, I'm told. Have Ike get his British pals to put one of those things right on Fort Driant."

"What good would that do, George? You've been bombing and shelling the living daylights out of that fort for a couple of weeks now. If you added it all up, you've probably dumped a hundred times that much explosive on the place. And it hasn't done a damn bit of good."

"But Brad, we're talking *six tons of HE*, all concentrated on the exact same spot, at the exact same time! Not scattered all over the place like our little bombs and artillery shells. I don't care what kind of steel and concrete they made that fort out of. The Brits blow up dams with those bombs, right? Nothing could withstand that blast."

Bradley dithered a few moments before replying, "I don't think it's a good idea. The last I heard, the Brits prefer to fly their heavy bombers only at night. The target would have to be well lit up for them to even find it."

"No problem," Patton said. "My artillery will light the place up all you like."

"Forget it, George. The Brits will no more fly through an active artillery area than our boys will."

"Well, they'll just have to do it in the daytime, then."

"Don't be ridiculous," Bradley replied. "I'm not going to waste Ike's time with this. He's got enough problems."

"Come on, Brad...at least run it by your air staff. Let's get Pete Quesada on the landline."

While the communications officer had his switchboard operators work their magic, Patton moved back to the original issue. "I can't just isolate and bypass Metz, Brad. There are at least two German divisions in the city and the surrounding forts. To keep them out of our hair would require at least two of my own divisions to bottle them up. I need those divisions to exploit Fourth Armored's breakthrough east of Nancy. My army is on the best route into Germany, and you know it. Look, Brad, I'm telling you I can be across the Saar in—"

"George, you're not listening to me. You're not going to be *exploiting* anything for a while. Ike wants your lines tidied up...and since it doesn't look like you'll be advancing past Metz anytime soon, that means you'll have to pull Fourth Armored back. It's that simple."

The debate went on for another five minutes—with arms waving and fingers stabbing at points on maps—

before the communications officer announced, "General Quesada on the line, sir."

Brigadier General Elwood "Pete" Quesada was commander of IX Fighter Command, USAAF, an expert on tactical air support and the man responsible for providing that support to Bradley's 12th Army Group. He listened as Patton and Bradley expressed their needs and concerns. When they were finished, he asked, "Is this line secure, sir?"

Patton looked to the communications officer, who nervously replied, "As secure as possible, General. There's no guarantee any line is perfectly secure."

When told that, Quesada said, "Not good enough, sir. I have some information that might be of help to you but it's classified. I can fly over to your headquarters first thing tomorrow morning, if that's okay?"

Not caring he was stepping on Bradley's toes, Patton rushed to reply, "Make it today, Pete. You've got great flying weather for a change."

A silence fell over the line as Quesada tried to figure out how to respond. He'd just been given an order from a man he did not work for while the man he did work for seemed suddenly mute, neither confirming nor overriding Patton's presumptuous directive.

Not wanting to step on his boss' toes, Quesada prodded, "General Bradley, is that your wish as well?"

Red-faced and glaring at Patton, Bradley replied, "If it's not too much trouble, Pete."

"No, sir. I need to clean up a few details here first, but I can be there by 1400."

Once the call ended, Bradley added, "George, I put up with a lot of shit from you because, quite frankly, you're worth it. But don't ever fucking embarrass me like that again. Am I clear, General?"

Like a contrite schoolboy, Patton replied, "Yes, General. Perfectly clear."

But it was all an act, and Bradley knew it. The bottom line was simple: *George Patton had gotten away with it again.*

★★★★

It was a few minutes before 1400 when Pete Quesada landed his AT-6 *hack* near 3rd Army Headquarters at Verdun. A jeep whisked him from the airstrip to the chateau where Patton and Bradley were waiting.

This time, Bradley would be doing the talking. He began by asking, "What's such a secret you couldn't tell us over the phone, Pete?"

"Well, sir," Quesada replied, "if you want one big bang on the target, the Air Force has a way to do it."

"Let me guess," Bradley said. "You've borrowed some RAF heavy bombers that can carry that big bomb?"

"Negative, sir. We've got a bomb of our own. Let's just say the RAF *inspired* us."

Patton murmured, "*Inspired*, my ass. *Jealous* of the Brits' bigger planes is more like it. It's classic *dick-measuring.*"

"Actually," Quesada continued, "it's a *flying bomb.* We modify some tired B-17s and B-24s for the job. Strip them bare, load them up with explosives, and fly them right into the target." Seeing the stunned look on their faces, he added, "Unmanned, of course."

Bradley looked skeptical. "Unmanned? How the

hell do you get them into the air?"

"Let me clarify that, sir. For safety reasons, a pilot takes the plane off. Then he bails out and radio control takes over."

It took several minutes and a few diagrams to explain the workings of *Operation Aphrodite*. Bradley seemed flummoxed by the whole proposition. "Has the Air Force actually used any of these *flying bombs* yet?"

"We've tried eight missions so far, sir, all very *hush-hush*. None of them have gone well. Four crashed before we got the remote-control system upgraded and working halfway decently. The rest got shot down by flak or missed the target completely, due either to bad visibility or human controller error. By the way, the Air Force has lost two pilots due to parachute mishaps. The Navy tried a mission, too. That one went even worse."

Bradley asked, "What do you mean, *worse*? And what the hell does the Navy have to do with all this?"

"Well, sir, it was worse because the two Navy pilots on board got killed outright. Plane blew up right after takeoff. Nobody's sure why. As to why the Navy's involved, I suppose they didn't want to get left out. They've got maritime patrol bombers that are worn out and headed for the scrap yard, too. So why not try to put them to good use one last time?"

Patton couldn't keep his silence any longer. "It isn't *good use* if it doesn't work, Pete. How's all this *failure* going to help me?"

Quesada smiled. He knew that question would be coming. He'd been polishing his answer all day. "I think there's a high degree of probability we can put a *baby* on that fort of yours without much problem, sir. My pilots in the area, the ones flying your ground support, know exactly where it is—hell, they've been hitting it every damn day—and the flak in the area's reported as fairly light. There's very little Luftwaffe presence, as well, so chances of the *baby* being shot down are pretty small. As long as we've got halfway decent visibility, we should be able to blow that fort to smithereens."

It was Patton's turn to smile. "So in other words, the Air Force is looking for an easy target to redeem this *Operation Aphrodite* disaster?"

"In a nutshell, sir, that's it."

"Outstanding," Patton replied. "Now what flyboy's ass do we have to kiss to make this happen?"

"That would be General Spaatz's ass, sir."

"Ahh, the theater commander himself." Patton looked to Bradley, adding, "Sounds like pretty high-level shit to me. Well, Brad, do you want to talk to *Tooey*, or should I?"

"Good lord, *no*, George," Bradley replied. "Let me handle it. And I think Ike might have something to say about it, too."

Patton laughed out loud. "Ike will only care if we're trying to take something away from his precious little Montgomery. And we're not doing that, are we, Pete?"

"No, sir," Quesada replied. "We wouldn't be doing that at all."

Chapter Six

The men of 37th Tank Battalion thought it was a good sign: a convoy of fuel trucks was rumbling into their assembly area under cover of darkness. Soon they'd have the gasoline to push ever closer to the German border, less than forty miles to the east. It was what they wanted most: to drive on Berlin, end the war, and go home.

It was also what they feared most: fighting on the soil of the Fatherland. The closer they got, the more the equations of fighting and dying changed. There had only been one enemy in France: Germans in uniform. If a Frenchman fought as a partisan, he was fighting with the Allies.

Would it be different inside Germany? Whose side would the civilians be on now? Would there be saboteurs in every village, picking off GIs one by one and then vanishing into the populace? Worse, there were rumors fanatical SS units—far more fierce and proficient than the unskilled troops they'd faced lately—would be in the forefront of homeland defense. If the Allies— American, British, and Russian—were fought to a standstill at the German frontier, would this war end in stalemate under a negotiated armistice?

There was one possibility no man of the 37th dared speak out loud: the Allies could still lose this war. It wasn't impossible. Maybe those rumors of *Nazi superweapons* might be true, and the resulting devastation in France, England—and maybe even the US—would force the Allies to sue for peace.

Or perhaps all of Germany would be overrun by

nobody but the Russians, who would proclaim themselves the sole victors. From what the GIs had heard, the *Ivans* were a swarming horde, fueled by the need to avenge four years of invasion, plunder, and genocide at the hands of the Third Reich. Their steamroller advance westward to Berlin only seemed to be gathering unstoppable momentum and bloodlust on a daily basis. Maybe they wouldn't stop at Berlin, flooding right up to the stagnant American and British lines in France and the Low Countries.

The Americans and British, at best, were plodding, bickering, and blundering their way slowly eastward. Their momentum was anything but assured and, at the moment, nonexistent. A sluggish American or British army might still find itself enveloped, encircled, and forced to surrender, just like the Germans at Stalingrad. And with that surrender would come the somber knowledge that every one of their comrades killed in the fight against Hitler had died for nothing.

Sergeant Sean Moon tried to push all that pessimistic speculation from his mind as his Sherman tank—*Lucky 7*—eased alongside the fuel truck. *This gas is going to take us across the German border*, he told himself. *With a little luck, we'll be wrapping this thing up real soon and going home.*

As his crew clambered down from the tank to stretch their legs in the cool night air, Sean remained perched on her rear deck, smiling as the precious gasoline quenched his Sherman's thirst.

A voice called to him out of the darkness: "That sure is a sweet smell, isn't it, Sergeant?" It was his company commander, Captain Newcomb.

"You got that right, sir," Sean replied. "I'm betting

this gas can take me and my guys all the way to Saarbrücken."

He'd expected enthusiastic agreement from his captain. But all he got was an awkward silence until Newcomb said, "I'm afraid that's not the plan, Sergeant Moon."

"What do you mean, sir?"

"I mean 37th Tank isn't pushing east. We've been called back to the Moselle."

"You mean we're *withdrawing*, sir?"

"No," Captain Newcomb said, "Fourth Armored's not withdrawing, Sergeant. The rest of the division will hold the line east of Nancy. But our battalion is going back to help out with something. Don't know what exactly it is yet, though."

Sean could feel the anger rising in him; *getting his Irish up*, like they said back in Brooklyn. He jumped down from the tank's deck to stand face to face with the captain.

"With all due respect, sir," Sean said, "how the hell—"

But Newcomb interrupted him. With the calm but unmistakable authority a man acquires as a combat commander, he said, "Knock it off, Sergeant Moon. This isn't my first dance, and I've got a pretty good idea what *with all due respect* really means. If you've got something to say, let's hear it, man to man."

The captain's words chilled Sean's ire like a cold shower. "Honest, sir, no disrespect or anything. But ain't it a real kick in the teeth—after all we've done here—to be finally getting some gas just so we can retreat?"

"I'm telling you, Sergeant, we're not retreating. Now I don't know what they've got in store for us—I'm

not even sure Colonel Abrams knows at the moment—
but it must be pretty damn important if they need 37th
Tank to do it."

Newcomb's words worked their magic. Even a
hardened veteran like Sean Moon, who'd survived more
than enough combat in North Africa and France to be
irredeemably jaded, couldn't help but feel the unit pride
welling up inside him.

"I see your point one hundred percent, sir."

"Excellent, Sergeant. Your platoon will be ready to
roll at sun-up, then?"

"Affirmative, sir."

★★★★

Lieutenant General Carl "Tooey" Spaatz, USAAF,
commander of US Strategic Forces in Europe, was
annoyed he'd been awakened in the middle of the night
for this conference call. Since it was General
Eisenhower's switchboard that had put the call through,
however, he had no choice but to get on the line.

"Tooey," Omar Bradley said, "this is Brad, and I've
got George Patton here with me. How's everything back
in England?"

"It's dark, Brad. Very dark. And very late. To what
do I owe the pleasure of this call?"

Bradley told him what Pete Quesada had proposed
the Air Force do to Fort Driant.

"Absolutely not, Brad. Ike specifically said
Aphrodite missions were only supposed to be flown
against strategic targets. What you're describing sounds
strictly tactical."

"George and I consider this far more strategic than

tactical, Tooey. This is the twentieth century. We can't get our soldiers bogged down in a sixteenth century siege when we've got the technology to blow that fort sky high. Ike agrees with us. He says if you've got the wherewithal, we should go ahead and do it, and as quickly as possible. There should be a communiqué from him coming over your headquarters printer to that effect as we speak. We wanted to call you first so you didn't get blindsided."

"I appreciate that, Brad. But let me ask you and George something. I'm guessing Pete's already filled you in on all the problems we've had so far with this remote-controlled bomb project. Do you really want to let one of those things loose when you've got your own troops in the vicinity? You could be begging for something far worse than the *Operation Cobra* fiasco. We only killed about a company's worth of men that time. Are you trying for a battalion's worth now?"

"I'd be lying to you if I said I wasn't concerned about another disaster like that," Bradley replied, "but we need serious firepower—far more than we've got at our disposal at the moment—to take Fort Driant down. And the only people who can provide it are you or the RAF."

"Forget about RAF Bomber Command," Spaatz said. "They work alone in Arthur Harris' own little world, and they lost interest in daylight precision bombing a long, long time ago. This isn't the job for them, even if they were up for it."

"Better we keep it an all-American operation, anyway," Patton added. "The Brits would just start with those full-of-shit lies about how they bailed out the *inexperienced* Yanks again."

"Hold on a minute, both of you," Spaatz said. "I haven't said I'm going to be able to help you out yet. There's going to be a lot of logistics involved, a lot of details to work out. It might even be out of the realm of possibilities entirely."

"When will you know?" Patton asked.

"I can give you an answer in a couple of days. If it's a *go*, it'll probably take a week or two to put it all together."

"Can we hurry it up a little, Tooey?" Patton asked. "I've got good men dying here."

Even through the phone lines, they could sense the sudden anger in Spaatz's voice. "We've *all* got good men dying, George. I just don't want any more of them to die by accident. And I'm afraid there's a real good chance I just might kill a bunch of your men—again— and maybe some of mine."

Before Patton could get in another word, Bradley replied, "We're not arguing that point, Tooey. We just need your help...in the worst way."

"I know, Brad. I know. But if I can do this for you, I want one thing perfectly clear: I want it in writing from Ike's headquarters that I recommended *against* using remote-controlled bombs on Fort Driant."

"Duly noted, Tooey," Bradley replied.

Tommy Moon couldn't sleep, so he wandered across the ramp to watch maintenance being pulled on the squadron's aircraft. He'd always marveled at the deep knowledge the young mechanics possessed and how they never quit on a new and nebulous problem until they'd found the solution. It seemed they could tear the P-47 apart on a nightly basis yet always have it back together and ready to fly at first light. They loved the machines as much as the pilots who flew them. Maybe more so.

Their stamina impressed Tommy, too. They rarely slept at night; there was always so much maintenance to do on the planes. When their aircraft was out on a mission, then—and only then—would they nap until the word came the returning ships were in range of the field. Then they'd drive to the end of the runway and wait, counting the jugs on final approach, praying theirs wasn't among the missing.

If their prayers weren't answered, they'd suffer the agony of wondering if maybe something they did—an errant adjustment, some bolt not properly installed, an electrical connector not secured—had caused their ship and her pilot to go down rather than German gunnery. That agony might persist for the rest of their lives, too, because unless the pilot survived to tell his story, the reason for a lost aircraft was rarely, if ever, known in full. *Failed to return* on the mission status board glossed over myriad reasons and exonerated no one's sense of guilt.

Tommy found his crew chief, Tech Sergeant McNulty, sitting in his truck, poring over his plane's maintenance records. He also noticed two of McNulty's mechanics busily opening wing panels.

"What's the matter, Lieutenant?" McNulty asked, checking his wristwatch. "It's three-fucking a.m. Can't sleep? Or are you just getting back from *searching the femmes* in town?"

"I've had enough sleep, thanks. Just thought I'd see

what you guys were up to. What are they doing up on the wing?"

"Well, sir, I don't see in these here documents where they ever did no gun heater check at the depot," McNulty said, "so we did it tonight. And guess what...two of them flunked. Pulled *zero* amps. Good thing it ain't real cold yet and you don't fly real high anyway. A couple of guns woulda been froze up on you, for sure." He pointed to the two mechanics. "So those two fine young *wrenches* are changing them heaters out for you."

"I appreciate that, Sarge," Tommy replied. "Anything else I should know about?"

"Nah, you're babying her just fine, Lieutenant. No problems. Not so far, anyway. The rest of the ships in *Blue Flight* are in good shape, too."

A fine, cold rain began to fall. The mechanics on the wing scrambled for a tarp to protect themselves and their wiring work from the rain. Tommy joined McNulty in the truck's cab.

"Don't look like you gentlemen will be committing no aviation anytime soon," McNulty said. "Forecast is for low clouds, rain, and fog all damn morning."

"Yeah. Looks that way."

"I'll bet them ground-pounders will be cursing you flyboys all over again, not being able to support them and all."

"I wish there was something I could do about that, Sarge. I really do."

McNulty closed the logbook on his lap. In the glow of the flashlights they'd rigged in the truck's cab, he looked troubled, like a man with a confession to make.

"You know, Lieutenant...I still feel kinda bad about

that thing I said yesterday."

"What thing, Sarge?"

"That thing about saying *fuck all this* and sitting out the war in Switzerland. I think I was just feeling a little homesick or something, that's all. I don't want you to be *misconscrewing* no meanings."

Tommy smiled. His syntax might be tortured, but McNulty's heart was usually in the right place.

"I don't remember you saying anything like that, Sarge."

"Oh yeah? Then what did I say, Lieutenant?"

"Something about if I fucked your airplane up again, you'd be kicking my ass all the way back to Brooklyn."

Now McNulty was smiling, too. "And don't you never forget it, neither, sir."

Chapter Seven

In the thick fog of pre-dawn, the men of 37th Tank Battalion were about to receive their orders. One tanker held his hand out in front of his face and said, "I always thought my old man was joking when he said *can't see your hand in front of your face.* But it ain't no joke, is it? Not this morning, anyway."

Colonel Abrams, the battalion commander, told his assembled officers and NCOs, "Here's the deal. We're going up to Metz and help Fifth Infantry Division take some of those forts blocking their way into the city. It's about a forty-mile drive. Should take us a good three or four hours provided nothing slows us down."

A grumble of disgust swept through his audience. "That isn't even Fourth Armored's AO," Captain Newcomb, Baker Company commander, said. "Isn't Sixth Armored supposed to be direct support for the Fifth?"

There was irritation in Abrams' voice as he replied, "Areas of operation are wherever Corps decides they are, Captain. And yeah—that's where Sixth Armored has been working, but now the 37th is going to be helping them out." He paused to scan the downcast faces before him, the shadows, no doubt, hiding just how unhappy they were with the news.

"Are there any more questions?" the colonel asked.

There were none. The rumble of tank engines warming up was the only sound.

"The S3 will now hand out the operations order with your various routes of march described in detail," Abrams said. "Since the companies are so spread out, we won't form into a battalion column until we all meet up just short of Nancy."

Captain Newcomb scanned Baker Company's orders with his platoon leaders. They found one thing troubling: they'd never been on some of the roads they were to take in their drive west toward Nancy. "We're gonna be driving along the division's northern flank," Sean Moon said as he studied the map. "There could be Krauts to our right in force. We'd better hope they're as blind in this pea soup as we are. Otherwise, we're gonna be bobbin' along just like targets in a shooting gallery."

The fog hadn't lifted a bit. Baker Company's tanks crept along, their drivers struggling to keep their vehicles on the narrow pavement and off the marshy shoulders. Keeping the tank in front of them in sight without running into it when it suddenly stopped was a challenge. Reading the few road signs was proving difficult in the poor visibility, too. As another signpost loomed out of the mist, Sean Moon, commanding the lead tank in the company column, stopped his Sherman, got out, and walked over to read it.

He didn't like what the sign told him.

Captain Newcomb, who'd been several vehicles back in the column, jogged up to join him. "I guess I fucked up, sir," Sean said. "I must've missed the turn. According to this damn sign, *Freezin' Soul* is two kilometers behind us."

Freezin' Soul: the GI's tortured pronunciation of the town Fresnes-en-Saulnois.

"Shit," Newcomb mumbled. He had no reason to

doubt Moon was right; it was hard to be sure at their slow pace, but he reckoned they'd been headed down this road for much too long. There was no reason to lay all the blame on Sergeant Moon, though. Neither Newcomb nor anyone else in the column had spotted the turnoff they were supposed to take as they rolled past it in that *pea soup*.

"Don't worry about it, Sergeant Moon. I don't know where the fuck we are, either."

Spinning a column of fifteen tanks around on a narrow road was asking for trouble. Maybe some of them would get stuck in a roadside ditch or bog. Precious time and gas would be wasted hauling them out. Even if they managed the *about face* without disaster, they'd still be blundering through the same *soup*, just in the opposite direction.

Silently, Newcomb speculated, *At least if there are any Kraut tanks or 88s nearby, they can no more see us than we can see them at the moment. But German infantry with panzerfausts—they could walk practically right up and blow us to Hell.*

"Keep going," Newcomb told Moon. "About two more miles, there should be a dirt road—probably more of a farm trail—to the left. Take it. It should get us back to Highway Seventy-Four pretty quick. I'll radio Battalion about our change of plans."

Sean traced the proposed route on his map. "Yeah, I see it. But what about the river, sir? We already missed the bridge we were supposed to take. There ain't gonna be any other bridges that can support a *Zippo's* weight. You sure it's gonna be shallow enough to ford with this rain we've been getting?"

"I don't think the Seille river is over three feet deep

anywhere around here, even with all the rain," Newcomb replied. "We'll cross it."

Let's fucking hope so, Sean thought.

Somewhere above this dull, back-lit murkiness, the sun shone brightly. *But it's sure taking its sweet time burning this damn fog off*, Sean told himself. Still on the paved roadway, they were making no more than five miles per hour. *And we'll be making a lot less when we're on that dirt trail...if I even find it. I've already fucked up once this morning. Please don't let me do it again.*

He did the rough math in his head one more time: *two miles at five miles per hour. It should take a little over twenty minutes.*

He checked his watch. They'd been on the move again for nineteen.

"Kowalski," he said to his driver, "hold up a second. I'm getting out."

"*Getting out*? Where the hell are you going, Sarge?"

"I'm gonna be your ground guide, *Ski*. Can't miss the fucking turn again. Try to keep me in sight and don't run my ass over, okay?" Then he told his gunner, "Fabiano, you're in command of this vehicle until I get back. Don't fuck up."

Walking along the road, Sean felt cloaked in some strange, mythic armor. It was as if his invisibility in the fog protected him better than the steel hull of his Sherman. Jogging faster than the tanks could drive, he was soon well ahead of them, so far that the hum of their engines at low throttle no longer masked the sound of his heavy breathing. Or the pulse pounding in his ears.

The darkened silhouettes he saw ahead seemed like nothing more than dense roadside shrubbery at first, like the bocages of Normandy where they'd fought three months before.

But the emerging shapes were too regular—too hard-edged—to be vegetation. And there was a sudden roar, like the Maybach engine of a panzer revving up. And a voice shouting commands that were definitely German.

Sean turned and sprinted back to his tank. He hadn't realized how far ahead of it he'd gone; it seemed like forever before it loomed back into view through the mist.

He jumped onto the forward hull and told Kowalski, "Stop right here. Don't go another foot."

Then he climbed to the turret and grabbed the radio headset from Fabiano.

"*Papa Gray 6* from *Papa Gray 2-6,*" he called to Captain Newcomb. "We got trouble ahead. Need you up here on the double."

Newcomb was there in seconds. Together, he and Sean walked forward into the *soup*, toward the German tanks.

"How many you figure?" Newcomb asked.

"I can only see three, sir. Don't hear any more than that, either. Can't tell for sure what type they are, but I'm betting Panther."

"And they're broadside to the road," Newcomb said, peering into the mist. "That isn't any way to set up a roadblock."

"I don't think they're a roadblock, sir. I think they're as lost as us. I could hear one of them yelling *Zurich* or something like that. Ain't that how the Krauts say *go back*? Or maybe *back up*?"

"Yeah, the word's *zurück,* I think. But I don't imagine he's talking about going to Switzerland, although that doesn't sound like such a bad idea right about now."

Sean said, "If they ain't gonna move for a minute, why don't me and Spinetti creep up on them and let 'em have it? The ground's firm enough here for off-road, two abreast. They'll never hear us coming over the racket those Maybachs are making. And they sure as hell won't see us until it's too late."

"Do it," Newcomb replied. "Just don't miss."

"At this range, it'd be harder *not* to hit them, sir."

As they jogged back to their tanks, Sean said, "Funny thing, sir. If I hadn't dismounted we wouldn't've seen or heard those Krauts until we were right on top of them. They could've had us for lunch."

In a few quick bounds, Sean was back in his commander's hatch. Spinetti's tank—the next in the column—pulled alongside *Lucky 7*. Together they slowly advanced—*why did the distance seem farther driving than on foot?*—until the dark shapes of the German tanks could be seen as if floating in the fog. The panzers were moving now, *going back*, perhaps, in the direction they'd come. Still showing their vulnerable flanks, they were no more than fifty yards away.

With the gunners' shouts of *On the way*, both Shermans fired, one hitting the lead tank, the other the trail tank. Sean's loader rammed in another round—and with it, Fabiano dispatched the tank in the middle.

Three brilliant orange blazes—the funeral pyres of three panzers—pierced the veil of fog like floodlights, proving Sean correct: those dying tanks were alone.

As the column rolled past the burning panzers, Sean took a moment to reflect: *I'm one lucky bastard, I guess. How many times is it now that I shoulda been dead...but I ain't? Well, I fucked up but good today and got away with it. But those Krauts fucked up, too...and they bought it.*

The dirt road they were looking for proved not as hard to find as they'd feared. Fresh, muddy tank tracks on the pavement—German, no doubt—led them directly to the turnoff, a wide and well-churned thoroughfare cut through marshland.

This soft, wet crap ain't exactly tank country, Sean thought as *Lucky 7* pivoted onto the dirt road. *Let's just hope those fresh tracks came from those three panzers we just turned into ovens...and not some other Krauts still hanging around here.*

As if the Germans weren't enough to contend with, Mother Nature wasn't finished throwing obstacles into Baker Company's path. The fog had finally dissipated, yielding to a steady rain that turned the dirt road beneath their tracks into a morass almost as treacherous for vehicles as the marshland bounding it. Sean Moon saw it this way: *It looks like they took all the cow shit in France and tried to make a road out of it.*

It was slow going, still; three of Captain Newcomb's fifteen tanks lost traction and slid into the marsh, bottoming their hulls in the soggy earth so firmly that tracks spun uselessly over their sprockets and road wheels, propelling nothing. They'd need a tow from other tanks—sometimes two working together—using steel cables to pull the mired ones out while struggling not to slide off the trail themselves.

The rain had finally brought the mixed blessing of at least partial visibility. They'd be less likely to blunder into Germans as they had just an hour ago. From a distance, though, in the veil of rainfall, their column could look very German to nervous, trigger-happy GIs who might be in the area.

As every GI was all too aware, friendly fire killed you just as dead.

Sean's radio came alive with Captain Newcomb's voice. "*Papa Gray 2-6*, this is *6*. There should be a bridge over the Seille in a couple hundred yards. Take a look—let me know if it's a good place to ford."

There was a bridge. It was old, made of stone, and only wide enough for a farm tractor, the cart it was pulling, or a small car. Sean doubted the old structure would support more than a ton or two. Certainly not a Sherman, even if a tank could fit between its railings.

Worse, swollen with rain, the Seille was swift and seemed much deeper than the three-foot fording depth of the company's Sherman and Stuart tanks. There was only one way to know for sure. He told Kowalski to stop the tank.

Climbing down from the turret, he stripped off his pistol belt and jacket, took a long, thin rope coiled on the tank's deck and began to tie one end around his waist. As he did, he told his driver, "Ski, come here and tie this rope off to the towing shackle."

"Where the hell are you going now, Sarge?"

"I've got me a new job—*depth gauge*. Be thankful I ain't making you do it. You're the next tallest after me."

Kowalski said nothing in reply. He *was* thankful

Sean hadn't designated him the *depth gauge*. Though only about thirty yards wide at this point, the Seille looked cold and more than powerful enough to sweep a man away to drown. It looked sinister, too, with a ghostly mist rising off its surface like the moors they'd seen in Scotland, when they were awaiting Overlord and the plunge into France.

"If I go under," Sean said, "you better pull me out or you're gonna be on my permanent shit list."

Fabiano yelled down from the turret, "Hey, I'm already on his permanent shit list. It ain't no big deal."

Sean smiled and said, "Congratulations, Fab. You just rose to the top of the list. See how big a deal that's gonna be."

Draping the Thompson submachine gun across his shoulders, Sean walked to the river bank. "Now, Ski," he called back, "if I get halfway across and it don't go over my belt buckle, bring the old girl across and tell the captain we found the spot."

He slogged through the bulrushes at the riverbank and waded into the water. The current was swift, but he managed to keep his footing even as the water level approached his waistline. *Don't get no deeper than this,* Sean silently urged the river, *or I'm gonna have to do this all over again someplace else. Hell, maybe I'll make it Kowalski's turn next time.*

He was surprised that once he was down in it, the mist rising off the river obscured his vision just as thoroughly as the morning's fog had done. Walking a few moments more, he started rising out of the water with each step. He was beyond the river's midpoint; it was shallow enough for a Sherman to ford. But when he turned to signal Kowalski to bring *Lucky 7* across, he couldn't see the tank through the mist.

And if I can't see them, they can't see me.

Sean felt the bullets whizzing over his head before he heard the sound of them being fired. He looked up to see tracers flying in both directions, like surreal streaks of brilliant white light blazing their way through his hazy world.

Starting back toward his tank, he heard her engine rev. The rope suddenly tightened around his waist and he was jerked off his feet, being pulled through the water—sometimes under the water—until, flat on his back, he was dragged up the muddy bank and into the bulrushes.

He heard *Lucky 7* squeal to a halt and the rope went slack. He could see her now through the tall stems, her turret traversing left, the tube elevating a bit, as machine gun bullets from across the river bounced off her hull and turret.

Then her main gun fired.

An explosion resounded from the far side of the river.

His tank fired again.

Another explosion, and the German bullets stopped coming. Sean scrambled to his feet and sprinted to his tank.

Fabiano called down from the turret hatch, "You okay, Sarge? We didn't drown you or nothing, did we?"

"No, not quite, *numbnuts*. But why the fuck did you back up like that?"

"Had to, Sarge. Couldn't get a good shot with that fucking bridge in the way."

Once up in the turret, Sean could see what his crew had done. Two German half-tracks sat burning in a tree line beyond the river's far bank.

Sean asked, "When the hell did they pop up?"

"As soon as you went into the water. Is it okay to cross?"

"Yeah, but not yet. Let's get the rest of the platoon up here first and cross all together and cover each other...just in case there's still some Krauts over there with *panzerfausts* and what-have-you."

"I did good, right, Sarge?" Fabiano asked. "You know, second-in-command taking over in the heat of the shit flying and all?"

"Don't pat yourself on the back too hard, Fab. It's what the gunner's supposed to do when the *TC's* not around."

"But I did good, right?"

"Yeah, you did good."

"So...am I off the shit list now?"

"Not *off,* Fab. Just a couple of notches lower, maybe."

Sean glanced down to see the muddy water dripping off him, forming a puddle on the turret floor. "Dammit," he said, "I didn't figure on *swimming* to Metz, though."

Chapter Eight

HEADQUARTERS, USAAF STRATEGIC FORCES, EUROPE

It was exactly the solution General Spaatz, C.O. of US Strategic Air Forces in Europe, had been looking for. He'd wanted no part of Bradley's plan—*No, make that Patton's plan*—to use an *Operation Aphrodite* remote-controlled bomb against some silly, obsolete fort in France. Since that phone call with them last night, he couldn't stop asking himself, *What the hell's wrong with these ground-pounder generals of ours, anyway, who seem so eager to fight a slogging, medieval battle in the age of fast-moving mechanized combat? But Ike is all for it, too, so I've got to play along.*

But here was the US Navy, surprisingly eager to bounce back from its latest deadly fiasco—one that killed a scion of the prominent Kennedy family—and take on any mission he'd give them. To Tooey Spaatz, their act of volunteering was a gift from heaven. Although he'd never wanted the Navy attached to his strategic bombing domain, in this case he'd gladly pass them the responsibility for executing this foolish enterprise—even though there was nothing in the least bit nautical about this landlocked target some three hundred miles inside France—and save him and his Air Force the trouble.

There was just one big problem: General Arnold, Commanding General, Army Air Forces, back in Washington had promptly caught wind of Spaatz's decision; an ocean bridged by telegraph cables and radiotelephone systems was little impediment to intraservice gossip and backstabbing. He sent a cable ordering Spaatz to reverse that decision without delay. *Only Army Air Force planes and pilots are to support Army troops in the field,* Arnold decreed. *Lack of procedural uniformity between the services would result in confusion and increased risk to our ground troops.*

Tooey Spaatz was beginning to wish he'd never heard of *Operation Aphrodite*, with its unreliable radio-control systems and its penchant for killing American airmen and missing its targets. It had seemed like such a great idea at first, a *win-win*: crash explosive-laden, unmanned bombers, which were going to be cut up for scrap anyway, into Nazi targets. In the process, the USAAF would be showing up the RAF by fielding a weapon with a bigger punch then their vaunted *blockbuster* bombs.

If only the damn things would work like they were supposed to.

FORWARD AIRFIELD A-90, TOUL, FRANCE

The rain didn't stop until 1300. It took another hour for the solid overcast to scatter. As soon as it did, the pilots of 301st Fighter Squadron were handed their mission for immediate execution: *Support 4th Armored Division forces in vicinity of Arracourt.*

Lieutenant Jimmy Tuttle, pilot of *Blue Two*, took a long look at the situation map. Then he said to Tommy

Moon, "Hmm. Arracourt...same place as two weeks ago. You think this is going to be a turkey shoot like it was the last time, Half?"

"Let's hope so," Tommy replied. "Kind of strange they're still in the same area, though. That's not like Fourth Armored at all. You figure they'd have moved a lot farther east in two weeks."

"Well, at least today we won't be throwing rocks at *the fort that refuses to die*," Tuttle said.

The pilots of *Blue Flight* were over their area of operations in less than ten minutes' flying time. They hardly had time for one orbit when the first request for air support came in. Tommy Moon was fairly sure he recognized the voice of the ASO on the ground: a pilot from the 301st named Rich Menifee, a young lieutenant from Alabama. Even the nasal filtering of the aircraft radios couldn't disguise a southern drawl as distinctive as his. It seemed ridiculous to go through the authentication process of challenge and response to confirm you were talking to an actual friend rather than a foe masquerading as one, but to not do so invited disaster, as Tommy knew all too well: *Some of these Krauts speak damn good English, and it isn't too hard to fake an accent. Fall for that crap and you get tricked into shooting up your own guys.*

Menifee reported German mechanized forces threatening an American infantry regiment in a thickly forested area. Tommy was pretty sure he and his three pilots were looking down at the right place. All they saw was the tops of trees and an occasional whiff of smoke.

No troops, no trucks, no tanks. Just glimpses of vehicle tracks imprinted in the soft, wet ground.

Menifee added, "We're real close, too. *Danger close.*"

Tommy radioed, *"Quarterback, this is Gadget Blue.* Request *goal posts*, over."

Goal posts: marking an approach line for aircraft to a ground target with white phosphorous airbursts high in the sky.

"Negative, *Gadget Blue*, negative," Menifee responded. "No goal posts. Artillery unable to comply."

Well, ain't that some shit, Tommy thought. *Usually when the artillery's too busy, there are big fat columns of smoke rising somewhere in the battle area from the pasting they're dealing out, and the ASO is screaming at you to stay clear—there are rounds in the air! But I don't see any of that stuff going on here.*

"We need help, *Quarterback*. Target not identified. Repeat—target *not* identified."

"Best we can do is white smoke from the eighty-ones," Menifee replied.

Great...mortar smoke. About as visible from up here as a black cat in the dark. But if that's all they have...

"Give it a try, *Quarterback*. Standing by."

Blue Flight barely had time to reverse direction to keep the area in view when Menifee reported, "Splash, over."

Five seconds later, an indistinct plume of white smoke appeared, wafting lazily up through the thick trees. In a few seconds, another puff of smoke materialized, hundreds of yards away from the first and just as difficult to see.

"*Quarterback*, this is *Gadget Blue*. Confirm number

of smoke rounds fired."

"One round, over."

"You're sure?"

"Affirmative."

"Then we've got ourselves a copycat, *Quarterback*."

Tommy was fairly certain one of those smoke rounds had been fired by the eavesdropping Germans, and it had probably landed somewhere in the American position. Menifee just hadn't realized it yet. It could be a ruse, a deadly decoy. And if Tommy led his flight against that target marker—whichever one of the two it was—there was an excellent chance they'd kill GIs.

And my brother could be one of those GIs down there.

But not providing the air support they so desperately needed could get his brother killed, too.

What the hell am I supposed to do? If we fly high, we won't see a damn thing. If we fly too low, we're moving too fast to see a damn thing.

There was another option, however, and as if on cue, it appeared out of nowhere as a voice on the radio: "*Gadget Blue*, this is *Rocket Man*. Need some eyes *low and slow*?"

Rocket Man: every GI in 4th Armored knew who he was, but the pilots of the 301st had only heard stories that seemed too fantastic to be true. He was an artilleryman—a major named Bob Kidd—who flew spotter missions in an L-4, the Army's version of the Piper Cub. He'd been doing much more than merely spotting for the big guns, though. Flying *low and slow*, he'd come face to face with panzers, often close enough to spit on them. Not willing to stop there, he'd mounted *bazookas*—the standard, shoulder-launched anti-tank rocket the ground-pounders carried—on the wing struts of his little L-4 and wired them up to firing buttons in his cockpit. And by flying *low and slow*, he could actually get close enough to the panzers—one hundred yards or less—to knock them out of action with rockets, something the speedy fighter aircraft could rarely do with any regularity, despite countless claims to the contrary. It was simple ballistics: compact, moving targets such as panzers were difficult to hit with rockets fired from a fast-moving aircraft. It was like trying to throw a ball from a speeding car into a bucket on the road ahead.

"Rocket Man, this is *Gadget Blue Leader*. Sure could use your help figuring out where to drop our stuff."

"Roger, *Gadget Blue*. Stand by."

Rocket Man's procedure for target marking would be a bit different—and a bit safer for the GIs on the ground. He'd drop a colored smoke grenade on the target and then ask the attacking fighters to identify the smoke color they saw. If their report agreed with the color he dropped, they were clear to attack.

Orbiting to the west to get out of *Rocket Man's* way, they watched in amazement as the slow-flying L-4 got down to treetop level—probably even drawing fire—as he made several passes over the forest, turning on a dime after each run and going back for another look. From that height, he'd be able to spot the details that distinguished Germans from the GIs. He could even see startled faces beneath Wehrmacht *coal scuttle* helmets looking up at him, some in disbelief, others in anger, as they raised their weapons for a fleeting shot at the L-4.

I don't get it, Tommy told himself. *These crazy guys in their fragile little airplanes putter around right over the Krauts' heads all day and live to tell about it. I saw a couple come back from missions with huge chunks of the fabric skin shot away from their wings and fuselages, but they still flew and got their pilot home. Shoot up a jug like that and it's probably going down...and taking you with her.*

On his fourth pass, *Rocket Man* dropped a smoke grenade. Tommy was too high to see such a small object fall into the trees, even with the wispy yellow trail it was leaving behind. But several seconds later, thick yellow smoke rose in a thin but distinct plume.

"*Gadget Blue's* got yellow smoke," Tommy reported.

"Affirmative, *Gadget Blue*. Now get in there and knock them silly, before some clever Kraut picks the damn thing up and throws it away."

Blue Flight wasted no time dropping their 500-pound bombs on the yellow smoke. As the last of the four jugs pulled up from her bomb run, Lieutenant Menifee—*Quarterback*—said, "Right on the money, *Gadget Blue*. Beautiful! Great job!" The radio failed to mask his excitement and relief just as it couldn't mask his southern accent.

"Good to hear, *Quarterback*," Tommy replied. "Do you need a gun run in the same area?"

"Standby, *Gadget Blue*. This may be under control."

"Roger," Tommy replied. "*Rocket Man*, you still on frequency?"

"Affirmative."

"Hey, we owe you a beer. Stop by A-90 anytime."

"I'll take you up on that, *Gadget Blue*. Great

working with you."

Blue Flight drifted back toward the Moselle, loitering in wait of another call for ground support. *Looks like this is shaping up to be a slow afternoon,* Tommy thought. *But I'm betting it wouldn't be this way if Third Army was actually advancing somewhere. If you ask me, I think they're digging in for the winter already. Doesn't look like anyone's going to be home by Christmas, that's for sure.*

Chapter Nine

It had been a full week since Sean had "swum" in the Seille, and he was still wearing those same filthy tanker's coveralls. But it was the cleanest uniform he had; *Maybe that damn swim had been good for something after all,* he told himself. *It was the only laundry service I've seen in months. Traded out a little dirt and grease for river silt. But still, if I ever take these duds off, they'll stand up all by themselves. Maybe even walk away. At least we got ourselves a hot meal last night, though. Hot food beats clean clothes any day.*

The hot meal—fried Spam and eggs any way you liked them—had been ordered by 5th Infantry Division's commanding general as a morale-booster. No GI would ever turn down food at any temperature, but the old hands of *this man's army*—men like Sergeant Sean Moon—weren't blind to the hot meal's real purpose: *Whenever the brass are about to get our asses killed in a big way, they try and pump us up with something first. Maybe it's a hot meal, maybe the padre shows up to dish out more of the "God is on our side" bullshit. But it all means the same thing: we're going into some serious action, and real soon.*

He asked Captain Newcomb, "So what's the big plan this time, sir? We've been pussyfooting around this damn fort for days now, getting blown to shit in the wire. If it ain't anti-tank ditches, it's mines. When are we gonna bust it all down for good?"

"Fifth Division G2 figures the fort's weakest defenses are on the east side—the back side," Newcomb said.

"That's also the steepest slope, too, sir. *Real* steep. *Mountain goat* steep."

"We know that, Sergeant. We also know there are no anti-tank ditches back there."

"That don't mean there ain't no mines, sir."

"We know that, too, Sergeant. But if we can breach the barbed wire network in at least three places on that back side, they figure we can push enough infantry through to actually get into the fort and hold it. Maybe two battalions' worth."

"But I hear they've already been inside," Sean replied, "and once you're in there, it's worse than house-to-house fighting with all them tunnels. They can get in, but they just get pushed right back out. At least the ones still alive, anyway."

"Yeah, you're right, Sergeant. The casualties have been pretty heavy. But they've never gotten more than a company inside the fort. Still, there can't be *that* many Krauts in there."

"I don't know, sir. Every swinging dick's beating his gums that the casualties are something like forty percent."

"Don't believe everything you hear, Sergeant. Gather up your tank commanders and report to the CP at 0800 hours. The engineers are going to give us a class."

Sean checked his watch. "You gotta be kidding, sir. That's less than an hour from now. The guys are still pulling maintenance."

"Do I look like I'm kidding, Sergeant Moon?"

"But a class, sir? On what?"

"Bangalore torpedoes," Newcomb replied.

Sean knew exactly where this was going. His reply: "Oh, my aching ass."

✮✮✮✮

The four P-47s of *Blue Flight* had taken off just after dawn, flying into the rising sun to look for German columns on the roadways east of Nancy. The blinding glare of sunrise was brutal even with tinted goggles, and it heightened the anxiety all Allied pilots lived with every time they left the ground: *Beware of the Hun in the sun.*

That's why I've got to keep us low and fast, Tommy told himself. *We're hard to see from above down here...and we'll flash past any flak gunners so fast they'll never have a chance to get a bead on us.*

Within a minute he was proved right. "*Blue Two* to *Blue Leader*," Jimmy Tuttle broadcast, "we've got two FWs, straight up overhead, maybe three thousand feet, heading northwest."

Tommy craned his neck to look out the top of his razorback jug's *birdcage* canopy. "Yeah," he replied, "I've got them. Good eyes, Jimmy." Within seconds, the German fighters had sped out of view.

"Doesn't look like they got us, though," Tommy added. He couldn't help but feel his tactics had just been validated.

And my wingman's definitely on the ball.

Finding the French roads strangely deserted, they prowled farther east to the town of Dieuze, where a number of highways intersected.

Maybe the pickings will be better there.

They were.

On a stretch of highway running through a thick woods—the *Bois de Morsack*—just west of Dieuze, they saw a column of trucks. *Twenty, maybe more*, Tommy counted, scattering among the trees at their approach. But even in concealment, their exhaust smoke and tire tracks in the soft earth had given the trucks' positions away.

They'd attack in two waves, Tommy and Tuttle making the first pass, strafing with their .50 calibers to keep the heads of any German gunners down. Right behind them would come *Blue Three* and *Blue Four*— Lieutenants Joey Nardini and Pete Iverson—to drop their 500-pounders in a glide bombing run.

It all went so well at first. Tommy and Tuttle riddled the trees just one hundred feet below their wings. They couldn't see much of the Germans below the treetops, but felt a vicious bump of turbulent air as something—maybe a fuel tanker, maybe an ammo truck—exploded beneath them. They wouldn't know what it was for a few moments, not until they could turn their ships and see the target area again. The color of the smoke would give it away: thick black for a fuel fire, grayish and wispy for ammunition.

Nardini in *Blue Three* saw it first. "You want us to use that smoke for a target marker?" he asked.

"Yeah, Joey, but drop your stuff a little beyond it, okay? I'm pretty sure that's the tail end of the column."

"Roger. Here we come."

Circling wide of the target area, Tommy and Tuttle had a front row seat as *Blue Three* and *Four* put their bombs right where they were told. As he pulled out of his shallow dive, *Blue Four*—Iverson, flying *tail-end Charlie*—reported, "Looks like a lot of Krauts running to the south side of the road. I'm talking *a lot* of Krauts."

"Okay," Tommy said, "let's swap hats. Joey, you and Pete do the strafing run this time, then Jimmy and I will get rid of our bombs. Keep it wide, guys…if they're running, they'll cover a lot of ground in the minute it takes us to get back on them."

"Maybe they're going to stop and dig in close on the south side, boss," Jimmy Tuttle said.

"Not likely," Tommy replied. "Once you start running, it's pretty hard to stop. And there's not enough time for them to dig deep enough. Like I said, play it wide."

Blue Three and *Four* were rolling into their strafing run. "How wide is *wide*, boss?" Iverson asked.

Tommy replied, "Come on, Pete, you've done this before. Put Joey's plane so it just fills the two squares in your canopy frame."

"Okay, okay. I've got it."

Nardini and Iverson were firing now, streaking so low across the treetops that Tommy thought they might vanish into the greenery. But they stayed in plain sight. When they reached the edge of the woods, Nardini pulled up. Iverson didn't.

His voice rising an octave in panic, Iverson said, "I'm not getting any power. And the whole ship's vibrating like hell. Can't keep her up much longer."

Shit, Tommy thought, *he hit a tree, I'll bet. He hit a fucking tree. It isn't the first time someone did that.*

"THE PROP'S RUNNING AWAY," Iverson shrieked.

"Just pull it back, Pete," Tommy said, fighting to stay focused and keep his own voice calm as he and Tuttle released their bombs. Then he added, "Jimmy, you and Joey give us top cover. I'll stay with Pete."

"Roger, boss."

Tuttle climbed away while Tommy closed in on

Iverson's wingtip. His altimeter read only two hundred feet. He could swear he was lower than that. More disturbing was his airspeed; matching pace with Iverson, they were barely making one hundred forty miles per hour.

It only took a quick glance at the nose of *Blue Four* to confirm Tommy's guess as to what had happened. There were several feet shaved off the normal thirteen-foot diameter of the propeller arc. The front lip of the elliptical engine cowling was bashed in all around its circumference. The oil coolers in the bottom of that cowling—if they weren't ruptured and leaking precious engine oil—probably had their airflow blocked by the misshapen cowl lip.

Yep, he hit a tree.

"How's your oil temp, Pete?" Tommy asked.

"Climbing."

Yeah, no kidding. Those coolers aren't getting any air.

"I'll tell you what we're going to do, Pete. Set your manifold pressure to twenty-eight inches. Can you do that?"

"Yeah, boss. It's about there now."

"Good. Now bring your RPM down until your jaw stops rattling."

There were a few moments of silence on the radio as Iverson teased the prop lever backward. "There," he reported. "It feels okay at twenty-two fifty."

"And the oil temp's still on the gauge?"

"Yeah, boss. Seems to be holding...for now."

"Swell. But we've got to get you a little higher if we're going to get you all the way home...but at that power setting the climb has to be *verrry* gradual. And your airspeed might get scary slow."

"Maybe I should just bail out," Iverson said.

"Negative, you're too low. Now listen to me. First thing we're going to do is a gentle right turn, about twenty-five degrees. That'll put us on a heading straight back to A-90."

It'll also put us straight into the high ground west of the Moselle if we don't gain some altitude.

They made it through the turn without a loss of altitude.

But they did lose a few miles per hour of airspeed.

"Pete, I'm going to start orbiting above you. Slow as you are, I can still keep pace that way, but I'll have a better view of what's going on around us."

He didn't say the rest of what he was thinking: *So if you go in, maybe we can have a place picked out where there might not be any Krauts.*

Four minutes later—and two miles from the Moselle River—Iverson said, "I can't hold her, Tommy. Airspeed's down to one-oh-five. Oil temp's pegged out. Where should I put her down?"

"The road junction dead ahead, Pete. Put her there. It's nice and flat."

With a violent shudder that threatened to loosen every rivet in his ship, Iverson's engine seized.

"Well, I'm landing for sure now. I'm gonna belly her."

"Affirmative. Belly her."

It was just a matter of seconds before *Blue Four* was plowing through the soft mud, her lower fuselage digging in like a knife through butter. She came to a quick stop still upright, something that would have been unlikely if Iverson had tried a wheel landing in all that muck. She would have flipped on her back almost certainly, and he would have been trapped inside.

But escape might have been a moot point if his skull was crushed or his neck broken.

Her seized engine smoked but nothing was on fire. Exiting the aircraft was as simple as climbing over the canopy rail and stepping off her wing to the soggy ground only inches below.

Tommy breathed a sigh of relief as he watched Iverson jog away from his aircraft. That relief didn't last long, though. A few hundred yards to the north, a light vehicle churned slowly across the muddy ground toward the wreck. A squad of men on foot hurried behind it in a ragged column.

That truck doesn't look GI issue to me, Tommy thought.

Any doubts he might have had vanished as pieces started to fly off the downed jug. *They're shooting her up. Got to be Krauts. And it looks like there's a heavy machine gun on that vehicle.*

He couldn't see Iverson anymore, but at last sight he'd been somewhere on the far side of *Blue Four* from the Germans, moving away from them.

Probably running like hell now, too, the poor bastard.

Tommy put *Eclipse* into a diving turn and locked the vehicle—now obviously an armored car—into his gunsight. He was sure the German machine gunner had seen him coming by now and was lining up on him, too.

First shot wins...and I've got the range over him.

Tommy's first burst of .50-caliber bullets splashed short. With gentle back pressure on the stick—*Put her right on the pip, Moon*—he walked the next burst across the armored car. It veered crazily—seemingly unguided—as *Eclipse* roared past.

When he pulled around for another pass, the car was motionless. The squad on foot was nowhere to be seen.

Now where the hell is Iverson?

Tommy could see several boxy, lumbering shapes rolling across the ground to the west, headed for the wreck. He knew exactly what they were: *Shermans.*

He did a wide orbit around them, displaying the jug's silhouette and markings as clearly as he could, to lessen the odds a trigger-happy GI gunner might mistake him for the enemy. As he completed the circle, he could see them waving at him as a man scrambled onto the deck of the lead tank.

That's got to be Iverson. Lucky bastard'll be back at A-90 before the sun goes down, probably.

He climbed to rejoin Tuttle and Nardini, who'd been orbiting high overhead, too high to make out what was happening on the ground below.

"Did you get that last call from *Halfback*?" Tuttle asked.

"No," Tommy replied. "Been a little busy. What'd he want?"

"They need some eyes over that damn fort again. Sounds like something big's going on down there."

"Did you tell them we're low on ammo and down a ship?"

"Yeah, but they didn't care, boss. They say they need help now, and we're closest and available. By the way, I'm positive the voice on the radio was Clinchmore."

If it was Lieutenant Herb Clinchmore—a pilot from the 301st doing duty as an air support officer with the ground troops—that meant the unit calling for help was probably 37th Tank…

My brother's outfit, Tommy told himself.

Chapter Ten

Sean Moon wasn't sure what aggravated him more: leading the tanks of Baker Company up this narrow, treacherous switchback along the steep hill leading to the back side of Fort Driant; the fort's howitzers firing noisily but harmlessly over their heads; that even on this clear morning they had no air support covering their flanks; that the *class* they were supposed to be receiving was actually *on-the-job* training under fire in the use of Bangalore torpedoes; or the thought that Colonel Abrams might still be pissed off—even days later—over his navigation error in the fog that had delayed their arrival and kept 37th Tank under strength and forced to cool its heels for the better part of a day.

And if the colonel's still mad at Baker Company, maybe that's why we got assigned this shit detail with the engineers and their stupid Bangalores. I fucked up, and now my whole company's getting fucked over.

It didn't matter that Captain Newcomb had assured him nothing could be further from the truth; the colonel knew better than to expect things to always go perfectly. *Everybody has problems*, *Alvin,* Abrams had told Newcomb, *but it's what you're doing about them that matters. And what you did about your little mistake turned out okay.*

Still, Sean was convinced that error—*his* error—had moved Baker Company to the top of Colonel Abrams' shit list.

Another salvo from the fort's batteries—100 and 150-millimeter howitzers in steel turrets—roared over the tanks of Baker Company. The howitzers were no threat; they couldn't be depressed low enough to engage them as they climbed the road to the fort. But they were firing toward the Moselle, no doubt at GIs trying to cross that river in assault boats just south of Metz. If this attempt to cross was like all the others before, the guns of Fort Driant would shatter those flimsy boats and send the surviving GIs treading water back to the riverbank from which they'd come. It didn't matter if they tried to sneak across at night, either; the German guns had the Moselle valley around Metz zeroed in.

It pisses me off, too, Sean thought, *because Fourth Armored's already been across the Moselle—waaaay across the Moselle—down by Nancy. But the brass think that place ain't good enough to move the rest of Third Army across. So Patton wants to take the direct route, crossing at Metz and blasting straight to the Saar River and into Germany...but this fucking fort won't let him.*

And so far, ain't nobody made a dent in the damn place.

A fort...can you believe it? Where the hell are we, in the Middle Ages or something?

Captain Newcomb's voice came over the radio. "All right, this is the place," he said. "Provide cover and suppressing fire for the engineers while they put these contraptions together."

Contraptions: the Bangalore torpedoes. A long, thin explosive charge made up of pipe sections that could be assembled to a fifty-foot length, pushed into a field of barbed wire, and then detonated to cut a path through the wire and set off any integrated mines. The tanks had transported several dozen of the unassembled torpedoes on their hull decks. Now it was time to put this technology from *The Great War* to use against a fort of the same era.

"This gotta be the thickest fucking barbed wire setup I've ever seen," Sean called down from the turret hatch to the engineer sergeant supervising the unlashing of the Bangalores from *Lucky 7's* deck. "You sure we got enough of these things to blow all the way through?"

"My captain says three torpedoes, full length, at each breach point should do the job," the engineer replied.

"You mean we gotta push one through, blow it, and then set up another one, push *it* through—"

"Yeah," the engineer interrupted, "you've got the picture. Just make sure you keep the Krauts' heads down while we're laying this pipe out."

"You ever used a tank to push one of these *thingamajigs* before?"

The engineer didn't bother to answer, but Sean could tell from the look on his face the answer was *no*.

"I thought so," Sean said. "Ain't infantry supposed to be the ones shoving these things through the wire?"

"They tried, over on the other side of the fort," the engineer replied, "but most of them got killed before they set off even one torpedo. We had to wait until dark before we could untangle and retrieve their bodies." Then he added, "Besides, this hill is much too steep to push the Bangalores by hand. They weigh almost a hundred pounds at full length. That's why you're here."

"I've got news for you, pal," Sean replied. "This hill's too steep for these *Zippos*, too. Maybe we can creep up them a ways in low gear, but that's gonna be about it."

He glanced down the slope, where several companies of infantry were assembled to assault through the wire once paths were blown open for them. "It might even be too steep for those poor bastards to climb on foot, lugging all that ammo and shit."

Sean scanned the parapet high above them with his binoculars as Fabiano manned the .50-caliber machine gun on the turret roof. "Over there, Fab…two fingers right of our muzzle…some Jerries are taking a peek at us. Play 'em a little chin music."

A long burst from the .50 cal made the Germans drop back behind their fortress wall. The noise of it also scared the daylights out of the engineers working on the ground behind *Lucky 7*.

"Keep it up, Fab," Sean said. "They'll be sending more Krauts over to this wall once they figure out what we're doing."

The engineer sergeant ran his hand across the tank's name painted on the turret. "How'd you come to call her this, anyway?" he asked.

"Easy. She's my seventh tank since North Africa," Sean replied.

"What happened to the other six?"

"What the hell do you think happened to them?"

"So what makes this one lucky, Moon?"

"Call it wishful thinking, okay? Now let's hustle it up with them damn stovepipes, before I have to christen *Lucky Eight*. We've been sitting still too damn long."

Sean looked into the distance to see a flight of P-47s orbiting wide of the fort. "Oh, great. Look who finally showed up. At least now we'll know if any Kraut armor's coming up the road behind us."

The engineer sergeant asked, "Why the hell are they all the way over there?"

Sean gave him a look like that was the world's

dumbest question. "Because they don't want to get knocked down by one of them big lead eggs the fort's throwing at the Moselle, that's why."

Blue Flight was orbiting north of Fort Driant, being the *eyes in the sky* the ground-pounders had requested. Tommy watched as the fort's howitzers fired, trying to follow the tiny dot of each round before it vanished from sight as it arced the few miles east to the Moselle. *There must be GIs trying to get across there*, he told himself. *Doesn't look like they're doing too good.* Even from this distance, the river's surface looked like it was being churned by geysers. The riverbanks were faring no better, the thick smoke of countless fires rising from them in ominous black columns.

A lot of vehicles burning, Tommy told himself. *GI vehicles.*

Looking down on the turrets of Driant, he couldn't believe how impervious they'd been to anything thrown against them, from high explosives to white phosphorous to napalm. Nothing had made a difference. This fort—this monument to another age of warfare, an age everyone had thought long obsolete—was proving invulnerable to everything the US Army had in its arsenal.

The GIs had long known the observation posts on Fort Driant—high, strongly reinforced towers protruding from the central blockhouse—gave the fort's gunners a superb view of the Moselle valley for miles above and below Metz. From that vantage point, they could direct the fire of the other Metz forts, as well.

I'd love to shoot up those OPs, Tommy thought, *but it'll be just like all the other times—it won't do a damn bit of good. It'll just make those artillery observers keep their heads down for a second, maybe even give them a headache or make their ears bleed, but that's about all. It's just like those flak towers we try to shoot up. Unless you can knock the damn thing down, you're just etching your name in the concrete and steel. And once you're gone, they're back to business as usual.*

I wish to hell we could do more for our guys on the ground.

Somebody's got to do more.

It seemed to take forever to get the first Bangalore torpedoes rigged. *Lucky 7*—Sean Moon's tank—was the first to move forward, pushing the torpedo's long pipe into the barbed wire with a bumper the engineers had fabricated from a log and hung low off her bow. The whole enterprise must have sounded so easy on paper.

"Hold up, Ski," Sean called to his driver before the tank had moved fifty feet. "We ain't pushing nothing, dammit. The *snake* just slipped under the hull."

The Bangalore torpedo—*snake* in GI slang—was snagging in the wire, kinking the pipe sections and disengaging the contraption from the tank's makeshift bumper. The other two tanks pushing the torpedoes up the hill weren't doing any better, either. Standing in the turret hatch, Sean motioned for the engineers huddled behind his tank to get out of the way so she could back up. Not thrilled to lose their cover, but not looking to get crushed, either, they reluctantly complied.

"Okay, Ski," he said, "they're clear. Back her up."

"What's the matter?" the engineer sergeant called up to Sean.

"Your little toy's falling apart. Go straighten it out so maybe we can get this shit job done sometime this fucking year."

The engineers kept shooting apprehensive glances skyward, as if expecting holy hell to come crashing down on them at any moment.

"Don't worry about the Kraut artillery from the other forts," Sean told them. "Not yet, anyway. They ain't gonna shoot at us unless we clear this wire. They don't like to waste rounds, either."

Right now, clearing the wire was anything but a certainty. They all knew it.

Machine gun fire from the fort's parapet began to chew up the ground around *Lucky 7*, sending the engineers scampering for cover behind her hull again.

"Let me put a couple of rounds from the big gun up their asses, Sarge," Fabiano pleaded as he returned fire with the .50 caliber.

Sean could tell his gunner was getting nervous manning the big machine gun out in the open. He was sure Fabiano's real motive for wanting to fire the main gun was to be back inside the steel cocoon of the Sherman.

"Negative," Sean replied. "They'll just bounce off those walls like all the other rounds we've fired. Just keep putting fifty cal right past their fucking heads, like the rest of the platoon is doing."

Fabiano did as he was told. The German machine guns stopped firing abruptly.

"There," Sean said, "that'll keep their heads down.

And keep your drawers on, Fab. Those Kraut *MGs* are too far away and with too much of a vertical interval. It'll be pure luck if they hit anything at all."

"But I've got the same bad vertical interval as them, Sarge."

"Yeah, but you're shooting bigger bullets with better range and a flat trajectory. Just keep scaring the shit out of them."

The engineers were still clustered behind the tank. Sean yelled down to them, "You guys having a prayer meeting or something? Get this fucking show of yours on the road before we take our marbles and go home. Where you gonna hide then?"

Tommy could see them a long way off: a column of vehicles snaking their way up the winding road out of Metz toward Fort Driant. *They're moving too fast to be tanks*, he told himself. *They've got wheels, not tracks. Probably armored cars. Kraut armored cars. About twelve of them.*

We've got to stop them.

"*Blue Leader* to *Blue Flight*," he radioed, "let's hit them out of the east as soon as they're on that next bend."

Out of the east meant *out of the sun.*

It would be a tricky approach to the targets. The Germans were driving along the side of a steep hill, paralleling an intermediate ridgeline. One miscalculation by a pilot—one moment of target fixation—and his jug would fly right into the rising terrain just beyond his quarry.

"*Blue Two*, you're with me," he told Tuttle. "We'll take the head of the column. *Blue Three*, you take the tail."

A classic ambush technique, applied from the air: knock out the front and rear of a column and trap all the other vehicles in the middle, forcing them to a stop. It would be so much easier, though, played out on flat ground. And easier still if *Blue Four* was still in the air and not a pile of fresh scrap metal lying in the French countryside.

At least Iverson's okay...I think, Tommy hoped.

Flying low, the three ships of *Blue Flight* swung a few miles east before turning back to their targets. Leading the way, Tommy told himself, *Okay, we're far enough out and the sun's behind us. They won't even see us coming...*

Not on the first pass, anyway.

He was right. Their attack run worked exactly as planned, knocking out several of the lead and trail armored cars. Those trapped in the middle were now stalled on the narrow road. Their only hope of escape was to push the burning hulks blocking them over the road's shoulder to career down the steep slope.

Nice pass...but this isn't any time to celebrate, Tommy reminded himself. *Sun in their eyes or not, they know we're here now. They may not be able to move but they can still shoot.*

Better mix it up.

Putting the high ground between *Blue Flight* and the stalled German column, Tommy announced their next move. "I'll strafe their line north to south. As soon as I'm done, you two do the same but from the opposite direction."

Tuttle asked, "Which way are you going to break after your run, boss?"

"Straight up," Tommy replied. "I'll stay out of your way better if I do it like that."

"You sure you don't want to break east, away from the slope?" Tuttle asked. "Going up might put you in somebody's sights for a long, long time."

"It'll be the same either way, Jimmy. I'm more worried about being in your way. I'll just do the old *zoom and boom*."

"Roger, boss. So be it. Good luck."

Hugging the contour of the hill, Tommy barreled his plane down the road, banking sharply right to follow the curve in the switchback as tightly as he could. The view out the right side of his canopy was enough to make his heart pound: the terrain was far too close to his wingtip for comfort and towered high above him.

Halfway through the pass, his guns stopped firing. They were *dry*, out of ammunition. But he finished his sweep along the line of vehicles, pulling sharply up as he reached its end to make way for Tuttle and Nardini, who had begun their headlong sprint toward him.

"You taking any fire, boss?" Tuttle asked him.

"Can't tell, Jimmy. But I don't think so."

"That's good news. See you on the other side of the mountain."

By the time they'd finished their pass, Tuttle's and Nardini's guns were dry, too.

"Funny thing," Tuttle said as *Blue Flight* re-formed north of Fort Driant, "but I think those Krauts ran away, just abandoned their vehicles. I don't think anyone fired at us, either."

"Can you blame them?" Tommy replied.

Orbiting at two thousand feet now, they could see the Shermans the ASO had advised them of, clinging to the hill on the fort's east side. They weren't calling for air support, but it didn't relieve the sick feeling in Tommy's stomach:

That could be my brother down there. And there's not a damn thing I can do to help him right now.

He felt as if he was committing an act of betrayal as he told *Halfback* that *Blue Flight* was returning to base to rearm.

Sean's tank was still trying to push its first Bangalore torpedo deep into the wire. They were on their third try. The first two had been a circus of misguided design and the mistakes of terrified men under threat of enemy fire.

Those engineers are trying their best, I guess, Sean told himself, *but we ain't gonna get nowhere with these piece of shit snakes if they're too scared to get out in front of the tanks. But that's where they gotta be—at least to put those pipe sections back together. Unless...*

"Hey," he called to the engineer sergeant, "get your guys to fit those fucking pipes together *under* the tank. You can build the whole *shebang* beneath this little rolling bunker of mine...even hook it to the front bumper without having to hang your asses out for Kraut target practice."

The engineer sergeant looked skeptical. "I don't think we've got enough room to work underneath the tank."

"Sure you do," Sean replied. "We crawl in and out

of that escape hatch in her bottom all the time, dragging all kinds of shit with us. There's plenty of room. Of course, if you'd rather stand outside in the shitstorm, that's up to you."

The sergeant thought it over for a moment. "Okay," he said, "we'll give your way a try."

"Just one little thing," Sean added. "When I say *CLEAR*, you'd better make damn sure that every swinging dick of yours is out from under this tank. I don't want to be running over no friendlies today."

As the engineers worked beneath *Lucky 7*, Fabiano asked Sean, "They ain't really gonna be pushing any of those snakes *under* her, are they, Sarge?"

"Yeah, they will. That's the whole point."

"Well, I take a pretty dim view of that," Fabiano replied. "That's all we fucking need—get blown up by one of those pieces of crap."

"Relax, Fab. Those engineers will only be killing themselves. It won't bother us none."

Promising as Sean's *ad hoc* procedure for assembling the Bangalores sounded, the next three attempts to push one deep into the wire were no more successful than the first three. The assembly was never designed to be pushed up a steep hill. The torpedo snagged constantly; the pipe sections bowed and disconnected.

On the seventh try, Sean thought he'd found a path free of obstructions. *Lucky 7's* crew and the engineers alike held their collective breath as the first pipe section slid into the wire. In a few moments of slow, steady progress, over half its length had been shoved into place. The torpedo finally snagged as the last few sections of pipe were crossing the wire's threshold.

Sean asked the engineer sergeant, "What do you think? Close enough?"

Before the sergeant could answer, the first German mortar round from Fort Driant landed no more than ten yards from *Lucky 7.*

"Dammit," Sean said. "I was wondering when they'd start with that shit."

The threat of a mortar barrage was more than enough to loosen the engineer's standards. He grabbed the trigger and squeezed it.

Nothing happened. This Bangalore was a dud.

Calling Captain Newcomb on the radio, Sean said, "No dice, sir. I'm ready to throw in the towel on this *fubar* exercise."

Newcomb couldn't agree more. None of his tanks had succeeded in pushing a Bangalore deep enough into the wire to do any good. Sean's idea had seemed to be the only potential bright spot in the whole disappointing affair, but now that, too, had been a bust. Add the deadly inconvenience of incoming mortar rounds, and there was no doubt it was time to call it quits. The infantry they were supporting had already started their withdrawal. Newcomb radioed his company, "Fall back to the Assembly Area Dog."

Today's *on-the-job-training* in the use of Bangalore torpedoes—and with it, today's attempt to breach Fort Driant—had come to yet another inglorious end.

Chapter Eleven

It took less than ten minutes for *Blue Flight* to make it back to A-90. When they were a few miles out, Tommy requested clearance for his three-ship flight to land. The tower's reply wasn't what he expected: "Can you hold, *Blue Leader*? We've got high-priority inbound traffic in the pattern."

"Affirmative, we can hold," Tommy replied. "We're good on fuel for the moment. How long will it be?"

"About five minutes, *Blue Leader*."

"Roger, we can do that."

Level at 2,000 feet, they picked up the *racetrack* holding pattern just south of the airfield. Below the patchy cloud deck, Tommy had a great view of A-90 and its incoming traffic. The delay grated on him, though. He wanted to rearm, refuel, and get back into the fight as soon as possible, before the weather shut down flight operations.

To soothe his impatience, he began playing the control stick gently in his fingers, putting *Eclipse* through some playful *s-turns*. He marveled at how responsive and nimble a lightened P-47 could be when empty of ordnance and down to just reserve fuel. *Eclipse's* responses to stick and rudder inputs now seemed direct and instantaneous, as if no longer being interpreted and delayed by that intangible elastic link between pilot and aircraft when she was heavily laden. For this brief moment, Tommy couldn't contain his sheer joy of flying: *Usually, it's like flying a Mack truck when she's loaded for bear. This is a lot more fun. Wish*

I had the time and fuel to really play around.

Jimmy Tuttle's voice in his earphones shattered his reverie. "You got ants in your pants, boss, or are you just trying to waste more gas? I'm getting a little nervous watching you jink around like that in front of me."

"Relax, Jimmy, I'm just passing the time, waiting to see who this *high-priority traffic* is."

They didn't have to wait long to find out. Like lumbering dragonflies, two four-engined bombers—one in olive drab paint, the other a garish yellow—turned below them to final approach at A-90. Trailing a mile or so behind the bombers—too small to be seen until they were seconds from touchdown—were two miniscule single-engined aircraft painted that same decidedly non-tactical shade of yellow.

"Holy crap, they're B-17s," Tuttle said. "And what the hell are those little toys chasing after them? Are they going to the circus or something all painted up like that?"

"Good question," Tommy replied. "But why the hell are they landing here? I don't think a *Flying Fort's* going to be able to take off from A-90, short as that runway is. Not with any kind of load, anyway."

The tower controller broke in: "*Blue Flight*, you're clear to land. Wind's two-six at ten. Altimeter two-niner point four."

Crap, Tommy thought as he watched the clouds thickening above them. *Baro's dropping. It's going to sock in and rain again, real soon.*

And when it did, *Blue Flight*—and the rest of 301st Fighter Squadron—wouldn't be able to help the ground-pounders even if they could get airborne.

Once on the ground and taxiing to the *hot pad*, they

could see the B-17s—the Flying Fortresses—and their *little yellow friends* tucked into a far corner of the field, away from any other installation. Half a dozen jeeps were forming a protective cordon around the parked aircraft.

They look like MP jeeps, Tommy thought.

The familiar faces of *Blue Flight's* ground crews guided the jugs to parking spots on the pad, where fuel tankers and tractors towing trailers loaded with bombs and machine gun ammo waited. Tommy could see the apprehensive look on Iverson's crew chief—a young, mild-mannered staff sergeant named Boone—as he waited like a man who'd just been jilted. He'd need to learn everything he could about what happened to his pilot and his plane—yes, *his* plane—for ground crews always felt the planes really belonged to them, and they merely loaned them to the pilots for a few hours a day.

Boone and his crew would need whatever assurance he could muster that the loss of a pilot and plane wasn't their fault.

Tommy's crew chief McNulty was on the wing beside the cockpit before *Eclipse's* prop had stopped spinning. "Any problems with my little girl?" he asked Tommy.

"No, she's good, Sarge. Just get her ready to go again as quickly as you can."

Boone was now on the wing, too. Before he could say a word, Tommy told him, "I think Lieutenant Iverson's okay. Looks like an armored unit picked him up the other side of the Moselle. The plane"—he stopped himself and rephrased—"*your* plane's done for, I'm afraid."

He knew that bit of information wouldn't be enough

to satisfy Sergeant Boone, though. He'd need to know *why*.

Tommy could ease Boone's tortured soul by simply saying, *Your guy screwed up. Flew a perfectly good airplane into a tree.* But he was pretty sure Iverson would be back in the squadron, probably that day. And when he did return, he'd be a hell of a lot wiser—and a hell of a lot better pilot—than he'd been this morning. But he'd be facing these same mechanics whose plane he'd just lost. Tommy didn't need them bad-mouthing one of his pilots. Nobody needed the drag on morale such dissension would create. His flight—and the whole squadron—ran so much better when mutual respect flowed between its members.

We've all made mistakes—lord knows I have—and we'll all probably make a whole bunch more. All that really matters is that we're learning from them.

He told Boone, "He was strafing and something hit her in the engine. Tough break, but your ship held up swell and got him down safe and sound. Nicest belly landing I ever saw."

Tommy watched the wave of relief pass over Sergeant Boone. In a few moments, he'd be able to watch that same relief pass over Boone's crew, who were anxiously awaiting word from him.

With Boone gone, McNulty asked, "That really what happened, Lieutenant?"

"It's close enough, Sergeant." Anxious to change the topic, Tommy pointed to the other side of the airfield and asked, "What the hell's going on over there with those B-17s?"

McNulty shrugged. "Nobody's told us shit, sir, except that if we got near them, we'd get our asses thrown in the stockade. Some MP outfit got that part of the field all locked up."

"Yeah, I figured they were MPs," Tommy replied. "I wonder what it all means?"

"Call me a *pestimist*, Lieutenant, but if it walks like a duck and talks like a duck, it's still gonna shit on your head."

★★★★

The mission debrief had just ended as Colonel Pruitt walked into the operations shack. "I've got good news," he told Tommy. "Just like you thought, Lieutenant Iverson is okay and in the good hands of Fourth Armored. That's your brother's outfit, isn't it?"

"Yes, sir," Tommy replied. "Thirty-Seventh Tank Battalion, Fourth Armored Division. But where are they, exactly? Last thing I heard, the Fourth was farther east of where Iverson went down."

"The call came in from a CP near Metz. That's all I know about it, Lieutenant. But there's something else I want to discuss with you. Alone."

As they walked to Colonel Pruitt's office in the adjacent Quonset hut, Tommy wondered what was so important they had to talk in private. The more he thought about it, the more worried he became:

The way he just talked about my brother's unit and all—that doesn't sound like he's got bad news about Sean, does it? Or maybe something happened to the family back home? Nah, they send the Red Cross out for that kind of stuff.

And it can't be my turn to be an ASO with the ground-pounders again. Hell, most of the pilots in the squadron haven't done it yet, and I've already had a turn. It's never been any secret when you got picked to go, either.

So what the hell did I do wrong?

As they stepped into the office, Pruitt said, "Shut the door, Half."

Uh oh, Tommy thought, *when the brass start getting real familiar with you, you might as well bend over and grab your ankles...because here it comes.*

"You can say no," Pruitt began, "but I hope you don't. Because the judgment and experience which make you such a good combat leader are going to be sorely needed in the project I'm about to describe."

That sounds like a setup if I ever heard one.

"Understand that everything I tell you from this point on is classified," Pruitt continued, very serious, all business. "Were you to repeat a word of it to anyone— whether you sign on to this project or not—it would be a court-martial offense."

Some advice his brother gave him the last time they were together popped into his head: *Try not to be conspicuous, Half. It draws fire.*

Tommy knew that was great guidance in *this man's army*, even if it wasn't doing him a bit of good right now.

"Should I continue, Lieutenant?"

"Yes, sir. By all means." Considering his apprehension, he was surprised how easy that answer slipped out. But he'd never given a moment's thought to any other response.

His tone suddenly relaxed, almost jovial, the colonel said, "Very good. Now let's get down to brass tacks. I'm sure you've noticed we have some very unusual visitors here at A-90."

"Yes, sir, I sure have."

"They're here for a very specific purpose, Tommy. The problem Patton's having with the Metz forts— especially Fort Driant—calls for extraordinary measures. Now I don't know any of the technical details, but it boils down to this: that *Flying Fortress* all painted up in yellow is actually a pilotless flying bomb. It's part of a secret enterprise known as *Operation Aphrodite*."

"Pilotless, sir? That thing landed here without a pilot?"

"Oh, no, Tommy. It was ferried here by real live pilots. When it's loaded with explosives, though, it's under radio control from a mothership. That's the other B-17, I'm told. Actually, both those ships have different designations in this role. The flying bomb is called a BQ-7. The mothership is a CQ-17."

"What about the little planes that came with them? What are they called?"

"They're called PQ-14," Pruitt replied, "and yes, they were flown here by real live pilots, too. They were built to be target drones for anti-aircraft gunner training. They're just wooden airframes built around a small engine. You never saw one before?"

"No, sir. Never saw one before in my life. But I'm confused. What do target drones have to do with all this?"

"They fly with the same radio-control system used on the B-17....excuse me, the BQ-7. I guess I'd better start getting my terminology right. Apparently, the geniuses who thought all this up want to use them to test for radio interference in this area before they put up the *big bomb*."

"I see, sir. That BQ-7 sitting out there—it didn't

land here loaded with explosives, did it?"

"Of course not, Tommy. That'd be much too dangerous. Besides, it couldn't get off the ground loaded with all those explosives plus enough fuel to make it to us in one hop, and having to make a refueling stop en route would increase that danger exponentially. So it'll be armed here, before it's launched on its mission."

"Whew...that's a relief. So where do I fit into all this, sir?"

"You'd ride with the mothership and act as liaison for the radio wizards so they figure out how to hit the right fort and not endanger any of our own troops. That ship can do a catastrophic amount of damage if it comes down in the wrong place. I can't think of a man better suited to this task than you, Tommy. You've got the talent for getting conflicting sides of a situation to work together. And you move on from setbacks better than just about any junior officer I've ever served with. And from the little I've been told about *Operation Aphrodite*, *setback* seems to be its middle name."

Colonel Pruitt let it all settle in for a few moments before asking, "So what's it going to be, Lieutenant. Are you in?"

"Absolutely, sir."

The sudden onset of hard rain on the metal roof of the Quonset began its noisy symphony. There would be no more flying for the 301st today.

"The weather guys say we're probably in for a couple of days of rain and low ceilings," Pruitt said. "It'll be a good chance for you to get familiar with the *Operation Aphrodite* personnel and equipment. And remember what I said, Tommy—not a word, not even a hint, about the project and what it's supposed to do to anyone."

"Yes, sir. I understand."

"Good. I'll tell you what, Tommy...since you won't be going anywhere the rest of the day, I'll have the Aphrodite project officer come over here to get you all indoctrinated and set up with the necessary clearances. Can't have you getting shot by the MPs the minute you set foot on *Zebra Ramp*."

"Zebra Ramp, sir?"

"Yeah, that's what we've named that area where the Aphrodite ships are parked."

✳✳✳✳

Major Rick Staunton wasn't a pilot. In fact, he didn't wear airman's wings of any kind. But he was an electrical engineer—a *radio wizard*—and he was the man in charge of *Operation Bucket*, the plan to put an Operation Aphrodite flying bomb on Fort Driant.

He looked anything but a field grade officer. His ill-fitting khakis were smudged and rumpled, hanging on his short, pudgy frame as if they'd been stuffed into a damp and dirty duffle bag for days. The major's leaf and Air Force insignia pinned to his open collar were carelessly out of alignment. The thick *Coke-bottle* lenses in his wire-rimmed eyeglasses seemed impossibly heavy and about to fall out at any second. He raced about with short, rapid steps as if speed walking, always seeming preoccupied with matters elsewhere.

He asked Tommy what he knew about radio and electronics and then seemed annoyed with the honest answer: "I don't know much of anything about it, sir. I can tune a dial. That's about it."

"But you are a pilot, aren't you?" Staunton sputtered, seemingly oblivious to the silver wings embossed on his flight jacket and the leather flying helmet, complete with goggles and dangling headset wires, in his hand. "Don't tell me I've been sent someone who's not a pilot."

Tommy took a long, hard look at this strange little man standing before him and came to two conclusions. First conclusion: *He's shorter than me. I just barely made the height requirement to join the service. He wouldn't make it.* Second conclusion: *This guy's one of those academics they dragged into the service for some special job in this war, gave him enough rank so everyone but the big brass would have to leave him alone and didn't bother explaining anything else about the military and how it worked. How else could he possibly not know I'm a pilot just by looking at the get-up I'm wearing?*

"No, sir," Tommy replied, pointing to the wings on his chest. "They sent you a real live pilot."

The major replied with only a grunt. Tommy couldn't tell if it meant he had accepted the obvious or was simply underwhelmed by it. Without saying another word, Staunton walked outside into the pouring rain and took the wheel of a parked jeep, gesturing impatiently for Tommy to *get in.*

"It's just rain, Lieutenant Moon. Not even an almighty pilot will melt in it."

Tommy's smile belied what he was thinking: *This guy's sure got the art of condescension down pat.*

Tommy figured the drive to the other side of A-90—a circuitous run around the airfield's perimeter—would be made in stony silence. He was surprised when

Staunton turned to him and said, "If you ask me, Lieutenant, the use of our *babies* against some insignificant target like this fort everyone's so concerned about—this *Operation Bucket*—is a colossal waste of an expensive strategic asset."

"*Babies*, sir?" Tommy replied. "You mean the flying bombs?"

Staunton didn't bother to hide his annoyance. "Yes, of course that's what I mean, Lieutenant."

"And you consider Fort Driant an insignificant target, sir?"

"Do I stutter, Lieutenant? Don't ask me to repeat myself again, if you don't mind."

"Well, sir…with all due respect, the GIs fighting and dying in droves trying to take that damn fort don't consider it insignificant. For them it's a matter of life or death."

"It wouldn't be if they knew what they were doing, Lieutenant."

"Begging your pardon, sir, but competence isn't the issue here. It's firepower. And right now, the advantage is with the Germans. Take my word for it. Those GIs need all the help they can get right now. And if we can give it to them, I'll be glad to help."

Staunton smirked, rejecting Tommy's assertion as if he and he alone knew some truth the rest of the US Army Air Force did not. They fell into silence, listening only to the murmur of the jeep's engine and the patter of rain on her canvas roof until they arrived at Zebra Ramp.

✯✯✯✯

General Bradley had wanted this discussion with George Patton to be face-to-face, but the bad weather was keeping his personal plane on the ground just like every other Allied aircraft in eastern France. A shouted conversation over a staticky, barely readable landline would have to suffice.

"George," Bradley said, "when do you plan to tell your corps and division commanders about using the *Operation Bucket* flying bomb against Fort Driant?"

"I don't plan on telling them a damn thing, Brad, until that contraption is ready to take to the air."

Bradley wasn't sure he heard that correctly through the static. "Say again," he said, "slower this time."

There was no mistaking Patton's words on the second try.

"Dammit, George, you've got to give them plenty of warning. We don't want any of our boys within five miles of the fort when that thing gets airborne. They'll need time to pull back."

"Believe me, Brad, when I give them the word, they'll get out of the way on the double."

"But George, this whole thing is so fantastic—and so unknown, even to your generals—that if we do it your way, they might not have enough time to appreciate the uncertainty of this thing and react accordingly. You need to tell them now, so they can make the appropriate plans to protect their men."

"Bullshit, Brad. This weather's not going to break for several days. Maybe a week. If I tell them now, they'll just sit on their hands until *the big bang* comes. But I'm going to keep trying to take that damn fort right up to the last damn minute. If it turns out I don't need the favor from Tooey Spaatz and his *Buck Rogers* contingent, well...*c'est la guerre*."

"No, George, that won't do. I don't want any poor son of a bitch caught with his pants down when this thing falls out of the sky. Consider this an order: your men in the Metz area are to have twenty-four hours' notice before *Operation Bucket* is executed. Not a minute less."

The landline connection was deteriorating steadily. Bradley wondered if Patton had actually understood the order when he replied, "Okay, Brad. I'll do that."

No bickering, no counterproposal. Just "Okay, Brad." That's so unlike George Patton.

Of course, Bradley knew all too well Patton's talent for interpreting—or just plain ignoring—orders he didn't like. Maybe that's the game he was playing right now. And in Omar Bradley's mind, that game could come to a disastrous conclusion.

Bradley would send a communiqué reiterating the order immediately. If it was in writing—even without a specific reference revealing the nature of *Operation Bucket*—at least his ass would be covered should the unthinkable happen. But in the long run, it would make no difference. Barring a needless catastrophe costing the lives of hundreds—maybe thousands—of his GIs, Bradley knew he could never impose a price on George Patton for ignoring it.

I might as well shoot myself in the foot, Bradley thought. *George is like a cat. He's got nine lives, and he's only used up three of them by my count.*

Besides, I need him, warts and all.

Chapter Twelve

Tommy Moon had been inside a Flying Fortress before. The 301st Fighter Squadron had shared an airbase in England with a USAAF heavy bomber squadron, and the pilots from each had spent some time getting a good look at how the other half lived. The bomber jockeys were always jealous of the fighter's speed and maneuverability. The fighter jocks yearned for the spacious cockpits the B-17 crews worked in, with room to move around and stretch your legs occasionally. You could even pee and defecate in a chemical toilet if necessary. But the bomber boys insisted that actually using the toilet was too inconvenient at altitude, requiring the user to peel off multiple layers of flight clothing in the subzero cold and lug a portable oxygen bottle with him lest he pass out on the can. For the gunners, a toilet break was out of the question. Any one of them not at their station during a mission could get them all killed if German fighters suddenly attacked.

Their solution? They urinated in empty beer bottles and threw them overboard when they reached their target. Sometimes they didn't wait that long.

Still, to a fighter pilot, trapped in his seat for the duration of a flight, it sounded better than trying to use the P-47's facility, a relief tube of small diameter. Using it while trying to fly at the same time was an awkward affair and usually resulted in pissing on your legs and at least one hand. If you tried to use the tube a second time on the same flight, the outlet would undoubtedly be frozen, causing the tube to quickly overflow into the cockpit.

Should a fighter jock have to defecate before making it back to the ground and the nearest latrine, well…that's why he had more than one uniform.

This B-17, though—*correction, this BQ-7*—looked far different on the inside than the ones he knew back in England. Its interior was practically empty, except for the cockpit instrument panels, flight controls, and the two pilot seats. Everything else—machine guns, powered turrets, oxygen system, bombsight, navigator's station, bomb racks, even the chemical toilet Tommy so envied—had been removed to save weight.

He did notice some components the operational bombers didn't have, electronics units and wire bundles jury-rigged haphazardly into place. He wasn't sure what they did, but he was about to find out. It would be Tech Sergeant Ira Dandridge's job to give him the *two-dollar tour.*

"You'll get used to Major Staunton, sir," Sergeant Dandridge said, rolling his eyes in acknowledgement of his boss' many quirks. "He's a brilliant guy. The trouble is, he doesn't mind telling you. But he knows more about this project than all the rest of us put together. Bear with him and you'll learn a lot."

"If you ask me, the guy needs a good dose of the front lines," Tommy replied.

"But don't tell him that, okay? Let's get you started here, Lieutenant."

They settled into the pilots' seats. Directing Tommy's attention to an odd-looking box suspended behind the left seat, Dandridge said, "That's one of two television cameras on board. Are you familiar with television, sir?"

"I saw it at the New York World's Fair in '39, but

that's about it."

"It's pretty amazing stuff, actually," Dandridge continued. "Basically, the camera breaks the image it sees before it into several hundred horizontal lines of video information and scans the entire field of those lines from top to bottom many times a second. This creates video frames similar in concept to the frames in a strip of movie film. We broadcast this video information to the mothership—the CQ-17—where the drone operator—that's me, by the way—can see it on a video monitor, just like I'm looking at it right now."

"I think I get it," Tommy said. "This camera lets you see all the flight and engine instruments, just like a pilot would."

"Just the flight instruments, sir. The engine gauges are out of frame."

Sensing Tommy's concern, he added, "It's not like we could do much if we had an engine problem, anyway. We control the throttles and absolutely nothing else."

"Yeah, I see your point. You said this was one of two cameras. Where's the other one?"

"It's in the nose, where the bombsight used to be. We'll take a look at it in a little bit."

"And that one gives you the view ahead of the ship?"

"Correct, sir."

"Okay," Tommy said, "you're looking at these television images in the mothership. What happens then?"

"I use what I see to actually fly the *baby* remotely."

"By radio control?"

"That's right," Dandridge replied. "I have a control box with a joystick and switches that let me control the elevators, ailerons, rudder, and throttles." He pointed to a device that looked like a small electric motor bolted to the center instrument panel. A metal rod extended from a crank on the motor to the throttle levers. "This is the servo that gives me control of the throttles," he continued. "For the elevators, ailerons, and rudder, we're wired into the baby's autopilot." He tapped the controller for the C-1 autopilot mounted at the rear of the center pedestal. "We use the autopilot amplifiers and servos to control those flight surfaces."

"Why couldn't you couple your remote-control stuff directly to the control column like you did with the throttles?" Tommy asked. "Why go through the autopilot?"

Dandridge sighed, like that was a sore topic. "That's how it was originally configured, sir," he replied, "but it was a disaster. The baby was much too easy to overcontrol. We wrecked four of them before we gave up—nothing but stalls, spins, and smacking into the ground. Then we wired it through the autopilot, and that gave us much gentler responses."

The rain was falling harder, sounding like a continuous stream of ball bearings was being poured on the thin aluminum skin of the bomber. To Tommy, it sounded too much like the sound of bullets striking his aircraft, something he'd heard more times than he cared to remember.

To Sergeant Dandridge, though, the driving rain presented a different nightmare. "These old ships leak like sieves in the rain," he said, pointing to thin but steady streams of water running into the cockpit from deteriorated window seals and the big sheet metal patch where the top turret used to be. "We've got to be very careful to keep the water out of the electronics units and wiring. A short circuit—even a little corrosion on the connectors—could cause us to lose radio control of the baby."

Dandridge pointed to several black metal boxes strapped to the floor behind the pilots' seats. Wire cables like stout rope were plugged into the boxes. "That box there is the transmitter that sends the TV signal to the mothership," he said, pointing to the nearest one. "The one beside it is the receiver that picks up my signals from the mothership and feeds them to the autopilot and throttle servo. Those boxes behind them are the inverters and power supplies. These units pull a hell of a lot of juice. It's a good thing so many of the ship's systems that used electricity have been removed or deactivated. Otherwise, her electrical system wouldn't have been powerful enough for all them and this *Castor* set-up, too."

"Castor?" Tommy asked.

"Yeah, that's the name they gave this upgraded control system. It replaced something called *Double-Azon*. That was our original control system for Aphrodite, but it just didn't work worth a damn on the babies. Too crude."

"I heard about that *Azon* project," Tommy said. "It stood for *azimuth only*, right?"

"That's right, sir."

"So you were trying to use two of those systems together, with one for azimuth, the other for pitch?"

"You catch on real fast, Lieutenant."

"Yeah, we knew about those radio-guided bombs with Azon. It was like giving the bombardier one more chance to get it right after he pickled them away. Didn't work real well for that, either, though, did it?"

"No," Dandridge replied, with a sad shake of his head. "It sounded great in theory, but…"

After a moment of awkward silence, Dandridge said, "Let me show you the rest of the installation here, sir, and then we'll check out the mothership."

They crawled into the nose compartment. "Here's the forward-looking camera," Dandridge said. "As you can see, sir, it looks straight out through the plexiglass nose. Once we're about ten miles from the target, I switch my video monitor to this camera for the final approach."

Tommy smiled: the term *final approach* took on a far more literal meaning when applied to flying the baby.

Back in the main cabin, Dandridge pointed to a panel on which two switches were mounted. "Those are the arming switches for the Torpex explosive, which, of course, hasn't been loaded yet." Then he began pointing out electrical cables draped throughout the cabin and bomb bay, each cable ending in a plug connected to nothing at the moment. "These plugs will hook up to the squibs that fire the Torpex," Dandridge said. "About ten tons' worth."

Trying to imagine it all, Tommy said, "That's a lot of *bang* all in one place."

"You'd better believe it, sir."

"So where's all this Torpex now?" Tommy asked.

Dandridge replied, "It's being shipped across the Channel and then trucked across France. Supposed to be here 12 October—three days from now."

"Why so long?"

"The way I understand it, sir, General Spaatz didn't want to waste the stuff if the planes didn't get here intact."

****

The rain hadn't let up at all, forcing Tommy and
Sergeant Dandridge to make a mad dash across the ramp
to the mothership. Once inside the CQ-17, Tommy could
see it looked much more like the bombers he'd toured
back in England.

"Unlike the baby," Dandridge explained, "she's still
got all of her original equipment. Since she's not
carrying any bomb load on these missions, weight isn't
much of an issue, even with the addition of the Castor
sets. We still have about four thousand pounds to play
with before hitting her max gross weight."

They moved into the nose compartment, where the
bulk of the equipment Dandridge used to control the
baby was located. The sergeant gave the video monitor's
glare hood a loving pat and said, "This CRT—the
cathode ray tube—is my eyes on the mission, sir.
Whatever those cameras in the baby show, I see it right
here on this screen."

"If everything works right," Tommy added.

"Yeah, of course, sir." Dandridge seemed a little
ruffled that Tommy was alluding to *Aphrodite's* less-
than-stellar success rate again. "But the goal is to
succeed, right?"

"That's always the goal, Sergeant. Not always the
outcome, though. Things tend to go to hell in a
handbasket real fast when the shooting starts. But go
on...show me the rest of your stuff."

"Sure, sir. Over here is the controller. This is where
I input the commands to fly the baby."

It was a compact metal box that could be hand-held or shelf-mounted, with a cable connecting it to the aircraft's electronics. A joystick, a few switches, and a row of indicator lights were clustered on its face.

"So that's it?" Tommy asked. "You make flight control inputs with the stick and control the throttles with this switch?"

"Yes, sir. That's exactly how it works."

"Okay," Tommy continued. "So with you sitting up here in the nose, I'm guessing you keep the baby ahead of you to maintain visual contact with her?"

"That's right, sir. We stay behind and well above."

"Well above...how high is that, Sergeant?"

"About twenty thousand feet, sir."

"And how high is the baby flying?"

"About two thousand feet, sir."

Tommy let out a shrill, skeptical whistle. "That's some altitude spread, Sergeant. Why is the mothership so high? Can you really keep track of the baby visually from so far above her?"

"We manage, sir. The view from the nose, the fact that she's painted bright yellow, plus the video image on the screen..."

Tommy's skepticism hadn't faded. "It seems to me that you've got a snowball's chance in hell of hitting anything smaller than Yankee Stadium. And even that might be a struggle. I don't know what you've been flying against, but Fort Driant—big as it is—is going to look pretty damn small from twenty thousand feet."

"Well, sir," Sergeant Dandridge replied, "if you've got some suggestions on how we can do it better, I'm sure Major Staunton would love to hear them."

"That's why I'm here, supposedly."

Tommy had noticed right away that Dandridge wore no aircrew wings of any kind, just like Major Staunton. Before getting any deeper into the technical details of what they were doing, this seemed the time to ask the question:

"Are you a pilot, Sergeant?"

"No, sir. I'm not classified as a pilot. My MO is 993—drone radio mechanic."

"How'd you get this job, anyway?"

"I was a technician at RCA Labs in New Jersey when the war broke out, sir, working on television development. I guess the Army figured I was a natural for this stuff."

"You sure don't sound like you're from Jersey."

"That's because I'm not, sir. I'm from Indiana originally. I just moved there to find a job. Wasn't a lot of ways to earn a living in Indiana. You sound like you're a New Yorker, though."

"Yeah. Brooklyn."

"Thought so," Dandridge said. "Funny thing—both the Army and Navy were looking for guys with my background. The recruiters were sort of fighting over me."

"Why'd you pick the Army?"

"I pretty much knew what my job would be, and I didn't want to do it in the Pacific. I heard about all the weird tropical diseases and such. Wasn't much interested in living there, even temporarily."

"Can't say I blame you, Sergeant. Let me ask you something, though…did they ever consider using an actual pilot to guide the drone?"

Dandridge flinched at the question. "You'd have to discuss that with Major Staunton, sir. That's a real sore point in some quarters, and it's way over my rank to decide something like that. I just do what I'm told."

Chapter Thirteen

On the west side of Fort Driant—the opposite side from the Bangalore torpedo fiasco—a company commander from 5th Infantry Division had made a startling discovery. "I'm not believing this," the commander—a captain—told his platoon leaders. "It looks like we can walk right into the damn place."

The commander could tell by the looks on their faces that his platoon leaders weren't buying it. They hadn't been forward with his recon party, so they hadn't seen it with their own eyes. He realized he was making this assault sound easy, and nothing so far had been easy about Fort Driant. For all the casualties they'd taken the past few weeks in their quest to conquer the Metz forts, they'd gained not one inch of terrain. But today just might be different.

The captain continued, "All that artillery fire the other Kraut forts have been dumping on us around Driant must've chewed up the barbed wire at the southwest corner something awful. Doesn't look like we'll have to cut hardly any of it to get through."

But the platoon leaders were still not convinced. One said, "Maybe it's a Kraut trap, sir. Lure us onto that slope between the wire and the parapet—get us canalized in there—and then slice us to shreds."

Another added, "That slope's a natural killing field, sir. We know that from hard experience. There's hardly any cover. Machine guns and rifles on the fort's walls can rake it just like it's level ground."

"That may not be much of a problem right now," the commander said. "According to Battalion, the Krauts seem to have shifted their infantry defenders to the east wall to counter another attack by the tanks and Bangalores."

"Are the tanks getting through, Captain?"

"No word on that, I'm afraid."

The platoon leaders knew to a man what that really meant: the tanks had definitely not broken through to the fort.

"But it doesn't matter right now if the tanks got through or not," the captain said, hoping he sounded more convincing to his lieutenants than he did to himself. "Just so they keep the Krauts distracted, that may be all the break we need. Don't forget that all this rain's going to make us harder to see, too."

"It's going to make everything muddy and slippery, too, sir."

"It's been raining for weeks, for cryin' out loud," the captain replied. "You guys should be used to that by now. Okay, here's how we'll do it. We'll advance in column, with Second Platoon in the lead, followed by First and then Third." Turning to his Weapons Platoon leader, he asked, "Are all your machine gun teams in place with the rifle platoons?"

"Affirmative, sir."

"And your mortars are dialed in?"

"Affirmative, sir."

"Excellent. We'll have additional fire support from the tank destroyer platoon on the ridge to our right."

A rifle platoon leader asked, "What about the artillery, sir?"

"Are you asking about ours or the Germans, Lieutenant?"

"Both, actually, Captain."

"Well, according to Battalion, the Kraut artillery is concentrated on our guys trying to force a crossing of the Moselle. That's why none of it has fallen around the fort all morning, even with the tanks trying to push in on the back side."

"But what if we actually get inside the fort, sir? Won't they shift some of it—maybe all of it—on us?"

"Once we're inside the fort, Lieutenant, we'll have all those great bunkers the Germans were nice enough to build for us to take shelter in."

The Weapons Platoon leader spoke up: "And what about *our* artillery, Captain? Will we get support from them?"

No matter how the company commander responded, he knew it would sound like a betrayal. But the question had to be answered honestly.

"We won't be getting any artillery support today, gentlemen," he replied. "Priority of fire goes to the river crossing." He paused, taking in the disconsolate faces of his platoon leaders, and then added, "Are there any further questions?"

Their silence was a ringing accusation, an inaudible but anguished cry of men who knew they were getting screwed again. Or perhaps sentenced to death.

"All right, then," the captain said. "We move out in ten minutes."

Maybe the company commander had been right after all. The advance through the shattered field of barbed wire was nearly effortless, with no serious opposition offered from the Germans on Fort Driant.

116

Effortless…until a machine gun in a concrete emplacement at the fort's southwest corner began to cut down GIs advancing up the slope.

Within seconds of the German gun opening fire, several rounds from the tank destroyers providing fire support struck its emplacement. Like all those rounds fired at the fort before, it seemed to have no effect on the structure itself.

But unlike all those times before, the machine gun fell silent. And it stayed silent long after the smoke and dust of the rounds fired against it had drifted away.

"Now ain't that some shit," a veteran platoon sergeant said. "That son of a bitch is either dead, shit his pants and run, or he's curled up in a ball mumbling for his mama. That's a fucking first."

A terrified young GI asked, "But what if he starts shooting at us again, Sarge?"

"We make sure we're not still standing here with our dicks in our hands, son. Get your ass moving."

The Americans were only yards from the southwest corner of the fortified infantry trench encircling the fort. Every man now knew—with pants-wetting certainty— why they'd fixed bayonets before starting up the hill to Fort Driant:

It's going to be close-quarters fighting. Maybe hand to hand. It's hard enough shooting them from a hundred yards away. Now we've got to look them in their fucking eyes, too.

And those German eyes would be as wide and terrified as those of the GIs spilling into Fort Driant's perimeter.

But the trench was empty. As the GIs scaled its stout concrete face and dropped into the sunken passageway behind, they stopped to stare in wonder that this magnificent defensive position—with its enclaves of thick overhead cover and excellent fields of fire—had been abandoned. The Germans had been here just moments before—rifle cartridges littered the rain-puddled floor as the odor of expended ammunition hung in the air; a cigarette left on the ledge of a firing aperture still glowed, its paper nearly consumed, its finger-like column of ash perfectly intact.

A few GI riflemen started to *whoop and holler*—the yells of men convinced they'd just routed their enemy.

"Knock it off, you morons," a sergeant yelled. "This ain't near over yet. Stop dancing around like a bunch of little girls and cover your sector, dammit."

The company proceeded along the southern boundary of the fort, one platoon in the narrow confines of the trench to make sure it was clear of Germans, the other two outside the trench's front wall. It seemed to make tactical sense: *If we start to take fire from inside the fort's perimeter—especially those two big bunkers between us and the gun batteries—everyone has cover this way*, the commander told himself.

The fort's artillery batteries—standing amidst the craters of so many ineffectual bombs and shells in their impregnable turrets of domed steel—continued to fire toward the Moselle River, seemingly oblivious to the Americans in their midst. But the howitzers were no threat to the GIs; just as with the tanks attacking the opposite side of the fort, they were beneath the howitzers' minimum elevation and too close to be effectively engaged, even if the turrets traversed to point directly at them. Still, it was unnerving to be so close— only a few hundred feet—to the turrets the American pilots called *Easy Battery*, with its three 150-mm howitzers belching fire and steel several times a minute.

What was more unnerving was the realization that the Americans were not *inside* Fort Driant. They were merely on top of it, walking the cratered moonscape of its barren, napalm-scorched earthen roof. The heart and soul of this installation—and the bulk of the men who manned it—were deep beneath the surface of this hilltop, secure behind armored doors, shrouded in the thick concrete walls and ceilings of the corridors and compartments in which they lived and worked.

"But they've got to breathe, Sarge," a PFC who looked far younger than his eighteen years told his squad leader. "I see some pipes sticking out of the ground near those bunkers. They've got to be ventilators or chimneys. A couple of grenades down those pipes oughta shake up those Kraut bastards pretty good."

The squad leader wasn't impressed with the idea. "You could be kicking a hornet's nest, too, kid. Let the lieutenant come up with the bright ideas, okay? That's what he gets paid for, not you."

But the lieutenant had overheard. "I think that's a great idea, Sergeant," he told the squad leader. "Do it."

The PFC and two of his buddies climbed from the trench and set out toward the pipes with all the grenades they could carry. They hadn't covered fifty feet across the open terrain of the fort's roof when three bullets cut them down, a split second apart, one for each man.

"Fuck," the lieutenant said, "we've got snipers out there somewhere. Anybody see where they are?"

Not a man in his platoon could answer that question with any certainty.

Farther down the trench, another squad came to a

steel door recessed into the inner wall. They called for their bazooka man, but he took one look at the situation and shook his head. "I've got no place to fire it from. I'd have to get way outside the trench, and even then I've got a shitty angle. Besides, ain't you guys heard? There's snipers all over the place. I'd be a dead duck before I could get into position."

"Never mind," the company commander said. "I'll call for the engineers to blow the door."

But there were no engineers to be had. They were all still tied up on the other side of the fort with the Bangalore torpedoes.

"Maybe we can just knock and the Krauts will open it up for us," a GI said, trying to make a joke. But no one laughed.

"Let's try to blow it with some grenades," a sergeant said. "Put 'em against the door and pile whatever crap we can find on top. Maybe we can get enough of a bang to blow the door off its hinges."

"Aw, that ain't gonna work, Sarge," a corporal said. "You see how thick that steel is?"

"How the hell can you tell how thick it is, being on just one side and all, numbnuts? Cough me up some of them fucking grenades. That's an order."

The rest of the squad gathered a tattered mattress, a few concrete blocks, and some weighted sacks that resembled sandbags, rummaged from the trench's shelters.

The sergeant asked, "Any of you clowns got any cord?"

A GI surrendered a bundle of twine.

"Good enough, if I double it up," the sergeant said. "Now give me that big hunk of wood over there."

The four grenades were lined up in a row against the base of the door, backed by the concrete blocks and the sacks. The spring-loaded arming levers of the grenades were facing away from the door. The sergeant tied the twine to the stump of a nail protruding from the wood, and pulled hard, testing its strength. Then he placed the heavy length of wood across the arming levers. Gingerly, he pulled the safety pins on the grenades one at a time. Restrained by the wood, the handles stayed in place.

"Any one of y'all who ain't got a set of balls better get the hell outta here," the sergeant announced. "On my count of three…"

He didn't have to look around to know he was suddenly all by himself.

"Oh, what the hell," he said, and then counted, "One…two…three."

In one swift motion, he pulled the twine and pivoted to sprint away from the door, stealing one last peek over his shoulder as he did.

Handles flew from the grenades. *But did I see four handles come off, or only three?*

He knew all too well the timing of a grenade's fuse was variable, somewhere between three and a half and five seconds from the instant the handle flew off until it exploded. *But hey…if one blows up first, it'll blow up the rest of 'em too, right?*

Once he'd counted to *three one thousands* on the dead run, he dove to the trench's floor, lying prone, his head away from the imminent explosion. It seemed he'd barely gotten his head down when the always-disappointing *pop* of grenades detonating echoed down the trench, blowing a storm cloud of dust and debris with it.

But was that four? Or only three?

When he opened his eyes, there was a grenade lying inches from his face. Its handle was gone. A thin wisp of whitish smoke spewed from its burning fuse.

And in that last split second of his life, the sergeant knew only three handles had flown off when he'd pulled that piece of wood away.

When the fourth grenade detonated, it not only killed the sergeant, it wounded two GIs who were rushing to his aid, showering them with fragments channeled down the trench. When the company commander arrived, he couldn't make sense of the scene—three of his soldiers were down, two alive but with multiple wounds oozing blood through shredded uniforms, and one dead, missing most of his head.

"What the hell happened here?" the commander asked. "A Kraut mortar?"

"Negative, sir," the corporal replied. "We were trying to blow off that door over there." He pointed to the dead man. "It was Sarge's idea. You know, use grenades. Looks like one got launched down the trench...or...I don't know...maybe it was just a slow burner. That's what got the sarge. Got Smitty and Allen, too."

But the door hadn't budged. It stood there as if nothing had happened. Perfectly intact. Still locked. Still impassable.

The few moments of indecisive silence that followed were shattered by more explosions along the trench line, each far more powerful than the cluster of grenades had been.

The commander shrieked, "Mortars!" And he was right this time.

"I've got to get my men out of this trench, sir," the platoon leader begged. "The Krauts got it zeroed in. We're getting slaughtered here."

The survivors of his platoon weren't waiting to be told to clear the trench. Their survival instinct had sent them scrambling over its escarp and deeper into the landscape of the fort. They sought cover in shell craters half-filled with rain that provided poor shelter from mortar rounds falling almost straight down.

But burrowed against the sides of the craters, at least they were still safe from the bullets fired by well-concealed Germans raking the air above their heads, if just for the moment.

And through it all, the gunners in the turrets of Fort Driant continued to throw their shells toward the Americans trying to cross the Moselle as if nothing of any great consequence was going on outside their steel and concrete cocoons.

Suddenly, it all stopped, like the abrupt onset of quiet after a storm. The howitzers fell silent in their turrets; the torrent of mortar shells on the GIs ceased; the bullets slicing the air like scythes brought their harvest of death to an end.

The company was far too disorganized to take advantage of the lull and continue their assault, and the commander knew it all too well. Any further thoughts of attacking the bunkers between his scattered unit and the nearest turrets were a fool's game. His choice became very simple: *We can die here or we can withdraw and maybe survive this god-awful fuckup.*

Withdrawal: the only tactically sound thing to do now. Men under his command had died before—plenty of them. But not another GI needed to die here today.

To hell with the mission. It's already a lost cause.

He called for his platoon leaders to pull back the same way they came in—the only escape route available—and rally their men beyond the wire, outside the boundary of the fort. His radio operator had barely spoken the first few words of the withdrawal order into his microphone when a bullet pierced his chest and flung him to the ground like a discarded rag doll.

Then there were German soldiers everywhere. They'd risen from the ground like spirits from the grave—maybe fifty, maybe five hundred of them— exiting their subterranean shelters through armored doors like the one the GIs had just failed to open. Their mission was simple: repel the Americans from the roof of Fort Driant by any means possible.

Driven by the bloodlust born of primal fear, the opposing forces quickly mingled, like exhausted boxers drawn together in a clinch. Often at less than arm's length, they were so close that rifles couldn't be brought to bear as firearms. The fight atop this archaic fort had devolved to the old-fashioned methods of hand-to-hand combat, just as the GIs had feared at the start of this assault. Rifles with bayonets affixed to their muzzles became broadswords and lances; the stocks of those weapons were now bludgeons.

And when even those ancient weapons couldn't be brought to bear, there were still blows from fists, desperate wrestling, and the chokeholds of men for whom the slogan *kill or be killed* was no longer just words.

But this was merely death in slow motion. There had to be a better way to win this.

There was. The same imperative seized both sides: *Take back the trench!*

The brawl dissolved to a frantic fifty-yard dash as Germans and GIs raced for the trench. The side that got there first with the most would win this skirmish. Men in the trench could bring their rifles and machine guns to bear on those still exposed in the open. It would be point-blank slaughter: if enough Germans got there first, they'd vanquish the Americans. If the GIs won the race, they'd be right back where they started. But they'd have fewer Germans blocking their escape from the fort.

The race ended in a tie. Even in the trench, there would be no respite from the hand-to-hand fighting. It would just continue in these narrow confines.

It was a battle of attrition now. Mortally wounded soldiers fell on each side until there were more Americans still standing than Germans. The battle had reached *critical mass*—that point when both sides knew for certain who was winning and who was losing.

No one needed to give an order; the Germans still on their feet fled, hoping to vanish back into the secret passageways from which they'd come before a GI's bullet struck them down. The Americans, exhausted from this brief but intense fight, hurled poorly aimed shots after them.

This was not a victory to be savored. It was not a victory at all. The GIs grabbed their wounded and filed quickly from the trench and withdrew through the damaged barbed wire field from which they'd come. The dead from both sides, some still locked with a foe in lethal embrace, were left behind, nothing more now than numbers on some adjutant's casualty report.

At the battalion CP, the company commander couldn't understand why his colonel was so upbeat about the attack. The post-action report was dismal: One hundred twelve men had started up the hill to the fort little more than an hour ago.

Sixty-eight had returned. Nearly half of that number were wounded.

A seventy percent casualty rate. Astronomical by any standard.

I get kicked off that hill and had to leave forty-four of my men behind. So where the hell is the silver lining in this disaster that the colonel's so high on?

His voice little more than an exhausted whisper, the company commander said, "Sir, we can't take that fort. Not this way. It's a maze—we don't know where the hell the Krauts are going to pop up."

"But you got inside, son," the colonel replied. "I'm proud of you and your men, Captain. You got inside. No other unit's done that. The rest of Fifth Division—hell, the rest of the whole damn Third Army—can learn from you. As soon as you get cleaned up, you'll be briefing the general on how you did it."

Fighting back his tears, the company commander said, "Begging your pardon, sir—and with all due respect—but we didn't get inside of anything. Not a damn thing. Hell, we didn't even scratch the surface. And these Krauts aren't the same scared old men and little boys we were capturing back at the Falaise Pocket. These guys are tough. At least the ones that showed their faces were, anyway. I'm thinking we had them outnumbered three to one and they were still kicking our ass. I'm telling you, sir, if we can't blow that whole damn hill to kingdom come, we'll never force those Krauts out of there."

Chapter Fourteen

Zebra Ramp had a sprawling operations tent all its own. At the moment, twenty-seven men were huddled inside it, seeking shelter from the cold, driving rain. In addition to Major Staunton and Sergeant Dandridge, there was the nine-man crew of the CQ-17 mothership, the two pilots who'd fly the BQ-7 *baby*, one pilot for each of the two PQ-14 drones, three electronics techs, eight aircraft mechanics, and Tommy Moon.

A telephone line had been strung to the main switchboard at A-90. Tommy was on that line, getting an update on the weather situation. Plotting furiously on a chart, he grabbed for a straightedge. The best thing within reach was a slide rule. He put it to use.

Staunton bellowed, "THAT'S NOT A GODDAMN RULER, LIEUTENANT."

He snatched the slide rule away. "This is a precision instrument. We don't use it around here for doodling." As he stalked off, he told Dandridge, "Get that officer a proper straightedge, Sergeant."

He lowered his voice, mumbling one more thing that was still heard by everyone in the tent: "Fucking pilots."

Tommy checked the faces of the other flyers in the tent. They didn't seem surprised, upset, or annoyed by Staunton's slur.

I guess they've heard it all before. Must be like water off a duck's back.

Tommy hung up the phone and moved to the briefing board. "It's about time," Staunton said. "So what's the weather going to be, Lieutenant?"

"The rain's going to continue both here at A-90 and over the target area through around 1200 hours tomorrow," Tommy said. "We won't see a break during daylight until then. After that, we're supposed to get about a week of clear days."

The mothership command pilot, a lieutenant named Paul Wheatley, asked, "Are your Ninth Air Force *metro* guys usually on the money, Moon?"

"They're not too bad. I'd take that time of 1200 as an approximation, though."

"That's all?" Wheatley replied, winking at the other bomber pilots. "We can usually consider the whole damn forecast from Eighth Air Force as an approximation."

Everybody seemed to be laughing except Major Staunton. He waved his arms impatiently to silence the tent and then said, "Let's get this briefing started." Pointing to the maps and aerial photographs hung on the tent sidewall, he added, "Lieutenant Moon, tell us everything you know about this Fort Driant."

For the next twenty minutes, Tommy explained the topography, defenses, and vulnerabilities—or lack thereof—of the fort. Using an aerial photograph giving a view of Driant from directly above, he said, "The best chance to destroy the *whole* fort in one shot from the air is to blow up one of these four gun batteries in the main fort. Everything of any importance is underground— ammunition, generators, fuel, living quarters, the whole bit. The only thing that sticks up above ground are these armored gun turrets, and even they retract so they're flush when not firing. There's got to be an enormous tunnel system connecting it all together. If we can blow up just one of these batteries, the blast force and hot gasses funneled down those tunnels should kill or incapacitate just about every Kraut in the place. We've never been able to put enough concentrated explosive force against one of these batteries to do it any damage at all, though."

Lieutenant Wheatley asked, "You said there's very little flak?"

"Yeah, that's true. We've never seen a flak position in the fort itself. There have been a few mobile ones in the vicinity, though."

"You'd bet your life on that, Moon?"

"I do every day, Wheatley." The air of certainty in his voice put an end to the skeptical line of questioning.

Major Staunton was at the map, jotting notes, making computations with the slide rule. He wasn't happy with what the numbers were telling him.

"Lieutenant Moon," he said, "how high does the concrete structure of a gun battery protrude above ground level?"

"I can't give you an exact figure, sir."

"Then give me your best guess, Lieutenant." The irritation in his voice was as cringeworthy as nails on a blackboard.

"Well, sir, as you can see in these oblique photographs, it's not very much. A couple of feet, tops."

Staunton went back to working the slide rule. In a few moments, he had his answer. "We're eight degrees beyond limit, dammit," he said. It didn't sound like an admission of defeat by some insurmountable obstacle. Just another equation—a very complex one—that needed to be solved.

Dandridge knew exactly what *limit* the major was talking about. He was the only man in the tent who did.

He told Staunton, "Maybe we'd better explain, sir."

The major nodded, adding an accommodating arm sweep that meant *be my guest.*

"What Major Staunton's getting at," Dandridge began, "is there's almost no vertical aspect to our target. It's flat on the ground, for all practical purposes. To have a decent chance of hitting one of those batteries, our dive angle is going to have to be steeper than we'd hoped for, so the baby impacts it from above rather than laterally. But we're limited by the maximum elevator authority of the autopilot. It wasn't designed for dive bombing, more for simply holding altitude or pitch attitude."

Tommy asked, "But we can still do it, right?"

"Theoretically, yes," Dandridge replied. "But unlike the gradual descent we've usually employed, our trajectory down to the target is going to be a tight arc, much tighter than we've ever tried before. And more difficult. Our numbers are going to have to be dead on the money or our chances of a bull's-eye are pretty small."

"Very small, indeed," Major Staunton added.

There was an uncomfortable silence in the tent, broken only when Tommy asked, "Sergeant, you actually fly the baby into the target, right?"

"Of course, sir. We already—"

"I know we've already talked about it," Tommy interrupted, "but I need to ask this: why aren't actual pilots flying the baby?"

The other aviators in the room clenched their teeth. They'd been there before and had learned not to go there again. They felt sure they knew what was about to happen.

And they weren't disappointed. Major Staunton bolted from his chair, snarling like a feral mother protecting her young. Spittle flying from his lips, he hurled his answer at Tommy.

"Let me enlighten you on what the rest of the Air Force knows all too well, Lieutenant. We studied this at great length back in the States and the entire air staff came to the same conclusion: a pilot is no more capable of flying a remote-controlled drone than a technician who understands the equipment so much better. In fact, pilots have a far longer learning curve, because they have to *unlearn* so much to become drone controllers. And since they think they all know so damn much, that unlearning is a monumental task. We crashed countless test drones with pilots at the controls due to *operator error*—wasting a tremendous amount of time and resources—until we learned this lesson. We're eternally grateful for a pilot's ability when it comes to taking off, finding his destination, and landing. But for remote control in the air and crashing into a target, our enlisted technicians have consistently given us better results. And they're far cheaper to train. Faster, too."

Paul Wheatley, the mothership pilot, shot Tommy a look which featured arched eyebrows. He knew what it meant: *You see the bullshit we have to put up with?*

Nobody expected Tommy to challenge Staunton's pronouncement. But there he was, standing toe to toe with the major. Two diminutive men about to lock horns in a cerebral turf fight.

"Be that as it may, sir," Tommy said, "but let's get back to the original problem. Are you actually telling me you don't think you can get an airplane to go *down*?"

The question left Staunton confused and silent. He'd

expected a challenge from the fighter jock, just not this one. The air in the tent was suddenly infused with excitement, like the moments before a street confrontation suddenly escalates to the first punch.

Tommy continued, "Well then, sir, I'm here to tell you that getting an airplane to go down is the easy part. Getting it to go up—now that's a little harder."

It took a few seconds, but the other men in the tent—especially the pilots—began to laugh. Softly at first, but it grew to a joyous chorus of agreement with the practical wisdom in Tommy's words.

An added bonus: seeing how much it pissed off Major Staunton.

"Let's talk specifics," Tommy said. "Why do you think it's going to be hard to fly a steep descent to the target?"

"We're not flying a nimble dive bomber here, Lieutenant," Staunton replied. "These ships handle like trucks."

"Yeah, but like I just said, sir, getting an airplane—*any* airplane—to go down is a cinch. Especially one making a terminal dive."

Staunton frowned and shook his head as if he was tired of suffering fools. To a lesser degree, Dandridge was doing the same.

"I know what you're going to say, Lieutenant—just chop the throttles and she'll fall like a brick," Staunton said. "But I'm afraid you just don't understand the equipment we have to work with. The autopilot elevator servo has—by design—very little authority, just enough to keep the ship straight and level. To expect it to be able to guide the ship through a steep descent that's somehow controllable is—well—simply wishful thinking. We still need the ability to *aim* the baby so it actually strikes the target. And those servos give us only a very limited ability to do that."

Now it was Tommy's turn to suffer fools. "Major," he said, "I've been on more dive-bombing runs than I care to remember, and not once did I need a lot of elevator input to keep the dive on target. The only time I needed a lot of elevator was for pulling out, and that's a problem we're not going to have here."

"Again, Lieutenant, you don't understand the equipment we're working with."

"Maybe not, sir, but an airplane's an airplane. And I sure as hell know how to fly one. Let me ask you this— have you ever even *tried* a steep dive?"

The blank look on Staunton's face provided all the answer he needed.

"Here's a proposition for you," Tommy continued. "Why don't we use those little drones you brought along—the PQ-14s—and give a steep dive to target a try? You say the explosives aren't going to even show up until 12 October—that's three days from now—and I'm betting it's going to take a while to get them installed in the baby, right?"

"Yes, approximately twenty-four hours to install the Torpex and ensure the triggering system is working correctly."

"Great," Tommy said. "So once it stops raining tomorrow, we've got at least three days to play with. Plenty of time for a little target practice."

Dandridge didn't have to say a word; it was obvious from the look on his face he liked the idea. Staunton was deep in thought and harder to read. But at least he hadn't said *no*.

Lieutenant Wheatley took the opportunity the silence provided to ask a question of his own: "We *will* have escort fighter coverage, right? We're not going to be tooling around over the Kraut lines on our own, are we?"

"That's Ninth Air Defense Command's job," Tommy replied. "They fly a couple of squadrons of jugs and one with P-38s."

Wheatley's brow furrowed. "They any good?"

"Never seen them in action."

Wheatley rolled his eyes and mumbled, "Oh, brother."

✶✶✶✶

It was midafternoon when the briefing finally ended. Before Tommy could leave the tent for the jeep ride back to his quarters across A-90, Sergeant Dandridge pulled him aside.

"Lieutenant," Dandridge said, "you'd better take it easy with Major Staunton. He's got horsepower way above that gold leaf he wears on his collar. The brass at Eighth Air Force Headquarters consider him some kind of indispensable genius. They give him anything he wants. You try to shit on him, and they might just shit on you. If you get my meaning, sir."

Tommy smiled and gave Dandridge a friendly pat on the shoulder. "What's he going to do to me, Sergeant? Get me sent into combat?"

"Gee, no, sir...that's not...that's not what I meant...not at—"

"Look, Sergeant, I attack ground targets for a living, and I do it nearly every damn day, weather permitting.

There's not a whole lot your major can do to make my life worse."

"I understand that, sir. And I respect it. I really do. But he can make *my* life a whole lot worse."

"Well then, Sergeant, let's see if you and I can make sure that doesn't happen, okay?"

"I'd like that, sir," Dandridge replied. "Sounds like a plan."

"It's going to be great working with you, Sergeant."

"Same here, sir."

****

Back at 301st Fighter Squadron's operations shack, Tommy went looking for Colonel Pruitt. "He's out on the ramp with Sergeant McNulty, getting his ass wet," the operations sergeant told him. "He's fixing to take your section while you're on special duty, Lieutenant."

Tommy found the two just where the ops sergeant said they'd be: doing a walk-around of *Eclipse of the Hun II*.

McNulty threw open his arms and said, "Well, well, well…if it ain't the *indisposable* Lieutenant Moon, coming back to visit us mere mortals."

Tommy replied, "I hope you meant *indispensable*, Sergeant."

"Ain't that what I said?"

Pruitt added, "I wasn't expecting to see much of you, Lieutenant. What're you doing back over here?"

"Got to pick up my kit, sir…and I've got a little request."

"Shoot."

"I'd like to take some leave tonight and try to run

down my brother. I think his unit may not be too far from here."

"That's fine by me," Pruitt replied, "but can the *cloak and dagger boys* across the field live without you?"

"They've seen enough of me for today, sir. Won't be needing me again until we can fly. Sometime tomorrow afternoon, hopefully."

"Well, then, stop wasting time yakking with us and go find your brother, Lieutenant. I promise to take good care of your ship in the meantime."

As Tommy walked back to Operations, Pruitt called after him. "Lieutenant Moon, take someone with you to ride shotgun, close as you'll be to the Krauts and all."

Chapter Fifteen

Lieutenant Jimmy Tuttle was getting nervous. It was pitch-dark, and the rain was still falling, silvery-white pellets coursing through the narrow beams of the jeep's blackout headlight. The windshield wipers could barely keep up with it; he and Tommy Moon could only read the road signs by stopping right next to them. Worse, the canvas roof above him was starting to leak. He'd put on his steel pot to keep his head dry.

"You really think we've got a snowball's chance in hell of finding your brother's outfit, Half?"

"Relax, Jimmy. That last sign said we're only two miles from Fifth Infantry Division HQ. Thirty-Seventh Tank's got to be around there somewhere."

"All I can say is the next bunch of guys we come across better not be speaking German." Tuttle tightened his grip on the carbine across his lap, mumbling, "Why the hell didn't I sign out a Thompson instead of this little pop-gun?"

A long column of American trucks raced by in the opposite direction. "There," Tommy said. "A GI convoy. Feeling better now?"

"Only if they're not running for their fucking lives. I'm telling you, Half...don't make me regret tagging along with you."

Neither spoke for another minute or two, until Tuttle said, "At this rate, we should be driving right through the front gate of Fort Driant any second."

"Don't be silly," Tommy replied. "That's at least a few more miles up the road."

Somehow, that didn't come out as confident and

reassuring as he'd hoped.

"Hey, slow down, Half. We've got more signs up ahead."

Next to a French sign at an intersection announcing their arrival at Pont-à-Mousson was a standard GI signpost. There were several wooden arrows affixed to the post, each with a unit's designation printed on it.

"Okay, now we're talking," Tommy said. "Fifth Division's that-a-way."

A few hundred yards down the road, they came to an MP checkpoint. Challenge and password were exchanged—*homer* and *bambino*—both casually blended into sentences about Babe Ruth.

"Ain't you aviators a little lost, sir?" an MP corporal drawled. It was impossible to miss the silver wings on their leather flight jackets.

"Negative, Corporal," Tommy replied. "I'm looking for my brother. He's with Thirty-Seventh Tank. I hear they're around here somewhere."

"They the outfit from Fourth Armored that showed up in these parts about a week ago, sir?"

"Could be. I'm just working on a hunch here, Corporal."

"Well, sir, if it's the tankers I'm thinking of, their bivouac's just down this road about half a mile. Don't miss it or you'll go swimming in the Moselle."

Jimmy Tuttle asked, "You guys see Krauts around here much, Corporal?"

The corporal looked down to the rain-slick pavement below his feet. "Right here? No, sir." Then he pointed north and added, "But over yonder a mile or two, there's plenty."

✳✳✳✳

An armored unit was bivouacked right where the MP said it would be. Sentries stopped the jeep at the perimeter, the *Ruthian* password drill was played out once again, and they were escorted to the farmhouse that served as 37th Tank Battalion's CP.

The same master sergeant Tommy had come to know from his previous visits to the 37th was at the desk. "I guess you're looking for your brother again, Lieutenant," the sergeant said. "But you ain't never gonna find him in the dark, the way we're spread out here, sir. I'll get his C.O. to round him up and send him over."

He cranked the field phone on his desk and told the switchboard operator to connect him with Baker Company.

"Lieutenant Tuttle here is just along for the ride," Tommy said. "Think you could find him a place to bunk for the night?"

"Sure thing," the sergeant replied. "I can put you up in the G3 section with our ASO."

Tommy asked, "That wouldn't be Lieutenant Clinchmore, would it?"

"That's affirmative, sir. You gentlemen know him?"

"We'll all from the same squadron, Sergeant," Tommy replied.

"Yeah, we sure do know him," Tuttle added. "Maybe you have someplace else I could bunk?"

Tommy gave him a surprised look, but Tuttle shook his head and, in a hushed tone, said, "You were happy just to have gotten rid of him, and that's fine. But I haven't forgiven him for the shit he pulled. Not by a long shot." He didn't want to say any more in front of an NCO; their unfinished business was none of his affair.

"Yeah, sure, sir," the sergeant said. "We got some extra cots in the liaison officers' bunkhouse, if that suits you."

Ten minutes later a jeep roared up to the CP. Sergeant Sean Moon climbed out—now wearing the *three up and two down* of a tech sergeant on his sleeve— and strolled reluctantly into the farmhouse. When he saw his younger brother, he broke into a grin. "I didn't figure it would be you come for a visit, Half...I mean, *sir*."

"That's for damn sure," the master sergeant said. "It's usually the MPs looking for our Sergeant Moon."

"You and them can lock me up in the stockade any-damn-time you want, Top," Sean replied. "At least nobody'd be shooting at my ass in there." He grabbed Tommy by the arm. "C'mon, *Lieutenant*. Let's go some place we can talk, just you and me."

As soon as they left the CP, the master sergeant said, "Hard to believe them two are brothers, with one a big bad bruiser and his kid brother some tiny little—"

Jimmy Tuttle cut him off. "At ease, Sergeant. Lieutenant Moon is no kid. He's one hell of a pilot and one hell of a fighter. Size doesn't have a damn thing to do with it, and don't you ever forget it."

"I was *just saying*, Lieutenant. Didn't mean no disrespect."

"Well, next time, Sergeant, try engaging your brain before you open your mouth, so maybe nobody will take you the wrong way."

Dodging the raindrops, Tommy and Sean dashed across a courtyard to a huge barn that had been appropriated as a maintenance shed, slipping past the canvas hung over the open doorway to provide light discipline. "Hey," Tommy said, "congratulations on the new stripe, big brother."

"Thanks, Half. It was about time, if you ask me."

In the dim electric light inside, several Shermans were getting new tracks. An M5 Stuart light tank was in the middle of an engine change. The dark shapes of half a dozen tanks sat outside the barn waiting their turn at heavy maintenance.

"Cadillac makes the M5, you know," Sean said, pointing to the Stuart. "Should be top of the line, right? But it's still got that puny little main gun. Absolutely worthless against another tank. But they ain't bad for recon work. They can run away like hell when they have to."

The industrial racket in the barn couldn't mask the continuous drum roll of distant artillery. The GI mechanics didn't seem to hear it. They toiled on as if immune to its message.

His mood darkening, Sean replied, "When's this fucking rain gonna quit, Half?"

"Tomorrow, around noon, I'm told. What the hell are you guys doing in this spot, anyway? I thought Fourth Armored was down south of here, and way out ahead."

"Most of the Fourth still is," Sean replied. "Except us. We got fucked over. Detailed back here to help break these fucking forts."

That was the last thing Tommy wanted to hear: his brother being fed into the meat grinder at Metz.

"Ain't that the same thing you've been doing, Half? I mean, trying to knock out these forts? We see the jugs up there every day. At least when it ain't raining,

142

anyway. That Fort Driant is a real pain in my ass. I've been close enough to spit on it, but that's about all the good I did."

He somberly described the fruitless assaults, the Bangalore torpedo fiasco, the mounting casualties. "How long can those fucking Krauts hold out? They gotta be running out of everything—food, water, ammo, generator fuel. They gotta be."

"From what I hear, Sean, they stocked some of those forts to hold out for months."

"Oh, my achin' ass! We been hearing the same shit."

They fell silent, two men consumed with thoughts of their own and each other's mortality, trying to come to grips with a common enemy from totally different perspectives.

It was Sean who broke the silence, with none of the brash confidence his voice carried in better days. Instead, Tommy heard nothing but dread. His big brother's voice was without hope.

"What do you think, Tommy? The brass just gonna let them pick us off until we finally starve 'em out? Or is there a way to bust this thing wide open?"

He'd seen Sean like this before: so fatalistic that death was the sole, inevitable escape from war's horror. Just like he'd been a few months back, before the tide seemed to turn for the Allies at the Falaise Pocket.

He couldn't blame him. Sean had been through enough in this war. Most men who'd earned as many Purple Hearts were in far worse shape physically and emotionally. Or they were six feet under.

Tommy would give anything to ease his big brother's fears. He couldn't tell him about *Operation*

Bucket, though. No matter how much he wanted to.

But he's my brother, dammit. Maybe if he knew something big was coming, it might...

No, I can't. I can't tell anyone. Those "Bucket" planes are so easy to knock down, slow as they are and flying all alone. The wrong word slips out, the Krauts get a heads-up, and the whole plan goes to shit. A couple of flak guns near Driant would be all it takes. Or the Luftwaffe showing up.

I can't do it. I can't tell him. I'm sworn to secrecy.

But maybe a hint. Nothing specific. Just a hint that something's in the works to buck him up a little.

Sean sat with his back against the wall, his knees drawn up, his head hung down. Tommy put a hand on his brother's shoulder.

Here I go again, playing big brother to my big brother. War really fucks things up and spins them around, doesn't it?

"I've been hearing rumors there's a big change coming, Sean."

A glimmer of hope shone on Sean's face, like a condemned man who thought he'd just heard the word *reprieve* mentioned.

"What *kind* of change, Half?"

"I wish I knew."

Sean's expression shifted to the glower of an accuser. "Don't bullshit a bullshitter, Tommy. What the hell do you know?"

Tommy just leaned back against the wall and shook his head.

"Son of a bitch, Half. You never could lie worth a shit. You're up to your ass in something, ain't you?"

He gave no answer.

"You didn't volunteer for some crazy shit, did you?"

Still no answer.

"How many times I gotta tell you, *don't volunteer for nothing.*"

"That's a double negative, Sean. You're really saying *volunteer for something.* Maybe everything."

"That ain't what I mean and you know it, you stupid little jughead."

"That's *Lieutenant Jughead* to you, Sergeant."

"Oh my god, you really did it." There was the same uncanny certainty in Sean's voice, something Tommy had heard so many times before in their lives. Whether it was a cheating girlfriend, a conniving boss, a neighborhood con man, or just a run-of-the-mill liar, Sean could always sniff them out, long before anyone else was even suspicious.

And now he's sniffed me out. He can read people. He always could. You can't fool him.

But I still can't tell him shit.

"You don't remember nothing I ever taught you, do you, Tommy? And you're supposed to be the smart one."

"I'll tell you what I do remember, Sean. I remember you telling me it was all *just a matter of time.* Well, brother, I'm here to tell you it still is. The clock on this *fubar* exercise at Driant is running out. So let me give you a piece of advice, too."

"Yeah? What's that?"

"Don't you go volunteering for anything either, okay?"

Sean mulled it over for a few moments. Then he said, "Okay. Deal."

A welder's torch flared just a few feet away, bathing them in its harsh light. Now out of the shadows, Tommy liked what he saw in his brother's face. The tension and despair had drained away, as if the sparks of the torch had kindled new hope deep within him. If nothing else, watching the weld in progress directed Sean's attention back to the realities of a tanker's life.

"Hey, numbnuts," Sean called to the welder, "that's the worst fucking weld I ever saw. A light MG could knock that patch off. Clean it up and do it again."

"Ain't a goddamn thing wrong with it, Sarge," the welder replied. "I know what the hell I'm doing."

"The fuck you do," Sean replied as he stood to his full, imposing height and snatched the torch from the startled welder's hand. "Let me show you how it's done, pal. Give me those fucking goggles."

Tommy smiled as he watched his brother deftly wield the torch. He breathed a sigh of relief, too. He hadn't spilled any beans about *Operation Bucket*. But his cryptic message had done its work: *The old Sean's back again.*

The brothers talked long into the night, spirited discussions about news from home, the winter clothing Uncle Sam still hadn't gotten around to issuing, Ike's questionable decision to give the bulk of their gasoline to Montgomery, the foolishness of having a World Series when all the best players were in the service, and plans for drinking beer in Berlin. Or, better yet, at home in Brooklyn.

Then the conversation drifted to a more private

matter. Sean asked, "When're you gonna see that French tomato of yours again?"

"You mean Sylvie?"

"What? You got another one, too?"

"No. Just her. But I have no idea when I'm going to see her again. Alençon is a long way from Toul."

"Hey, you got an airplane."

"It doesn't work like that, Sean. I got a couple of letters from her, though."

"So you've been chatting, then."

"I wouldn't call it that. I'm not really sure how I'm getting her letters, as screwed up as the mail is and all. But I'm pretty sure she's not getting mine."

"So you miss her, then?"

"What do you think, Sean?"

He'd expected his brother's reply to be some crude sexual gesture. But he was in for a surprise.

"Can't say I blame you, Half. She's something special, that Sylvie Bergerac."

Tommy expected him to follow up with something like *don't see what the hell a dame like that's doing with a chump like you...*

But he didn't.

Exhaustion was catching up with them. They both had things to do and places to be once the sun rose in a few hours, and they'd need whatever recharge a few hours' sleep might provide. There'd still be time for more talk over breakfast.

And maybe, on another rainy day, they'd be close enough to see each other again.

✯✯✯✯

Tommy had been able to smell breakfast cooking as he tossed and turned, listening to the patter of rain on the canvas over his head, trying to get comfortable on the rickety cot the tankers had loaned him. He'd set up that cot in Baker Company's CP—his brother's company. He would've been perfectly happy sleeping in the squad tent with Sean and his tank crew, but they wouldn't have him.

"Sorry, Lieutenant, but this tent ain't no place for gentlemen," Sean had said. Walking his brother to the CP, he'd added, "I feel real bad about this, but you know how it is, Tommy. Can't be fraternizing. Even with family."

The sun was still a long way from rising when Sean roused him.

Through bleary eyes, Tommy thought, *Look at him. He looks like he just got ten hours' sleep.*

And I feel like warmed-over shit.

The field kitchen was a huge tent—a *circus tent* in GI lingo—with four mess section deuce-and-a-halfs backed up to one end. The serving line's specialty of the morning: scrambled egg sandwiches—the eggs piled thick within slices of fresh-baked bread—with all the fried Spam and hash browns your mess kit could hold. Of course, they were powdered eggs—most GIs hadn't seen a fresh egg since their time in Great Britain, and that was only if they'd been lucky—but the cooks tried their best to fluff them with some bartered-for fresh milk and season them liberally so they almost tasted good.

Sean asked, "You remember what this means, don't you, Half?"

Tommy just nodded. He remembered his first

morning as an ASO with 37th Tank back in August. He'd
learned its meaning then: scrambled egg sandwiches—
considered a delicacy by the GIs—meant you were
going into some big action that day.

"This wouldn't be related to that *thing* you were
talking about last night, would it, Half?"

"Nope."

"Oh, yeah?" Sean replied. "You mean we still got
more surprises coming?"

"Afraid so, brother."

There were tables set up in the tent for the officers.
Tommy glanced their way and did a double take. Seated
at one of them was Jimmy Tuttle and Herb Clinchmore,
engaged in what seemed like friendly conversation.

*What the hell's going on here? Last night, Jimmy
said he hadn't forgiven him. This morning, they look like
asshole buddies. That sure was a quick change of heart.*

Tommy still hadn't forgotten—or forgiven—that
Clinchmore, once a member of *Blue Flight*, had
abandoned that flight during combat and fled back to
base. Questioned why he'd done such a thing, he lied
and claimed there was a problem with his airplane's
radio.

There hadn't been a thing wrong with that radio.
When confronted with that fact—and after a few too
many drinks in an Alençon café—he'd loudly
proclaimed that he didn't give a damn about the ground
troops he was supposed to be supporting. A bunch of
equally inebriated infantrymen who'd overheard him
would have beaten Herb Clinchmore to within an inch of
his life if Sylvie Bergerac hadn't artfully defused the
situation.

Being drunk was no excuse, though; that comment

got him shipped off to ASO duty for *re-education*. True, Colonel Pruitt had issued the order sending him away, but it had been at the instigation of Tommy Moon, his flight leader.

Lieutenant Herb Clinchmore could have been court-martialed for running out on his flight. Or at the very least, become a pariah in the squadron, a festering sore of disunity and discontent. Neither the colonel nor Tommy wanted either of those options; morale is a delicate and finicky commodity, easy to lose, difficult to regain. Sending him off to learn a hard lesson had seemed a much better solution.

There was a third officer seated at the table as well, a major wearing a flight jacket with pilot's wings. He seemed more interested in his chow than the lieutenants' conversation.

Tuttle caught sight of Tommy and waved, bidding him to come over.

"You've got to hear this," Tuttle said as Tommy drew closer. "Ol' Herb here's found religion now."

Clinchmore was on his feet, pumping Tommy's hand like a politician on the stump. "I'm glad you're here, Half—may I call you Half?"

"Yeah, sure, Herb. Why not? You always did before."

"Well, Half, I just wasn't sure, after…well, you know. And I'm sorry about all that. I really and truly am. But you were right. I needed time with the ground troops. It sure has changed me…for the better. In fact, I've put my papers in for a transfer."

"A transfer? To what? A ground outfit?"

"Well, sort of, Half. I'm going to be an aerial observer, just like Major Kidd here." He turned to introduce the man, who was hurriedly washing down his latest mouthful with a big gulp of coffee so he could actually speak.

"Holy cow! Major Bob Kidd," Tommy said, offering his hand. "You're *Rocket Man*, aren't you?"

"In the flesh," Kidd replied. "But if I keep getting good chow like this, I'm going to be in too much flesh. Never thought that would be much of a problem over here."

Tommy found the comment odd, since the major was as skinny as most GIs. *Four bones stuck together*, as his grandmother used to describe it back in Brooklyn.

"We worked together not too long ago," Tommy said. "I'm Tommy Moon, *Gadget Blue Leader* from the 301st, the jug outfit out of A-90."

Kidd's face brightened as recognition set in. "Yeah, I remember you guys. We worked over some *panzergrenadiers* in a forest east of the Moselle. You guys put those bombs right on the smoke. Great job."

"Couldn't have done it without you, sir. And the invitation for a beer at A-90 still stands, anytime. So you're ready to take on Herb Clinchmore, eh?"

"I sure am. He's got the knack for it…sees things from above and below pretty darn well. I could tell the first time he rode with me. And he's figuring out how to handle one of those *rag bags* pretty darn fast, too."

"*Rag bag*, sir? You mean an L-4?"

"Yeah. Good nickname for a bunch of sticks covered in fabric, don't you think? So what brings you to these parts, Lieutenant?"

"Just visiting my big brother." He nodded toward Sean, who'd avoided the officers' area entirely and parked himself on a crate in a corner of the tent. "He's a tank platoon sergeant here. If you'll excuse me, sir, I'm going to go join him. No telling when we might see each other again."

"Sure thing, Lieutenant Moon. Good meeting you. You jug boys keep giving them hell, okay?"

"You bet, sir. You do the same." He nodded to Tuttle and said, "As soon as we're done with breakfast, we'd better hit the road."

"Yeah, great," Tuttle mumbled. "My turn to drive, right? And you get the leaky roof."

"Sure. Your turn." Then Tommy nodded to Clinchmore, offered a smile, and said, "You take care of yourself, Herb."

Back with his brother, Tommy relayed the story of Herb Clinchmore's conversion. "I guess it worked out pretty well for everyone concerned," he concluded.

"Nah, you should've broken it off in his ass the minute he pulled that shit, Half. Anyone who fucks his buddies like that ain't worth a bucket of warm piss."

"C'mon, Sean, we all make mistakes. No one's perfect."

Wordlessly, with one sour look, Sean managed to reject Tommy's opinion and express his unremitting belief that his kid brother was too often a naïve fool.

The food vanished from their mess kits all too quickly. Captain Newcomb, Sean's company commander, had hurried by, telling Sean to be at a battalion briefing in fifteen minutes. There was nothing left to say except goodbye.

Tommy was startled by the ferocity of his brother's hug as he said, "Listen up, Half. You already fucked up and volunteered your scrawny little ass for some bullshit, whatever the hell it is. Don't make it worse by having

Mom and Dad read what a fucking hero you were off some goddamn telegram from the War Department. The one that tells them where you got buried. If they ever find your body, that is."

"I could say the same to you, Sean. Hell, I *should* be saying the same to you."

When their clinch finally ended and they could look into each other's eyes, neither tried to hide his tears.

"See you whenever," Sean said.

"Yeah, count on it, brother."

As Tommy turned to walk away, Sean said, "Hey, Half...this *thing* you were talking about. It's gonna be real soon, right?"

"Yeah. I think so."

Jimmy Tuttle cursed his luck. It had only been a few minutes since they'd driven away from 37th Tank's bivouac, and already the rain had slowed to a gloomy drizzle. "Son of a bitch," he said. "When you were driving, the rain poured through that leaky roof all over me. Now you're riding the right seat and it's slowed down to almost nothing. I'm telling you, Half...you're one lucky bastard. You must've backed into the golden doorknob or something."

"I can't help you with that one, Jimmy. Take it up with Mother Nature."

Suddenly, there were dark shapes looming just ahead. Tuttle slammed on the brakes: an elderly farmer was urging his herd of reluctant cows across the roadway. Over the jeep's idling engine—its clattering *purr* like the sound of a hundred sewing machines— and the foghorn *moos* of the annoyed cows, he and Tommy could hear the shrill, terrifying whistle of artillery shells passing high overhead.

"It's coming from the forts, I'll bet," Tommy said, looking up anxiously into the dull gray overcast. "Sounds like they're shooting up the Moselle crossings again."

Tapping his fingers nervously on the steering wheel, Tuttle added, "That's one thing about artillery...it works just the same no matter how screwed up the weather is. We of the *aviator persuasion*, on the other hand, get to sit on our asses whenever the weather turns to shit and do fuck all."

"*Fuck all*, Jimmy? Now there's an expression I haven't heard in a while. Are we back in England all of a sudden?"

"I wish," Tuttle replied.

A line of GI trucks was backing up behind the jeep, waiting for the bovine roadblock to clear. "Maybe I ought to have a word with this guy and get him to hurry it up a little," Tommy suggested, "before those trucks behind us start mowing those cows down."

"Yeah, good idea, Half. At least you can *parlez vous* their stupid language. To me, it always sounds like they're trying to spit out something that tastes really awful."

But you didn't have to be fluent in French to see the farmer was in no mood to be hurried. After a few moments of unsmiling conversation, punctuated by the Frenchman's provocative hand gestures, Tommy was back in the jeep.

"I'd say that farmer hates Americans only slightly less than he hates Krauts," Tommy said. "I didn't get a couple of the words—probably curse words anyway—but he basically said that every minute he wastes having to talk to an *Ami imbecile* like me is another minute the road stays blocked."

Tuttle laughed. "How about that, Tommy? We've run into a wise man. And here I was, thinking he was just another ungrateful *frog*."

They watched in silence as the rear guard of animals began to lumber across the road.

It was Tuttle who broke that silence. "So you're not even going to give me a hint about this *top secret project* of yours, are you?"

"Look, Jimmy...you broke my chops all the way out here and I didn't tell you a damn thing. What makes you think the ride back's going to be any different?"

"Suit yourself, Half. I'll bet you told your brother, though."

"Negative, Jimmy. Negative."

"So you're all clammed up, eh? But you know, there's been some talk around the squadron...and we think we've got a couple of ideas what you're up to."

"Whatever the hell they are, keep them to yourself. Tell the other clowns to do the same, dammit."

Tuttle looked surprised. "Really? It's that big a deal?"

"It could be, Jimmy. It just could be." He paused, measuring his words, before continuing, "We don't need any bigmouths screwing it up, even if they don't have a damn clue what they're talking about."

"You mean like *loose lips sink ships*?"

"Yeah, Jimmy. That's exactly what I mean."

Chapter Sixteen

It was a little after 1000 hours when the jeep bearing Tommy and Tuttle drove onto A-90. The rain had finally stopped for good about an hour before, but a low overcast still hung over northeastern France. "Doesn't look like we'll be doing any flying until that stuff breaks up," Jimmy Tuttle said as he scanned the gray cap of clouds. "Where do you want to go first, Tommy? Operations or quarters?"

"Let's sign in at Operations. Then I'll have to get back over to Zebra Ramp and see what the hell's going on over there."

"Okay…and when you come back, maybe you'll be ready to tell the rest of us?"

"Don't count on it, Jimmy."

Tommy didn't think anything of the ladies' bicycle with its mud-splattered fenders parked by the operations shack door. There were no fences around A-90, save the recently created bastion known as Zebra Ramp. French civilians frequently visited, sometimes just to watch the airplanes, sometimes bearing small amounts of food and wine as gifts for the airmen and ground crews. The more cynical among the Americans—Tommy's crew chief Sergeant McNulty was in this group—were sure the French came bearing their modest gifts just for the chocolate bars and cigarettes they received in return. The rest, more sympathetic to what the French had gone through in the Occupation, harbored no such suspicions and were more willing to accept the gifts as tokens of appreciation. Besides, some of the visitors were young French women, and to be in the presence of *any* woman—even one with whom you couldn't manage a conversation—was better than *no* woman.

And occasionally, a guy could even get lucky. According to Sergeant McNulty, it wasn't uncommon to encounter several trysts going on at the same time in the supply shed or an amorous couple sequestered in the bed of a parked truck. He'd never had the heart to break up a rendezvous, though. To do so would have been counterproductive, anyway; the encounters rarely lasted longer than a smoke break and were far more conducive to morale.

Tommy's first impression when he walked into Operations was that there was no one there. Then he heard spirited voices and laughter from a far corner of the room and realized every man on duty was huddled in that corner, obviously enchanted by something—or someone—in their midst.

From inside that circle of men, a voice emerged—a young woman's voice, engaging, confident—speaking excellent English but obviously French.

Even though he couldn't see her yet, hidden by that crowd of admirers, he had no doubt to whom that voice belonged.

As if in slow motion, the men parted, fell silent, and revealed the woman who'd been captivating them…

Sylvie Bergerac.

She walked toward him slowly, a beautiful vision in ordinary clothes suitable for cycling: full pleated skirt, wool jacket, oxfords and socks on her feet, a black beret on her head. In her hand was a bottle of Coca-Cola, a straw protruding from it like the stalk of a plucked flower. An obvious offering from her American admirers.

She looked like so many American girls relaxing with friends at a stateside soda fountain. But no American girl ever had to do what Sylvie Bergerac had done as a member of the Resistance. A sobering thought crossed Tommy's mind as she closed the distance between them:

Sylvie is the only person in this room who knows for certain she's killed Germans. We pilots probably have...but maybe not. Where's our proof? Maybe it's better we don't have it.

And the ground personnel—the staff officers, the mechanics, the armorers, the admin clerks—have never been in a kill-or-be-killed situation and probably never will be.

But she knows. She's seen the faces of men she's killed.

Looked into their eyes.

And yet she seems an angel...

An angel who's tougher than all of us put together.

An angel who sleeps at night with no regrets about what she's done.

Then she was before him, close enough to touch, close enough to kiss.

He was grinning like an idiot but couldn't seem to move a muscle.

The words that escaped his mouth did nothing but restate the obvious: "You're here."

A voice called out, "Moon, if you don't kiss her, I sure as hell will."

She held him in a curious gaze, sure of herself but not so sure of him. In French, she said, "Have you forgotten me already, Tommy?"

He was grateful she'd spoken in French. Now they

could converse in private despite the prying eyes and ears of the operations staff.

"Are you joking?" he asked. "Forget you? How could I?"

"That is my question, too—how could you? Did you get my letters?"

"Yes. Surprisingly, I did. Did you get mine?"

She shook her head. "You replied, then?"

"Yes, of course! That explains it," he said. "Maybe we ought to try carrier pigeons or something."

"Yes, maybe so—" She was going to say more, but he'd figured out how to move again. He was kissing her full on the mouth.

They ignored the whistles and catcalls. Then, as if of one mind, they ended their long kiss, turned, and bowed theatrically to their audience. That display finished, they sauntered out of the operations shack arm in arm.

Once outside, he pointed to the bicycle and asked, in English, "You didn't ride that thing all the—"

Her burst of laughter cut him off in mid-sentence. "No, silly boy. It's nearly three hundred miles. I took a bus from Alençon. The bike is borrowed from a friend here in Toul."

"Gee, you've got friends and family all over, don't you?"

With the tip of her finger, she tapped the black beret on her head, the mark of the Resistance: the *maquis*.

"Even strangers are friends when you wear the beret," she replied.

"But you're finished with all that stuff now, right? I mean, the Germans are gone."

"They are not completely gone from France,

Tommy."

'But you are *finished* with the Resistance, aren't you?"

"For God's sake, lower your voice," she pleaded.

"Oh, crap! You're still playing soldier."

"We are not *playing*, Tommy." She pulled back a step, a kaleidoscope of emotions whirling across her face: defiance, anger, hurt, pain, desperation, need—and at last, a hopeful plea: "Can't you be happy just to see me? Please?"

That didn't seem like too much to ask. He pulled her into his arms, letting his tight embrace answer the question.

Another long kiss, and then he said, "Can we start again?"

"Yes, please."

They found a place to sit that wasn't wet from the rain, a just-delivered crate of aircraft parts. She explained that she was now a courier for the Free French, no longer a fighting member of the Resistance. Still, she might occasionally have to operate in German-held areas, not as a spy, femme fatale, assassin, or saboteur, but merely a messenger.

To emphasize the point, she said, "I don't even carry my pistol anymore."

Then she explained that she was on her way to Nancy, carrying urgent personal messages to soldiers in the French 2nd Armored Division. "*La Poste* works as poorly for the French as it does for you Yanks, I suppose."

"You're going to Nancy? I just passed through it. My brother's up north of there."

"Is he fighting at the forts of Metz?"

"Yeah. I am, too, actually."

Her face saddened. "Those forts...they are a very bad business. For decades, they did nothing, not for the French, not for the Germans. They were useless, monuments to petrified thinking. And now, suddenly, against all reason, they are important and powerful."

"You know about those forts?"

"They are part of our history. We studied them in school, Tommy."

"Yeah, I guess you would."

Desperate to change the subject, he asked, "How's your papa?"

"He still hates you."

A moment of stunned silence, and then her face broke into a mischievous smile. "But he hates all Americans. Not as much as he hates the *Boche* and communists, though."

"At least I'm in good company," Tommy replied with a smile of his own.

Then he got serious again. "And Bernard?"

"Our annulment will be announced eventually. The Church shall not be hurried. But I don't need their piece of paper to know I am rid of him."

A P-47's engine roared to life. Sylvie asked, "Should you not be flying, too?"

"He's not going to fly. That's just a run-up for maintenance. The weather's still too socked in. Besides, I'm not with—"

He'd stopped himself cold. He was about to let slip he was on a special project.

A *secret* project.

"You're not with *what*, Tommy?"

He hesitated, stumbling through some evasive

gestures before he said, very coldly, "I can't talk about it."

"Are you in some sort of trouble? Have you been grounded?"

"No, nothing like that, Syl."

She watched him squirm for a few moments, at first confused that this sweet and guileless American she'd taken as a lover these last few months could seem so conflicted. There had never been anything terribly complicated about Lieutenant Tommy Moon. He was always open, honest, intelligent, and driven by duty.

And he speaks almost intelligible French! So rare for an American.

"Yet you can't tell me," she said.

He hung his head as if betraying her, but his lips remained sealed.

She allowed herself a brief interval to pity him. And then she broke into thunderous laughter.

"What the hell is so damn funny, Sylvie?"

It took her a minute to catch her breath before she could articulate an answer. Once she had, she threw her arms around him and said, "Oh, Tommy, this is so perfect. Forgive me for finding the irony in this so…so…what is the word you *Ami* use? When you laugh so much?"

"Hysterical?"

"Yes, yes! That's it. It's hysterical! *Hystérique!*"

"Sorry, but I don't get the joke here."

She wiped the tears of laughter from her eyes, took a deep breath, and began her explanation.

"Ever since we first met, Tommy, you never fully understood—maybe never fully respected, either—the need I had for absolute secrecy as a *maquisard*. But I just assumed all American men were like that, living in their perfect world where everything was black or white, regarding women as mere accessories to their very important lives."

"How can you say I didn't take it seriously, Syl? Of course I did. You saved my life, for cryin' out loud! That's pretty damn serious. But every second I was terrified something would happen to you."

"And you didn't think I was just as terrified? For myself...as well as for you?"

"Well...I suppose so."

"You'd better *suppose so*, Tommy Moon, because what I had to do was every bit as important as what you had to do."

"Okay, fine. No argument there. But why do you find it so funny, Sylvie?"

"Because now *you* have a secret, Tommy. And all of a sudden, you expect me, without question, to respect it, to take it very, very seriously. But you're so uncomfortable with this secret. You're not used to living with them in your little black and white world, so it's tearing you apart."

She smiled coyly, and then added, "You're dying to tell someone, aren't you?"

The sheepish look on his face was the only answer she needed.

"Well, I know the importance of keeping secrets better than you, Tommy. So here's my promise: I'll never ask you to tell me what it is. Never. You have my word on that. So you can stop being so uncomfortable with it. At least around me."

Nestled against each other, they fell quiet, relieved that the storm between them had passed, leaving no damage in its wake. She slipped a piece of paper into his hand. "This is where I'm staying. It's not far from here."

Chapter Seventeen

As far as Sean Moon was concerned, it had started like every other time they'd tried to attack Fort Driant: *Just one damn SNAFU after another.*

But then, the *dozer tanks*—Shermans with bulldozer blades rigged to their bows—made a startling discovery: although they couldn't move earth fast enough to fill in the deep, steep-sided ditch protecting the front—or west—side of the fort from tanks, they could certainly bury the pillbox at the end of that ditch in no time flat. The pillbox covered the ditch's length with grazing machine gun fire, making it a deathtrap for infantry as well as armor. The bullets from inside the fort *clanking* off the dozers' blades were no impediment to this improvised earth-moving project.

The pillbox silenced, infantrymen of 5th Division spilled through the narrow, suddenly undefended gap at the south end of the ditch. The barbed wire field they skirted was quickly found to be free of mines, so the four Shermans of Baker Company's 2nd Platoon—the platoon Sean Moon led—were ordered to smash through it, enter the fort's perimeter, and protect the infantry with roving cover and fire support. The infantry, in turn, was to protect the tanks from German sappers.

The constant *ping* of bullets off the tanks' hulls and turrets kept them buttoned up. *I'd give my eye teeth to be able to open this hatch and have a really good look around*, Sean thought, *but the view out this damn periscope will have to do. At least I can tell where we are—coming up on Bunkers 3 and 4. Beyond them are those two batteries—six guns total, three domed steel turrets each. They ain't firing at nothing...they're retracted into their concrete shells like turtles pulling themselves in and covering up.*

Can't see a friggin' Kraut anywhere...not even the outline of a fucking helmet.

But somebody's shooting out of them bunkers, that's for damn sure. All those firing ports...they're like windows without glass, and they ain't that big. They can't shoot anything out of them but rifles and MGs. If they got any anti-tank guns inside the perimeter, they would've been firing at us already.

We still gotta watch out for them fucking panzerfausts. But I'm betting the Krauts will have problems firing one of them things from inside those bunkers because they got two wrong ends, just like a bazooka. Try to fire it in a tight space and you cook yourself and everyone around you with the rocket blast.

And now that we're inside, ain't the other forts supposed to be laying down fire on us?

Not that I'm complaining, mind you.

Just so the dogfaces keep them jokers with grenades off our backs

Still, this is fucking nuts, driving around inside this place—or on top of it, or wherever the hell we are— being target practice for Krauts we can't see and can't touch. What's that old saying? Try not to be conspicuous. It draws fire?

Gee, no shit.

And we sure as hell won't be getting no help from the flyboys. Not with this overcast.

It was hard to keep track of where the GI infantry was through the limited view of the tank commander's periscope. Usually, a squad or two would be bunched behind *Lucky 7*, desperate for the cover her hull provided. But sometimes, the infantry was nowhere to be seen.

At least my tankers are on the radio...and they're doing what they're told just like they're supposed to.

But the dogfaces...their radios don't talk to ours. Not directly, anyway. Sure, they can get a message to us through Battalion, but that takes too damn long. So when we gotta be buttoned up like this and we can't yell at each other, I have no idea what they need unless one of them's talking to me on the phone hanging off the ass end of the tank.

And right now, none of them corn plaster commandos are telling me a damn thing.

Sean led his tanks around the back side of Bunker 3, the one nearest the place they'd breached the wire. The tankers weren't expecting the sight that met them.

"Holy shit," Sean said. "Get a load of this!"

Although the bunker was built into a hill, its back side was completely exposed, as if a quarter of the hill had been scooped out and the structure built to fill the excavation. Viewed from this side, it was so much more than just the ground-level blockhouse atop the hill they'd been facing before turning the corner. In actuality, the bunker was a two-story monolith of concrete and stone, almost one hundred yards wide. Its back side faced a broad, sunken courtyard and featured dozens of firing ports. There were big steel doors at each corner of the facade. Even from two hundred yards away, those doors looked impenetrable.

Couldn't tell it looked like this from them aerial photos.

The anxious voice of an infantry lieutenant at *Lucky*

7's external phone crackled over her intercom. "Battalion wants us to take this bunker. Can you knock those doors down?"

"We can try, sir," Sean replied. "But we can't quiet down all those Krauts shooting at us. How the hell are you gonna get across that courtyard?"

"We'll be behind you."

"You're gonna have to come out in the open at some point, Lieutenant. Then they're gonna riddle your asses."

"I've got that covered. Smoke's on the way."

The main guns of four tanks traversed to target the doors. But within seconds, smoke shells from the infantry's mortars began to blanket the courtyard in a dense white cloud.

Fabiano, Sean's gunner, banged his head against the gunsight in frustration. "Who turned on the fucking smoke? How the hell am I supposed to hit something I can't see?" Over the radio, Sean's other tanks were reporting that they, too, were suddenly blind.

"Take your best shot," Sean told them. "That's all you can do."

The tanks fired. Just as fast as the loaders could shove in another round, they fired again.

The infantry lieutenant's voice was back in Sean's earphones. "Cease fire, cease fire. We're moving in."

Through his periscope, Sean could just make out the ghostly shapes of infantrymen running forward, only to disappear into the smoke in their dash to the bunker. By the time they reached its doors, the smoke screen was drifting away in the breeze. Seconds after that, they were sprinting back to the shelter of the tanks.

The doors stood fast. True, they were dented and

scorched; a few of the tanks' rounds had been direct hits. The rest had hit the concrete walls around them. They were chipped and scorched, too.

But those doors were still closed tighter than a bank vault. The walls were perfectly intact.

Sean told himself what he already knew too well: *These damn seventy-five millimeters can't punch through much more than a cardboard box. Ain't got the muzzle velocity.*

As the smoke cleared, withering fire from the bunker raked GI infantrymen who hadn't yet reached the tanks. The suppressive fire from the Shermans couldn't hope to deter every last German gunner.

They'd be lucky to silence half of them. Temporarily.

"We're pulling back," a terrified voice said over *Lucky 7's* intercom. It could only be coming from one source, an infantryman on the tank's external phone. Probably the same lieutenant from before, just more scared now.

"Not so damn fast, sir," Sean replied. "My tanks are going to pull forward a little. Pick up your wounded and put them on the rear decks. We'll carry them out."

The four Shermans pulled forward, cutting the distance to the bunker down to less than a hundred yards. "Let me have another crack at 'em," Fabiano said. "I can put a round right through one of those fucking windows, we're so close."

"Okay," Sean replied, "bottom floor, third window from the left. Put that fucking MG out of its misery."

"Got it," Fabiano said. "On the way."

The round struck with a thunderous *SLAM* and then a rippling shudder, like the tremors of an earthquake.

Fist-sized chunks of concrete rained down like meteorites; thick gray dust shrouded the bunker's façade.

But the dust settled quickly. When it did, the machine gun in that window began spewing its mechanized death all over again.

Fabiano smacked his gunsight in disgust. "Shit! I fucking missed."

"You made their ears bleed, at least," Sean said.

"Let me take another shot, Sarge."

"No can do, Fab. We're pulling back now."

"Ahh, c'mon, Sarge. Just one more."

"I said no, dammit. How many times I gotta tell you...don't waste rounds while we're moving. You won't hit nothing that way."

The periscope view satisfied him that there were no GIs still huddled behind his tank, so he gave the order to Kowalski, his driver, to back away.

Through the periscope, Sean could see his other three tanks backing away, too, with GIs riding their hulls. Some were lying flat, probably wounded, while others crouched over them. There wasn't anyone on *Lucky 7's* deck.

I can't tell how many they got wounded, but it sure looks like we took a shellacking.

As the tank rumbled backward, Sean kept up a panoramic sweep with the periscope, watching for threats from any direction:

I heard how them Krauts pop up out of nowhere in this place, like there's hidey holes everywhere. That's all I need right now—some clown with a panzerfaust appearing like magic—because I don't see no GIs covering my ass.

But he wanted to make damned sure they didn't

accidentally run over any GIs, either.

Just because I can't see 'em through this tiny little scope don't mean they ain't there.

"How long you want me to keep her in reverse, Sarge?" Kowalski's voice.

"Until I tell you different."

The other three tanks were pivoting and then shifting into forward gear to retrace their steps out of Fort Driant. Sean told Kowalski to do the same. They'd be the last tank in the exodus back to the assembly area, far behind the rest.

He swung the periscope for a view back to the bunker, now off the tank's right side as she plowed forward.

At first, he wasn't sure what he was seeing: *Am I looking at GIs running for the wire? Or have Krauts come out of the woodwork to try and cut us off?*

"Ski," Sean called to his driver, "give me a quarter turn right."

"That ain't the way out, Sarge."

"I ain't asking for a map reading lesson, Corporal. Just do it."

He pressed his face against the periscope, trying for a better look—an *identifying* look—at the soldiers they were fast closing on.

Dammit, I can't see shit.

He popped open the hatch and stuck his head out.

It only took a second to tell they were Germans. The shape of their *coal scuttle* helmets gave them away. The sound of bullets striking the turret and hull was so much louder with the hatch open.

Pulling his head back inside, he told Fabiano, "Traverse right, thirty degrees rough. Krauts in the open,

171

range forty yards. Hit 'em with the coax."

The gunner swung the turret to Sean's mark. "Yeah, I got 'em." Then he hesitated. "You sure they're Krauts, Sarge?"

"Yeah. Fire that fucking thirty cal, dammit."

Under his breath, Fabiano mumbled, "God forgive me, maybe." Then he pressed the foot switch that fired the turret's coaxial machine gun.

"There you go," Sean told his gunner. "Now keep firing, traverse as necessary."

Then he told Kowalski, "Ski, turn right to two o'clock."

"We're gonna be driving right at 'em, Sarge," the driver replied, his tense voice climbing in pitch.

"That's the idea." Then he addressed Bagdasarian, his brand new assistant driver, sitting next to Kowalski, manning the bow machine gun. "*Bags*, anything in front of us now is fair game. Knock them down. Got that?"

"Affirmative, Sarge. Loud and clear."

Gotta love these new guys, Sean thought. *They don't talk back to you. They don't know shit, either, but Ski will keep him straight.*

Within seconds, Kowalski was doing just that, shrieking at Bagdasarian, "SHOOT HIM. SHOOT HIM, FOR GOD'S SAKE."

In the split second it took Sean to pivot the periscope forward, Bagdasarian had begun to fire. But the rounds were short, splashing on a low parapet, doing little more than spraying dirt at a German soldier with a *panzerfaust* on his shoulder.

It seemed everyone on board *Lucky 7* was screaming, "SHORT! SHORT! BRING IT UP!"

Fabiano didn't need to be told to traverse the turret

and bring the coaxial machine gun to bear. But that would take precious seconds.

Through the prism of the periscope, Sean watched the life-or-death struggle unfold—like he had so many times before—in slow motion.

Here we go again. One lunatic Kraut with nothing but his uniform for armor—with one crappy little rocket on his shoulder—against us here in the belly of this iron beast.

He's gotta be some stupid volunteer, all hopped up on Dexedrine or something, like all them hardline Krauts are.

The fucking idiot.

But that fucking idiot is just a second away from killing us all.

It probably happened all at once: the German squeezing the *panzerfaust's* trigger; the tank's bullets ripping him apart.

The rocket streaked past the turret, missing by little more than a foot.

Then Sean and his crew heard nothing but the sound of their hearts pounding in their ears, louder even than the roar of *Lucky 7's* engine.

Another shriek from the bow. Kowalski again, this time without words.

Just an anguished cry.

"What happened, Ski?" Sean asked.

It took a few seconds for Kowalski to put together his answer. "Ahh…ahh, shit…it's…it's nothing. There was another Kraut out there. I just ran over him."

"Did he have a rocket?"

"Don't think so."

"Well," Sean said, "it don't matter now, does it?

Turn left to ten o'clock. Pour the coals on. Catch up with the rest of them."

There was a *thud* from the rear of the tank. The engine faltered for a moment as the acrid fumes of explosives assaulted their senses.

Kowalski backed off on the drive levers, let the engine recover, and then resumed the race out of the fort.

"What the fuck was that?" Fabiano asked. "We blow a fan or something?"

"I don't know," Sean replied. "Ski, what's your panel telling you?"

"Temps are all going up. Still making good RPMs, though."

"Then get us the hell out of here."

They made it back through the breach in the wire before *Lucky 7's* engine got balky. Kowalski was able to keep her crawling along at far from top speed. But it was enough to get them back to the assembly area.

Once they'd gotten well beyond the wire, Sean finally felt safe to open the hatch and ride with his head out. When he looked over the rear of the tank, though, he got a surprise: there was a dead German hanging off her aft deck. He was missing an arm and most of his face. Also missing: half of the engine air inlet grille. There was nothing but mangled metal where it used to be.

Son of a bitch! That Kraut must've cut the grille away and tried to stuff a grenade down the manifold. Wasn't his lucky day, though: doesn't look like the grenade went all the way down. If it had, we might all look just like him right now.

So I guess it's our lucky day.

It took a close second look to realize why the German was still attached to the tank: his web gear was hooked on the pickaxe strapped to the aft deck.

His own grenade ripped him to shreds. He couldn't even get himself blown off the old girl. Stupid bastard...that's what you get for volunteering.

At first, the battalion intel officer, a captain, had no interest in the dead German. But he returned a few minutes later with a booklet on Wehrmacht uniforms and insignia in hand.

"This guy's an officer cadet," the captain said. "We heard some rumors that Driant was staffed with cadets instead of line troops, but this is the first actual proof we've seen."

"Figured," Sean said. "Officer cadets. *Volunteers.* Uncle Adolph's got those lunatic bastards hook, line, and sinker."

Fabiano asked, "So what's the big deal, Sarge? That means they're rookies who don't know nothing, right?"

"No, you moron. It means they probably take this *fight to the last man* bullshit real serious. You won't see no cadet throwing up his hands and yelling *kamerad* like when them run-of-the-mill Krauts surrender."

Sean looked to the intel officer and said, "So maybe it makes more sense if we just *go around* this fucking city, sir, and stop getting our brains beat in?"

"That would be nice, wouldn't it, Sergeant? But there's just one thing: it would take at least two more divisions than we have at Metz right now to pull that off. If we just *go around*, we won't have anybody keeping all these *lunatic bastards* fixed in place. Our backsides will be wide open. We'll walk ourselves right into a trap—a double envelopment."

Sean smiled knowingly. "So let me guess the rest, Captain. We won't have enough troops in place until we get the gas to bring them all here, right?"

"You catch on real quick, Sergeant."

Chapter Eighteen

By 1400, the overcast had finally broken up. There were nearly four hours of prime flying time left before sunset, and the P-47s of 301st Fighter Squadron roared into the sky to make the most of it in support of 3rd Army.

Once all the fighters were airborne, the CQ-17 mothership got her turn on the runway. Tommy Moon was riding in the nose in what was usually the navigator's position. Since it was a local flight in visual conditions, he—the only person on board familiar with the area—would be the navigator, for all practical purposes.

Just forward of him was Sergeant Dandridge, in what would have been the bombardier's seat if this aircraft was on a conventional bombing mission. The Norden bombsight had been removed, replaced by Dandridge's remote-control equipment.

"Pretty good view," Tommy said as he looked through the plexiglass nose. "I've never gotten to see the runway ahead of me drop away like that."

"Really?" Dandridge replied, a little surprised. "How come, sir?"

"Simple. My ship's big ol' nose is always in the way."

There was one other difference between taking off in the jug and this modified B-17: speed. In the three minutes they'd been airborne, the swift jug would've been halfway to Nancy. This lumbering beast was barely beyond the Toul city limits. But the unobstructed scenery unfolding before the mothership's plexiglass nose was spectacular to behold: the muted yet gorgeous colors of the French countryside in fall, the red brick clusters of quaint towns which—from this distance— looked out of a storybook rather than the scenes of recent, brutal combat. Gazing to the horizon, Tommy knew he was looking into Germany, whose border was some fifty miles to the east.

"Here's the procedure," Dandridge said. "In a minute, we'll do a one-eighty and keep climbing. Once we're at about three thousand feet, they'll launch the PQ-14."

"And there's no pilot in it, right?"

"That's right, sir. The team on the ground will control the drone through takeoff and climb. Once I visually acquire it, control will pass to me."

"You've done this before, I take it, Sergeant?"

"Oh, yeah. Lots of times."

"So it's okay to put the little ones up without a pilot, but the real deal—the *baby*—always needs actual pilots to get off the ground?"

"That's right, sir. We just don't have enough control authority through the baby's autopilot to risk a takeoff. The system's good…but it's not *that* good. It's only designed for gentle maneuvers at cruise. With the PQ-14, though, there's no autopilot involved. We've got direct control of its stick, so we can do anything a pilot can do. Of course, it helps that it flies like a big toy, too."

As Dandridge did a final check of his equipment, Tommy said, "I'm a little surprised Major Staunton isn't coming with us."

"He never comes on the missions, sir. Maybe we should have brought this up earlier, but…well, here's the deal: Major Staunton is prone to airsickness. They say it could be dangerous if he flies."

"Hell, yeah, it could be dangerous," Tommy replied. "Puking into your oxygen mask is a great way to choke to death."

"He's come along on a few of the low-level test flights we've done, when we didn't need to use oxygen. But it was a nightmare each time. And the smell...it takes forever to get rid of it."

A voice in their headphones reported the *Culver* was airborne.

"Culver?" Tommy said. "That's the code name for the PQ-14?"

"Not really a code, sir. That's the name of the company that makes it. It's as distinctive as anything, I guess."

"So we're dealing with *motherships, Culvers* and *babies.*"

"Exactly, sir."

The mothership had almost completed its 180-degree turn, giving them a view back toward A-90 through the expanse of the plexiglass nose. Tommy thought it would be easy to spot the little airplane painted bright yellow climbing toward them.

But he didn't see it. "Where the hell is she?"

"It's pretty hard to spot when you're looking at it almost dead on, sir."

"But do you see her, Sergeant?"

"Yes, sir. It's at eleven o'clock, about in line with the third rivet from the bottom on the optically flat panel."

Tommy slid closer to share Dandridge's point of view. It took a lot of squinting, but he could just make out the forward silhouette of the tiny Culver. Just barely.

"It'll get a lot easier to see once it turns, sir," Dandridge said. "Those yellow wings will be hard to miss."

The drone's ground control team was on the radio again. "*Almighty Four-One*, this is *Groundhog*. We have good control. Standing by for acquisition."

His face pressed against the television monitor's hood, Dandridge fiddled with its knobs, trying to get a stable image from the Culver's single camera. With a few careful adjustments, what was just a pattern of slowly rolling diagonal lines on the screen became a steady image of the Culver's very spare instrument panel and the view over her nose.

"There," Dandridge said, with a hint of relief. "That ought to do it."

Then he was back on the radio. "*Groundhog* from *Almighty Four-One*, video acquired. Repeat, video acquired. Level the Culver on heading two-four-zero for handoff."

"Roger, *Almighty*."

Dandridge told Tommy, "If all goes well, sir, once we take control we can fly it over the target area and make sure there's no interference of any kind. Then we'll see if we can actually pull off a steeper approach to target, like you suggest."

"How's that going to work, though?" Tommy replied. "Don't the Culver and the baby have very different flight characteristics?"

"Sure they do. The Culver, as you can see, is much more nimble. But I can tone down the gain on the controller to make her respond more like a B-17."

"I see," Tommy replied. "Sounds like a plan."

He glanced at the airspeed indicator on the

bombardier's panel. It read 120 miles per hour.

"I realize we're still climbing," Tommy said, "but won't we be going a good bit faster once we're up at altitude?"

"Not on this flight, sir. The Culver climbs at about this speed and cruises at one-fifty. We need to keep her in front of us so we can maintain visual contact."

"How about with the baby?"

"A little faster, sir. About one-eighty. If we go much more than that, it gets harder to precisely put the baby on target. If your aim's off a little bit, you may not be able to correct in time."

Tommy was silent for a few moments, recalling the discussion at his first briefing with Major Staunton, where getting the baby to descend steeply seemed to be presenting a challenging aerodynamic problem. As far as he was still concerned, that was the least of their problems. But he wasn't surprised at their failure to comprehend. They were electrical engineers, not pilots.

"I'm still a little amazed you guys are worried about getting an airplane to go *down*," he said. "Hell, at those speeds, you're close to dropping out of the sky, anyway."

"You fighter pilots really like going fast, don't you, sir?"

"You bet, Sergeant. Speed is life up here."

Dandridge was on the radio with the ground controllers again. Everyone was happy with the flight's progress so far. The countdown to changeover of control from ground to air was begun:

"Three...two...one...TOGGLE. Your airplane, *Almighty."*

"I've got it," Dandridge replied. He played with the

switches on his control box, putting the Culver through a few test maneuvers. First, a series of s-turns, and then a brief drop of the nose followed by a sharp nose up. Finally, he put the drone through a barrel roll.

"Everything feels good," Dandridge said.

"Pretty responsive," Tommy added. "I assume you haven't turned down the controller's gain to mimic a B-17 yet, right?"

"Correct, sir," Dandridge replied, his tone polite but with a distinct touch of *Can't fool you, can we?*

To save time, the mothership would only climb to 10,000 feet, half her usual operating station of 20,000. Still, it would take twenty-five minutes to get there in her unhurried, spiraling ascent, as she gradually worked her way north toward the fortress of Metz. Every minute they climbed, the Culver—which Dandridge had leveled off at 3,000 feet— was slipping farther below them.

"This is crazy," Tommy said. "When you're at twenty thousand and the baby's way down, almost on the deck and out in front of you, she's about five miles away. Aren't you afraid you'll lose her?"

"No, sir," Dandridge replied. "It'll be leaving a smoke trail from that canister on her tail. And it is painted bright yellow. But once we're on course to target and the cameras are working right, I don't need to see the baby at all."

"That's all well and good, Sergeant, but maybe we should experiment with how to put her into a steep dive first, while we're still within a mile or so of the Culver and can see exactly what she's doing. At least we'll be high enough to make mistakes and get away with it."

"Sure, we can do that."

Dandridge called to Lieutenant Wheatley, the

mothership's pilot, and asked that he start s-turning so as not to overtake the Culver during the experiment.

"Okay," Wheatley replied, "but I don't know why we're bothering. Four degrees pitch down is all you're going to get if you're simulating the baby. We did the math on this a long time ago."

Dandridge turned down the gain on his controller to mimic a B-17's responses. Then he put the Culver through the first test dive. True to Wheatley's word, a shallow, four-degree descent was the best the controller could wring out of her.

"It's just like we're bringing it in for a landing, sir," he told Tommy.

"That's great if you're trying to hit the Empire State Building, but I'm betting you won't even see your aiming point on top of Fort Driant at that angle. Hell, you may not be able to see the fort at all."

Dandridge looked perplexed. "So how do we do it differently, sir?"

He didn't sound like he expected a viable answer.

"I'm saying we stall her, Sergeant, let her nose drop all by itself, then just make gentle adjustments to the dive as necessary."

The look on the sergeant's face was as if he'd just heard blasphemy. "But, sir, we went through this already. The system doesn't have the elevator control authority for that."

Tommy replied, "We know you don't have the control authority to *order up* a steep dive, but I'm betting you sure have enough elevator authority to make the minor corrections necessary to keep her on target once she dives all by herself."

"How can that be, sir?"

"Believe me, Sergeant, I do this for a living. Like I told you before, the only time you'll need a lot of elevator authority is when you want to pull out of a dive real fast. We're not going to have that problem when we attack the fort."

"But what about *now*, sir? Will we be able to pull out of the dive?"

"With the altitude cushion we've got? Probably. Only one way to find out, though."

"We're going to be in deep shit if we lose a Culver doing unauthorized maneuvers, sir."

"These things were meant to be destroyed, Sergeant. They're *target drones*, for cryin' out loud. If what we learn saves the lives of a whole lot of GIs on the ground, it'd be a small price to pay if we wreck one. Or both."

Dandridge didn't seem convinced. "I want to believe you, sir. I really do, but…"

"But what?"

"It's just that…I don't…oh, never mind. Can we at least do it my way, though?"

"Your way?"

"Yeah. Let's get everybody a couple of thousand feet higher. I want that altitude cushion to be really fat."

They relayed their plan to Wheatley. He didn't object but had a question: "We *are* still over friendly territory, right?"

"Yeah," Tommy replied. "We're a good ten miles behind the lines right now. By the way, any word from our escorts?"

"Affirmative," Wheatley replied. "They're up at *angels twenty*, keeping an eye on us."

As Dandridge turned down the gain on his controller, he told Tommy, "We're going to need something to aim at."

"I've got a point picked out already," Tommy replied. "Look at one o'clock. There's a road junction that forms a *t*, with a railroad crossing just beyond the junction."

"I see it, sir. But couldn't we use one of those little towns all around instead?"

"Bad idea, Sergeant," Tommy replied. "There's likely to be GIs in those towns. They might not understand why some aircraft type they've never seen before is diving straight for them. Don't be surprised if they start shooting at her. A road junction's a lot safer—especially one with no traffic on it."

"I see your point, sir."

"Have you ever stalled a Culver before, Sergeant?"

"No, sir."

"It would've been nice if we could've spoken with the pilots who flew the Culvers out here. They could tell us whether she drops a wing or not when she stalls. Or maybe even goes into a spin. Where the hell did they go?"

"Major Staunton sent them back to England, sir. Apparently, Eighth Air Force didn't think they'd be needed here anymore."

"Well, if we wreck both Culvers those pilots certainly won't be needed."

The look on Dandridge's face made it plain once again: he didn't like that prospect at all.

He lined the Culver up on the road junction, still several miles distant. But another problem presented itself. "How will I know when to start this dive, sir? I can't even see the target in the monitor. It's off screen, low."

"Then we're going to have to use our eyeballs, Sergeant. I'll tell you when you're at a good point to start diving. Wait for it…"

Ten seconds later, Tommy said, "Now."

"Okay, here we go," the sergeant said. "Throttling back, easing back on the elevator."

Dandridge kept his eye on the television monitor, watching the Culver's airspeed steadily sink from 120 miles per hour down to 60. She'd only lost about one hundred feet of altitude, but she didn't want to slow down any more.

"I can't hold her nose up, sir. It's started dropping already," Dandridge said. "That's keeping it above stall speed. I told you I wouldn't have enough elevator."

"Give her a minute, Sergeant."

But the Culver wouldn't stall. She just kept mushing forward in a gentle descent.

"I didn't think this would work, sir."

"Wait a minute," Tommy said. "Try this—kick her rudder left and right."

"What'll that do?"

"Slow her down."

"But I can't control the rudder separately, sir. It's coordinated with the ailerons. I'd have to uncouple them…and that'll take a minute. We'll miss this pass."

"Then kick the ailerons, Sergeant."

Dandridge began moving the joystick rhythmically left and right as he held back pressure on the elevators. The Culver waggled, trembling on the brink of a stall. He couldn't read the Culver's airspeed indicator on the video monitor because the image was shaking violently.

"She's in a pre-stall buffet," Tommy told him. "Keep it up. She'll stall. Give her a chance. Just watch she doesn't spin."

It didn't take long. The wing waggle bled off what was left of the Culver's flying speed and pushed her into the stall. Her nose dropped sharply and the little ship began a steep downward plummet.

"Okay, good," Tommy said to a very nervous Dandridge. "Pretty clean stall, no spin. Do you have the road intersection in the camera?"

"Nope."

"Yeah, I figured. You're looking short. She'll raise her nose a little as she gains some speed. Help her out with a little up elevator."

A few anxious moments later, Dandridge said, "Okay! I've got the target. Gee, Lieutenant, you're right! I don't have to give it much elevator at all to stay on track."

"Okay, don't get target fixated. When she's at twenty-five hundred feet, start to pull out."

It only took a few more seconds for the Culver to drop to that altitude.

"Okay, I'm easing in up elevator," Dandridge said.

"Good. Now watch her airspeed and feed in the throttle when it starts to bleed off. You'll lose about another thousand feet or so before she starts to climb again."

Two minutes later, the Culver was back cruising at 3,000 feet, with the mothership in trail at 8,000 feet.

Tommy asked, "Do you think you'd have any trouble keeping her on target in a dive like that?"

"No, sir. I don't think so. It seemed to work just like you said it would."

Wheatley's voice came over the interphone. "The nose kept getting in the way with all that s-turning, so we didn't get to see the whole thing. But what we did see looked pretty good. I didn't think that Culver was ever going to stall, though."

"I'm betting the baby's going to stall a whole lot easier than that," Tommy replied.

Dead serious, Wheatley said, "You can count on that."

"Well, what do you think, guys?" Tommy asked. "You want to try another one?"

No one could think of a reason not to.

The second practice dive went even better than the first one. There were no jitters this time. Dandridge took the Culver through the stall and into the target run like he'd been doing it his whole life.

"Only one thing bothers me, sir," he told Tommy. "We're not going to get a practice run with the baby."

"Why not? We've still got two days before the Torpex shows up."

Dandridge's face turned ghostly pale. "Oh, I don't know about that, sir. Major Staunton's not going to like that idea. Not one bit."

"Can't hurt to ask, though, Sergeant."

"Just so it's you doing the asking, sir."

They were over Fort Driant now, flying the Culver in a wide orbit to check for radio interference to both the television and flight control systems. There seemed to be no problems; the television reception was excellent, and even in the low gain setting that simulated a B-17's control responses, the little drone was operating perfectly.

"Okay," Dandridge said, "the first test for interference passes with flying colors."

From 10,000 feet altitude, they turned their attention to the defenses of Metz stretching below them. Being totally familiar with the terrain, Tommy could pick out five of the forts easily. Dandridge and the mothership's pilots couldn't pick out one on their own.

"They blend into the terrain pretty well, don't they?" Tommy said as he pointed out each one. "All the forts west of Metz are contained within the two rivers that flow together at Ars-sur-Moselle. That's the town just off our right side, built along the banks of the Mance River. Ars is further identified by the two highways intersecting on its east side and the railroad track crossing the Moselle. Fort Driant is the one about a mile west-southwest of the highway intersection."

"I see it," Dandridge replied, "but it doesn't look like much of anything."

"True, but look real close inside the bell shape of the fort. You see those four rectangles with three dots lined up in each of them?"

"Yeah, I see them, sir."

"Those rectangles are the gun batteries. The dots are the individual gun turrets. We're going to be aiming for one of those two batteries in the middle."

"And those batteries aren't visible from low altitude, sir?"

"Hardly at all, Sergeant. You can't tell real well from up here at *angels ten*, but the fort is sitting on a very steep rise. From the base of that rise, where our GIs are, you can't see anything of the fort at all. Even flying toward it at the same height as the peak, you can't see much of it. Everything on the premises barely sticks up above ground level."

"That's not good, sir."

After another orbit of Driant, Dandridge said, "I think we've got a problem, sir. The Culver's camera is only about two miles from the fort right now, but I can't make out any of its details on the video at all. I mean, looking at it with just my eyes, I can see the details because of the variations in color—and there's really not much of that, just different shades of brown and gray. But the camera only does shades of gray. I have no idea how I'm going to put the baby right on the money with this image to work with. I'm going to need something prominent to aim at. Every place else we've targeted has something tall sticking up, some big structure or something."

He paused, a distraught look on his face, and then added, "If I don't have the target acquired by the time we're two miles out, I'm probably going to miss, for sure."

"Maybe we should try some approaches to target from a couple of different directions," Tommy said, "and try to get the sun angle and shadows working for us."

But Lieutenant Wheatley's voice was in their headphones. "Okay, we did what we're supposed to do. We're heading back now."

Tommy keyed his mic to ask Wheatley to delay the return to base and then thought better of it. There was a good chance the discussion would turn acrimonious, so he'd prefer it to be face-to-face, without the entire crew hearing it. Few things short of bald-faced cowardice tended to diminish officers in their men's eyes than watching them engage in a pissing contest. He already suspected Wheatley was a *prune*: an *inefficient* pilot in Air Force slang. *Inefficient* was just a polite way of saying *lousy, poorly skilled, chickenshit*, or any other derogative term you could think of.

I think the guy's a little flak-happy, he told himself, meaning Wheatley's concern over anti-aircraft fire seemed all out of proportion to the threat. *He's going to balk at anything keeping us up here a second longer than necessary.*

Tommy made the awkward crawl from the nose into the cockpit. He explained to Wheatley the need for more experimenting with the video image. Before he was halfway through his explanation, the pilot was shaking his head.

"No way, Moon," Wheatley said. "That's not authorized for this mission. All we're supposed to do is test your *stall and dive* theory and check for radio interference. We've done all that, so I don't see any reason to keep stooging around up here, making a target of ourselves."

"I think you're worrying about flak a little too much, Paul. I'm telling you, I fly this patch of sky every damn day. Unless you're down on the deck, you aren't going to draw any fire...and we aren't anywhere near the deck. Near as we can tell, nobody's even shooting at the drone way down below us. If we're going to have a problem with the television setup, we'd better know about it now."

"Not going to happen, Moon. Checking out your harebrained schemes isn't part of my orders. Better find yourself a seat because we're heading back to A-90 now."

"I think that's a mistake, Paul. We're not flying over Hamburg or Berlin here. We're pretty safe at 10,000 feet…and we've got fighter cover overhead just in case the Luftwaffe decides to make one of its very rare appearances."

"I don't give a damn what you think, Moon. This is my ship and you're just a fucking little guest along for the ride. Now get lost, because I'm busy here."

Little really rubbed Tommy the wrong way. It wasn't just a generic adjective; it was an insult a tall man would hurl, meant specifically for a short guy like him.

Insulted or not, there wasn't much point trying to continue this argument while they were up in the air, so Tommy returned to the nose compartment. But he was now sure of one thing: *I'm right…this guy's a prune. And an asshole. Yeah, it's his ship and all, but he's a weak sister if I ever saw one.*

Dandridge's unenthusiastic reply to the news the mission was over: "I figured as much, sir."

He went back to struggling with the video equipment as he piloted the drone in a gentle orbit far below the mothership, having one last try to get a picture of the ground he could use. But Tommy could tell by the look on his face he wasn't getting it.

Chapter Nineteen

Major Staunton's answer was a firm, if apologetic, *no*. "There won't be any *test dives* of the BQ-7 *baby*. We can't risk it. It's the only aircraft we've been allocated for this mission. We've proven your theory with the Culver, Lieutenant Moon, and that will have to be good enough."

Then he showed a tactful, almost fatherly side neither Tommy nor Dandridge had ever seen before. "And I'll do you the favor of not bringing up your little suggestion to the baby's pilots. They didn't sign on to this project to be guinea pigs."

True, the pilots would be on board—but not in control of their ship—as a test dive was conducted by remote control. All they'd have to do was manually fly the plane out of the dive from an altitude that yielded plenty of cushion. Of course, they'd have to do the takeoff for the test and land the ship afterwards, but that was routine stuff.

He's got the guinea pig analogy all wrong, though, Tommy thought. *Hell, every pilot flying combat is a guinea pig. But it's not my call. If the brass think the test we did today answers their aerodynamic questions, well...so be it.*

"Besides," Staunton said, "we could never get the baby heavy enough without the Torpex on board to simulate her actual flight characteristics for the mission. We'd have to load her full of fuel, which introduces a host of problems all its own."

"What kind of problems, sir?" Tommy asked.

"First off, there's the problem of getting the fuel

load authorized. I'm sure Eighth Air Force will say *no*. Second, we wouldn't use much of that fuel. Either the baby flies around for hours burning it off, which is incredibly wasteful of precious aviation gasoline and increases the chances of it being shot down or simply malfunctioning, or it lands overweight and has to be defueled. I'm sure you'll agree, Lieutenant Moon, that landing overweight is asking for trouble. And as I understand the SOP, any fuel we pump out will be unusable in another aircraft."

Tommy didn't know anything about what Air Force higher-ups would or would not approve, but as to flying around just to burn off fuel, the major was dead right: it would be incredibly wasteful. An overweight landing ran the risk of structural damage to the ship, maybe even resulting in a gear collapse and threat of a raging fire. A *crash and burn* item, in pilots' jargon.

One thing the major had wrong, though: the business of not being able to reuse gasoline defueled from one aircraft in another. That might be the stateside regulation—or something done in an Air Force that had more fuel than it knew what to do with—but here in a combat theater, starved for aviation gasoline as they were, they'd have no qualms whatsoever about putting that fuel in their jugs. Whatever the technical objections to doing so—be it water buildup, contamination, or anything else the tech boards could come up with—the guys under the gun in the field would find a way to use it.

That left the daunting question of targeting Fort Driant through the indiscernible view of the television camera. "Obviously, there's too much contrast in the image," Staunton said.

"I tried the full range of contrast available at the

monitor, sir," Dandridge replied. "Nothing made much difference at all. You can't paint any contrasts in the image if everything in it is at or near the same point on the gray scale. And if we turn the gain down on the camera any more, the image will probably just white-out on us."

There was a thoughtful silence, broken when Tommy said, "We'll have to mark the target to make it more distinguishable."

Staunton asked, "Are you thinking of marking it with smoke, Lieutenant?"

"No, sir. I was thinking *fire*, actually."

"Right," Dandridge added enthusiastically. "Smoke will be hard to pick up on the monitor. And it drifts, too. But flames—they'll show up real good."

Staunton scratched his head. "How on earth do we start a fire in the precise spot we want on that fort?"

"We get my squadron to drop napalm on it, sir."

Skeptical, the major asked, "Can we involve your pilots without compromising the secrecy of this mission, Lieutenant? You're fully aware it must remain a secret."

"Sure, sir, we can keep it a secret. We're told to do lots of stuff without being told *why* we're doing it."

Staunton fell deep in thought. It was impossible to tell if he was reasoning why the idea might work or scheming how to shoot it down. When he finally spoke, it was as if he wasn't yet sure which side of the issue he was on.

"We'll get the artillery to do the marking," he said. "That will be simpler and less compromising to our mission."

"No, sir, it wouldn't be," Tommy replied.

"What would you know about artillery, Lieutenant?

I thought you were a pilot."

"I am a pilot, sir. But I've spent some time as an ASO with the ground troops coordinating air support for them, so I've learned quite a bit about artillery, infantry, and armor operations."

"ASO...that stands for what, exactly?"

"Air support officer, sir."

"All right, then," Staunton said, "share some of this *expertise* you've acquired with us." He made *expertise* sound inconsequential.

"First off, sir, the artillery doesn't shoot napalm. The closest thing they have is white phosphorous, and all that'll do is make clouds of white smoke—"

Dandridge jumped in: "Which I won't be able to do much with, anyway."

"Exactly," Tommy replied. "And even if you could see it clearly on the monitor, the smoke from *willy petes* could get so dense it'll cover the entire top of the fort, so we'd lose our aiming point completely."

The light was starting to go on in Staunton's mind. He seemed ready to buy into the idea.

"Also," Tommy added, "the marking will have to be very tightly time-controlled with our mission, to keep the aiming point precise. Like a minute before the baby hits. No more than that. A napalm fire can spread, or it can go out all by itself, too. Even if the artillery could shoot what we needed, we can't talk with them directly to coordinate. Our radios don't work on the same frequencies. But we can talk directly with the jugs."

Staunton was almost there. He wanted to believe, but he had another question.

"And your pilots can put napalm on the *exact* spot we need to target, Lieutenant?"

"Have you ever heard the expression *close enough for government work*, sir?"

"Yes, of course I have."

"Well, then, sir...you have your answer."

"Very fine," Staunton replied. "How much advance warning do your boys need for a napalm mission?"

"Just a few hours, sir. Most of that is the time needed to bomb-up the aircraft."

"And they don't need any mission details other than the target point?"

"That's correct, sir. And it won't be anything they haven't done before, so they won't suspect what's really going on."

After another thoughtful pause, Major Staunton said, "I like this, Lieutenant Moon. I like this very much. I'm entrusting you with coordinating the target marking."

"Very good, sir. It'll be my pleasure to do it."

Dandridge asked, "Will we be flying any more missions with the Culvers, sir?"

"Absolutely," Staunton replied. "Let's get in all the practice we can manage."

"Speaking of practice, sir," Tommy said, "would it be all right if we crashed a Culver or two into simulated targets? You know...just to see how good our aim really is?"

Dandridge cringed. He'd thought this was already a dead issue.

Staunton had that near-wild look in his eyes so common to men under extreme pressure to succeed. But his answer was not what the sergeant expected.

"That's what we brought them for, Lieutenant. They're disposable aircraft, so let's make the most of them. Just make sure we continue to perform the interference checks on a daily basis…and anything we crash comes down in Allied territory, so the Germans can't get their hands on our equipment."

"No problem, sir," Tommy replied. "How about we put them into the area we dump our unused ordnance? Everyone steers clear of that place…civilians and GIs."

"Sounds like that'll work just fine, Lieutenant."

✳✳✳✳

Tommy unfolded the paper with the address Sylvie had given him earlier that day. He read it aloud: "Thirty-Seven Rue de Claret."

How hard can it be to find a street named after wine? Or is it some famous guy's name, too?

Once the MPs had dropped him off after the drive across A-90, he'd hoped to slip unseen into his quarters—a small shack with no amenities other than a decent roof he shared with three other flyers—and change into fresh khakis before hurrying into Toul to be with Sylvie.

He'd hoped for too much. Fresh from their mission debrief, the pilots of the 301st descended on him, eager to pump him for information on what he was up to over on Zebra Ramp. This time, they weren't asking questions; they were floating theories.

"I know what's going on, Half," a pilot from *Red Flight* said. "You guys are doing some kind of special photo recon of the West Wall. Those little remote-control jobs go right down on the deck so they can see every Kraut pillbox and fox hole. Maybe even take portrait shots of the Krauts themselves."

"Ah, bullshit," his flight leader said. "That wouldn't

explain what that B-17 painted yellow is all about. I'm betting that's the formation ship for a whole squadron of heavy bombers they're gonna put right here to support the *Russkies* coming through the Balkans. I'm right, aren't I, Moon? And just you watch…when those heavies show up, we're going to get kicked out of here."

Tommy didn't bother to answer. He just kept packing his AWOL bag.

"Going somewhere, Tommy?" Jimmy Tuttle asked. "You're looking all spic and span, like you got a hot date. So I guess it's true that a certain lady friend from Alençon is in town, isn't she?"

"Yeah, that's it, Jimmy. You've figured out my secret. Now if you guys will excuse me…"

A pilot from *Green Flight* blocked his path. "No, wait, Half. You didn't tell us who's right about what you're up to over on Zebra."

"And I'm not going to, pal."

"Ah, come on, Tommy. Cut us a little slack."

"How about you guys cut *me* some slack?"

"Well, suit yourself, Half. But I'm telling you, I— and *only* I—know exactly what's going on over there. I've been talking to a buddy over at Ninth Air Defense Command, and they say you're probing Luftwaffe air defenses around the West Wall with those disposable little drones. And they should know, because that's their business. But it doesn't look like you've lost any of those little crates yet, so I guess you're not probing real well."

Another pilot piped up, "Or the Krauts are too smart to take the bait."

Yet another added, "Once you offer up that big yellow B-17, though, I'll bet you they take that bait. Did you volunteer to fly that thing, too?"

"I didn't volunteer for anything," Tommy said, fully aware he was one of the world's most unconvincing liars.

"Bullshit. That's not the Tommy Moon we all know. That doesn't make you a bad person, though. A little crazy, maybe…"

Tommy just shook his head and made for the door. But before stepping outside, he turned back to them all and said, "Really interesting theories, guys. Don't lose any sleep over them, okay?"

Sergeant McNulty was waiting behind the wheel of a jeep. Tommy hopped in and told him, "Get me the hell out of here before I say something stupid."

McNulty tossed a half-assed salute toward the other officers and then dropped the jeep into gear. "Sounds like they're breaking your balls, Lieutenant. Maybe driving you nuts with all that *specification*?"

"You mean speculation, right?"

"Yeah, that's what I said, ain't it?"

"Then I guess you're right, Sarge. They *are* breaking my balls."

"Well, that just pisses me off, then," McNulty replied. "I'm your crew chief. That's supposed to be *my* job. That, and looking out for your ass."

✻✻✻✻

Tommy woke from the dream with a start. Sylvie's bemused face hovered above his, her elbow propped on the pillow they shared, her hand supporting her head.

"You kept mumbling *bucket, bucket*," she said. "What were you dreaming about?"

"Dream? More like a nightmare," he replied, his

voice still groggy. "I don't remember anything about it, though. Just that it was awful."

"But what does a bucket have to do with your dream, Tommy?"

"Maybe it comes from a conversation I think I remember overhearing. It was about this military operation—*Operation Bucket*. But that wasn't the original name. It was supposed to be *Operation Trebuchet*—with proper French pronunciation and all. You know, that thing that hurls boulders and—"

"I know what a trebuchet is, Tommy," she interrupted.

"Yeah, I guess I'm not surprised. But the Americans, as usual, couldn't pronounce the French right. So they started calling it *three buckets*, and finally just *bucket*."

"So you think this conversation actually happened in real life?"

"Yeah, maybe so. But I'm still half asleep. Not real sure of anything right now."

"Well, it's certainly believable," Sylvie said. "If you GIs are any example, Americans are not the most linguistically talented nation on Earth." Then she kissed him on the forehead and added, "Except you, my Tommy. Imagine! An American who almost speaks two languages!"

She fell back on the pillow, giggling like a schoolgirl, leaving no doubt she was poking fun at him. "What should I expect, though, from someone who learned his French from Irish nuns in America?"

"Hey, not just any place in America—Brooklyn, New York. The hub of civilization."

She shot him a withering look. "I doubt that very much, Tommy."

"Okay, Miss Worldly-Wise. If you know so much, how about you tell me about these forts at Metz? You said you studied them in school."

"Is that what's really giving you nightmares? The forts?"

"They're giving everyone nightmares, Sylvie."

She pulled him close, as much to comfort as share the warmth of their naked bodies beneath the threadbare blanket. "Maybe I can help you, then," she said. "Yes, we studied the forts at school. They are part of our history, after all. Where to begin?"

She fell silent for a few moments, staring into the darkness of the boarding house's little bedroom as if looking back in time.

"We should start," she said, "with the War of 1870. You Americans, as well as the British, I believe, refer to it as the Franco-Prussian War."

Sylvie paused, looking for a glimmer of comprehension in his sleepy face. After a moment, she realized she wouldn't get it. Recalibrating the depth of her lecture to a more basic level, she launched back into it.

"As I'm sure you're well aware, we French and the *Boche* have rarely been on friendly terms. In 1870, when Germany was still just a collection of independent states, the most powerful of them was Prussia in the north. Bismarck, the Prussian chancellor, wanted to consolidate the southern German states into a powerful Prussian confederation to dominate France. We could not tolerate this prospect and attempted to destroy the German forces massing on the border between Metz and Luxembourg. Unfortunately, the army of Napoleon the Third was not victorious. Ultimately, in 1871, Metz and the entire region surrounding it was taken from France to become part of a unified Germany. Metz was then, as it is now, a fortress city and strategic transportation gateway between Germany and France, with abundant road and rail facilities. The Germans fortified it further, building additional forts around the city, equipping them with the advanced artillery that had just been developed. But they fully intended to use Metz as a secure base for attacks against France, too. By the time of the Great War, all the forts you're encountering today had been built."

She took a sip from the wine bottle on the nightstand. "Ahh, that feels much better," she said. "I am talking so much, my throat is dry. Now where was I? Oh yes...the Great War. Oddly enough, after all that construction the forts played almost no role in it. And at the end, of course, Germany had lost, and the region with all its forts was returned to France. Eager to make sure the Germans could never again invade France, those forts became part of the Maginot Line."

"And we all know how well that worked out," Tommy said. He didn't mean it as an insult. But as soon as it came out of his mouth, the angry look on her face made him wish he hadn't said it. At least not that way.

She hissed her reply: "We were betrayed in 1940 by our allies as well as our enemies."

"Okay, fine. I don't want to fight about this, Sylvie."

"Good. Then be quiet and let me finish." She wasn't annoyed with him, and he knew it. But he also could tell how much she was enjoying playing the stern schoolmistress, so he resolved to lie quietly and just listen.

"In the early years of the German occupation," she

continued, "the forts again served no strategic role. Their artillery was scavenged for Hitler's Atlantic wall, and the structures themselves were used merely as storehouses and training camps. Only in the summer of this year, as Patton's army rolled steadily to the Moselle, did the cannons return and the fortress line manned to at least partial fighting strength. It is so ironic that after fifty years and two wars, those forts are finally fulfilling one of the purposes for which they were built: to keep a foreign army out of Germany."

Tommy asked, "How'd you know all that stuff that happened since 1940? You were already out of school, weren't you?"

"Out of the *lycée*, yes. But after that, the *maquis* was an even more demanding school."

There was that word again: *maquis*. She was still part of it, even if she no longer fought with the Resistance and was just a courier now, as she claimed. But the thought of it still terrified him.

"How long are you going to be here in Toul, Sylvie?"

"I leave in the morning for Nancy."

"Do you know how long you're going to be there?"

"I'm not sure. A week, maybe more. But I suspect I'll be there until Sixth Army Group moves up from southern France to join forces with Patton. Half of Sixth Army Group is the French First Army. I expect I'll be doing much work for them."

"I've been to Nancy already," Tommy said.

"I know. You told me."

"I told you my brother's around there, too, right?"

"Yes, you did. When you go there again, find *Café Rimbaud*. Ask for Isabelle Truffaut."

"Who's that?"

"It's me."

"You mean like a pseudonym?"

She gave him an exasperated look. "Yes, Tommy. Of course it's a pseudonym."

Asking why she needed one would be pointless because he already knew the answer: she was still doing dangerous things. Things that might get her killed.

And she'd never tell him what those things were, anyway.

Courier, my ass, he told himself.

"So when I ask for this *Isabelle Truffaut,* what happens then?"

"They'll get a message to me. I will come to you. If I can."

Chapter Twenty

The sound of a jeep's engine on the deserted streets of Toul was unmistakable in the stillness of predawn. Tommy looked down from the bedroom window as it rolled to a stop in front of the boarding house. He was already dressed and ready to go. Sylvie was awake but still in bed, trying to summon the courage to throw off the covers and leap into the chill of the unheated bedroom. She was in no hurry, though. Her bus didn't leave for hours.

They kissed for what was probably the thousandth time since falling into that bed last night. "See you in Nancy," he said as he stood and grabbed his AWOL bag.

"I hope so," she replied. "Be safe."

Even in the shadows, she could see the yearning in his face as he repeated her farewell: "You, too. Be safe. I mean it. I'm not kidding."

"Neither am I, Tommy."

Sergeant McNulty seemed surprised when Tommy came bounding out the door only a minute after he'd pulled up to the curb. "Ain't this a *serendeputy*," he said. "I figured I was gonna have to come in there and drag you out in your birthday suit."

Tommy started to correct his crew chief's fractured syntax once again but thought better of it: *serendeputy…serendipity…at this hour of the morning, it's all the same.*

"Weather report for today's good, surprisingly," McNulty said as they rumbled over the cobblestone streets. "I guess you and the *mystery planes* across the field gonna be flying again, doing whatever the hell it is

206

you do?"

"Yeah, no doubt we will. What about the squadron?"

"You know the old song, Lieutenant: *blue skies, jug flies.*"

Tommy asked, "Is Colonel Pruitt taking good care of our ship?"

"Not to worry, sir. I wouldn't have it any other way. Where do you want to get dropped off?"

"Take me to Ops, Sarge. I've got to talk with the colonel."

"Sure thing. But let me ask you something, Lieutenant. You got any idea how long this secret project of yours is gonna go on?"

"A couple more days, Sarge."

The answer surprised McNulty. "That's all?" he said. "Hell, you took leaves longer than that."

Tommy's discussion with Colonel Pruitt lasted all of five minutes. They were on the same wavelength from the opening sentences. "I agree," Pruitt said. "There's no better way to put this *practice* napalm down for you guys than to have me—and only me—do it. That way, it won't fuel any more speculation in the squadron than we already have."

"And from the speculation I've heard, sir," Tommy replied, "nobody but you and I know what the hell is going on, anyway. The rest of them don't know their ass from a hole in the ground."

"Let's try to keep it that way, Tommy. Just a couple more days until this is all over, right?"

"That's the way I understand it, sir. The Torpex is supposed to arrive tomorrow, 12 October. We should be ready to fly the mission on Driant the following day. Weather permitting, of course."

"Yeah, the damn weather," Pruitt said. "We'd better do it by then because it's supposed to turn crappy again on the fourteenth. So where are we going to do these practice runs?"

"I was thinking we'd do them in the ordnance jettison zone, sir. It's in the middle of nowhere, and everyone on the ground already knows that area's off limits." Tommy went over to the map and pointed to a spot in an area outlined and cross-hatched in red. "This trail junction—it's in the middle of a burned-out part of the zone and it's pretty easy to spot from the air. But because it's all burned-out like that—and nothing but shades of black and brown—it might be a little hard to distinguish on the television gear, just like the top of Fort Driant is. So put some napalm right on that spot. We'll see how well the camera picks the flames up."

"And if you're happy with the picture, you'll try to crash a Culver right on it?"

"Yes, sir…we'd like to see how well we can do that, too. This steep dive-angle attack is something new to the drone guys. I think it's going to work, though, just as long as we have a good aiming point."

"What time will the drone fly today?" Pruitt asked.

"We don't plan on taking off until after 1200 hours, sir," Tommy replied. "We want to practice under the same conditions as the actual attack, with the sun behind us so we don't get glare in the camera. Any Kraut flak trying to take a shot at us will be looking into the sun, too."

"Excellent," Pruitt said. "That gives me half the day to get ready. By the way, I'm taking real good care of your ship."

"So I heard, sir. Thanks."

****

Thirty minutes later, Tommy walked into Zebra Ramp's operations tent. It was strangely quiet, the tension in the air akin to a roomful of errant schoolboys waiting to be paddled for their transgressions. Each man went about his work silently, head down, as if raising it would single him out for punishment.

Major Staunton's voice broke the silence, a tirade booming from the far end of the tent: "IS THERE ANYONE IN THIS ENTIRE GODDAMNED ARMY CAPABLE OF COORDINATING EVEN THE SIMPLEST OF PLANS? HOW HARD COULD IT BE TO GET FOUR TRUCKLOADS OF EXPLOSIVES ACROSS THE CHANNEL AND THEN DRIVE IT THREE HUNDRED AND SIXTY-FOUR MILES ACROSS FRANCE? IF A FUCKUP OF THIS MAGNITUDE HAPPENED IN THE CIVILIAN WORLD, HEADS WOULD ROLL."

It didn't take a genius to figure out what this *fuckup* was: the Torpex had been delayed. Maybe even lost. Or maybe it had never left England.

Whatever the reason, one thing was obvious: they wouldn't be trying to blow up Fort Driant on the thirteenth of October. Then, the window of good flying weather would probably close on them until who-knows-when.

Sergeant Dandridge approached Tommy and said

softly, "Let's you and me be someplace else for a while, sir."

They walked over to the adjacent mess tent to grab some coffee. It wasn't a field kitchen, just a small circus tent with a serving table and a few picnic tables, all scrounged locally. The MPs brought the food over from the kitchen at the 301st each mealtime. It was strictly self-serve; no unauthorized personnel—such as cooks and KPs—were allowed on Zebra Ramp. From the looks of the scraps left in the marmite cans, everyone had already eaten. There was barely enough coffee left for two half-cups.

Tommy asked, "So what's the whole story with the Torpex?"

"Some SNAFU with paperwork once they kicked it off a boat in Normandy, sir. The supply people couldn't figure out what kind of explosive it was, so they didn't know which rules for trucking it across France applied. And get this: the fastest way to get it here is straight through the outskirts of Paris. Can you imagine the flap if that stuff were to blow up anywhere near there? If it didn't have EXPEDITE-SHAEF HIGHEST PRIORITY stamped all over it, they might have just pushed it off into a corner of some ammo dump and forgotten about it."

Tommy asked, "Any idea how long we're going to have to wait for it, then?"

"Eighth Air Force G4 is estimating it won't show up now until the thirteenth—a day late."

"And right into the teeth of more crummy weather," Tommy added. "Anyway, I've got the practice napalm lined up for today. We're still flying at 1200 hours, right?"

"Yes, sir. That's the plan. What do you think...should we crash one of the Culvers today?"

"Let's see how it goes," Tommy replied. "The jug will be carrying three napalm bombs. We can start with one and see how good that fire looks on television. If it doesn't show up real well, we'll drop the other two and see if that makes it any easier to see. And if we're happy with it, I guess then we can plant the Culver."

"I'm really looking forward to doing that, sir," Dandridge replied.

At 3rd Army Headquarters, George Patton had just gotten the word that *Operation Bucket* would be delayed another day beyond 13 October, possibly longer. He considered the news a mixed blessing. While he had high hopes that Tooey Spaatz's *flying bomb* would end the vicious headache of Metz in one fell swoop, he had no intention of putting all his eggs in one basket. He'd continue to wage ground actions against the forts—especially that prime obstacle Fort Driant—right up to that twenty-four-hour deadline Bradley had imposed on him to get his troops well out of the way.

And if I miss that deadline by a few hours, or maybe a little more, who's going to know? I sure as hell will not break off an engagement that promises success just because Brad wants to be overcautious. Hell, airplanes can always be called back, right up to the last damn minute.

Patton had gotten another piece of crucial news in the last hour, too: during 7th Army's sweep north from southern France, an intelligence unit attached to that headquarters had located the architectural plans for Fort Driant in a Lyon archive. Those plans were on a courier plane to 3rd Army HQ at that very moment. They'd be in Patton's hands in just a few hours.

And once we know where all their secret tunnels and little trap doors are, he told himself, *we can hit them where they live. There will be no more surprises in store for my men at Fort Driant.*

Chapter Twenty-One

By 1300, all the players in the day's practice mission for *Operation Bucket* were in the air. Colonel Pruitt, flying *Eclipse of the Hun II*, was airborne with her load of napalm, high above the mothership and her drone.

They were using the second Culver for today's run, and there had been a problem with her that almost aborted the mission. Before she had even left the ground, they couldn't get a stable picture from the drone's camera on the airborne mothership. The ground crew had hastily rectified the problem on the runway, reporting something about an antenna cable being loose at the drone's television transmitter.

"I'm not sure I'm buying that, sir," Dandridge shouted over the big bomber's ambient noise, not wanting to broadcast his comments to the entire crew over the interphone. "It's not a real good omen."

Tommy shouted back, "But you've got a good picture now, right?"

"Yeah," Dandridge replied, "but I've never been a big believer in the *reseated connector* theory of maintenance. You've probably run into that before, sir. That's just a bullshit way to kick something over the fence without really finding or fixing the problem. Nobody's touched that transmitter since we got here. Those plugs don't come loose all by themselves."

It bothered Tommy that he was sensing so little trust among the other members of the *Operation Bucket* technical team. He thought of his relationship with the mechanics who maintained his aircraft; how he always marveled at their dedication, their skill, and their belief that to let another member of the team down, be it the pilot, the crew chief, or a fellow mechanic, would betray a sacred trust. Doing something haphazard or shoddy just to launch an airplane—to *kick it over the fence*—was not even in the realm of possibilities. Someone's life—most likely Tommy's—could be at stake.

Something else occurred to Tommy, too: *Maybe that's what comes with only having to deal with disposable airplanes: not a lot of time or interest to build up a bond. I guess that's why they refer to a drone as "it" instead of "she."*

Clearly unhappy, Dandridge added, "If there wasn't so much pressure from upstairs for this program to succeed, I'd refuse the handoff and pull the plug on this flight right now." His next comment was mumbled, as if talking to himself: "I could end up on some stinking jungle island on the other side of the world yet."

"Not to make the pressure on you any worse," Tommy said, "but I've got my own reason for wanting *Bucket* to work. I've got a brother—a tanker—down there butting his head against that fort. Me and my jugs haven't been doing a damn thing to help him out. Nothing we do seems to make a dent in Driant. So that's why I volunteered for this duty. I'm just trying to keep my brother and all the guys who fight alongside him alive. And maybe this'll be the way to do it."

Dandridge nodded respectfully. "I understand, sir. That's a shitty deal, though…for your brother, I mean, getting thrown into a meat grinder like that." He gritted his teeth and went back to work.

While the mothership loitered at 5,000 feet, the Culver finally took to the air, piloted by the ground control team. "We'd better not let it get out of our sight," Dandridge said, his face pressed to the video monitor's hood. "If the video craps out again, and we've lost visual, we may never get it back in time to save it."

Tommy's eyes locked onto the little yellow bird, now climbing toward them and visible through the left side windows. "I've got it," he told Dandridge.

A few minutes later, the Culver was at 2,000 feet. "Okay, start the countdown to *toggle*," Dandridge told the ground controllers.

The handover went without a hitch. As the mothership climbed to 7,000 feet, the drone was climbed to 5,000.

"Do you have any checks you need to do before the target run?" Tommy asked.

"I'm already doing them, sir. Everything seems okay." If you went by the apprehensive tone of Dandridge's voice, though, everything was *not* okay as far as he was concerned.

"You've still got good video, right?"

"Yes, sir. Still got it. Control of the drone's good, too."

Then Dandridge got an idea. "Hey, sir, would you like to handle the sticks for a little while?"

He offered the remote-control box to Tommy.

This is some quick change of heart, Tommy thought. *First he's convinced she's got problems, and then he wants to drop her in the hands of a raw rookie.*

Or maybe he just wants someone else to take the fall when everything goes haywire.

Sensing Tommy's reluctance to take the box, Dandridge said, "Really, sir, it'll be fine. I've got good visual on the Culver. If it starts acting funny, I'll just take the box back."

That helped Tommy's reluctance a little. But not enough.

Dandridge added, "I really think it would be a good idea if you got to see what it's like through the camera, sir...before the whole thing goes to hell."

Then he added, "Besides, I don't buy the story Major Staunton's putting out on why real pilots don't fly the drones. The way I heard it, it was strictly a manpower decision. They weren't any worse than an enlisted man at doing it. They just couldn't waste trained aviators flying drones, that's all. Hell, if I could learn to do it, anyone could."

Tommy took the box and peered into the video monitor.

"Hey, it's just like being in the cockpit," he said, happily surprised. "I just can't turn my head."

"There you go," Dandridge replied. "Why don't you put it through a few fighter maneuvers?"

Tommy complied with a barrel roll, an Immelmann turn, and then a wing-over to get back on the same heading as the mothership. He found the Culver responsive and very easy to control. He had little trouble adapting to the realm of remote control.

"Try the stall and dive," Dandridge said. "Just remember to pull out at 3,000 feet."

"You sure you'd rather not be getting the practice, Sergeant?"

"I'll get a couple more chances, sir. Go ahead...get the feel of it. After all, it was your idea."

"Okay," Tommy replied, "but tell *Gadget Blue Six* to stand clear. Don't want the colonel to think we're starting the show without him."

Dandridge made the call to Pruitt.

"Roger, *Almighty Four-One*," the colonel replied. "*Gadget Blue* standing by. Don't want to hurry you boys or anything, but be advised I'm burning gas like crazy up here. Can't hang around forever."

"Tell him we understand," Tommy said. "Then tell him we'll do one dive for practice, and right after that, we'll need him to light that fire."

Dandridge made the transmission. Pruitt's reply: "That's what I'm here for, *Almighty*."

As Tommy maneuvered the Culver into position to begin the dive, Dandridge asked, "How come he's flying your plane, sir? Doesn't he have one of his own?"

"He's waiting on a new one. His old ship got *retired*. She'd been through the wringer...had more patches on her than original skin. Even something as sturdy as a jug doesn't last long when it keeps taking ground fire. At least they tend to get you home, though."

Tommy leveled the Culver at 5,000 feet, cut the throttle, and held her nose up. When she started to *mush*, he waggled her wings to bring on the stall. Just like all the times before, she began to plummet nose down toward the target.

Dandridge asked, "Can you see the intersection okay in the monitor, sir?"

"Yeah...not very distinct...but I've got it."

Then he announced, "I'm going to let her get down to two thousand before I pull out."

Eyes glued to the video scope, he couldn't see the panicked look on Dandridge's face.

"You sure you want to go that low, sir?" Dandridge asked, more a plea than a question. "I thought we agreed on three thousand."

"Relax, Sergeant. It'll be all right."

"I sure as hell hope so, sir. By the way, aren't you aiming a little short? You sure you've got the right target identified?"

Then Dandridge noticed Tommy's fingers weren't even on the control stick.

"Yeah, I'm aiming short. But it should all work out. Remember when you were doing the diving, you had to keep some nose down pressure on the stick to stay on track? You had the target centered in the monitor, didn't you?"

"Yes, sir, I did, but—"

"But *nothing*, Sergeant. Even though she's nose down and dropping like a brick, with all that speed her wings have lift. Lots of it. And that lift is pushing her forward, toward the target."

"So you're saying she's going to line up on the target all by herself?"

"You didn't forget I do this for a living, did you, Sergeant?"

Pressed against the plexiglass of the nose dome, Dandridge nervously watched the Culver streak toward the earth. He was sure the lieutenant had already let it descend too far to pull out. But he was growing convinced of one thing: if Tommy didn't pull out, the little yellow drone was going to plant itself perfectly in the middle of the targeted road intersection.

"Okay, coming down to two thousand," Tommy said, and then quickly counted off, "Two thousand three…two…one." His fingers back on the control stick, he eased her into the pullout.

From the mothership's vantage point, the Culver, now in level flight, seemed to be just inches off the ground.

"What does the altimeter read, sir?" Dandridge asked.

"One hundred feet, give or take a couple."

"Cutting it a little close, aren't we?"

"Close only counts in horseshoes and hand grenades, Sergeant."

"I've got to admit, sir, you just scared the living shit out of me."

Tommy had the Culver climbing back to the start point for the dive: the IP, or *initial point.* "Your turn, Sergeant," he told Dandridge. "Ready for the handoff?"

"Affirmative, sir."

Tommy gave him the control box. "Your airplane."

"I've got it," Dandridge replied.

"That was a piece of cake," Tommy said as he did a few quick calculations. "It's not fair you non-coms get to have all the fun."

Dandridge looked ready to hand the box right back. "You want to do the napalm run, too, sir?"

"Oh, no, Sergeant. Wouldn't dream of taking your job. I'm going to get the colonel into position now."

In less than a minute, Colonel Pruitt was ready. The jug screamed down from 8,000 feet in a near-vertical dive. The crew on the mothership didn't even see her until she'd slashed through their altitude.

"Notice that he's doing the same thing I did?" Tommy asked Dandridge. "He looks like he's aiming short, but he'll end up releasing the eggs right on the money."

"How do you guys train to do that, sir?"

"Actually, the gunsight doubles as a bombsight and does all the work for you. Just keep the pipper inside the reticle and it works like magic."

Colonel Pruitt flashed through 3,000 feet, released one napalm canister, and pulled sharply out of the dive. The canister struck the road intersection nearly dead center, spreading a ring of brilliant fire around it.

"I'm betting you'll see those flames pretty darn good with the camera," Tommy said.

The Culver was at the IP. "Here we go," Dandridge said. He stalled the little drone like an expert. As her nose came down and the dive commenced, he said, "Holy cow! I've got no problem seeing those flames at all. Gee, it's almost like we're painting them in color!"

"If you want to do the dive like I did," Tommy said, "put the target at the very top of your monitor picture."

"Yeah, I've got it."

"As you get closer, she'll slide toward the center of frame. You'll need just little blips of elevator to keep her on target."

A few seconds later, Dandridge said, "Oh, brother! This is going to be so fine! Lit up like this, we could probably even bomb through light cloud cover."

"One thing at a time, Sergeant. Just put her on the money."

That's exactly what Sergeant Dandridge did.

There was quiet contentment in the mothership as she winged her way back to A-90. But despite their undeniable success, a new concern had crept into Tommy's mind.

"It just occurred to me," he told Dandridge. "Now that we're pretty sure we can put the baby right where we want her on top of Driant, how are we going to be sure we really knocked that fort out? Unless we set off some spectacular explosion that blows off the top of that hill, it might look just like it did before we attacked, minus a gun battery or two. I mean, everything and everybody in that damn place is underground. Suppose enough Krauts survive to keep an even damaged fort operational and deadly?"

Dandridge looked perplexed. "Wouldn't the concussion from the baby's hit be enough to kill or cripple everyone in it, sir?"

"I'd like to think so," Tommy replied, "but I'd rather we come up with a way to be sure. A way that wouldn't involve ground-pounders walking into another trap."

"That's kind of over my rank, sir," Dandridge said.

Tommy knew the sergeant was right. And he knew something more: *It's over my rank, too.*

As the mothership touched down on A-90's runway, the answer to Tommy's question was sitting on the 301st's ramp, plain as day, in the form of an L-4 spotter plane. He recognized her markings as well as the bazooka tubes mounted on her wing struts; she belonged to Major Bob Kidd—*Rocket Man.*

That's the guy who can get in low and slow enough to see exactly what's going on.

Major Staunton was waiting for the mothership on Zebra Ramp. They'd already advised him while still in flight that the practice run was a great success. No one in *Operation Bucket* had ever seen him so jubilant. He even gave Tommy a congratulatory slap on the back.

But he didn't share Tommy's concern over confirming the results of the baby's strike. "That's not really my call, Lieutenant Moon. But believe me, if we hit that place *on the money*, as you and Sergeant Dandridge say we should, there won't be enough left of it to worry about."

True, 20,000 pounds of Torpex would yield a far bigger explosion than Tommy had ever seen. Still, he pleaded his case, if not for his sake, for his brother's.

Tommy was glad he hadn't mentioned anything about using *Rocket Man* to confirm their success, because the next words out of Staunton's mouth were, "And of course, anything that divulges information about *Operation Bucket* in advance to unauthorized personnel is expressly forbidden."

Then, with breezy indifference, he added, "So arrange whatever you want, Lieutenant. Just so it doesn't compromise the execution of *Operation Bucket* in any way. Anything that happens after that execution is not my concern. Our job is complete once the baby impacts, another page in the history books."

By the time Tommy made it across the airfield to the 301st's ramp, Rocket Man's plane was still there. His P-47, piloted by Colonel Pruitt, was just pulling into its parking spot. Its weapons pylons were now empty. Pruitt had rid her of the two napalm canisters they hadn't used in the Culver's terminal practice run.

The colonel gave a *thumbs up* to Sergeant McNulty as he turned over the ship's logbook to the crew chief. Then he jumped off the wing and approached Tommy.

"Great machine you've got here, Moon," Pruitt said. "I hope my new one flies as sweet as she does."

"Yes, sir, she's a keeper," Tommy replied. "Where'd you dump the rest of the napalm?"

"Some tank outfit around Driant was asking for it, so I was happy to oblige."

Shit. A tank outfit near Fort Driant is in contact with Krauts as we speak. Good chance that's Sean.

Stay out of trouble a little bit longer, big brother. If you can.

Tommy motioned toward Major Kidd's L-4 and said, "You know whose plane that is, sir?"

"Sure. It's Bob Kidd's. I've known him a long time."

"I just met him yesterday over at my brother's outfit," Tommy replied. "Maybe he can do us a favor, sir." Then he explained his concerns about damage assessment after the baby's attack on Fort Driant and how he figured only a low and slow flyer like Rocket Man could tell them what they needed to know.

The colonel didn't seem taken with the idea.

"I'm not as well versed on this *Operation Bucket* as you are, Half, but I thought the plan was to blow that fort to kingdom come. Do you really think we're not going to be able to tell if we did that or not?"

"From whizzing around high up in the air? No, sir, I don't. And I really think we owe the ground-pounders some good information so maybe they won't have to pay a price in casualties finding it out for themselves. I'm thinking someone in a spotter plane—someone who knows how to do low-level recon—is just the ticket for getting that information. And I can't think of anyone better at it than Major Kidd."

Pruitt mulled it over a few moments, knowing full well what was behind Tommy's request: *He's looking out for his brother. Can't fault a man for that. But still...*

"Don't you think you're asking a lot of the major, Tommy? I mean, he could get his ass riddled to shit flying low over that fort."

"From what I've seen of him in action, sir, he's kind of used to that risk."

"Yeah, you're probably right. Tell you what...let's go talk to him."

"But, sir, you know we can't tell him—or anyone—about *Bucket*."

"Nobody's going to tell anybody anything, Half. Just leave it to me."

✷✷✷✷

They found Major Kidd in the officers' mess, drinking coffee with a few pilots from the 301st. Pruitt told Tommy to take a seat at a table on the other side of the mess. Then he called out to Kidd, "Hey, Bob, grab a seat with us for a minute. Need to talk to you about something."

"Good to see you, sir," Kidd said, "and good to see you again, too, Lieutenant Moon. Wasn't it just yesterday we were having breakfast together?"

"Yes, sir, it was. Over at Thirty-Seventh Tank."

"That's great," Pruitt said. "Glad you two know each other. You going to be hanging around long, Bob?"

"Just as long as it takes to get some gas for my bird, sir. Usually, the armor boys fill me up with some of their supply. But they don't have any to spare today."

"Yeah, no kidding," Pruitt said. "I just did a little work for them myself. Looks like they've got their hands full."

Tommy tried to hide the apprehension all this talk about the tank units being in battle was causing him.

Kidd asked, "So what'd you want to talk to me about, sir?"

"Well, Bob...me and Lieutenant Moon here have a little project we're working on, and it involves that damn Fort Driant. We're going to need some *up close and personal* bomb damage assessment...and I figure you're just the guy to do it."

"The photo recon guys can't handle it, sir?"

"When I say *up close and personal*, that's exactly what I mean, Bob. I'm not talking pictures from ten thousand feet up—or even low-level obliques—that take hours to be developed and interpreted. I need real live eyes on the scene who can get that assessment to us *on the double*."

"So I've got to buzz Fort Driant, in other words." He wasn't brimming with enthusiasm for the idea.

Colonel Pruitt looked at him as if what he'd just asked was the most natural thing in the world. "In a nutshell, Bob, yes."

Tommy marveled at the great snow job the colonel was throwing down:

Some guys just have the knack for getting you to do things you ordinarily wouldn't even think of doing in your right mind. You trust everything they tell you. I guess that's what the military calls leadership. It worked on me when I "volunteered" for Bucket, that's for damn sure. He's got Kidd on the hook already, and he hasn't given up one piece of information about who's doing what, either.

Amazing.

"When is this supposed to happen, sir?" Kidd asked.

"In three days, Bob…the fourteenth. Weather permitting, of course."

"Well, sir…*weather permitting*, I don't know who exactly I'll be supporting in three days. I may be miles away from where you need me."

"Don't worry about that, Bob. We'll get orders temporarily attaching you to us here at the 301st. I'll take care of it personally." Then the colonel, a big grin on his face, turned to Tommy and asked, "Lieutenant, did you ever hear the story of how ol' Bob here almost got himself court-martialed?"

Incredible! The colonel's got him on the hook, so now he's changing the subject, pumping the major up real good, like he's already part of the team. I guess this is going to be a funny story, so I might as well take the bait and keep this con game going.

"No, sir," Tommy replied, "but I'd sure love to hear it."

"You tell it, Bob," Pruitt said.

"Well, it was like this," Kidd began. "I was having a little trouble with my ship, so I was on the ground with this tank unit I'd been flying aerial observer for. Great timing on my part, because just then some Kraut tanks attacked. It was total chaos…I ended up in the turret of a Sherman whose tank commander was missing. Next thing I knew, *I* was the tank commander, standing up in that turret, telling the crew who to shoot at."

He took a sip of coffee and then continued, "Right in the middle of this brawl, this *thing* starts coming straight at us…I had no idea what it was. Never seen anything like it. Looked like a big box with a gun sticking out of it. Figured it was some kind of new-fangled German tank…so I told them to shoot it."

Pruitt was anticipating the punch line now, trying to keep himself from laughing out loud.

"Turns out this *thing* I was looking straight at was the blade of one of our *dozer* tanks," Kidd said. "We blew that blade halfway to Paris before I realized I'd ordered the tank crew to shoot at one of our own. Fortunately, the blade was the only thing that got hurt. The GIs in that tank were all okay. We didn't know that, though, until after the Krauts had given up and withdrawn."

Pruitt, knowing what was coming next, was now red-faced with laughter.

"Turns out some regimental commander decided I was fighting for the other side. Brought me up on charges."

"And that's a firing squad offense," Pruitt added, still laughing.

Kidd continued, "He added *willfully destroying US Government property* to the charge sheet, too. I guess he was trying to cover all the bases."

Pruitt added, "Have you ever heard anything so dumb? That *regimental commander* couldn't find his ass with both hands."

"So I'm guessing there was no court-martial?" Tommy asked.

"Ahh, you catch on fast, Lieutenant Moon," Kidd replied. "Ol' George Patton shit-canned the charges and gave me a medal instead. Said my actions were *a major contributing factor* to the Krauts being defeated in that battle."

Sergeant McNulty popped his head through the mess hall doorway. "Major Kidd," he said, "that little bag of sticks you call an airplane is good to go. Your little fueling problem has been *dissolved.*" Then he vanished just as quickly as he'd appeared.

Looking confused, Kidd asked, "*Dissolved*? You guys from New York sure got an interesting way with the language."

"He probably means *resolved*, sir," Tommy offered. "He's my crew chief. I get to translate for him a lot."

Kidd stood to say his goodbyes. Pruitt asked him, "So we can count on you to help us out, Bob?"

"I guess so, sir," Kidd replied. "Hell, it isn't something I don't do every day, anyway."

Then he left them and made his way to the ramp.

Pruitt smiled serenely at Tommy and said, "You see how easy that was, Lieutenant? I'll bet you're happy now."

"Yes, sir. It couldn't have worked out better. Thanks."

"You're welcome, Half. Now, if you'll excuse me, I've got to do a little politicking on the landline."

Bob Kidd touched his L-4 down on the grass landing strip at 4th Armored Division HQ just as the sun was dropping below the trees. *That was cutting it close,* he told himself. *Another minute or two and I would have needed a vehicle with its headlights on to point me to the runway…and keep me out of the trees.*

A messenger was waiting as he shut the L-4 down. "This just came in for you, sir," the messenger said. "It's from Third Army, and it's marked *urgent*."

Kidd pulled out his flashlight to read it. In the typically terse language of military orders, it directed him to report to A-90—with his aircraft—not later than 1000 hours, 13 October 1944, for temporary assignment to 301st Fighter Squadron.

Thirteen October. The day after tomorrow. Colonel Pruitt didn't waste any time, did he? Hell, I was just having coffee with him a couple of hours ago.

Chapter Twenty-Two

Lieutenant Jimmy Tuttle walked in on Tommy as he was packing his AWOL bag. "Where you off to tonight, Half?" he asked.

"I'm going over to Nancy—"

"Ahh, shit, Tommy. Don't tell me you're going to commandeer the jeep all to yourself. A bunch of us are planning to go into Toul. C'mon…don't make us walk."

"No, Jimmy, you guys take the jeep."

"Gee, thanks, Half. But how the hell are you getting to Nancy? That's fifteen miles. You aren't going to hitchhike, are you?"

"A couple of our mechanics fixed up some derelict motorcycle they found laying around. They're letting me borrow it for the night."

Tuttle let out a whistle of surprise. "A motorcycle, eh? They're like gold in these parts. Just make sure you secure that thing real good, or it'll be gone in no time flat, for sure."

"Don't worry, Jimmy. You ought to see the padlock and chain that comes with it."

✳✳✳✳

The sound of the motorcycle—a *Moto Guzzi* with a loud and distinctive industrial rasp—attracted quite a bit of attention as Tommy cruised the streets of Nancy, searching for *Café Rimbaud*, the place he hoped to find Sylvie. But he was having no luck. And he was half-frozen from the brisk ride on this chilly October evening.

Well past sunset, there seemed to be no one on these

streets except aimlessly wandering GIs searching for entertainment of their own. He finally saw a civilian, an old man walking a leashed dog. His noisy approach set the dog to frenzied, uncontrollable barking.

The annoyed old man yelled something in French at Tommy that he didn't quite get, but it was obviously not *How nice to see you this fine evening, my friend.*

Summoning what he hoped was his best French, Tommy apologized for upsetting the dog and explained he was lost. A glimmer of recognition replaced the old man's scowl, if just for a moment, when he spoke the name *Café Rimbaud.*

But the scowl quickly returned. Without saying another word, the man hurried away, pulling the yapping dog behind him.

This better not be like back in Alençon, Tommy told himself, *when her own relatives would protect Sylvie's maquisard identity by pretending not to know her. Maybe that Café Rimbaud is a maquis front or something. If it is, no Frenchman's ever going to tell a stranger how to get there.*

Or maybe he's just pissed off I scared the hell out of his mutt.

Nancy was a big town, but he was prepared to search each and every one of her streets until he found *Café Rimbaud.* Even if it took half the night.

Which it just might.

He remembered Sylvie saying the café was on a main street near the river. Tommy checked the Michelin map he'd stuffed into his leather flight jacket. *She must mean the Meurthe River. That's the eastern border of the town. Looks like there's about ten streets on that side of town this map considers "main" roads.* He found a street sign at an intersection, got himself oriented, and composed a search plan.

He had just turned onto the third street in his search plan when he came across a rowdy knot of GIs. One of them ran into the thoroughfare as if to flag the motorcycle down. The soldier was yelling something unintelligible over the racket of the *Moto Guzzi*. He was waving like a madman, too, as if trying to flag him down.

The guy must be drunk. Or an MP.

As he braked the bike to a stop, Tommy realized the GI was definitely not an MP. In fact, he recognized him. It was Fabiano, his brother's gunner.

"Ain't this one hell of a coincidence, Lieutenant," Fabiano said. Despite the distinct odor of alcohol about him, he sounded surprisingly sober. "We've been hearing that bike of yours tooling around town for God knows how long. You ain't looking for your brother, are you, sir?"

"Sergeant Moon's here? Sean's here?"

"Yeah, he's just up the block, finishing his supper. C'mon, I'll show you."

Fabiano hopped on the motorcycle's back seat and pointed straight ahead. "This way, sir."

They'd only driven about a hundred feet when Fabiano yelled, "This is it, sir...that little place on the right."

Tommy wondered, *Maybe he's more drunk than I thought? Hell, I could have pushed the bike to here. But still, I owe him my gratitude.*

"Right in there, sir," Fabiano said. "He's chowing down with some of the other *big wheels*."

Tommy began the tedious process of securing the motorcycle to a streetlamp's steel pillar, unwrapping the chain from the seat post. "You don't have to do that, Lieutenant," Fabiano said. "I'll watch it for you."

"Don't you want to get back with your buddies?"

Before Fabiano had a chance to reply, an MP jeep screeched to a halt beside them. The driver, a burly, snarling buck sergeant with a foghorn voice, said, "You two *touch-holes*...what do you think you're doing with that *motor-sickle?*"

Any GI who'd been around long enough to earn three stripes should have known even in the dark of night that Tommy Moon was probably an officer, and an Air Force officer at that. The *crusher* cap, the leather flying jacket, and the khakis—something ground troops in action rarely carried or were even issued due to their constant need of laundering—were dead giveaways. Yet he'd spoken that profane and insubordinate slur.

As Tommy turned to face the jeep, the glow of the streetlight reflected off the silver lieutenant's bar on his shirt collar like a beam of rectitude. The MP's tough guy façade shattered and his body stiffened, as if trying to come to a seated position of *attention*. "Gee, Lieutenant, I'm sorry. Didn't realize you—"

Tommy cut him off. "What's your name, Sergeant?"

"Dickens, sir. Lamar J. Serial number 3462—"

"Hold on a second, Sergeant Dickens. You're not a POW. I just asked for your name."

"Sorry, sir." He really did sound sorry, too.

The other MP in the jeep, a PFC with his face in shadow, fidgeted in silence in the passenger's seat, hoping to have no part in the reckoning about to come.

Just a short distance down the street and out of earshot, the rest of Fabiano's group seemed to quiver in place, as if trying to decide whether to flee the MPs or just stand and watch the show unfold.

"I tell you what, Sergeant Dickens, Lamar J., I'll do you a favor by not pressing charges if you do me one, too."

"What'd you have in mind, sir?" He sounded tentative, like he knew he was trying to bluff with a very weak hand.

"Two things, Sergeant. First off, this man standing here with me and those other men over there—yeah, they've been drinking, but they're not being disorderly and not bothering a living soul. Just helped me out in a big way, in fact. So I want you to leave them alone. If I hear that their balls got busted in any way tonight, I'll suddenly remember your insubordinate outburst just now."

That seemed like a good deal to Dickens. He nodded eagerly.

"Second," Tommy continued, "do you know a place called *Café Rimbaud*?"

"I sure do, sir. It's off limits to all personnel."

"That's too bad, Sergeant Dickens, because you're going to escort me there in a couple of minutes, just as soon as I make a quick stop inside this bistro."

Dickens didn't seem as enthused with this second condition as he'd been with the first. Still, Tommy wasn't very worried he wouldn't agree; it was a hell of a lot better than losing his stripes or spending time in the stockade.

MPs don't do real well in the slammer. Too many GIs in there with scores to settle against authority, and anyone who'd worn the MP shoulder sleeve is fair game for retribution.

This time, Dickens' nod of agreement was less enthusiastic.

"Good," Tommy said. "Wait here. I'll be right back."

In a back corner of the bistro, three NCOs sat at a small table, enjoying an after-dinner smoke. They were freshly showered in clean fatigues and brushed boots, quite unlike the usually grimy condition of men in combat. Sean Moon did a double take as Tommy approached.

"What the hell, Half?" Sean said as he wrapped his much smaller brother in a bear hug. "I get to see you twice in the same week? You following me around or something?"

He looked to the other sergeants and added, "You guys remember my little brother Tommy, right?"

A master sergeant jumped to his feet and replied, "Can't forget the best damn ASO we ever had, could we? When are you going to be joining us again, sir?"

Tommy didn't say a word. The look on his face said it all: *Not for a long time, if ever, I hope.*

The other man, a tech sergeant, peered warily toward the front window. "We ain't in some trouble with the bulls, are we, Lieutenant? This is all on the up and up. We've got twenty-four-hour passes."

"No, everything's fine with the MPs," Tommy said as he shook their hands. "In fact, they're going to help me out in a minute."

"Now that's a first," Sean said. "The MPs helping someone. Oh, wait...I forgot. You're an officer. You get away with all kinds of shit. Like that bike. That ain't government issue. Where the hell'd you get it?"

"It isn't mine, Sean. It's borrowed."

"So you could come looking for me?"

"Actually, finding you was a bonus. I'm trying to find Sylvie. She's here in Nancy somewhere. I've got the name of a café where I'm supposed to meet up with her."

"Wow! Ain't that special, Half? She got a girl for me, too, maybe?"

"I don't know…why don't you come along and see?"

Sean threw down cash for his share of the bill and bid his fellow non-coms goodbye. Then the brothers headed for the door.

"Just one thing, Sean. This place I'm supposed to look for her…it's off limits. So if you're worried about—"

"Who gives a shit?" Sean interrupted. "I've got my little brother the lieutenant to protect me." Then he shrugged and added, "Besides, it'll be worth it, right?"

"Let's hope so."

With a theatrical bow and sweep of his arm, Fabiano turned over the motorcycle to the Moon brothers. As Sean hopped on the back, he told Fabiano, "Now don't you guys go getting your asses locked up, you hear me?"

"Don't worry, Sarge. The lieutenant here took care of everything."

Tommy kick-started the *Moto Guzzi*. Yelling over the engine noise to the MPs, he said, "All right, Sergeant Dickens, lead the way."

They didn't have to go very far. After a few minutes' drive, they rolled to a stop on a darkened street. Nestled in a block of clustered two and three-story buildings stood the *Café Rimbaud*. A dim, yellowish glow escaped from its windows, barely lighting the sidewalk. Only a carved wooden sign, small, weathered, and unlit, in the shadows above the doorway announced its name. Tommy thought, *Man, I would've never seen that sign in a million years.*

There was another sign stuck in the window. Handwritten and haphazardly installed, it read, *OFF LIMITS TO US PERSONNEL, BY ORDER OF XII CORPS PROVOST MARSHALL.*

Sean was busy locking the bike to a street lamp as Tommy dismissed the MPs. Those chores done, the brothers stepped into the café.

It was close quarters inside, dark and smoky, just as they'd expected. Something else they'd expected: they were the only GIs in the place. A dozen or so men and women—civilians all—sat at tables scattered across the floor opposite the bar. All eyed the Americans with expressions that ranged from curiosity, to annoyance, to contempt.

"What're you having, Sean?" Tommy asked.

"How about a beer, little brother?"

"Coming right up…I hope."

Turning on the *français*, Tommy wished the bartender a *good evening*. Then he ordered two beers.

As the amber brew flowed from the tap, Sean leaned in and whispered, "I sure hope your girlfriend is here, somewhere. Maybe she can stop these frogs from kicking our asses."

"You really worried about that?"

"There's a lot of them, Half. And the *janes* look tougher than the *joes*. Unless you think you can charm them with that Brooklyn French of yours."

The bartender placed the tall glasses in front of

them. Pointing to the sign in the window, he asked, "That does not concern you?"

"Not tonight," Tommy replied.

"Well, soldier, I am glad to take your money. But what made you come to this place?"

Tommy replied, "I'm here to see Isabelle Truffaut. Please tell her I am here."

The bartender paused, giving him a look that, if not exactly welcoming, was at least accommodating. "You are the *moon man*?" he asked.

Stifling a laugh, Tommy replied, "Yes, that's me."

Pointing to Sean, the bartender asked, "And him?"

"He's a *moon man*, too. My brother, in fact."

Without saying another word, the bartender walked into the back room. He emerged a few moments later, escorted them to an empty table in the corner, and said, "You wait."

"All right, we'll wait." Tommy replied. "How long?"

The bartender just shrugged, as if the unpredictableness of women was something he had no interest in contemplating.

As he made his way back to the bar, there was a sharp exchange between the bartender and a few of his patrons. Tommy didn't get all of it, only the bartender's insistence that the Americans were *invited*.

As they nursed their beers, Sean asked, "Hey, Half...that big thing you were dumb enough to *volunteer* for. It happen yet?"

"No, but soon, Sean. Very soon."

Soon. The thought of that made Tommy feel very good. Thanks to his brother's twenty-four-hour pass, he might not be anywhere near Fort Driant when the *Bucket boys* blew it to smithereens.

The day after tomorrow. Just so the damn weather holds out.

And then, maybe Sean—and a whole bunch of other GIs—wouldn't have to deal with that damn fort anymore.

"And this *thing*...you're not gonna get yourself killed or nothing doing it, right, Half?"

"Probably not, Sean."

"You better not." He shook his head and mumbled to no one in particular, "He *volunteered*. Can you fucking believe it?"

The entry door swung open. Framed in its arch was the silhouette of a woman in flared skirt and heels, backlit by the same street light holding the *Moto Guzzi* in its steely grip. The café was suddenly silent, still, and attentive, as if a magistrate had entered her courtroom. Tommy couldn't see her face yet.

He didn't need to.

She walked forward, the respectfully nodding heads of every patron rippling behind her like the wake of a mighty ship.

Sean whispered, "What the hell? Is she the *Queen of France* now or something?"

"Nah. I guess they just know she's a real-live heroine of the Resistance."

The brothers rose to greet her.

"You didn't waste much time getting here," Sylvie said to Tommy, delightedly cradling his face in her hands. If there'd been any lingering doubt how delighted she actually was, her deep kiss put an end to it.

"And isn't this lovely?" she added. "Both Moon brothers in the same room!"

The kiss hello Sean received—a peck on each cheek,

French style, delivered on tiptoes—lacked the passion she'd bestowed on his brother but none of the warmth. She was truly glad to see him, too.

Then, her voice low, she cautioned them, "Just remember, you must call me *Isabelle* in public."

Before they could take their seats, she asked, "Are you both staying the night?"

When Tommy said they were, she raised a finger as if to say *one minute* and hurried to another corner of the café. She whispered something to a pretty young woman standing there and then brought her back to the brothers' table, seating her next to Sean.

"Gentlemen, I'd like you to meet Delphine," Sylvie—*Isabelle*—said. "Unfortunately, she speaks no English, so we must translate for you, Sean."

"Oh, yeah?" Sean said, reaching for his wallet. "How much?"

"Don't be an imbecile, Sean," Sylvie replied. "She is not a whore. Now behave yourself."

"Okay, then," Sean replied. "Delphine, is it? Nice to meet you." Offering his hand, he asked, "Is that her real name, *Isabelle*?"

Tommy kicked him under the table as hard as he could without being too obvious.

"Hey! Knock it off, Half. I'm just asking, for cryin' out loud."

"Don't ask, Sean. Her name's Delphine. That's all you need to know."

Sylvie smiled approvingly at Tommy. In French, she told him, "I couldn't have expressed it better myself. I think you may finally be appreciating what life must be like as a *maquisard*."

"What are you ladies drinking?" Tommy asked in

English.

"Beer sounds wonderful," Sylvie replied. She posed those same words to Delphine, this time as a question in French. When she answered with an agreeing nod, Tommy headed for the bar.

"Get a pitcher, Half," Sean said. "Less trips for refills that way."

Tommy was standing at the rail when Sean called after him. "Better make that two. We've got a long night ahead of us."

Chapter Twenty-Three

The night may have been long, but they only spent an hour of it drinking in the café. Delphine and Sean had quickly become enamored with each other. Their inability to communicate verbally hadn't proved much of a hindrance. Their bodies were doing the talking.

Sylvie said, "She thinks you are very handsome, Sean. And so big and strong, too, just like she imagined the *Amis* would be."

"So she thought Americans would all be big and strong, eh?" Tommy asked. "She's not real keen on brains, then."

"Oh, no," Sylvie replied. "Not at all. She thinks you, Tommy, are very, very smart. Imagine…an American who speaks more than one language!"

"But big and strong is still better?"

She clutched his hand tightly and said, "Tonight, for Delphine, yes." She kissed him and added, "But only for her."

Sean and Delphine were paying no attention. What had begun as playful kissing had turned to full-on necking.

"We should all leave," Sylvie said. "There are better places to make love than here."

She led them all across the street and up a flight of stairs. The building's interior was cramped and had the stale, dingy air of a boarding house. Maybe even a YWCA, just without the *cohabitation police* at the front desk. Delphine clung tightly to Sean as if they were glued together.

"Take this room," Sylvie told Sean. "The toilet is at

the end of the hall. We'll be right next door. Have a wonderful night, Sergeant."

Then, in French, she told Delphine, "Be gentle with the poor boy, *tigress*."

Somehow, Tommy managed to keep from laughing out loud at her choice of words.

Once everyone was behind closed doors, he asked, "Go easy on *him*? Are you kidding? I don't know how long it's been since my brother had a woman, so I'm betting she's going to be the one begging for the gentle touch."

"You don't know Delphine, Tommy," she replied, undoing his khaki necktie.

Before they could get undressed—they were only up to removing their shoes—the sound of the bed next door rhythmically slamming against the wall startled them like gunfire. If they hadn't known better, they'd have sworn there was an accelerating locomotive beyond that wall, effortlessly working its way to top speed.

They could actually see the wall moving in and out like some pulsating membrane. The picture that hung on it swung, shuddered, and then crashed to the floor. In disbelief, they pressed their hands against the wall to confirm what their eyes were telling them. But they pulled them quickly away as if that tactile confirmation was somehow intruding on the fierce lovers next door, who were managing to satisfy their desires without a single word necessary between them.

Amazed, Sylvie said, "We rejoiced when Nancy was liberated without suffering any destruction. But those two seem intent on changing all that."

Then Sean and Delphine began to speak—*shriek*, actually—in two different languages, each surely incomprehensible to the other.

"YOU ARE THE MASTER," Delphine announced several times, as if singing an aria in French. "YOU ARE MY KING!"

The pounding on the wall took on the intensity of a jackhammer.

"YOU'RE LIKE DIPPING IT IN A BARREL OF HONEY, BABY!" Sean testified. "I'M GONNA DRIVE YOU TO CHINA."

That was more than Sylvie and Tommy could take. They collapsed on their bed, convulsed with laughter. Sylvie managed to ask, "Why is it funny when it is other people doing it?"

Intelligible words from the next room vanished, replaced by a duet of screams and grunts growing louder and louder, until suddenly there was a silence as thunderous as everything that had come before it, like the breathtaking, quarter-note rest just before the final, sustained note of a symphony.

After relishing the tranquility for a few minutes, Sylvie said, "I suppose it is our turn now?"

And then—with Delphine's cry of *ENCORE!*—the uproar of sexual congress from the next room began all over again.

Tommy turned to look at that common, pulsating wall, but Sylvie pulled his face down to hers. "Ignore them," she murmured. "This is our time, too."

And for a few blissful moments, it was...

Until the sounds of a siren, the engines of large trucks, and men shouting in the street claimed back that time.

From the window, Tommy could see an MP jeep parked in front of *Café Rimbaud*. Three deuce-and-a-halfs were lined up in the street behind the jeep, with an MP on the running board of each truck. On the sidewalk, a big MP—Sergeant Dickens, no doubt—was loudly berating several civilians. The café's bartender, who stood silent and defiant, with arms crossed over his chest, did nothing but shake his head.

Sylvie pressed up against Tommy to watch the drama unfolding on the street below, straining to hear what was being said there through the rumpus on the other side of the wall.

"They must be looking for me and Sean," Tommy said. "That MP knows we were in there. Hell, he brought us there."

"What are you going to do, Tommy?"

"Something big must be up. I'm going down there and see what's going on." He already had his trousers on.

"You are coming back, are you not?"

"I'll be back," he replied. "Just give me a minute to get the story."

✳✳✳✳

Even in the dim glow of street lights, Tommy could tell Sergeant Dickens was red-faced. He could see the deuce-and-a-halfs were full of pissed-off GIs, too.

"These frogs are lying to me, Lieutenant," Dickens said. Pointing to the chained-up *Moto Guzzi*, he continued, "They keep telling me there were no GIs in that shithole tonight, but I know damn well—"

"Of course you do, Sergeant," Tommy replied. "Now what's the deal with the roundup?"

"All Third Army leaves are cancelled, sir. We're to collect all personnel and return them to their units immediately."

"Any idea why, Sergeant?"

"That one's over my head, sir. I'm just following orders. So I suggest you and that tech sergeant you were with hop on—"

"Not so fast, Sergeant Dickens. First off, I'm not Third Army. I'm Ninth Air Force, so I guess your orders don't apply to me, right?"

"Well...no, sir. I guess not. But that tech sergeant...I know damn well he had a Fourth Armored patch on him. That makes him Third Army."

"That it does, Sergeant Dickens."

"So if you know where he is now, sir, I suggest you tell us and my boys will go roust his ass—"

"Again, Sergeant, not so fast," Tommy replied. "You recall our little deal from earlier this evening?"

Dickens looked at him suspiciously. "Yes, sir."

"Well, I'm afraid I'm forced to add another wrinkle to it."

"A *wrinkle*, sir?"

"Yeah. I'm assuming responsibility for returning said tech sergeant to his unit. For the record, my name's Moon, Thomas P., First Lieutenant."

"I can't do that, sir," Dickens replied.

"Well, then, Sergeant, I guess I'll just have to file those charges. Let me see...what was it again? Called an officer a *touch-hole*, I believe?"

"That's blackmail, sir."

"No, Sergeant, it's a test to see how smart you are. What's it going to be?"

Tommy watched as the process of decision-making churned across the MP's face. It didn't take very long.

"All right, sir, you win. But just one thing...I need

that tech sergeant's name."

"Hmm," Tommy said, "it was *touch-hole*, right?" He made a *tsk-tsk* sound, and then added, "What a shame. A busted-down private who used to be an MP in the stockade." He twisted his face into a grimace. "I hate to even think about it."

The MP bit his lip, about-faced, and walked back to his jeep. In moments, the entire procession of GI vehicles had driven off down the street.

When Tommy returned to Sylvie, Sean and Delphine were still going at it in the next room. "I can't believe that noise didn't carry all the way down to the street," Tommy said. "Is this *round two* or *three*?"

"It's still round two. So what was going on down there, Tommy?"

"Leaves are cancelled. I'm going to have to take Sean back right now."

Sylvie pointed to the pulsating wall. "Right now? Are you sure? They'll probably kill anyone who tries to separate them."

"I did plan to wait until they're finished," Tommy replied. "Seems the brotherly thing to do. But I'd better not give them a chance to start up again."

It was another ten minutes before round two ended. Tommy and Sylvie ventured into the hallway and knocked on Sean and Delphine's door.

"Go away or I'll break your fucking head!" Sean's voice.

"Sean, it's me," Tommy said. "Your leave's been cancelled. Something big must be going on. Those MPs were looking to come and grab you. I made a deal with them, but I've got to take you back to your unit now."

"Bullshit, Half. I ain't falling for that."

"No bullshit, Sean. I'm not kidding. Get dressed and get out here." Then, reluctantly, he added, "That's an order, Sergeant."

There was mumbling and shuffling from behind the door. A minute later, it swung open and Sean, back in uniform, stepped into the hallway. A confused and distraught Delphine, hair tousled, face flushed, and clad only in a full slip, lingered in the doorway. She looked just like a woman on the cover of a racy dime store novel, complete with ample breasts about to topple from the bodice.

Tommy explained to her in French why Sean had to leave. She understood, but disappointment was written all over her. Her only comment: "Merde!"

Sylvie followed the brothers down the hall. She asked Tommy, "Will you come back? It's not even eleven o'clock."

"I'll be back real soon unless I get arrested or stuck in a traffic jam."

Sean leveled an accusing gaze at his brother. "Don't you have to get back to your unit, too, Half?"

"No, Sean. Nobody's looking for the Air Force tonight. Sorry."

His brother's mumbled, aggravated reply: "You lucky son of a bitch."

On the street, Sylvie hugged Sean goodbye and bestowed him with kisses on each cheek once again. He ambled across the street to unlock the *Moto Guzzi*, casting longing glances at the building where he'd planned to spend the night.

As they kissed goodbye, Sylvie told Tommy, "You must come back tonight, because tomorrow I will be gone."

"Wait a minute. When will you be—"

She put a finger across his lips. "Do not ask. Just come back tonight."

He was back in Sylvie's arms by half past midnight. Finally free of distractions, they reveled in each other's bodies until sleep overtook them both. They didn't wake until the sunrise lit the room.

"There is fresh bread and coffee at the café," Sylvie said as she dressed.

"Great, I'm starving," Tommy replied. "When do you have to leave?"

"Ten o'clock this morning."

"And when will you be back, Syl?"

He needed only to see the sad look in her eyes to know she had no answer to that question.

Chapter Twenty-Four

It had taken far longer to round up all the 3rd Army troopers on passes than their commanders had planned. It was mid-morning before every unit around Metz could report their GIs were *all present or accounted for*. But that hadn't slowed down the preparations for the next assault on Fort Driant.

"We've got the plans to the damn place," Colonel Abrams told the officers and senior NCOs of 37th Tank Battalion. "We now know where every hidden machine gun nest, every tunnel, and every trap door in the place is located."

Hanging on the wall before them, the diagrams looked like an artist's renditions of some medieval citadel. Captain Newcomb, Sean Moon's company commander, took a good look at them and asked, "How do we know they're genuine, sir, and not some Kraut trick?"

"Because Third Army attests to their accuracy, Captain, and that's all we need to know. It took some great intel work to dig them up, I can tell you that. And we're certainly going to take advantage of it."

Pointer in hand, Abrams got down to the specifics of the attack's operations order. "Second Infantry Regiment is sending in a battalion with elements of Seventh Combat Engineers attached. They'll enter Driant's tunnel system at this point here, on the side of Bunker Number Three and—"

Abrams paused, acknowledging the raised hand of Sean Moon. "Begging your pardon, sir," he said, "but that's the same place where we got our asses handed to us a couple of days back." Murmuring voices in agreement with Sean floated above the assembled cadre like a cloud of discontent. "How the hell are we just going to walk into their secret tunnel entrance through all the lead they're going to be throwing at us?"

"I figured that question was coming," Abrams replied, "so I'm glad you asked it, Sergeant Moon. This is why having diagrams of the fort changes everything. We all know the Krauts are damn good engineers, and when they design something—like Fort Driant, or *Feste Kronprinz*, as they call it, as you can see from the legend on these plans—you can bet your life on its functionality."

As soon as he'd said *you can bet your life*, he wished he hadn't: that's exactly what every man in this room had done in that last assault. Some GIs no longer present had made that bet, too. And lost.

The murmuring, which had died out on its own, returned even louder.

"All right, all right," Abrams said, staking sole claim to their attention again. "I want you to take a good look at this diagram, especially the design of the entryway to the tunnel."

He paused, letting them focus on Driant's plans.

"Notice that you won't be in a field of fire from any fortified position inside Driant when you're at that door. That's because when the Krauts built this place forty years ago, they didn't have to worry about sappers with special explosives and welding torches. So, once our tanks lead the infantry around the northern flank of the bunker, the engineers will be able to blow the door to the tunnel without much interference from the Krauts. And then we'll be inside."

Sean's hand rose again. "Sir, we shot doors like that with seventy-five millimeter at close range. It bounced right off."

"As we expect it would, Sergeant Moon," Abrams replied. "This time, the engineers will be using shaped charges specially designed for this purpose. And as I've already mentioned, if that fails for any reason, we'll bring in the torches to finish the job."

The room fell into that usual, uneasy silence all combat briefings do when you've heard the plan, want to believe in it, but for some inexplicable reason, you don't. All you know is there's this voice deep inside of you insisting, *It's not going to work. It can't work…*

But even if it somehow does work, I'm going to get my ass killed doing it.

"Are there any questions?" Abrams asked, hoping there would be none. Maybe he was hearing that voice from deep inside himself, too.

But he got his wish. There were no questions.

"One more thing," the colonel said. "Ninth Air Force will be pasting the hell out of the adjacent forts during our attack, so interdicting fire from them on Driant should be at a minimum, if at all. Now, the S3 will go over your specific assignments." He checked his watch. "It's exactly 1045 hours. This operation kicks off at 1300 hours."

When Tommy arrived at Zebra Ramp, he found Sergeant Dandridge sitting on *Culver 1's* wing. From a distance it looked as if Dandridge was talking to the little plane.

"No, I wasn't talking to her, sir. Just myself," the sergeant told Tommy. "I was doing some preflight checks."

That's an improvement, Tommy thought. *He called the Culver a "her," not an "it." He's either getting attached to the things...or he's just starting to talk like a real pilot. Either way, I'll bet he's feeling bad we're going to crash her today.*

Inside the operations tent, Major Staunton rushed through the pre-mission briefing. Like yesterday, a target would be marked with a napalm fire. Then, the last Culver would be crashed into that burning target. Once that was finished, the mothership, while still airborne, would do a complete test of the baby's systems while that plane remained on the ground at A-90. This would be the last chance to check out the baby, for once the Torpex arrived tomorrow, there could be no power on the sacrificial ship while the explosives were being loaded or anytime after, until it was time for her final mission.

"I don't have to remind any of you," Staunton said, "that the smallest spark, the tiniest static discharge, will blow everyone on this airfield to oblivion. Absolutely no metal tools or other equipment, such as pens, keys, cigarette lighters, dog tags, collar brass, or belt buckles, will be on your person or within fifty yards of the aircraft while the Torpex is being loaded. Is that perfectly clear?"

Every man in the *Operation Bucket* team nodded. They knew the drill all too well.

★★★★

The mothership took to the sky just after 1300. Fifteen minutes later, the Culver was in the air as well, with control handed off to Sergeant Dandridge. All systems seemed to be working like a charm.

He pushed the control box toward Tommy and asked, "Want to fly her for a bit, sir?"

"Sure, I'll take her."

Tommy put the drone through a few simple maneuvers. She responded well, but he noticed something a little different in her handling today. "The weathermen weren't kidding," he said. "The winds aloft are a hell of a lot stronger than they were yesterday. If we do the dive out of the west—out of the sun—we're going to be doing it against a pretty stiff crosswind."

Dandridge asked, "You think that's going to blow us off the target line, sir?"

"Yeah, it will. But there are ways we can correct for it. Let me do a practice dive and see what it takes."

"But we're not over the target area yet, sir."

"Any reference point will do for now, Sergeant." He glanced through the nose plexiglass and picked a spot. "How about that little bridge a couple of miles ahead? There shouldn't be anyone there to get upset when the Culver comes screaming down on them."

"Okay, I see it, sir."

"Outstanding. Now get our pilot on a parallel course with the river while I get the Culver turned around. Oh, and tell Colonel Pruitt to stand by. This will only take a couple of minutes."

It all fell into place quickly. Satisfied with the Culver's *top-of-dive* position, Tommy closed her throttle and nursed her toward the stall.

"This is interesting," he said. "I think she may stall without the wing waggle."

"How do you account for that, sir?" a puzzled Dandridge asked.

"The crosswind's doing it. It's killing our airspeed...and our lift. Whoa! Here we go."

The Culver had stalled with no help from Tommy. Her nose dropped and the dive to the simulated target of the bridge began.

"Yeah, the wind's pushing her hard off track," Tommy reported. "I'm putting in some downwind aileron to correct for it."

"Couldn't we just uncouple the rudder and crab her to the target?"

"I suppose we could," Tommy replied, "but the rudder's not very easy to work with this box. Too much fumbling with switches. I guess the designers weren't planning on a lot of crosswind work, just *bank and yank*."

The drone had plummeted another thousand feet before he said, "The aileron correction's working. I'm dead on the bridge. I'll pull out at two thousand. Coming up on two thousand five...four...three...two...one."

He eased the Culver out of the dive. Once again, Dandridge thought he had her trimming the treetops.

"What's the altimeter read, sir?"

"One hundred fifty."

"Damn, it looks a lot lower than that."

"It always will from way up here, Sergeant."

Once the Culver was climbing again, he handed over the control box. "Here, Sergeant. You try it now."

Dandridge brought the drone back to altitude and

started the practice dive. "Oh, yeah," he said, "I see what you mean, sir. It's like a big hand pushing her sideways. I'm going to add in some rudder."

"You sure it's not going to mess up the other controls? You need them a lot worse right now."

"It's okay, sir. I know how to do it."

But after a few moments, Dandridge said, "It's not working as well as I thought. Hard to keep the target in frame with the rudder kicking the nose to the right like that." He flipped the switch on the box to return the controls to normal mode. "Now I'm trying it your way."

Within seconds, he added, "That's much better."

"Altitude?"

"Three thousand, sir. Two thousand nine...eight..."

Tommy smiled. Dandridge had gotten up the courage to take her down to 2,000 feet before pulling out, just like he'd done.

"Three...two...one..."

Tommy watched through the nose dome as the Culver pulled smoothly out of the dive and seemed to be skimming the ground. "What's your altitude now, Sergeant?"

"Two hundred fifty feet and starting to climb."

"See? That wasn't so hard, was it?"

"I'll let you know when my heart stops pounding, sir."

A few minutes later, with the Culver back at altitude, Tommy asked, "You need another practice dive? Or are you ready for the big time?"

"Definitely ready for the big time, sir."

"You're on," Tommy replied. Then he told Lieutenant Wheatley at the controls of the mothership to proceed to the target area. That done, he advised Colonel

256

Pruitt they were on the way.

Pruitt was more than ready to deliver the napalm. He told Tommy, "Standing by. But I'm sending you the bill for all this gas I burned tooling around up here on this beautiful day."

It truly was a beautiful day; a blue sky, clear as a crystal dome, the nearest clouds a hundred miles to the southwest. The airborne visibility was so exceptional that the mothership's eagle-eyed flight engineer, manning the top turret, saw the four distant specks—at a much higher altitude—off their left wingtip.

His voice tightened with each word as he said, "Engineer to Crew, we got bogies at nine o'clock high."

"Are you sure they're not our escorts?" Lieutenant Wheatley asked.

"Negative, negative. They ain't P-38s, that's for damn sure. Not with just one engine, they ain't. And speaking of P-38s, I'm looking all over but I don't see our top cover anywhere."

Wheatley asked, "How far out are the bogies?"

"Not far enough. They'll be on us before you know it."

"Pilot to Radio, have you got contact with our escorts?"

"Negative. No reply."

"Pilot to Crew, abort. Repeat, abort. We're turning back."

Tommy wanted to say something to stop what he considered a panicky rush to judgment. Looking through the navigator's astrodome, he could see the bogies now. But the engineer was right; they were too far away to identify.

Sure, they're unidentified, and all single-engine

fighters look pretty much alike from this distance. They don't even look like they're coming toward us. I've lost count of how many times I've seen Luftwaffe planes that just passed right by without ever trying to engage.

But this isn't my ship...and it isn't my call.

Still, the question needed to be asked: "Observer to Pilot, just what are we aborting, exactly?"

"This whole damn mission, Moon."

"So you're taking us back to A-90?"

"Damn right I am."

"So we can be a sitting duck on the ground?" Tommy asked. "At least up here, we might have a few options. If they really are Krauts, that is."

"Negative. We're on our own, and we're getting the hell out of here. End of story."

Tommy replied, "Well, Lieutenant, you can take your ship anywhere you please, I imagine. But it seems like Sergeant Dandridge can still run this drone mission...while *you're* running away."

Dandridge's eyes may have been pressed to the video monitor's hood, but Tommy could see his mouth break into an amused grin for just a moment. Watching officers cut each other up could sometimes be enjoyable. Even in the face of danger.

"Controller to Pilot, Lieutenant Moon is correct, sir. All I need is the drone on course with good video, and I've got that. It doesn't matter much where the mothership is at this point."

Colonel Pruitt was on the air now, too. "*Almighty Four-One*, this is *Gadget Blue*. Where the hell are you going?"

When told the mothership was fleeing the *bogies*, the irritation in Pruitt's voice cut through the airwaves

258

like a knife. "Negative, *Almighty*, negative. Your *bogies* are friendly. Repeat, friendly. And you might have noticed by now they're not tracking you, either."

The radio operator had this to add: "I've got the escort leader on *hailing freq*, sir. They had to switch over for a minute. Says we've got nothing to worry about."

"Oh, yeah?" Wheatley replied. "Just where the hell are they, then?"

"On station at *angels twenty*, sir. It's so damn bright out we probably won't even see them way up there unless the sun glints off them. But they can see us real good...and they can see those jugs passing us going the other way, too."

"*Almighty*, this is *Gadget Blue*. Can I drop this hellfire now, before I run out of gas boring holes in the sky up here?" Even the harsh filtering of aircraft radios could not distill the annoyance from Colonel Pruitt's voice.

Wheatley probably didn't intend to broadcast his next comment to the whole world, but his mic was keyed as he said, "Ahh, this is all fucked up."

His voice no less annoyed than a moment ago, Colonel Pruitt replied, "Not all of it, son. And not all of us, either."

Lieutenant Wheatley began the slow turn that would bring the mothership back toward the target area. He told his crew, "Resuming mission." He sounded as if saying those words was some sort of imposition on him.

Dandridge said, "Might as well tell the colonel to drop the napalm, sir. I'm ready to dive as soon as he marks the target."

Pruitt had one request: "You mind if I drop all three

canisters at once? I won't have enough gas to do this twice."

Tommy asked Dandridge, "That okay with you?"

"Yes, sir. That's how we're going to do it on the fort, right? I can make sure the fire's not so bright it makes the video bloom. And how come the colonel's always complaining about how much gas he's burning?"

"Fuel's pretty tight in these parts, Sergeant. We can't afford to top off the tanks for local training missions like this one, especially when we need so much for this four-engined beast here."

Since the mothership was still some distance from the target zone, those who could see forward in the CQ-17 had a spectacular view of Pruitt's dive from start to finish. It was breathtaking to watch the stubby fighter plummet like a projectile yet still be under perfect control.

"You weren't kidding about this crosswind," Pruitt said casually as the jug was halfway down to the release point.

But crosswind or not, the colonel dropped the three canisters of napalm squarely on target. "Okay, boys, that's the best I can do. See you back home."

"Like I told you, he can put it right where we want it," Tommy said. "Now let's see you do it, Sergeant."

Dandridge proceeded to do exactly that.

With the Culver dispatched to her fiery but productive demise, the mothership flew over A-90. The crew could see the BQ-7—the *baby*—being run up on Zebra Ramp. Dandridge said, "We've got to use ship's power for the operational tests of the video and *Castor* gear."

"How come?" Tommy asked. "What's wrong with using ground power units instead of wasting all that gas?"

"We've gotten some strange results with them, sir. For final checks, it's SOP to use nothing but ship's power. We've got to run her engines up to cruise RPM, too, to make sure the generators are stabilized." As if to confirm what Dandridge had just said, the ground crew reported they were coming up to cruise power, the signal that the testing of the video and remote-control equipment could begin.

Tommy glanced down at the BQ-7 through binoculars. The only personnel and equipment around her were two mechanics acting as fire guards and the large, wheeled fire bottles they were manning at a safe distance in front of the whirling props. Everyone else involved in the testing would be on board, Dandridge told him.

"Pretty funny," Tommy said, "but if we ran up a jug like that on the ramp, we'd have about ten guys sitting on her tail to shift her CG way back, hanging on for dear life in the prop blast, just to keep her from nosing over from all that thrust. Doesn't look like the baby is in any danger of going on her nose, though. Not as big and heavy as she is."

"And even though she's lightened up a lot for the mission," Dandridge added, "that tail still stays glued to the ground, even at high power."

The mothership quickly acquired the television signal from the baby. With a clear view of her instrument panel now, Dandridge took over her controls.

He told Lieutenant Wheatley, "Toggle is complete, sir. Ready to run the operational tests."

Each check of the baby's controls worked perfectly. As the testing progressed, the mothership put more distance between herself and A-90, flying higher and farther north. At nearly twenty miles straight-line distance, the television signal from the baby was finally lost.

"Well, that all passes with flying colors," Dandridge said. "As long as we're more than ten miles from the baby when we lose contact, we're good. I think twenty miles is some sort of record, though. And no sign of interference, either, even with weak signals."

Ahead in the distance, they could see Fort Driant and the city of Metz just beyond. It was Dandridge who made the suggestion, even though Tommy was thinking the same thing: "Let's have one last look at that fort before we try to blow it up."

Lieutenant Wheatley didn't think much of that idea. "I'll do one pass," he said, "but that's it. And we're not going any lower, so don't even ask."

Tommy wedged himself into the nose dome for a bird's-eye view of what, if anything, was going on below. He didn't need the binoculars to see the clouds of dust rising south and west of the fort: a sure sign American columns were on the move. With the binocs, he could identify American tanks, half-tracks, and trucks advancing toward Driant.

Shit, they're going to attack that damn fort again, Tommy told himself. *I'll bet that's why all those leaves got cancelled. But they'd better capture it real quick this time or get the hell out of there, because the day after tomorrow, the baby's going to be dropping in for a surprise visit…*

And my brother—and all his buddies—better be miles away from Fort Driant.

His thoughts were interrupted by the radio operator's voice in his headphones, passing along a message. It was a code word; Tommy had no idea what it meant.

Dandridge unraveled the mystery: "It means the guys on the ground have a big problem."

Back on the ground at A-90, the crew of the mothership assembled in the *Bucket* operations tent for the mission debrief. They didn't have much to talk about: their end of both the Culver practice run and the baby's checkout had gone according to plan. The ground team, however, had a much different and very troubling report.

"It's going to blow up, plain and simple," Tech Sergeant Rocco Inzetta said. The chief electrician's voice was choked with emotion, his pleading eyes welling with tears. "We've got stray voltage in the Torpex igniter wiring when it's under remote control, more than enough to set off the explosives. There shouldn't be a milliamp of current there until it impacts the target. It'll detonate just like that *Navy baby* that blew itself and its pilots to bits."

Major Staunton shook his head and replied, "We've been through this a dozen times before, Sergeant Inzetta. We just need better grounding for the transmitter's power supply. Once your men burnish and reconnect the leads to the ship's grounding bus bar, everything will be fine."

Dandridge whispered to Tommy, "Here we go again, sir. Remember what I was saying about the old *reseat the connectors* fix?" He motioned to the two pilots whose job it would be to get the baby airborne and then bail out once it was under remote control. "I don't think those two gentlemen are buying it, either. If they clamp their jaws any tighter, they're going to be breaking off teeth and spitting them out."

Tommy had been watching Staunton intently as he delivered his textbook solution. He'd sounded confident enough—*And who knows? Maybe he is right*—but Tommy was pretty sure he'd caught just a hint of uncertainty in his face. It seemed to him like Staunton was trying to convince himself along with everyone else.

One of the baby's pilots, a captain named Pym, whose hair was graying well before its time, asked, "Of course, Major, we *will* keep testing the system until we're absolutely positive there's no loose voltage on those wires, right?"

"Absolutely, Captain Pym," Staunton replied, his voice full of confidence.

But Tommy was sure he caught that hint of uncertainty in the major's face once again.

And Sergeant Inzetta's face had the disbelieving look of a man who'd just been told that *up* was *down*.

"This *Navy baby*," Tommy said to Dandridge. "What's he talking about?"

"The Navy flies these things, too, sir. A couple of months back, one of them blew up in midair, right after control passed to the remote operator. Nobody knows for sure, but they think it happened as soon as the pilots armed the explosives, which is the last thing they do before bailing out."

264

"So if there's already voltage in the wiring, the Torpex will blow as soon as it's armed?"

Dandridge replied with a somber nod.

"And this stray voltage problem has been seen before?" Tommy asked.

"Yeah, we've seen it from time to time, sir. It's like a phantom. Sometimes it goes away without us doing anything, so we're not real sure what the positive fix is. But the big brains are convinced that cleaning up the bus bar grounding connections takes care of everything."

"And nobody's got proof of that?"

"Correct, sir. I suggested months ago that we replace the bus bar, which is thin, flat aluminum, with something much more solid, like a copper rod or something, that wouldn't flex and arc with changes in temperature and pressure altitude. The Air Force wouldn't buy it, though…not without extensive testing back in the States. It would be like recertifying the design of the whole electrical system."

Tommy asked, "Are they doing that testing?"

He knew what the look of frustrated helplessness that came over Dandridge's face meant. It was the same look he'd seen a hundred times before on the faces of highly experienced NCOs, men who were expected to execute the policies of the military but despite their considerable expertise had no input in the making of those policies.

"Your guess is as good as mine, sir."

As Tommy and Dandridge emerged from the operations tent, they walked right into Lieutenant Wheatley reading the *riot act* to his flight engineer. His tone nasty and threatening, the pilot was dressing down his senior, most experienced enlisted crewman for *embarrassing* him when he called out those *bogus bogies*. It was like listening to a self-obsessed parent scolding a child for having the temerity to breathe.

Tommy grabbed Wheatley by the arm and ushered him around the corner of the tent, the much bigger man struggling to pull away the whole time. But he couldn't shake Tommy's vise-like grip.

"Get your fucking hands off me, Moon, or I'll have your ass court-martialed so fast your head will spin."

"Yeah, sure you will, Paul," Tommy replied. "Now shut up and listen. You might want to show that sergeant a little respect. Right or wrong, he was just doing his job. You were the one who made a horse's ass out of yourself by jumping to the wrong conclusion."

"Fuck you, Moon. And fuck all you fighter jockeys who think you're all such hot shit."

"Just out of curiosity, Paul, how many combat missions have you logged, anyway?"

Wheatley glared down at Tommy as if he was regarding a lower life form. That was all it took for Tommy Moon to understand Paul Wheatley:

He's one of those boys from the world of privilege who has always lived by a different set of rules than the rest of us poor slobs. And those jacked-up rules have followed him right into the service, too.

"Let me guess, Paul. Your daddy's a general or a rich man, right? Or maybe a congressman?"

Wheatley's head jerked back, as if the truth was a blow as effective as a punch.

Then Tommy added, "Only someone who's been told his whole life that the sun rises out of his asshole would treat a valued non-com like dirt. Especially the non-com who keeps your ship airworthy."

Wheatley's dismissiveness didn't soften a bit as he wheeled and strutted away. His only words in parting: "Go fuck yourself, *dwarf.*"

Tommy found Dandridge and the flight engineer lurking around the corner of the tent.

The engineer said, "Thanks for sticking up for me, Lieutenant. We could sure use a little more of that around here."

Dandridge added, "Boy, you hit that one right on the head, sir."

"Oh yeah? Which part?"

"All the parts. But especially the one about his daddy being a congressman. He actually is a congressman from Missouri, you know."

"No shit," Tommy replied. "And here I was, throwing things against the wall to see what stuck. Wait a minute...how much of that did you guys hear?"

"Probably all of it, sir," Dandridge replied. "I know we weren't supposed to be listening, but it was too good to miss. I loved when you asked him about how many combat missions he has. We can tell you the answer. It's two."

"Two? That's all? He must've made a real mess of things. Or he went crying to his daddy."

"Mostly, I hear it was the *real mess* he made, sir. I don't know any of the details, but they pretty much drummed him out of a bomb wing."

"And he ended up flying motherships? From what I've heard, you get bounced to transports if you can't cut it. Or you just get grounded, period."

The flight engineer chimed in: "Well, that brings us to the part about *crying to his daddy*, sir..."

Chapter Twenty-Five

As far as Sean Moon was concerned, the operations order for this latest attack on Fort Driant was proving too optimistic: *Having the plans to this place is great and all, but it's still a shitstorm. We're getting cut up by Krauts we can't even see, just like before.*

But the plans had taught the Americans some useful things about the fort, such as the locations of concealed entrances to the tunnel system that connected most of Driant's structures. While the broad attack order featured multiple simultaneous prods into the tunnel system at various points of access, the assignment for Sean's platoon was more compact: protect the engineers who were to blow the steel door at a hidden tunnel entrance between Bunkers 3 and 4. They'd be bypassing those bunkers—and their kill zones—to exploit and conquer the tunnel system beneath them.

This involved first covering the approach of the engineers' two armored half-tracks and then suppressing any German fire that might interfere with the demolition work. One infantry company would follow the engineers and storm the tunnel once it was opened. Another company of infantry would provide protection for the tanks and half-tracks from sappers. Per the ops order, these four attacking elements were to enter the fort in a close, mutually supporting column.

Sean's platoon should've had four tanks, but one had already broken down with transmission problems moving out of the assembly area to begin the attack. His remaining three tanks, with the engineers' half-tracks nestled among them, passed through the same breach in the barbed wire perimeter they'd used in the last attack. They would've been in position at their objective—the tunnel door—in just a few minutes, even with the slow pace necessary to not outrun the infantry. But in the face of withering fire, the infantry had slowed to a literal crawl. With the usual poor-to-nonexistent communications between buttoned-up tanks and foot soldiers, coupled with the self-preservation instincts of the tankers telling them not to stand still, the vehicles had soon gotten far ahead of the GIs on foot.

As they rolled up to their objective, which was down in a narrow trench below ground level, Sean could sense his tanks and the engineer half-tracks were without infantry support. "Circle the wagons," Sean called over the radio to the other two tanks in his platoon. "The *corn plaster commandos* didn't show. It's gonna be up to us to keep the Krauts off our asses. And try not to run over any of our own guys while you're at it."

The sound of bullets large and small bouncing off the hull and turret was maddening. "Kowalski," Sean called to his driver, "pull her up another ten yards, and make it snappy. We'll use the old girl to make a wall the engineers can hide their asses behind."

A burst of heavy machine gun bullets struck the tank like the rapid chattering of teeth, each round making a dull *THUNK* as it ricocheted off an unyielding piece of steel. "Better our paint job takes a licking than those poor bastard engineers," Sean said.

Circling the wagons put Sean's platoon in a rough triangle around the trench where the engineers worked, their bows pointing outward. The bow machine gun of each tank covered a narrow arc of the perimeter they'd formed around the engineers. The coaxial machine gun that traversed with each turret's main gun would have to provide cover from infantry attacks for the rest of the perimeter's circumference. If a major threat popped up, like an anti-tank gun, an exposed strongpoint, or—however unlikely—another tank, the main guns of the Shermans would be brought to bear.

Fabiano, Sean's gunner, was glued to his gunsight as he traversed the turret, looking for a target he could actually see instead of just the blast-pocked moonscape of the fort's earthen roof. Meanwhile, Sean tried to correlate the defensive positions marked on his sketch of Driant's plans to the incoming fire they were receiving. He could hear the main guns of his other tanks firing intermittently, but when questioned, they didn't seem very sure of what, if anything, they were shooting at. Through his periscope, he had a limited view of the engineers working behind his tank as they moved explosives into position against the tunnel door.

Sean was relieved that, at least for the time being, one part of the attack plan seemed to be working: they weren't receiving artillery fire from the adjacent forts. "The flyboys must be pasting the shit out of them other forts real good," he said, thinking out loud. "That'll keep those turrets retracted into the ground for now, but they can't keep that shit up forever. And as soon as them birds fly home, them guns will start spitting out shells all over again."

But what bothered Sean most: *We been standing still too damn long. We're dead meat if some joker with a rocket on his shoulder pops up and we don't cancel his ticket quick enough. But if we move, the engineers take it in the shorts. What's taking them so damn long, anyway?*

He didn't have to wait long for the answer. An

engineer lieutenant identified himself on the tank's intercom. Then he announced, "FIRE IN THE HOLE."

The explosion was disappointing, more dust and flying debris than noise. It didn't feel like the usual punch to the eardrums and scrotum that accompanied a blast.

But then there was another explosion, far more powerful, felt by every fiber in the tankers' bodies. They heard only the sirens screaming in their brutalized ears. Everything else was muffled, as if each man's head was packed in a box full of cotton.

Then came the dense smoke that began to fill the hull, tinted a lurid pink by the flames licking through ruptures in the engine compartment firewall.

"EVERYBODY OUT," Sean screamed, but no one heard him. In the world of the suddenly deaf, spoken words were useless. Actions were the only language.

Pulling his gunner and loader behind him, he leaned down into the driver's compartment, pointing frantically to the escape hatch in the bottom of the hull. Once the driver and assistant driver had made their way through the hatch, Sean and the other two from the turret followed.

They didn't need to be told to take their Thompson submachine guns with them. *Lucky 7* wasn't going to protect them anymore. They were foot soldiers now.

Beneath their crippled tank, there was no way to get out but forward, toward her bow. The way aft was blocked by burning puddles of gasoline, rapidly growing.

Sean started to yell an order but quickly gave up. He couldn't understand himself through his crippled ears. Nobody else's ears would be able to understand him, either.

He'd simply have to lead the way.

When they dropped into the trench leading to the tunnel door, they realized they weren't the only tankers now walking; three of the five crewmen from one of his other tanks were there, too. Those men couldn't hear much of anything, either.

Peering over the ledge of the trench, Sean could see both tanks *brewing up*, each with mangled metal on the aft hull where a projectile had penetrated. Across the triangle formation that had once been his platoon, the sole operational tank was firing her 75-millimeter main gun as fast as her crew could load it. The turret was traversed completely around so it was shooting across her aft deck, directly over the tankers and engineers in the trench. The added pressure on their eardrums from the 75 millimeter's firing wasn't helping the return of anyone's hearing. After getting off five shots, it fell quiet.

The engineers had retreated down the trench to trigger their blast and had now returned. The engineer lieutenant tried telling Sean something, but his moving lips—which made no sound—did nothing but emphasize just how hearing impaired the tankers were at the moment. It took some lip-reading, but finally Sean reduced what he was saying to just one word repeated over and over again:

Three syllables...panzerfaust.
Shit. Where the hell did they come from?

The engineers had broken out long crowbars to pry away what was left of the tunnel door. In the few minutes it took them to clear the opening, the tankers had regained at least some hearing, provided the speaker shouted loudly enough.

"You saw panzerfausts?" Sean asked the engineer lieutenant, a man of easy confidence and composure named Chenoweth.

"Yeah," the lieutenant replied. "A couple of 'em. Your tank over there...the one that still works. He took care of them."

"Great," Sean replied, "I'll get him a fucking medal."

They could feel the searing heat of the fires consuming the two shot-up Shermans.

"Those tanks of yours, Sarge. They're burning pretty good. They gonna blow?"

"They might, if that fire gets through the water jackets around the ammo."

"We'd better be inside that tunnel when they do blow," Chenoweth said.

"You seen the infantry anywhere, Lieutenant?"

"There's part of a platoon down the trench."

"That's all? *Part* of a platoon? There's supposed to be a whole fucking company."

"We've got enough men to go in, Sergeant," Chenoweth replied, as if nothing surprised or upset him much anymore. "There's not going to be a lot of room down there, anyway. If and when the rest show up, we'll get them involved somehow."

Then he fixed the tankers in a judgmental gaze and asked, "You going to join us in the tunnel? Not like you'll be doing much above ground anymore."

Sean replied, "There's a kinda ominous ring to what you just said, sir. That whole *not being above ground* thing..."

Chenoweth grimaced as if he was smelling something rotten. Or maybe the stench of gutlessness.

"Wait a minute, Lieutenant," Sean said. "We ain't yellow. We're in this fight one way or the other."

His face now a victorious smile, Chenoweth replied, "Never doubted you for a second, Sergeant. Now let's get those infantrymen up here and take the plunge."

"Let me just have a word with the TC on that buggy of mine that still works, sir. Maybe he can radio for some help over this way."

As he worked his way down the trench, Sean came to the three crewmen of his other knocked-out tank. The TC, Sergeant Spinetti, was not among them. The loader, PFC Bonner, wasn't there, either.

"Spinetti bought the farm," his gunner reported. "Don't know what happened to Bonner. He was with us when we bailed out, but..." His voice trailed off hopelessly.

"Yeah, yeah, I get the picture," Sean said. "Go with the lieutenant over there."

The gunner eyed him suspiciously. "And where're you going, Sarge?"

Sean pointed to the surviving tank. "I'm going over to tell Sergeant Lerner that he *is* Second Platoon now. I'll be back in a minute."

✶✶✶✶

Sean didn't think much of using the handset on the back of Sergeant Lerner's tank—it left him dangerously exposed. Instead, he crawled to the front of the Sherman and startled her driver as his face suddenly filled the armored glass of the narrow viewer. Sean made a quick hand signal *to open the bottom hatch* and dropped back to the ground. By the time he'd crawled under the tank to the hatch, it had been opened for him.

"Talk loud," he yelled to Lerner. "I'm still half fucking deaf. You got contact with the CP?"

"Yeah. They say Fourth Platoon is gonna come over and reinforce us. Or what's left of it, anyway. We're taking a beating in this fucking place all over again."

Impatiently, Sean replied, "No shit. Tell the captain we got one dead, one missing, and I'm taking who's left to work with the engineers in the fucking tunnel."

The look on Lerner's face could only mean one thing: *Better you than me, buddy.*

Sean had time for one more question: "Did you take out them Krauts with the panzerfausts? Or did they just *vamoose?*"

"It's the damnedest thing, Sean. Keller here"—he pointed to his gunner—"I think he actually shot one with the seventy-five while the bastard was lining up on us. I saw the whole thing through the scope. Watched the round go right at him. One second he's standing there, next second he fucking vanished. Kinda overkill, don't you think? The main gun shoots one hell of a big bullet."

"Whatever works, Lerner. Good job. You just watch your ass now, okay?"

Then Sean dropped down through the hatch.

When he got back to the tunnel entrance, Lieutenant Chenoweth was putting the finishing touches on his improvised plan of attack. He told Sean, "It's really close quarters inside the tunnel. There's fourteen of us armed with Thompsons—your guys and my engineers. Those are the only weapons compact enough to be worth a damn in there besides forty-five pistols. All the infantry guys are lugging M1s, with a couple of BARs and one thirty-cal machine gun thrown in. Those'll all be a little unwieldy where we're going."

He pointed to the infantrymen spread out down the trench. It was hardly a platoon, more like two squads, about seventeen men, at Sean's rough count. "There's only one non-com in the bunch," Chenoweth added, "a buck sergeant who just got the stripe about five minutes ago. So they're a little light on leadership. I'm thinking we keep them as rear guard in case we get Krauts from Bunker 3…or from lord knows where."

"They have any idea where the rest of their company is, Lieutenant?"

"I don't think any of them even know where they are themselves, Sergeant Moon. You tankers have any flashlights on you?"

"I got one," Sean replied, "and I think we can come up with a couple more between us."

"Good. You'll need them. Blowing the door shattered all the light bulbs in this part of the tunnel, I think. It's going to be pretty damn dark in there."

"One question, Lieutenant. What are you expecting to find once we're inside?"

"According to the drawings of this place, we'll probably find another armored door. One other thing…you guys have any grenades?"

"No, sir."

"Good. We don't want to be throwing them around in there unless we absolutely have to."

The tunnel reminded Sean of the New York City subways. He could picture himself just five years ago, before he'd joined the pre-war Army, walking those crowded, tiled corridors that led to the underground station platforms. The only difference to him was dimensional: the tunnels of Fort Driant were much narrower. Only two men could fit abreast in their narrow confines. And they'd be rubbing shoulders.

But, so far, they hadn't rubbed shoulders with any Germans.

There were two ways they could go: west, toward Bunker 3, or east, toward Bunker 4. Looking west—or left—they could see another armored door—closed and locked from the opposite side—leading to Bunker 3. Since the plan was to bypass that bunker completely, they made a right turn and headed east toward Bunker 4 and the gun batteries.

"This'll be pretty much a two-man fight," Sean said to Lieutenant Chenoweth. "One GI against one Kraut. Everybody else has someone in their damn way."

They advanced slowly, cautiously, crouching to be smaller targets. The only thing ahead in their flashlight beams was more tunnel. Sean asked, "How far you figure we've gone, Lieutenant?"

Chenoweth replied, "Not real sure. Maybe halfway to Bunker 4."

If he was right, that meant in the five minutes they'd been in the tunnel, they'd only crept about two hundred fifty feet into its inky, concrete-lined menace.

They could hear the faint hum of machinery and feel it in the walls. "Generators," Chenoweth said. "Hydraulics, too. Maybe those big turrets are getting ready to fire. I wonder what that's going to feel like?"

"It can't make my hearing much worse than it already is, Lieutenant," Sean replied. Then he dropped to one knee and said, "Hey, I think there's something up ahead."

He was holding the flashlight away from his body, as if that might attract the gunfire they hadn't encountered yet. Then he mocked himself for the pointless precaution.

This flashlight ain't gonna save you, you idiot. The place is so fucking narrow it won't matter where they aim. They just gotta point.

But the flashlight had caught something in its beam, a glint off another surface still far ahead but squarely in their path.

"It's the door I've been telling you about," Chenoweth said. He then used his flashlight to signal his demolition team to the head of the column. "Hold the rest of the men back," he told Sean.

"You know, Lieutenant, sooner or later there's gonna be Krauts behind one of these doors."

"No shit, Sergeant Moon."

"How far back you want the rest of us?"

"Fifty paces. Make them *big* paces."

It took three minutes to rig the charge. Chenoweth and his demo team came quickly back down the tunnel, unreeling a spool of wire behind them. When they reached Sean and the rest, the lieutenant said, "Everyone turn around and cover up. Especially your ears."

A few more seconds to hook the wire to the detonator, and then:

"FIRE IN THE HOLE."

Funneled down the confines of the tunnel, this explosion was infinitely louder and far more punishing to the body than the engineers' first blast. Smoke, dust, and debris swirled around the GIs, a choking cloud that had them all gasping for breath.

In a few seconds, they realized they weren't able to breathe at all.

"OUT! EVERBODY OUT," Chenoweth yelled. He tried to repeat it but gagged on the words. There was nothing he could do but push the stumbling, choking men back to where they'd entered the tunnel.

Once outside in the trench, the lieutenant caught his breath. Then he cursed his miscalculation. "Carbide gas, dammit," he said. "There's not enough airflow down there with all those doors buttoned up. The explosion sucked up all the oxygen. There's nothing left but the carbide. Everyone okay?"

Their nods might've been slow in coming, but once they'd regained their breath, every man had to admit he was all right.

Sean asked, "So how the hell are we going to get to the Krauts if there's no air to breathe, Lieutenant?"

"Slowly, Sergeant. One fucking door at a time."

"How long before we can go back in, sir?"

"Give it a couple of minutes. I think we blew all the way through that door."

"Kinda makes you wish we hadn't thrown all them gas masks away, don't it, Lieutenant?"

Chenoweth couldn't help his pained smile as he said, "Probably wouldn't have helped. GI gas masks are just filters, not oxygen generators. They don't work if there's no oxygen available to begin with."

But he knew Sean was right about one thing: just about every GI in France had managed to *lose* his issued gas mask a long time ago. The bulky masks were considered just another useless encumbrance strapped to their bodies. Everyone sensed the unwritten agreement: nobody would be hurling chemical weapons at the other side. Tear gas, nerve agents, pathogens, and other poisons would languish in depots for the duration.

Bullets, incendiaries, and high explosives were deemed lethal enough.

Chapter Twenty-Six

It brought a small measure of comfort when three Shermans from 4th Platoon arrived. The lead tank pulled up right next to the trench so it was easy, and somewhat safe, for Sean to use the phone handset on its stern.

"They've got Battalion on the horn," he yelled to Chenoweth. "Sounds like we're the only ones who've actually gotten inside a tunnel, so far."

He listened for a few moments and then added, "A couple more things from Battalion, sir. First off, they're sending more infantry our way."

Chenoweth was less than impressed. "Let's hope this bunch actually gets here intact. What else?"

"They think Bunker 3 is deserted. They want us to check it out."

"Tell them we don't have the people to probe a damn tunnel and a damn bunker at the same time," Chenoweth said. "If and when more infantry show up, maybe then it'll be a different story. Which one do they want done in the meantime?"

They had the answer in a matter of seconds: the tunnel.

"I'm gonna have them push the burning *Zippos* out of the way," Sean said. "If that's okay with you, Lieutenant."

"Good idea," Chenoweth replied. "They're making me nervous. We've got enough trouble with explosions right now."

"Sure. Anything else you need them to do?"

"Yeah. Try to keep our half-tracks covered. There's stuff in them we still might need. And ask them if they want any of this infantry we've got now for support."

"He says *roger* on the half-tracks, sir. And they'll take a squad of infantry, too."

"Good," Chenoweth said. "Divvy them up, Sergeant Moon, and then we'll go tunnel diving again."

★★★★

Lieutenant Chenoweth was right. They had blown a hole in the second door. Just not a big enough hole for a man to fit through.

But it was more than big enough for bullets to pass through. As Chenoweth's team crept up to the door, they were met with burst after burst of machine gun fire from the tunnel beyond. It didn't hit any of the GIs nearest the door. But two engineers at the rear of the group, far enough back that they hadn't felt the pressing desire to hug the tunnel's wall, were struck down. They thrashed on the tunnel floor, their echoing screams drowning out the machine gun's insistent chatter.

"LIGHTS OUT, EVERYONE," Chenoweth ordered.

The tunnel went dark immediately as flashlights clicked off. The only light now was whatever leaked through the breach in the door from the other side.

Sean sent Fabiano and Kowalski to drag the wounded engineers out of the tunnel. Then he and Chenoweth slithered through the blackness in a low crawl toward the door. Once they got there, they sat, hearts pounding, one on each side of the hole they'd blown through the thick steel, trying to see what was on its other side as bullets whizzed through the hole, hissing like angry insects, just inches from their faces.

Every now and then, there'd be a nerve-shattering

CLANK as the gunner exceeded his very narrow field of fire and one of his bullets struck the opposite side of the door.

They found the hole bigger than they originally thought, a jagged vertical tear in the steel almost four feet long. It was nearly a foot wide at its center but quickly narrowed toward each end. The area on the other side of the door was still well lit. A small fraction of that light spilled through the hole, casting a ghostly light on their faces.

As long as they stayed wide of the hole, they were safe.

"Be kinda nice if we had one of those grenades now," Sean said.

Chenoweth replied, "You wouldn't be able to throw it in there, not without getting your hand shot off. We've got to make him stop shooting for a second or two."

"Maybe some of them dogfaces got a rifle grenade, sir. We can shoot one through."

"Too chancy," the lieutenant replied. "It'll probably hit the door and bounce back on us."

He yelled to one of his men, "Shellnutt, get the *blunderbuss* and four grenades, *on the damn double.*"

Sean asked, "What the hell's a *blunderbuss*, Lieutenant?"

"It's an idea we borrowed from the Tommies back in England. Real handy for cleaning out pillboxes and bunkers in a *humane* manner." A weak, ironic smile followed the word *humane*. "But maybe we'll get lucky and the bastard will run out of ammo while we're waiting."

Three minutes passed before PFC Shellnutt returned, dragging what looked like a duffel bag as he low-crawled to them. The *bastard* beyond the door had not yet run out of ammo.

Sean watched in the dim light as Chenoweth removed a weapon from the bag. In Brooklyn, they'd call it a sawed-off shotgun or *hand cannon*, an ideal heavy-gauge weapon for close-in, wide-angle carnage. Then he pulled the four grenades out and slid them across the floor to Sean.

The lieutenant stuck his finger into the barrel of the shotgun as if testing its contents. He nodded to Shellnutt and said "Good job."

"What's in the barrel?" Sean asked.

"Rock salt. Packed full of it. Bounces all over the place and stings the shit out of you. Really incapacitating for a couple of seconds."

Chenoweth laid beneath the breach in the armored door and then nestled the muzzle of the *blunderbuss* into the base of the breach, the trigger guard resting on his chest. He told Sean, "As soon as he stops shooting, throw the grenades in."

Under his breath, Chenoweth muttered, "Fire in the hole."

He pulled the trigger.

The hammering of the machine gun stopped immediately, replaced by the sound of men screaming in pain, until the dull *poomh* of Sean's first grenade.

He threw the rest in sequence, waiting until the one before had burst, throwing each one harder than the last. As he pitched the fourth—and last—grenade, his arm inadvertently pushed against the door…

And it creaked open a few inches.

"Well, I'll be a son of a bitch," Chenoweth said. "Maybe we blew the bolt off and didn't even know it. It ain't like the Krauts to leave it unlocked. See if you can push it open a little more."

The heavy door yielded slowly but without complaint.

"At least we're not choking to death again," Chenoweth said.

"Pretty quiet in there," Sean added. "Should I push it open some more?"

Chenoweth brought his Thompson to the ready as he nodded his approval.

With a hefty shove of his foot, Sean flung the door all the way open.

They were staring into a smoke and dust-filled chamber that looked much like a building's concrete-walled basement. Most of the lights were still on. They could make out the machine gun, overturned and broken on a low berm of sandbags. One German soldier was slumped over the berm. Several others lay motionless on the floor nearby.

"We're going in," Chenoweth told his men. "Let's move out."

With two engineers wounded and two tankers acting as their litter bearers, they were down to ten men. But that was more than enough to cover this cellar, little bigger than a basketball court. None of the men had any doubt this windowless, damp chamber was anywhere but underground. And to their surprise, it even had a working toilet.

"How about that," Sean said as he used the sink to rinse the dust and grime from his hands and face. "All the comforts of home."

Two of the Germans weren't dead, but they were wounded badly enough to pose no immediate threat.

Sean didn't find it odd these casualties, both fully conscious, had never uttered the word *kamerad*, the German act of surrender. Despite their wounds, they glared defiantly at their captors.

"We seen those uniforms before, Lieutenant," he told Chenoweth as he checked them for hidden weapons. "These ain't your ordinary *fritzes*. They're officer cadets. Real hardcore Nazi lunatics."

"Yeah, I know, Sergeant. The ops order mentioned it. Put them over in that corner for now." He pointed to one of his men and added, "Schmidt, you're in charge of these prisoners. If they try anything—anything at all, even look at you sideways—shoot them. Tell them that in German."

In the center of the room were metal stairs leading up to another closed steel door. The stairs looked more like a ladder canted at a steep angle.

"Looks like we're in the basement of Bunker 4," Chenoweth said as he positioned men to cover that door.

Near the base of the stairs was a large, rectangular grate over a floor drain. There was another drain near the blown door through which they'd entered.

"We'd better pull them grates off, Lieutenant," Sean said, eyeing the door at the top of the stairs. "Those drains under them'll make great grenade sumps."

"Yeah, good idea."

On the far wall was yet another armored door. It didn't take any knowledge of German to translate into English what was written on it: *15 Centimeter Battery*.

For the first time since they'd teamed up, Sean saw indecision written on Lieutenant Chenoweth's face. *I know what he's thinking. We're holding the cellar of Bunker 4 by the skin of our teeth. Battalion wants us to*

*probe Bunker 3, too...and now, we're just one door
away from the gun batteries.*

We're gonna need a hell of a lot more guys...

*And either one of those doors could bust open any
second and the whole fucking Wehrmacht could come
spilling in here.*

"Sergeant Moon," Chenoweth said, "you're in
charge here until I get back. I'm going to go find a radio,
report in, and see what they want us to do next."

It had been an hour since Lieutenant Chenoweth left.
Sean and his improvised team of engineers and tankers
had heard nothing from the outside world except the
sound of gunfire from the building above their heads.
That all changed when Fabiano and Kowalski returned,
their arms loaded with boxes of K rations.

"The infantry finally got around to doing
something," Fabiano said to Sean. "There's a company
of our guys crawling all over Bunker 3. The rest of the
battalion's been trying to storm some of the gun turrets
but they can't get through the wire. They're taking a real
beating."

Sean started tossing ration boxes to the men, "Only
half of you clowns eat at a time," he instructed. "If
you're not moving your jaws, you're watching your door.
Is that clear?"

Then he asked Fabiano, "What'd you do with those
wounded engineers you hauled out of here?"

"We put them and a whole bunch of wounded
dogfaces on Sergeant Sokol's tank and drove 'em to the
aid station. There's plenty of wounded to go around, so

we made a couple more trips, too. Then we *liberated* these rations."

"Regular Florence Fucking Nightingales, ain't you? Look around you, Fab. What do you see?"

"I see a big fucking dungeon with three doors."

"Very good. Now pick a door."

Fabiano pointed to the one at the top of the stairs.

"Okay, see the three guys covering that door already? Go join them. Kowalski, go hook up with the guys covering the door to the gun battery. Now you see those big square holes in the floor?"

Both men nodded.

"Guess what they are."

Fabiano replied, "Grenade sumps, right?"

Sean asked, "Do you agree, Corporal Kowalski?"

"Yeah, Sarge. I do."

"Outstanding. Now you know as much as the rest of us."

"Hey, Sarge," Kowalski said, "it's getting dark out. We gonna be stuck in here all night?"

"Who knows, Ski. Besides, down in this tomb, it don't much matter if it's day or night, does it?"

An engineer tore open his ration box, held up the coffee packet, and asked, "Hey, Sarge, okay if we start a little fire for some hot joe?"

"Yeah, go ahead. I might even have some myself."

Sean waited until all of his men had brewed their coffee before he made his. Settling into a corner, he savored its aroma as he brought the canteen cup to his lips...

And then their subterranean refuge trembled as if an earthquake had struck, spilling the coffee all over his chest.

The earth kept shaking, one unsettling tremor every second or two, strong enough to make a man hold on to something for dear life. Strong enough to knock concrete dust loose from the ceiling, too. It drifted down on the GIs, coating them with a gray pall.

And the sound—it was like being inside a bass drum banging out the cadence of a quick march.

"What the hell, Sarge?" Fabiano said. "Are them turrets upstairs firing?"

"I don't think so, Fab. That's incoming. The guns from them other damn forts are trying to sweep our guys off the roof."

"I guess that means the flyboys are done bombing them other forts for the day, right?"

"Yeah, and it means something else, too, Fab. We're cut off down here now. Ain't nobody up top gonna be able to help us out. Those rounds from the other forts can't get us, but we're sure as hell on our fucking own."

A GI shouted, "THEY'RE COMING DOWN THE TUNNEL." His Thompson was leveled, cocked, and ready to fire.

A distant, echoing voice shouted right back, "LIEUTENANT CHENOWETH, NUMBNUTS. DON'T FIRE. I'M LIEUTENANT CHENOWETH."

It was more than just the lieutenant coming. With him was a mob of GIs—Sean couldn't count them, but they were many more than those already in the cellar. Most were lugging something as they ran. One of them even carried the musette bag of a medic.

"Good to have you back, Lieutenant," Sean said. "What's going on outside?"

Struggling to catch his breath, Chenoweth said, "All the other tunnel attacks got beaten back. We're the only ones who've actually gotten in."

"We really ain't into much of anything, Lieutenant."

"That remains to be seen, Sergeant Moon."

The equipment the new arrivals carried was piled up in the middle of the cellar. There was ammunition, more demolition equipment, more rations, and two field radios.

"The radios aren't worth a shit while we're down here," Chenoweth said, "but at least we can use them from the tunnel entrance. Once this fucking barrage stops, of course."

Sean asked, "That shelling hurting us bad, sir?"

The lieutenant nodded somberly. "You bet it is. We've got infantry down all over the place. It's forced our tank support to pull back, too."

Sean looked at all the munitions stacked on the floor. "It sure looks like we ain't done here yet, Lieutenant. I guess that means we won't be pulling out tonight?"

"No, Sergeant, we won't be."

There were shouts and then bursts from Thompsons at the base of the stairs.

Two German grenades—*potato mashers* in GI parlance for their long, wooden throwing handles protruding from tin can-like bodies—bounced crazily down the steps. Tumbling behind them was a soldier, apparently struck by the Thompsons' bullets. Like a sack thrown from a truck, the falling soldier struck the floor with a sickening *ploomp* at the base of the stairs. He remained motionless right where he landed.

One grenade hit the floor and rolled toward Fabiano,

who deftly kicked it into the grenade sump.

The other deflected backward through the open steps and rolled toward the two German captives.

Both grenades exploded within a heartbeat of each other, the one in the sump hurting nothing except the GIs' ears.

The other exploded next to the German captives. Too impaired by their wounds to scurry away, the grenade killed them both.

Schmidt, the engineer guarding them, had been too far from the grenade to get it into a sump. But he'd instinctively thrown himself prone on the floor. Still, he wailed in pain as he caught fragments in his leg and arm.

Sean shook his head vigorously, trying without success to clear this new concussive assault on his already damaged ears. Everyone else was doing the same thing, with the same lack of success.

Fabiano, his Thompson trained at the now-closed door at the top of the stairs, said, "Keep opening up, assholes. I can do this all night."

One of the engineers asked Chenoweth, "What do you want to do with these dead Krauts, Lieutenant?"

"Drag them way down into the tunnel before they start to stink."

After making sure everyone had been resupplied with plenty of ammunition, Sean sat down on a crate of explosives, the same type the engineers had used to blow the first two doors. He watched the metal latch on the crate rattle with each impact of artillery rounds on the surface above them. That rattling was making a sound, he was sure, but he couldn't hear it. He asked Chenoweth, "Which door we gonna blow next, sir?"

The lieutenant pointed to the one that led to the gun

batteries.

"We gonna have to evacuate the tunnel again when we blow it?" Sean asked.

"Yep. It's a shame, too, because this cellar's probably vented well enough so we wouldn't nearly choke to death like after blowing that last door."

"But the blast would kill us if we stayed close, right, sir?"

"Yep."

"And it ain't safe for all of us to leave the tunnel while those damn guns are firing," Sean said. "So I'm guessing we ain't gonna be blowing nothing until they stop, right?"

"Affirmative, Sergeant."

"And I'll bet they shoot until the sun rises and the flyboys can shut them up all over again." He blew out a weary sigh, adding, "It's gonna be a long damn night, Lieutenant."

"Yeah, you're damn right, Sergeant." He settled next to Sean on the crate. "I'm kind of pleased you and your tankers are still here. I wouldn't have blamed you if you hit the road."

"Where would we have gone, Lieutenant? It's not like we could just leisurely stroll back to the rally point. Not with all this lead whistling through the air."

"Well, thanks anyway, Sergeant."

"Just do me a big favor, Lieutenant. Don't go telling nobody I *volunteered* for this, okay?"

Once night had fallen over A-90, Tommy tried to avoid the other airmen. There were still too many questions about what was happening on Zebra Ramp. Every man in the 301st seemed to have noticed the absence of the first yellow Culver. Now the other one was gone, too.

But he couldn't avoid everyone. Especially his bunkmates.

"Krauts blew them out of the sky, didn't they, Half?" Jimmy Tuttle asked. "So what'd you learn from that?"

"That Culvers are easy to shoot down, Jimmy, that's all."

"It's still *too low and too slow, look out below*, I guess," Tuttle added.

"You've got that right."

"But come on, everybody already knows that, Half, except those maniacs like Rocket Man in their L-4s. So what the hell is really going on over there on Zebra?"

Tommy was running out of ways to deflect those questions. As he tried to think of a snappy evasion to this latest probe, he was interrupted by the rumble of trucks coming to a halt outside.

Tuttle glanced out the window. He did a double take and pressed his face against the glass. "You ain't going to believe this, Half, but there's a bunch of *darkies* driving those deuce-and-a-halfs. Wait...there's a white guy with them. He's a *first john*, too. They all look like they're lost to me."

They walked outside, but Colonel Pruitt was at the lead jeep before them. He asked the *first john*—a first lieutenant just like Tommy and Tuttle—where they were going.

The lieutenant shuffled some papers by flashlight and replied, "We've got orders here to deliver these truckloads to Five-Sixty-Second Bomb Squadron, sir."

The unit designation didn't ring a bell to the colonel. He looked at Tommy and Tuttle, who just shrugged.

Pruitt asked, "Any other clues on those orders, Lieutenant?"

"Yeah, hang on a second, sir." He began to shuffle the papers again, looking for something more. "Oh, here it is. A Major Staunton's supposed to sign for it. He around here?"

"Now you're talking," Pruitt replied. "Lieutenant Moon here can help you out. He'll take you over to the other side of the airfield. That's where you'll find the major."

"Give me a second to get into proper uniform," Tommy said. "I'll be right back."

As they waited, Colonel Pruitt and Tuttle took a hard look at the column of trucks. There were four deuce-and-a-halfs in total, with another jeep bringing up the rear.

"Your drivers are all Negroes, Lieutenant," Pruitt said. "Where'd you find them all?"

"Have you ever heard of the *Red Ball Express*, sir?"

"Yeah, but I have no idea what it does."

"Well, Colonel, at the moment, the *Red Ball* is how the whole danged Twelfth Army Group's getting its supplies. This special load we're carrying would've sat in some Normandy depot until the cows came home. Transportation units were working overtime figuring out how to avoid carrying the stuff. Only the Red Ball drivers would haul it. And most of those drivers are coloreds, by the way."

"What's so special about this *stuff*, Lieutenant?"

"It's ten tons of Torpex, sir."

The colonel and Tuttle took a spontaneous step back when they heard that.

Tommy reappeared and jumped into the back seat of the jeep. Tuttle asked him, "Did you hear what's in these trucks?"

"I think I already know, Jimmy. It's Torpex, right?"

Then the column drove off.

"What the hell are they going to do with all that explosive, sir?" Tuttle asked Colonel Pruitt. "Drop it on Hitler's house or something?"

"I think we're going to find out the answer to that question very shortly, Lieutenant."

Chapter Twenty-Seven

At first, Major Staunton was furious. "Who is responsible for entrusting this cargo to coloreds?" he barked at the convoy lieutenant.

"Well, sir," the lieutenant replied, "it says right here *by order of Commanding General, US Army Air Forces, Europe.*"

That meant General Spaatz.

"Oh, I see," Staunton replied, not nearly as belligerent as he'd been a few seconds ago. And as his ire cooled, his mind began to process opportunities that, until this moment, had seemed out of the question.

A few hours ago, he'd checked the weather forecast for the next few days. The climactic mission of *Operation Bucket* was in a race with a storm front due the afternoon of 14 October. The latest forecast had moved up that front's arrival almost twenty-four hours, to the afternoon of the 13th—*tomorrow*. Once the bad weather moved in, all aviation activities, to include *Operation Bucket*, would have to be postponed.

Staunton recalled a conversation he'd had with General Spaatz last month, when the major had sought to postpone an *Aphrodite* test for some minor technical issue. The general had made his displeasure with the delay clear. He hadn't actually uttered the sentence, but it was implicit, without a doubt: *any delay due to some piddling little technical issue would be considered a failure on your part, Staunton, and yours alone.*

Failure: just the thought of the word had stung like a paddling from a schoolmaster. *Aphrodite* had been nothing but a failure to that point. Those who'd contributed to that failure wore the big red *F* around their necks for everyone in War Department to see and remember for a long, long time.

Major Rick Staunton hadn't been saddled with the big red *F* yet, and he was not about to start wearing one now. They had eighteen hours until the weather was forecast to shut down flying. They'd need eight of those hours just to load the Torpex into the baby, but if they started immediately...

He put the brakes on his careening mind. Sure, they'd need eight hours; eight hours of *daylight*. Without it, the ordnance technicians couldn't see what they were doing. For safety's sake, you couldn't have any electricity on the aircraft during the loading to power the interior lighting, and explosion-proof electric lighting, like the kind used by coal miners, for example, was only available at maintenance depots. Any spark could vaporize everything and everyone within several hundred yards—to include the entirety of A-90—and cause a radius of damage far greater. And, of course, kerosene or gasoline-powered lamps, with their open flames shielded only by a layer of easily breakable glass, were out of the question as lighting sources. Sunlight was the only option to illuminate the work.

It was 2100 hours; they wouldn't see a glimmer of daylight until 0630 tomorrow morning. If the weather front was supposed to arrive by midafternoon, that would be cutting it mighty close.

But eight hours was the *book value*. The experienced ordnance techs of the *Bucket* team had done the job in as little as five hours when necessary, without any compromise of safety. *But that was under perfect stateside conditions, not at some makeshift outpost like*

A-90, Staunton told himself. *But surely we can find some way to do it again.*

That bridge crossed, there was another obstacle to clear: the repair to the arming system and its stray voltage had yet to be resolved. All the contacts on the grounding bus bar had been disconnected, burnished until shining clean, and reconnected. Five successive tests would have to be accomplished with no stray voltage found to consider the problem fixed. Each test was a complicated process involving simultaneous ground run-ups of both Flying Fortresses while the mothership simulated "flying" the baby by remote control.

Four tests had been completed during the course of the evening, with no voltage found.

On the fifth test, the flat green line spanning the cathode ray tube of Sergeant Inzetta's oscilloscope was suddenly transformed into a jagged freehand sketch resembling the peaks of a mountain range. The stray voltage—the *phantom*—was back.

"Impossible," Major Staunton fumed as he nudged Inzetta out of the way. Running his hands along leads connecting the oscilloscope to the ship's wiring, he added, "Have you considered this is just a poor test equipment connection, Sergeant?"

"We've got a voltmeter jacked in, too, sir," Inzetta replied. "It kicked a few spikes, just like the scope showed. They can't both be bad connections."

"You're sure of that, are you, Sergeant?" Staunton snarled as he disconnected the test equipment leads and then reconnected them, rocking the alligator clips on the ends of the wires in an attempt to seat them more firmly.

"Try it again, Sergeant. Run another series of tests.

I'll bet you get five out of five."

With groans of frustration, the technicians and mechanics began yet another tedious series of tests, cranking the engines and establishing radio control from the mothership. This time, the voltage spikes appeared on the third test.

Inzetta called a halt to the testing. "What now, sir?" he asked Staunton.

Like a man besieged, Staunton replied, "Burnish every damn connection on that fucking bus bar again, Sergeant. And try to do it right this time."

Inzetta let the offense in that statement pass. Calmly, like a man resolved to his involuntary role in this budding catastrophe, he replied, "That'll take all night, sir."

"Well, isn't that convenient, Sergeant, because you just happen to have all night. Now get your men back to work on the double."

As Staunton stormed off, Rocco Inzetta was sure he could hear the major mumbling, "Or do I have to do everything my goddamn self around here?"

He was still mumbling when he brushed past Tommy like he wasn't even there.

"Anybody see Sergeant Dandridge?" Tommy asked Inzetta.

"Some of the mothership crew went into town, sir. We don't need them to run these tests, so *Major Mumbles* let them go."

"Do you guys always call the major that?"

"Actually, it just came to me, Lieutenant. We usually call that pompous prick a lot worse..." Inzetta caught himself before any more insubordinate talk spilled out. Then he added, "With all due respect, of course, sir. But he does talk to himself a lot."

"We had a guy in the squadron like that once," Tommy said. "We called him *Major Disaster*. Thought he was the only man walking the planet with a lick of sense, even though he was accident-prone as hell."

"What happened to him, sir?"

"According to Axis Sally, he's cooling his heels as a POW in some Stalag Luft."

✯✯✯✯

Back at the 301st, Tommy found Colonel Pruitt in his quarters. When told of the change of plans—the one that would move *Operation Bucket* up an entire day—the colonel replied, "I figured as much. Did you see the weather forecast, Half? Good thing we told Bob Kidd to get here early tomorrow."

Tommy filled Pruitt in on the lingering problem with the baby's arming circuit. The colonel thought it over for a moment and then said, "Where are they planning to arm this thing once it's airborne, Tommy?"

"We figure over the jettison zone should be the safest place, sir."

"Yeah, you ain't kidding," Pruitt replied. "Too bad we don't have any oceans around here we could do it over. You're not planning on flying straight over Toul, either, are you?"

"Not if we can help it, sir."

Pruitt shook his head and said, "God help us all, Tommy."

They moved on to some planning details. Pruitt asked, "You got the escorts all coordinated?"

"Yes, sir. They were pitching a fit, too. Figured we

wouldn't be flying again until the fourteenth. They had to squeeze us back into their busy schedule, the poor bastards."

"Just so they keep the Krauts away," Pruitt replied. "Those big, slow Flying Forts make nice, fat targets."

"I was thinking, sir...can you imagine some *ME* or *FW* jockeys pumping incendiaries into the baby? That would be the last thing they ever did. When she blew up, they'd all be turned to dust. They'd go to Kraut heaven wondering what the hell they did wrong."

Pruitt scanned the mission roster for tomorrow. "I'm going to use Tuttle as my backup," he said. "If something happens to me, or I can't put the junk on the money, it'll be up to him to do the napalm honors. Every other ship in the squadron will go back to hitting Driant's sister forts at first light, along with the rest of Nineteenth Tac Command. That's the most we can do to make sure the baby doesn't get knocked down by a lucky round of Kraut artillery."

The colonel took another look at the weather forecast. "You sure they can't go earlier than noon, Tommy?"

"I think even noon is pushing it, sir."

"It's just that if this cloud cover moves in like the metro guys think it will, it's going to ruin your *coming out of the sun* plan. There won't be any sun. You're all going to stand out against the high cumulus like a sore thumb."

"At least it shouldn't ruin our visibility over the target, sir."

"Let's hope not," Pruitt replied.

The night air carried the rumble of distant artillery into the colonel's quarters. They could feel the impacts of shell with earth, each a faint quiver that passed right through the soles of their shoes.

They both knew what it meant. Somewhere around Metz, GIs were getting pounded.

Tommy had one more question. "Third Army, sir…do they know we're coming early? We know they hit Driant again today. They've got to be well clear of the place by noon tomorrow."

"You're worried about your brother, aren't you, Tommy?"

Before he could answer, a distant yet especially strong impact made the cups on the table rattle.

"You'd better believe it, sir."

"Well, try not to worry about it too much. The updated *Bucket* schedule went out to Bradley's HQ just before you walked in here."

✯✯✯✯

It was just past midnight when General Patton's aide woke him. "General Bradley's on the horn for you, sir. It's urgent."

"It better goddamn well be urgent," Patton grumbled as he climbed out of bed in the country estate near Arnaville, the *maison de campagne* he'd claimed as his headquarters.

Bradley came right to the point. "George, pull all your troops back from Fort Driant immediately. *Operation Bucket* has been moved up."

"Brad, it's the middle of the fucking night. Moved up until when?"

"Today, in the early afternoon. Maybe sooner. Get your men clear."

"Brad, are you aware I have a battalion holding ground inside Driant as we speak?"

"No, I was not." From the sound of his voice, Patton was fairly sure Bradley's face was red and his eyes were bugging out with rage.

"When the hell did this happen, George? And what exactly does *holding ground* mean?"

Patton tried to explain his men's successes so far inside Driant. Bradley sounded less than impressed.

"Pull them out. You're still running a siege, dammit. I specifically instructed you not to do that. I repeat, get your men out of there."

"I can't, Brad," Patton whined. "We're so close to taking the turrets. And once we do that—"

Bradley cut him off. "And once you do that, there's only about a dozen more forts you'd have to take, not to mention Metz itself. I don't want to still be sitting on the Moselle next summer, George, rebuilding your shattered army. Get out of the way and let the Air Force finish this for you."

"It may not be as easy as that, Brad. They've been under a barrage since nightfall. At least they're safe inside the fortifications, for now."

"Hear me and hear me good, George. I will not have another *Operation Cobra* fiasco on my watch."

"And you won't, Brad. You have my word. But do me one favor...I can take this fort. I'm almost there. Just give me some more time."

Bradley sounded cold as ice as he replied, "Oh-nine-hundred. You have until oh-nine-hundred to either take Fort Driant or have your men five miles away from it." He paused and then added, "And I mean oh-nine-hundred *today*, George."

"Thank you, Brad. You'll see...Fort Driant is as good as in the bag."

"Bullshit yourself all you like, George. But don't bullshit me."

Then Bradley rang off. There was a resounding *click* on the line as the circuit was disconnected.

To George Patton, that click sounded like the cocking of a gun pointed right at his head.

✶✶✶✶

To Sean Moon, deep in the cellar below Bunker 4, nothing seemed anywhere near *in the bag*. As unnerving as the continuous bombardment had been, they were safe from it below ground. What really bothered them was what would happen if the bombardment stopped.

"I think our biggest danger is Krauts coming from outside, down the tunnel," Lieutenant Chenoweth said.

"Yeah, you're probably right, sir," Sean replied. "Any Krauts trying to come through the door from the gun batteries or down those stairs are gonna be stepping into a slaughterhouse. Of course, if they manage to let loose with a bunch of grenades, they're gonna take some of us with 'em..."

They stood at the threshold of the door that led to the tunnel and the outside world, reviewing their defenses. The flashes of shells impacting near the far end of the tunnel lit that passageway as if a mass of paparazzi were storming the place.

Sean said, "The only thing that worries me, sir, is if some Kraut gets far enough down the tunnel that he can let loose with a panzerfaust or some other kind of rocket. But as long as this thirty cal here can keep firing, this tunnel's a natural kill zone."

"Yeah," Chenoweth replied, "but I was thinking of something else, too. What if our guys are still holding Bunker 3? I don't see why they would have run when the shelling started. They're as safe in there as we are down here."

"So?" Sean asked. "What's the difference if they're there or not, Lieutenant?"

"Well, they'd have a pretty commanding field of fire over anyone trying to get near this tunnel entrance. Plus, if we're holding Bunker 3, we'd be able to use the tunnel to get back and forth from here to there. And according to the fort's plans, there's no other way in or out of these bunkers, so no Krauts are going to come out of the woodwork on us, not as long as we hold this tunnel."

"We got radios, Lieutenant. Maybe we take a stroll toward the end of the tunnel and see if we can raise them."

"Sure, but if we don't raise them, it doesn't mean they're not there. I think we ought to confirm who, if anyone, is inside Bunker 3. If we find GIs in there, we need to all get on the same page. If there's nobody at all in there, we need to get some of our guys from the cellar to hold the bunker."

"So you're saying we launch a recon patrol…"

"Yeah, that's exactly what I'm saying, Sergeant."

Sean expected Chenoweth to say something more, but he didn't. He just stood there, fixing Sean in a questioning gaze.

"Oh, I get it," Sean said. "You want me to lead the patrol."

"I think you're the best man for the job at the

moment, Sergeant."

He knew the lieutenant was right about that. *It's either him or me that does it...and he's the one who's gotta take care of all the explosives and shit. Right now, I'm just another corn plaster commando with a lot of stripes.*

"All right, Lieutenant. I'll do it. Just remember I didn't volunteer for this shit."

Chapter Twenty-Eight

Sean took three of the tankers for his recon team. He left Fabiano with Lieutenant Chenoweth. "You'll need Fab if you get some trouble down here in the cellar, Lieutenant," Sean said. "He's a good man in a fight. One of the best, in fact. Just remember he's a little off his rocker."

The recon team made its way out of the tunnel, waiting near the door that led outside until the German artillery barrage had swept to another part of Fort Driant's roof. They'd been listening to the impacts sweep back and forth across the fort for hours and gotten the timing of that sweep down to a science. "One thing about them Krauts," Sean told his men, "they can be so damn dependable sometimes."

"How long can they keep this shit up, Sarge?" one of the tankers asked.

"As long as they got ammo, they can shoot," Sean replied. "Those barrels ain't gonna melt. We're listening to lots of guns firing just a couple at a time. I'll bet the gun crews are working in shifts, too. Especially the loaders. You do get beat after a while, dragging around them big, heavy rounds. Gotta get a break now and then."

Another minute passed before Sean said, "Okay, here's our chance. Move fast, but stay the fuck alert and stay close. No stumbling around in the dark."

After each man acknowledged with a nod of his head, he added, "Move out."

It was less than fifty yards to the northeast corner of the building known as Bunker 3, that two-story mini-fortress built into the side of a hill. This was the third time Sean had found himself in action against this bunker. But it was the first time he'd done it without being in the turret of a tank.

One thing they hadn't realized down in the tunnel: an armored observation post perched atop the central fortification was using a searchlight to scan the area within Driant's perimeter. But like the barrage, its sweep seemed to follow a specific pattern. Sean told himself, *Shouldn't be too hard to keep ourselves out of the spotlight.*

They rounded the corner of the bunker to its front face, the side facing away from the hill into which it was built. Just feet from the entryway, they paused, their bodies pressed against the wall for whatever cover it might provide, and tried to shake off the mortal fear that grips every man who doesn't know to what hell his next step will carry him.

Sean decided they wouldn't actually *step* into that unknown; they'd low crawl into it instead. Dropping to their bellies, Sean and his men slithered to the big steel door.

It was unlocked. They pushed it open and found no enemy to oppose them. But there was no friend to meet them, either.

The team rose to their feet. The entryway was a design they'd seen in German strongpoints before: after a straight run of twenty feet or so, there was an abrupt right-angle turn, where you met a setback blast wall with a narrow passage space on either side. Dim electric light leaked around the edges of the blast wall.

"They paid their light bill, at least," Sean mumbled.

There was a sense of emptiness beyond the blast

wall. The floor was thick with concrete dust just like they'd found in the cellar below Bunker 4, shaken loose from the walls and ceiling by the endless barrage. There were footprints in the dust Sean and his men hadn't made, and even in the dim light those footprints looked fresh.

Sean huddled his men together and said, "I'm gonna gamble that there's GIs in here. Stay behind this blast wall."

Before any of the men could ask what form this *gambling* would take, he yelled, "ANY GIs BACK THERE?"

A voice replied, "WHO THE FUCK WANTS TO KNOW?"

"MOON. THIRTY-SEVENTH TANK."

"MOON...THAT'S A PRETTY FUNNY NAME FOR A KRAUT," the voice said.

"YOU AIN'T TOLD ME YOUR NAME YET, PAL."

"CUTTER, TENTH INFANTRY. WHY DON'T YOU TELL ME WHO JUST WON THE WORLD SERIES, *HERR MOON.*"

"THE CARDS."

"SO YOU LISTEN TO THE RADIO, TOO, EH, *FRITZ*? THEN TELL ME THIS: WHO WAS THE WINNING PITCHER?"

"WHO GIVES A SWEET FUCK?" Sean replied. "NOW ARE YOU GONNA CUT THE SHIT AND LET US IN? WE CAN PROBABLY DO EACH OTHER SOME GOOD HERE."

"WHERE YOU FROM, MOON?"

"CANARSIE."

"WHERE THE HELL IN GERMANY IS THAT?"

"IT AIN'T IN GERMANY, NUMBNUTS. IT'S IN BROOKLYN. NOW HOW ABOUT IT?"

Sean could hear hushed voices in discussion but couldn't make out most of the words. There were several different speakers, and they seemed divided on what to do next.

Finally, Cutter said, "HOW MANY WITH YOU, MOON?"

"THREE. LOOK, IF YOU DON'T WANT TO PLAY BALL, WE CAN JUST LEAVE YOU TO FUCKING DIE HERE."

Another hushed conversation ensued before Cutter said, "ALL RIGHT, STEP OUT FROM BEHIND THAT WALL ONE AT A TIME, REAL SLOW."

Sean stepped out first, passing around the wall into a concrete corridor stretching the length of the bunker. Halfway down that corridor were three GIs huddled behind a low pile of rubble. Poking out of that pile was a .30-caliber machine gun aimed straight at Sean.

One of the GIs—a buck sergeant—stood and said, "Shit, why didn't you say you're a tech sergeant?" The voice left no doubt: this was Cutter.

"Why? You wouldn't shoot a Kraut pretending to be a tech sergeant? You in charge here, Cutter?"

He seemed reluctant when he replied, "Yeah, I guess so."

"You *guess* so, Sergeant Cutter? What fucking army you in, anyway? If you're senior, you're in charge, right?"

"Yeah...but I gotta show you something, Sarge," Cutter replied.

He led Sean farther down the corridor. Near its end, they stepped through a door into something that resembled an orderly room. It seemed unoccupied, until Cutter pointed behind a desk.

Huddled in the far corner was a US captain, seated on the floor, his knees pulled against his chest. He looked Sean's way without seeming to see him, the vacant stare through dark-rimmed eyes focused on something far away, perhaps in another dimension only the despondent could see. Sean had seen it too many times before. He'd even felt himself slipping into that hopeless certainty a few times: *you were already dead and there wasn't a damn thing you could do about it.* Officers weren't exempt, either. In fact, combining the extra pressures and responsibilities of command with the relentless slaughter of combat sometimes drove officers over the edge faster than ordinary dogfaces.

Sean asked Cutter, "So when did the captain here lose his marbles?"

"When all that shelling started. We were in the south trench. We tried to get back to the wire and get the hell out of here, but that artillery...it was like they had our number."

"So you guys weren't even supposed to take this bunker?"

Cutter looked at him like he'd just made a bad joke. *"Take the bunker?* Hell, no, Sarge..."

"Any other GIs in here besides your outfit, then?"

"No," Cutter replied, "but there's Krauts on the top floor."

"How many Krauts?"

"I don't know. A lot."

"What about the basement?" Sean asked. "The tunnel entrance?"

"There's nobody there."

"Good. How many guys you got, Cutter?"

"About half the company. Maybe forty guys...out of the eighty we started out with."

"And you're the top kick?"

"Yeah, I think so. All the senior non-coms and officers are dead or missing, maybe...except for the captain over there." Then Cutter shrugged as if to say, *But he's as good as dead to us, too.*

"Forty GIs, huh? That's a whole lotta guys if you're all inside a building like this. Too many, probably. You even *try* to clean out the Krauts?"

Cutter recoiled, as if the mere suggestion of attacking the Germans upstairs was enough to kill him. "Look, Sarge," he pleaded, "half of my guys are so green they still got creases in their pants. When we first came inside here, we walked right into the Krauts. A lot of shooting. Couple of our guys got killed right then and there. A bunch of the rookies just cut and ran. Don't know where the hell they are now. The Krauts went up the stairs, and ever since, it's been *we don't bother them, they don't bother us.*"

Something concerned Sean even more than the fact the Germans were in the building: the misinformation Lieutenant Chenoweth had received from Battalion was dangerously misleading. American troops were *not* holding Bunker 3. They were only hiding here, with no intention—or capability—of fighting anyone. He felt in jeopardy being among them, these men who felt that if they did nothing, perhaps, mortal combat would simply pass them by. They hadn't yet learned that when someone doesn't do his job, everyone dies.

Sean said, "I'll tell you what, Sergeant Cutter. We're gonna get rid of those Krauts on the top floor. Me and my guys just come from the tunnel to Bunker 4 and the gun batteries. There's a platoon of engineers down there who are gonna blow up them guns, but we need to keep the tunnel entrance covered so no Krauts can get in and run up their asses. And we need this bunker, especially the top floor, to do that."

Cutter looked like he was going to be sick. He sputtered, "But…we….we don't…"

"Knock off the blubbering, *Sergeant*," Sean told him. "In fact, me and my guys'll do the hard work for you. How many grenades you got?"

Cutter just shrugged and said, "I don't know. A lot, probably."

"Good. Get us eight grenades. Got any radios?"

"Just a couple of walkie-talkies."

Sean asked, "Do they work?"

"We can't raise anyone back at Battalion."

"Course not. You're too fucking far away. But can you talk to each other?"

"Yeah, I think so."

"Good," Sean replied. "I'll take them, too. Now what about bazookas? You got any?"

"Yeah, we've got two."

"I'll take 'em. How many rockets you got for 'em?"

"We ain't fired them, so unless we lost the rounds out there somewhere…"

"I'll make this easier for you," Sean said. "Get me four rockets."

Cutter looked horrified. "You're not going to try and go up the stairs, are you?"

"Fuck, no. How stupid you think I am, Cutter? We're going outside, up the hill, and fire them rockets through those big gun ports on the top floor."

"But…the barrage…the searchlight…"

"But *nothing*, Cutter. We just gotta synchronize with 'em. How the hell you think we got here? Besides, that searchlight is just like illum rounds. At these distances, you only see the movement, not the thing that's moving. If you freeze, you're invisible. Now get me that shit I asked for, on the fucking double."

Sean watched as Cutter tried to round up a few of his soldiers to collect the equipment. The sullen, unresponsive men were scattered in various rooms along the corridor, huddled together as if hiding from a bogeyman. One soldier, a tall, lean young man slouched with a few others in a corner of what resembled a ransacked kitchen, replied to Cutter's order with a raised middle finger. Sean took that gesture to be aimed at him, too.

Nudging Cutter out of the way, Sean asked the soldier, "What's your name, hot shot?"

Looking up at Sean with the same disregard he'd shown Cutter, the man defiantly replied, "Tillotson." He spoke with the slow, bassy drawl of a Texan. His rifle lay beside him in the floor's dust and grime as if it'd been thrown away.

Sean told him, "Pick up that weapon, Private Tillotson, and get on your feet, right fucking now."

"I ain't doing shit," Tillotson replied. "You're just another dumb fucker fixing to get us all killed."

Sean stood over him, glaring down. "Don't make me say it again, shithead."

Leaving his rifle on the floor, Tillotson rose to his feet with irritating slowness. He was taller than Sean by an inch or two and maybe even had a few pounds on him. Hands balled into fists, his deep voice became a menacing rumble: "Why? What're you gonna do about it, *Sergeant*?"

"How about this?" With the precise skills of an accomplished street fighter, he delivered a quick and powerful left jab squarely into Tillotson's face. Nobody who heard the *pop* doubted he'd just broken the man's nose. The splatter of blood confirmed it.

Tillotson collapsed to the floor like a house of cards. Holding his bloody face in his hands, he wailed, "You broke my fucking nose, you bastard!"

"That's *Sergeant Bastard* to you, pal," Sean replied as he jerked the man back to his feet. "But you're fighting the wrong guys." Then he retrieved the M1 from the floor and slung it over Tillotson's shoulder.

"Take the private here over to the doc," he told Kowalski. "Use the tunnel door downstairs. Tell Lieutenant Chenoweth he can have him, then get your ass right back here."

As he was led from the room, Tillotson whined, "I'm gonna press charges, Sergeant."

"Yeah, you do that, numbnuts. Now get him the hell outta here."

Then Sean turned to the rest of the stunned GIs in the room and said, "Anybody else here got a problem with authority figures today?"

No one said a word.

"Good. Then get up off your sorry asses. You got work to do."

He pointed to a soldier wearing corporal's stripes. "You with the two stripes, let's start earning that non-com pay. Roust the rest of these *sad sacks* from wherever they're hiding and assemble them in the corridor, on the fucking double."

✶✶✶✶

Kowalski slid the heavy iron bolt on the tunnel door in the basement of Bunker 3. Swinging the door open, he prodded Tillotson to walk into the tunnel entrance.

He wouldn't move.

"Look, pal," the tanker said as he pressed his Thompson against the back of the reluctant soldier's neck, "keep feeding me your bullshit and I'll shoot you right fucking here. Nobody'll ever believe the Krauts didn't do it."

Tillotson started walking toward the tunnel, slowly at first, finally reaching a normal pace.

"That's more like it, Tex," Kowalski said.

When they reached the tunnel entrance they'd blown open earlier, Tillotson said, "I'm gonna bring your Yankee ass up on charges, too, Corporal."

"First off, dimwit, I ain't no Yankee. I'm from Chicago. Second, every man in that room saw you take first shot at Sergeant Moon."

"That's a damn lie," Tillotson protested.

"Prove it, deadbeat. It'll be your word against the word of a veteran non-com whose shirts got more time in the laundry than your redneck ass has in this damn army. And as far as bringing me up on charges, I ain't gonna lose no sleep over that, either. Now you better stay close, because if we get separated, those GIs down there are gonna shoot your ass because you don't know the fucking password."

Tillotson had no answer for any of that. Shoulders slumped, holding his hand over his battered face, he looked like a boxer who'd just taken the *ten count*.

"Now get your ass moving, before you bleed out

through that *schnoz* of yours."

By the time Kowalski returned to Bunker 3, Sean had worked out how they'd deal with the Germans on the top floor. He and his three tankers would form two bazooka teams, with two rockets each. They'd exit the bunker the way they came in and climb the hill to its back side, where only the upper reaches of the top floor protruded above its peak. The few trees that had survived the relentless bombardments would augment the darkness to provide concealment—and perhaps some cover—for the teams. After expending their four bazooka rockets into the gun windows of the top floor, they'd immediately rush to those windows and throw their grenades—eight in total—into the bunker.

Sergeant Cutter's men had been organized into four teams: the first on the north staircase; the second on the south staircase; the third would cover the ground floor from any intrusion; the fourth would be in reserve and go wherever needed. Cutter would carry one of the walkie-talkies. Sean had the other radio, with which he'd signal the start of the bazooka teams' attack.

Any Germans not killed or incapacitated outright from the rocket and grenade attack would probably try to flee down the staircases. It would be the job of Cutter's team one and two to cut them down before they could form a new pocket of resistance on the first floor. Any Krauts who attempted to escape through the top floor gun ports onto the hill would be dealt with at close range by Sean's teams using their Thompsons.

Once Sean's teams had finished their work, it would

be up to Cutter and his men to climb to the top floor and secure it. "Make sure you don't rush the top floor from both staircases at once," Sean cautioned, "so you don't end up shooting each other."

Sean's last words to Cutter as his team headed out of the bunker: "Remember what my grandma always used to tell me...*Boy, don't fuck up.*"

As they started up the hill, Kowalski asked, "You think they're gonna be watching out those top floor windows?"

Sean replied, "Yeah, maybe."

"So what happens if they spot us?"

"Then the fight starts a little sooner than planned, Ski. But I'm betting they're more concerned with the GIs on the ground floor at the moment."

Sean's bet was a good one. They made it to a position among a few trees about thirty yards from the bunker without drawing any German fire. "One problem," Sean said softly. "We can't make out the fucking gun windows, dammit. We'll have to wait until the searchlight comes around again."

"But then we'll be lit up, too," Kowalski said.

"Yeah, but things better be happening so fast by then it won't matter."

Sean put the bazooka into firing position on his shoulder. He whispered to the other team, "You guys ready?"

They both answered, "Yeah, Sarge."

"Okay, I'll call your target as soon as it's lit up."

Sean told Cutter over the walkie-talkie, "Ten seconds."

The searchlight was sweeping back their way. Sean muttered, "Almost, almost..."

And then they were bathed in light harsher than any daytime sun. They could see four apertures in the concrete wall, gaping opaque rectangles much wider than they were high.

"TAKE THE TWO RIGHT," Sean called to his other team.

Then there was the *whoosh-whoosh* of the two bazookas firing. As the rockets streaked toward their separate targets, he was sure he'd seen the twinkling muzzle flash of a German machine gun...

Until the rockets flew inside and exploded. He'd barely had time to catch a breath when his loader patted him on the helmet, the signal the bazooka was reloaded.

He fired again. So did the other team.

The searchlight had panned past them. Suddenly, the beam skittered to a halt and reversed itself back toward the bunker. Sean could see clouds of smoke and dust spewing from the windows in the brilliant light. There were no guns firing, only the screams of wounded men inside.

Then, inexplicably, the searchlight resumed its scan across the fort.

"Pineapple time, boys," Sean said. "MOVE OUT."

Racing to the bunker, they hurled grenade after grenade into the windows until they had no more.

As the last one exploded, Sean called on the radio, "Cutter, take the top floor, NOW."

Sean's men climbed onto the roof, ready to shoot down any Germans trying to escape out the gun ports. It seemed like a safe place to be; not one round of the shifting barrage had landed on the bunker since they'd left the tunnel.

Fifteen, then thirty seconds went by with no sound

from the bunker other than the wailing of the wounded. They'd expected gun shots, shouting, any indication Cutter's team was on the top floor.

Sean spat into the radio, "Where the hell are you, Cutter?"

His reply: "We're still on the staircase."

"Why?"

"You blew out all the fucking lights. Pretty slow going in the dark."

Sean said, "In about ten seconds, the searchlight's gonna light the place up like Christmas. Move your ass."

The searchlight swept across Sean and his men as they lay motionless on the roof. It quickly moved on, not bothering to pause on them like some accusing finger.

"I guess they really can't see you if you ain't moving," Kowalski said.

Sean replied, "That's what they tell me."

Cutter was back on the radio. "Okay, we're on the top floor. There's about ten dead Krauts and maybe five or six wounded. There's no fight left in any of them."

"Any of your guys wounded?"

"No. We're okay. But what're we gonna do with *their* wounded?"

"You got a medic with you?"

"Negative, Sarge."

"Then take their weapons and move 'em out of the way."

There was a long pause before Cutter replied, "Roger."

"We're coming in through the windows now, Cutter. Do not fucking shoot us, you hear me?"

****

It was nearly 0430 when the baby's engines were fired up for the fifth—and final—test of the Torpex's ignition circuit. Sergeant Inzetta's exhausted technicians had toiled through the night, reworking every connection on the ship's grounding bus bar. Then they'd conducted four painstaking tests to ensure there was no stray voltage on the wires that would detonate the explosives prior to impact with a target.

Each of those four tests had passed. The trace on the oscilloscope had remained as straight as a ruler; the needle of the voltmeter connected as a confirming backup hadn't so much as quivered.

Just one more test. If it passed, they would've done everything required to ensure the baby's pilots would not be the victims of a premature detonation...

Like those two unfortunate Navy pilots had been.

Her four engines now stabilized at idle, the mechanic on the baby's throttles gently revved them to cruise RPM.

Inzetta's bloodshot eyes were glued to the green glow of the oscilloscope's cathode ray tube. He fiddled with some knobs on the instrument's face, getting the trace line as thin and sharp as it could be.

He knew he was tired, and being tired could lead to mistakes.

Mistakes that could get people killed.

But they just needed one more good test.

He nodded to the tech on the arming switches. "Go ahead, Bob," he told him. Those three words—so simple, yet so critical—nearly caught in his throat.

It was impossible to hear the *click* of those two

toggle switches over the engine noise. But Rocco Inzetta *felt* them being activated.

So did Major Staunton, who was looking over Inzetta's shoulder.

And at the very instant they felt the switches go over, Rocco Inzetta thought he saw that perfectly straight green line on the oscilloscope quiver, like a string vibrating as it was pulled taut.

It couldn't have lasted more than a fraction of a second.

"It's back," Inzetta whispered, surrendering to yet another soul-crushing failure.

Staunton barked, "What did you say?"

"It's back, sir. We've got stray voltage again. I saw it."

"BULLSHIT," the major said. "There was nothing there. Perfect flat line. We're good."

"No, sir," Inzetta replied. "With all due respect, I saw the line trace a little voltage. It was small, barely perceptible, but it was there."

"Sergeant, you're seeing things. I think you're too tired to be objective. But regardless, we've got the fifth good test." He pointed to the tech monitoring the voltmeter and asked, "Did the needle kick?"

The tech shook his head. Maybe it was because that's what he really saw.

Or maybe he knew that's what Staunton wanted as a reply.

"Then that's all we need to know," Staunton said. "The mission is on."

Rocco Inzetta was too tired to argue. As he felt himself surrendering to the unavoidable, he felt a wave of relief come over him:

It's out of my hands. It all belongs to Major Staunton now.

Chapter Twenty-Nine

Just before dawn, Sean made his way down the tunnel to speak with Lieutenant Chenoweth. Unfolding his sketch of the defenses he'd set up, he told the lieutenant, "We hold the whole bunker now, sir, from the basement to the top floor. That means we hold the whole tunnel from Bunker 3 to Bunker 4, too. As you can see on the drawing here, I've got two .30 cals on the ground floor, with interlocking fields of fire that protect the bunker as well as the outside tunnel entrance. The rest of the infantrymen are on the top floor, with good fields of fire in all directions."

Chenoweth nodded and then pointed to two arrow-shaped symbols drawn on the bunker's top floor, asking, "What're these?"

"Bazookas, sir. We've got two, with a couple of rockets between them. They're set up at the ends of the building so the backblast won't roast any of our own guys."

"Good plan," Chenoweth replied. "Best thing about it is that we don't have to wait for the Air Force to shut those guns up anymore. We won't need to go outside when we blow the door. We just go down the tunnel to your Bunker 3."

"*My* Bunker 3, sir?"

"Yeah, *yours*, Sergeant Moon. You stay there and keep those dogfaces you found straight. Take the big radios with you, too, so you can keep the whole damn Army informed of what we're doing."

"No problem, Lieutenant. Got you covered."

Chenoweth asked, "Those GIs with you...have they

eaten anything?"

"They won't starve for a while," Sean replied. "They scoffed down whatever food the Krauts left behind."

"Good, because we're about out of K rations. I can't even feed my own guys now. No way we can feed forty more."

"Yeah," Sean replied, "I hear you, Lieutenant. So when are you gonna be ready to blow the door?"

"In about five or six minutes, I think."

"And what happens after you blow it, sir?"

"We wait until the gas clears and then we storm ourselves a gun battery."

****

The sun still wasn't up when Tommy arrived at Zebra Ramp. There was a flurry of activity around the baby: pallets loaded with the Torpex were being positioned alongside the ship, waiting for the delicate loading process to begin at first light. But when he stepped into the operations tent, it was obvious that something wasn't quite right.

"Did the arming system test fail again?" he asked Sergeant Inzetta.

The despair in Inzetta's eyes seemed to be saying *yes*, but he was shaking his head *no*.

"What's wrong, then?"

"Dandridge got a little banged up last night, sir. Truck accident."

"Is he okay?" Tommy asked.

"I guess so, sir."

"Where is he?"

Inzetta pointed toward the mess tent.

When Tommy saw Sergeant Dandridge, he definitely didn't look okay. Both his eyes were blackened. There was a blood-spotted bandage covering half his forehead. He appeared to be favoring his left arm; moving it was obviously painful.

"I'm all right, sir," Dandridge told Tommy. "Just a couple of bumps and bruises, that's all. Damn truck we hitched a ride back to base on got run off the road. Ended up nose down in a ditch. The guys in the back— me included—got thrown around pretty good."

"No," Tommy said, "you're not all right. You've got a head injury. You can't fly with that. Not until a doctor signs you off."

"I don't need a doctor, sir. I told you, I'm okay."

Tommy wasn't having any of it. He took Dandridge by the arm—his good, right arm—and started to lead him out of the mess tent. "I'm taking you to see the flight surgeon, Sergeant. He'll decide if—"

"NO," Dandridge said, pulling his arm away. Then, less stridently, he added, "I mean, no, *sir*. Let's not do that. Please."

"Why the hell not, Sergeant?"

"Because I've got to fly this mission, sir. I've *got* to. It's important for a whole lot of reasons."

Tommy looked at him skeptically. "Is Major Staunton putting you up to this?"

"No, sir. This is my own decision. And putting the baby on the money is my job, nobody else's. I'm not going to let some fill-in take over now and screw everything up."

"I still wish you'd come with me to see the flight surgeon, Ira."

Dandridge was startled by Tommy's use of his first name. Never before in his time in the Army Air Force had an officer done so. But every reason he'd ever been given for that strict protocol—like the erosion of respect for superiors bred of familiarity—suddenly didn't seem to have any validity. He'd never respected Lieutenant Tommy Moon more than at that moment. And he could tell the feeling was mutual.

Within minutes, Sean and the radio operators were on the top floor of Bunker 3. With their antennas stuck outside the building through the gun ports, they quickly established contact with 5th Division HQ. When they reported how much of Fort Driant was in their hands, the voice from Division sounded as if he either didn't believe them or considered their transmission a German ruse. The voice requested the information be repeated three times, each request with a different challenge from the code tables. Only after each of the three challenges received its correct authentication did Division seem to take them seriously. The attack on the gun batteries was to continue without delay, they were told, and progress reports were to be sent every fifteen minutes.

"Sounds like they want us to do this all by ourselves," Sean fumed. "Might be swell if they sent some reinforcements."

But he knew it would be a while before they'd see any help. As long as the other forts were still hurling their protective fires at Driant, no GIs would be setting foot inside its perimeter. It would take the sunrise—and the ensuing return of Ninth Air Force planes over those forts—before that could happen.

Sergeant Cutter's walkie-talkies provided decent communication from floor to floor. Sean's set came alive with news from the ground floor: the engineers and infantry from the cellar of Bunker 4 were streaming in from the tunnel.

"Okay," he replied, "that means the door to the batteries is gonna blow any second now. Put the lieutenant on when he gets there."

Looking down from the top floor, they didn't so much hear the explosion as feel it; like the single *thump* of a heart's pulse beneath your fingertips. What they could see, however, was far more dramatic: the jet of dust, debris, and hot gas venting from the tunnel's outside entrance, forming a thick gray cloud spreading rapidly across a vast expanse of ground.

Lieutenant Chenoweth's voice spilled from the walkie-talkie now. "As you can see," he said, "we did the deed. I figure about an hour before we can go back in. Good thing that door between your bunker and the tunnel still works or we'd be getting a good dose of that blast down here in the cellar right now."

Sean replied, "When you do go back in, how about me and some of my guys go with you, sir? You could probably use the help."

"Negative. The best way you can help now is make sure no Krauts jump our asses. So stay where you are."

Kowalski looked at Sean and said, "Gee, Sarge, the lieutenant just did you a favor, and you look disappointed. You really want to go back down the tunnel that bad?"

Sean wasn't sure what bothered him most: that he really did want to go back into the tunnel and take those gun turrets or that Kowalski had read him like a book.

But there was little time right now for self-analysis.

"Mind your damn business, Ski. But if you really want to know, I think I've done a little too much volunteering for one week."

Sean keyed the walkie-talkie, asking Chenoweth, "What do you want me to tell HQ when I report in every fifteen damn minutes?"

"Just tell them the God's honest truth. If that's not good enough for them, tell them they can come out here and do it themselves."

Sean smiled. He'd relish the opportunity to say precisely that.

★★★★

As the morning sun began to climb above the horizon, Sean figured three things would happen shortly: the bombardment of Fort Driant would stop; the Germans within Fort Driant would try to take back Bunker 3 and the tunnel with an assault along the fort's earthen roof; GIs with tank support would re-enter Driant's perimeter to continue the assault.

By 0800, only two of those three events had come to pass. He'd seen the formations of American planes high overhead, on their way to pummel the Moselle forts for another day. Within minutes of their sighting, the guns of those forts ceased their bombardment of Fort Driant.

A few minutes after that, German soldiers—seeming like hundreds but probably no more than fifty—began to swarm from the north and east corners of Driant, converging on the battle-scarred terrain surrounding Bunker 3.

"What do we do?" Sergeant Cutter asked, the fear driving his voice up an octave.

"It's simple, Cutter," Sean replied calmly as he prepared map coordinates to transmit to headquarters. "We call in our own artillery now. Any Krauts left standing after that, we shoot them."

He called in the fire mission and then told Cutter, "Tell all your guys that when I call out *SPLASH*, duck down behind something real solid. A lot of those rounds are gonna hit real close, and some'll be airbursts. A bunch of shit may come flying through the windows."

A minute later, the rounds from several GI artillery batteries burst all around Bunker 3 in a time-coordinated volley. Sean was right; some shell fragments did *whiz* through the gun ports, bouncing around the corridor until their energy was spent. The only GI hurt in the bunker was a man who, in wonder, picked up a fragment after it came to rest on the floor. He didn't realize it would still be sizzling hot. It burned a few layers of skin off his hand.

The Germans outside weren't so lucky. Their assault force, suddenly thinned as if a steel rake had culled it, became disorganized and fell back.

"Gotta love those cannon-cockers," Sean said.

There was a call on the walkie-talkie from the first floor. "We got a problem, Sarge," the voice told Sean. "There's a runner here from Lieutenant Chenoweth. He says the door didn't blow."

"What? Send him up here," Sean replied.

The runner was one of the infantrymen who'd joined them in the tunnel yesterday. To Sean's incredulous question, he replied, "Really, Sarge, it's no bullshit. The fucking door did not blow. Bent a little, but it's still closed tight as a bank vault."

"Well, I'll be a son of a bitch," Sean said. "What's the lieutenant gonna do now?"

"He wants you guys to cover him real good, because the engineers got to go out to the half-tracks and get more C-3." The runner paused and then asked, "The half-tracks...they are still there, right? They didn't get blown up or nothing with all that artillery?"

Pointing him toward a gun window, Sean replied, "See for yourself. It's a fucking miracle, I guess...but they're still intact, near as I can tell. Probably got the shit dinged out of them, though. Okay, tell the lieutenant we got him covered."

A few minutes later, four of Chenoweth's engineers popped from the tunnel door and sprinted to the half-tracks.

"Hey, look," Cutter said, "the Krauts are rolling out some kind of gun from behind Bunker 4!"

Sean watched as the GI infantrymen tried without success to pick off the four-man crew pushing a 37-millimeter anti-tank gun into firing position. "You ain't gonna get 'em as long as they're behind the gun's shields," he said. "Let's see what those bazooka guys of yours can do."

"But what if they start shooting that thing at us?" Cutter asked.

"Just keep your fucking heads down, that's all," Sean replied. "That puny little peashooter can't hurt you in here. I shot this bunker up with my tank's main gun plenty and didn't hurt nothing or nobody."

The bazooka crew didn't think they could hit the German piece. "It's too far," the gunner said.

"Bullshit," Sean replied. "It's about one-fifty yards. Trust me. I've been here before."

The bazooka man gave him a skeptical look but lined up the German gun in his sights. "One-fifty, you say?"

"Yep."

Meanwhile, the German gun crew got off their first round. It struck one of Sean's dead tanks, exploding against its hull but damaging nothing.

"Not very smart," Sean mumbled. "That's a wasted round. Probably scared the shit out of them engineers in the half-tracks, though."

He tapped the bazooka man on the helmet. "You gonna shoot sometime today, pal, or what?"

With a deafening *WHOOSH*, the rocket left the tube and flew toward its target. It missed, striking the ground and exploding just a bit short, spraying a geyser of dirt into the air.

"Well, you got 'em dirty, at least," Sean said as the loader rammed in another rocket. "Bring your sight picture up just a hair."

The bazooka fired again. This time, it flew straight into the shield of the German gun, the ensuing explosion raising the piece several feet off the ground and flipping it over backward.

The four men of the German gun crew lay motionless and exposed around their overturned weapon. Whether they were dead, wounded, or just stunned, the GIs in Bunker 3 couldn't tell.

"You can shoot 'em to your heart's content now," Sean told Cutter.

Then they watched with satisfaction as the engineers, hands filled with crates of explosives, ran back into the tunnel.

Sean checked his watch; it read 0830. He walked over to the radio set.

"Gotta check in with HQ," he said. "Too bad we got a big fat nothing to tell them."

By 0900, Tommy had been back and forth between Zebra Ramp and Operations at the 301st several times, shuttling the latest weather reports to the Flying Fortresses' pilots and status updates for the squadron's switchboard to pass on to 3rd Army. The weather was deteriorating faster than anyone had imagined. Already, patchy clouds had yielded to the thick cumulonimbus announcing the coming of bad weather.

As he returned to Zebra Ramp once again, the baby was still cordoned off; the loading of the Torpex was still underway and probably would be for at least the next three hours. But it was a flurry of activity around the mothership that caught his attention. Her number 2 engine was uncowled, with mechanics clustered around it on A-frame ladders and oil drums serving as maintenance stands.

"What's going on?" Tommy asked the mothership's flight engineer.

"Oil pressure indication's going nuts, sir. Looks like the transmitter's shot. We just replaced the relief valve, but no joy."

"Got another transmitter, Sarge?"

"Yeah," the flight engineer replied as he pointed to the baby. "We got four of them hanging right over there, just as soon as we can get at them."

"You mean you're going to swap with one of the baby's oil pressure transmitters?"

The sergeant nodded.

Tommy puzzled over that for a moment. No jug pilot would ever even think about leaving the ground with a fluctuating oil pressure indication.

Surely, the pilots of a flying bomb wouldn't either, right?

He asked the sergeant, "You sure that's the smart solution?"

"It's the one Major Staunton wants, sir. And what the hell else are we going to do? There isn't a B-17 parts depot within three hundred miles of here."

"What about Captain Pym? He's the one who's going to be flying the baby."

"You'll have to ask him about that, sir," the flight engineer replied.

Tommy found Captain Pym in the operations tent, checking his parachute. When Tommy asked about having to contend with the fluctuating oil pressure indication, Pym just shrugged. "One way or the other, Lieutenant Moon, that plane will be written off a couple of hours from now. As long as that pressure needle's bouncing and the temp's normal, I'm good with it, and so is my co-pilot. Better you guys in the mothership have a reliable indicator. She's got a lot more flying to do."

Tommy replied, "I know what you're saying, sir, but aren't we throwing basic safety practices to the wind here? What's going to happen if you shut that engine down? Or worse, it seizes up, catches fire, and maybe tears off its mounts. You're sure as hell not going to try and land her, and we won't have enough control over her with the remote system to contend with the asymmetric thrust."

With a weary smile, Pym replied, "That won't be my problem, Lieutenant. I've just got to get her off the ground and then float myself back down." He paused and then added, "And it won't be your problem, either, because you guys can't even see the baby's engine gauges on the monitor. All you need to know is if she's flying where Dandridge points her or not."

Major Staunton was at the mission status board, revising the departure time for the *Bucket* mission. He'd just erased *1300*. In its place, he wrote *1400* in grease pencil.

"That gets us right up against the weather, sir," Tommy told him. "In fact, if that front moves any faster, it'll get us *behind* the weather."

And if they were *behind the weather*, they probably wouldn't see enough of the ground to put the baby anywhere near the target.

"It doesn't matter now, Lieutenant Moon," Staunton said. "We're committed. If it wasn't for that damn engine problem on the mothership now…"

He gave Tommy an accusing look, as if it was somehow all his fault.

★★★★

At exactly 0901, General Bradley was on the line to Patton's headquarters. "Time's up, George," Bradley said. "Where are your people?"

His voice had the tone of a drillmaster scolding a cadet.

Patton replied, "My men are on the verge of making

history, Brad. We're about to capture the gun batteries of Fort Driant."

"That's what you told me thirty minutes ago," Bradley said. "And thirty minutes before that, too. Withdraw your troops from the fort, General."

"Brad, listen to me. Nearly all my men are withdrawn to the five-mile line you've drawn. I've got less than a hundred men inside Driant's perimeter but they're—"

"No, George. You listen to your commander. I don't care if you have only ten men inside Driant. Or even one. I will not put American soldiers on the wrong end of friendly air power. Not again. And neither will you. Withdraw your men. *Now.*"

"I can't, Brad. I mean…it won't happen that quickly."

"And why not?"

"It'll be so much harder for them to withdraw than to keep attacking. They'll be running a gauntlet of German fire, surrendering the advantage they've gained so brilliantly. How can you ask me to sacrifice those fine men who are so close to victory? Besides, we have more time. We've just received word the *Bucket* mission's been pushed back another hour…and with the weather that's promised, I'm willing to bet they never come at all."

"Yes, I know about the delay, George, but it doesn't change a damn thing. I want those men at least five miles from Fort Driant, and I want them to start moving that way right now."

There was silence from the other end of the line.

Seething, Bradley asked, "Do you understand me?"

"Yes, Brad. I understand."

"Good. I eagerly await your next report, George."

Bradley rang off. Patton told himself, *And with any luck at all, that next report will be the one in which I announce the fall of Driant's guns...and Brad will forget all about that withdrawal order.*

In fact, he'll be pushing me to plow forward and take Metz.

Chapter Thirty

It was already past 1000 hours. The explosion from the tunnel Sean and the GIs in Bunker 3 were expecting still hadn't come. Instead, the men on the ground floor reported several brief bursts of gunfire, accompanied by dull *thuds* they took to be the detonation of grenades. Whose grenades they were, nobody could tell.

When they'd tried to make their report to HQ at fifteen past the hour, the radio operators made a startling discovery: both the radio sets were dead. The batteries had given out.

"Ain't you got no spares?" Sean asked.

The reply: "These *are* the spares, Sarge. We could try putting them out on the roof and let them bake in the sun for a while. Sometimes that rejuvenates them a little."

"Yeah," Sean replied. "I seen that done before. But how much sun you counting on seeing through them fucking clouds? I got a better idea. There's that kitchen downstairs. Where there's a kitchen, there's a stove. We can cook the bastards. That'll be faster, don't you think?"

"Worth a try," one of the radiomen said. He and his partner each tucked a bulky battery pack under an arm and trudged off down the staircase.

An out-of-breath infantry runner from Chenoweth's team passed the radiomen as he came up the stairs. "We got trouble, Sarge," the runner told Sean. "The Krauts in Bunker 4 got frisky again, dropped another couple of grenades down the stairs on us before we persuaded them to shut the fucking door."

"Anyone hurt?" Sean asked.

"Yeah, dammit. We got three wounded. One of them's the lieutenant. He's still on his feet and calling the shots, but he's beat up pretty bad."

"Shit. What about the other two?"

"Stretcher cases, but the doc says they're not gonna die or nothing. Not yet, anyway."

"Fuck," Sean mumbled. Then, at full volume, he said, "We gotta get our wounded the hell outta here."

"Actually, Sarge, the lieutenant's talking like maybe we all better get outta here. The grenades fucked up a lot of the engineers' stuff. We're all out of food, too, and the Krauts finally cut off the water. All we've got left is what's in our canteens. He's not sure we'll be able to blow anything else. But he's still trying."

★★★★

General Bradley was on the landline again, at 1045 hours. "I've been patiently waiting for your call, George," he told Patton. "But I'm out of patience now. Where are the men who were on Fort Driant?"

"I don't know, Brad. We've lost contact with them."

There was silence on the line for several seconds. To George Patton, those seconds felt like a lifetime.

Finally, Bradley said, "Dammit." Then he rang off.

Patton asked his G3, "What unit is that still inside Driant, anyway?"

"It's a hodgepodge, sir," the G3 replied. "From what we know, it's a mix of Fifth Division infantry and engineers, with some tankers thrown in. They're using a call sign from 37th Tank—*Papa Gray 2-6*."

"Tell every commander from Corps right down to

the battalions I want a pullback order transmitted to that call sign every ten minutes beginning now and until I say differently."

"Do you want to send it in the clear, General?"

Patton thought that one over for a moment and then replied, "Negative, Colonel. We're not that desperate. Code it."

A few minutes before 1100 hours, the ordnance section crew chief walked into *Bucket's* operations tent with surprising news. "The Torpex is loaded and wired, sir," he told Major Staunton.

The burst of elation Staunton felt was immediately snuffed out by suspicion and dread. "How is that possible?" he asked the ordnance chief. "It should have taken another hour or two, easily. You didn't take any shortcuts, did you, Sergeant?"

"No, sir. No shortcuts. Let's just say we're getting the hang of this."

Still skeptical, Staunton stepped outside to look at the two Flying Fortresses sitting on the ramp. Sure enough, the mechanics already had an engine opened up on the baby. They were busily installing something on that engine.

"They're clear to hang that oil pressure transmitter now, sir," the ordnance chief said. "Once they finish the swap on the mothership, they're ready to go."

Staunton ran back inside the tent. "Round up the flight crews," he ordered the operations sergeant. "We're going early. Get a message to Third Army to that effect. We're going to beat this weather yet."

"What time should I tell them we'll be over the target, sir?"

"Tell them 1230 hours, Sergeant."

It had only taken a few minutes to bring the coal-fired oven in Bunker 3's kitchen up to temperature. They put the radio battery packs on a cooking pan and slid them inside, not daring to close the oven door.

"We've got to keep a good eye on them," one radio operator told the other. "They're in cardboard cases, for cryin' out loud. If the case goes up in flames, we're fucked."

"Yeah," the other operator replied. "How long you figure we should keep them in there?"

"What do I look like, a scientist? How the hell should I know?"

The batteries answered the question for them. After about ten minutes, the cardboard cover of one began to singe. Using a scrounged towel to keep their hands from being burned, they pulled both batteries out of the oven. They'd tried to dampen the towel in the kitchen sink but found the Germans had cut off the water to Bunker 3, as well.

When plugged back into the radio sets, the radiomen found they'd restored enough juice to operate the receiver for a while, but trying to transmit depleted the battery immediately. Sean told them, "Put the one you just killed back in the oven. Don't broil it this time, just warm the bastard. Use the other one to monitor the command net. Maybe we'll get lucky and pick up something useful."

Five minutes later, the radio had, indeed, picked up something useful: a coded order for *Papa Gray 2-6.* They were to abandon Fort Driant and withdraw to the town of Gorze, some five miles to the west.

"You sure that order's on the level?" Sean asked.

"If it ain't, Sarge, the Krauts just broke our code book."

"You're right," Sean replied. He grabbed one of Cutter's infantrymen, telling him, "Get your ass down the tunnel and tell Lieutenant Chenoweth we've been ordered to pull out. You better haul ass the whole way, too."

As the runner set off down the stairs, Sean checked his watch. It read 1125.

The runner didn't have to *haul ass* for very long. As soon as he got to Bunker 3's cellar, he ran headlong into the rest of Lieutenant Chenoweth's men. They were all huddled together after their own dash down the tunnel, waiting for the next attempt to blow the door to the gun batteries. Chenoweth, battered as he was from the last grenade attack, had the detonator in his hands as an engineer connected the wires from the explosives.

"Hold up, sir," the runner called out. "Sergeant Moon's got orders for us to pull out."

"Oh, for cryin' out loud," Chenoweth said. "*Now* they want us to pull out?" He looked at the detonator in his hands like it was suddenly the most useless thing in the world:

Do I turn the handle on this thing or not?
If I don't, well...all this boils down to just another

stalemate.

If I do—and the door blows this time—maybe we kill a few more Krauts, even if we can't exploit it.

Will it change our orders if we actually blow the door open?

He told the runner to return to Sergeant Moon and have him ask HQ that very question.

"Don't know if he can, Lieutenant," the runner replied.

"Why not?"

"Looks like those radios can only receive, not transmit."

Chenoweth dropped the detonator to the floor, muttering, "Fuck it."

But he picked it back up and said, "Here goes nothing." Then he yelled, "FIRE IN THE HOLE."

He counted to three and then turned the crank.

He expected a roaring explosion.

He got nothing but a deafening silence.

"Shit. It didn't blow."

Slumping against the tunnel wall, Chenoweth felt whatever strength he had left drain from him. The grenade wounds were taking their toll in pain and blood.

Struggling to get some volume in his voice, he said, "Section leaders, get your men organized. We're pulling out."

He told the runner, "Better get Sergeant Moon down here before…"

And then he fell unconscious.

The mothership's engines were already running

when Dandridge finally arrived on the flight line. Tommy had seen how difficult his injured arm had made donning his flight suit and parachute harness. Climbing into the Fortress would be another problem. Usually, the men who rode in the nose entered through the hatch on the lower forward fuselage. To avoid unnecessary ground equipment around the ship that could easily be blown into whirling propellers, the crewmen would enter by grasping the hatch frame—some six feet above the ground—and swinging up into the aircraft like a gymnast. But it took two good arms to accomplish that feat. For this mission, Tommy had seen to it that the ground crew was standing by with a ladder so Dandridge could get through the hatch with the least amount of trouble.

As they settled into the nose compartment, Dandridge asked, "What if we have to jump, sir? I don't think I'll be able to do it."

"Sure you will," Tommy replied. "I had to bail out once. Smacked into the stabilizer on the way out and broke my arm. But I got the chute open somehow...even climbed down out of the tree I landed in. If I can do it, you can do it."

As the mothership taxied to the runway, Dandridge checked out the remote control gear. "I think I've got another problem, sir," he said. "The switch on the control box—the one that selects the other functions—I can't work it too well with my left hand. I'll either have to let go of the joystick to use my right or—"

"Or you tell me what you need with that switch, and I'll do it for you."

Dandridge sounded relieved as he said, "That'll work, sir."

Then they were airborne, climbing into the scattered cloud deck that seemed to be dropping lower by the minute.

Lieutenant Wheatley's voice came over the interphone. "Wheels up at 1202 hours."

On board the baby, Captain Pym and his co-pilot cranked her engines. As number 3—the one with the faulty oil pressure transmitter installed—settled into the mechanical purr of idle RPM, her oil pressure gauge reading was normal and steady as a rock.

"I don't see what all the fuss was about," Pym said. "It's reading fine."

His voice grew tense as he added, "Now let's see if we can get this widow-maker off the ground."

On the other side of A-90, Sergeant McNulty and his mechanics had just dispatched Colonel Pruitt and Lieutenant Tuttle, both their aircraft loaded with napalm. The other mechanics of the 301st were waiting for their jugs to return for the third refueling and rearming of the day. They stopped preparations to watch as the two Fortresses took to the sky. First came the one that looked like a normal B-17, its turrets bristling with machine guns. "She must be awful light," Sergeant McNulty said, "because she got off the ground like a scared cat."

The second Fortress, painted yellow and stripped of her guns—the one they didn't know was referred to as *the baby*—was now taking her place at the end of the runway. One of the mechanics asked McNulty, "Hey, Sarge, you got any idea what they were loading into that girl this morning?"

"Yeah, I think I do," McNulty replied.

"Well, you gonna tell us what it was?"

"Nope. Ain't none of your business."

Another mechanic asked, "Well, tell us this, Sarge—you think they're going to come back here after their mission?"

McNulty replied, "One of them, maybe."

Halfway down the runway, Captain Pym began to have serious doubts the baby would ever get airborne. She'd bounced into the air a couple of times, but after each bounce had settled back to the runway. He was getting as much power out of the engines as the book allowed.

But she still wasn't flying. And the trees at the end of the runway had never looked so tall.

Need more power!

He teased the throttles forward just a little more, watching the manifold pressures on the engines rise above 50 inches, well beyond the *Do Not Exceed* limits.

And she still wouldn't fly.

Maybe she knew her fate...and refused to accept it.

Maybe the ordnance crew had loaded the Torpex incorrectly, shifting her CG too far forward.

Or maybe she was just too heavy—and too war-weary—to break gravity's hold.

This is all wrong, Pym told himself. *I either throw the book away...*

Or I'm going to die right here.
And take this whole airfield with me.

It was just a simple reflex, requiring no thought, no calculation on Captain Pym's part: he jerked the control column all the way back.

And the baby rose. Hesitantly, but she was at least climbing.

He was sure he could count the leaves in the treetops as they cleared the airfield boundary.

Only as the co-pilot was retracting the landing gear did they notice the oil pressure indication on number 3—the one with the faulty transmitter from the mothership—had fallen to zero.

Major Bob Kidd—*Rocket Man*—was airborne, too. He'd wasted no time flying to A-90 that morning to join the 301st, hoping to beat the deteriorating weather. The orders he received from Colonel Pruitt were simple: he was to get airborne and loiter several miles west of Fort Driant, awaiting instructions from *Almighty Four-One,* the mothership, to perform a BDA—a bomb damage assessment—following a *special air operation.*

Once airborne, however, he decided to deviate slightly from those orders. He'd perform the BDA, no problem. But it couldn't hurt to have a look at the fort *before* the *special air op*—whatever that was—so he'd have a better frame of reference to determine if they actually had caused any damage. He'd been over Driant any number of times in the last few weeks, and no matter how it had been battered by shells and bombs, it always looked the same to him: pockmarked earth and impregnable structures that didn't seem to be harmed in the least.

They may have to blow the top right off this hill for me to tell if this special air op did any good at all.

The only stroke of good luck had been that both the engineers' half-tracks still ran, despite sitting still and in the open on Fort Driant since yesterday afternoon. They'd been battered thoroughly and punctured occasionally by shell fragments, but their thin armor, coupled with the defilade in which they'd been parked, had managed to save them from destruction. Still, both had useless radios due to severed whip antennas, and one had a shredded front tire.

"Don't matter it's got a flat," Sean told the half-track's reluctant driver. "It'll drive good enough to get you out of here."

But still, there were only two vehicles. A half-track was designed to carry a twelve-man squad of infantry. Their wounded alone—including Sergeant Cutter's battle-fatigued captain—filled up one vehicle bed.

The other half-track—the one with the shredded tire—would become an armored weapons carrier for the machine guns and their crews. The rest of the GIs— some fifty men—would have to walk.

"This pullout," Sean told the squad and section leaders, "it's gonna be in three groups, real orderly. We don't want no big crowd gathering in front of the bunker or the tunnel so one fucking shell gets you all. You guys on the top floor with me...we're gonna cover everybody else's withdrawal. We'll be the last ones out. The track with the wounded guys goes first. The infantry who was in the tunnel with the lieutenant will provide protection for it."

He drummed his fingers on one of the radio sets, still awaiting its batteries from the oven. "If we get one of these bastards to transmit, we'll try and call in smoke to cover us. If we can't...well, your mama told you there'd be days like this, right? Now, next out will be the engineers and the rest of the guys on the first floor. The gun wagon will go with you. Then us guys upstairs will bring up the rear."

Chapter Thirty-One

Captain Pym wrestled the baby through her slow, circling climb. The oil pressure on number 3 remained firmly planted at zero on the gauge. But the oil temperature indication was normal, and, most importantly, the engine was still running smoothly.

"By the book, we should shut her down," his co-pilot said.

"Fuck the book," Pym replied, "and we're not going to tell them shit about this, either. What they don't know won't hurt them. If that engine was really out of oil pressure, it would have crapped out already."

Level at 2,000 feet over the ordnance drop zone, control of the baby was passed to the mothership. Pym took a deep breath and said, "Okay, it's showtime."

Both pilots left their seats, snapped on their parachute packs, and moved aft to the arming switches for the Torpex. Carefully lifting the guards on the two switches, each pilot held one toggle in his fingertips.

Pym tried to push the thought from his mind that flipping that switch just might be the last thing he'd ever do. But his voice was full of that fear as he asked his co-pilot, "Are you ready?"

He wished he hadn't said it like that. It sounded too much like an abbreviated form of *Are you ready to meet your maker?*

The co-pilot tried to speak his answer but couldn't. Perhaps he, too, was feeling his imminent demise. The words stuck in his throat.

The best he could manage was an affirmative nod.

One more deep breath by each man, and then their

fingers began to push both switches toward the *Armed* position.

On board the mothership, Tommy watched as the two parachutes blossomed in the baby's wake. "Well, it looks like those guys got out okay," he said. "The baby's all yours, Sergeant."

But he didn't get an acknowledgement. When he looked to Dandridge to see why, he found his head slumped against the sidewall, the control box dangling from his lap.

"Someone get down here and take care of Dandridge," Tommy called over the interphone. "He's unconscious."

"Who's flying the baby?" It was Lieutenant Wheatley's voice, sounding panicky.

"I am," Tommy replied.

"So what the hell happened to Sergeant Dandridge?"

"I wish I knew," Tommy replied. "All I know is he's out like a light. That knock he took on the head...maybe it finally caught up with him."

"Can you really fly the baby, Moon?"

"I'm giving it one hell of a try."

Wheatley asked, "You're just going to dump her, right?"

"Yeah, I'm going to dump her...right on Fort Driant. Give me a left turn. Come around to a heading of one-zero-zero degrees."

Wheatley didn't sound convinced. "Are you sure you're going to be able to pull this off, Moon? You put that thing in the wrong place and—"

"Tell me something I don't already know. And yeah, I'm going to try my damnedest to pull this off. Now am I going to get that heading change, or what?"

Wheatley put the mothership into the turn Tommy requested. Then he said, "I need authorization for this, Moon."

"You do, eh? What are they going to say? No? Bring the baby back and land her? Or sure—go ahead and waste this chance by dumping her in the middle of nowhere? Are you out of your fucking mind, Wheatley?"

"Have it your way, Moon. But if this whole thing goes to shit, I'm blaming you."

Yeah, sure, pal. And if it works, you'll be first in line to take the credit, I'll bet.

The heated radio batteries were rejuvenated enough to work. Sean used the first one to call Division HQ, asking for artillery smoke to cover their withdrawal. He got to the last of the four parts in the fire mission request—*"Adjust Fire"*—when that battery ran out of juice.

The radio operator asked, "You think you need to repeat that, Sarge? They might not have gotten the last couple of words." He'd watched the transmitter's output meter sag and then drop to the bottom of its scale.

"Nah, I ain't gonna use up the other radio yet. If they can't figure out I'm gonna adjust fire by now, we might as well hang it up."

He expected it would take a minute, maybe a little

longer, for that first adjustment round to land.

Two minutes passed, and they still hadn't received the report of *Shot, over.*

"That other receiver…it is working, right?" Sean asked.

"Yeah. It's still got good juice, Sarge…until we transmit, anyway."

Thinking out loud, Sean said, "Let's hope somebody out there even has smoke shells. I seen 'em run out before."

One of his tankers was riding shotgun in the half-track carrying the wounded. Using a walkie-talkie, he broadcast, "Hey, Sarge…we're kinda sitting here with our dicks in our hands waiting for that smoke. We gonna move or what?"

What Sean and his men didn't know was that the light artillery, who usually fired the smoke from a mile or two behind the front lines, was withdrawing in accordance with Patton's belated order. The battery designated to take the fire mission was still on the road, almost four miles west of Driant. They had to stop right where they were, unhook their 105-mm howitzers from the deuce-and-a-halfs towing them, quickly lay the battery, break out their few boxes of smoke rounds, and start shooting. And while all this frantic activity was going on, the men in the battery's fire direction center had to use the map to determine, as close as humanly possible, where they were on the face of the earth, down to eight-place coordinates.

The base piece—the howitzer firing the adjustment phase of the mission—didn't get its first round off until nearly four minutes after Sean's request for fire.

When the call, *"Shot, over,"* finally spilled from the

radio, Sean acknowledged with the standard, *"Shot, out."* Then, after releasing the *push-to-talk* button on the mic, he mumbled, "About fucking time."

Fourteen seconds later, the smoke appeared, nowhere near where it was needed. Any smoke screen based around that first round would do Sean and his GIs no good at all.

"That's fucked up," Sean said, "but it ain't our fault. That gun battery don't know where the hell they're at, because we sure as hell know the coordinates for every inch of this damn fort by now."

But they didn't have a lot of time—or a lot of battery juice—to engage in a lengthy, multi-round precision adjustment. One correction would have to do.

"*Left* one-five-zero, *down* one-five-zero," he transmitted. "Shell smoke, fire for effect."

"Ooo, they ain't gonna like a shift like that," the radioman said. "Too damn big."

"Too damn bad," Sean replied. "We're the ones supposed to get what we want here."

The lone smoke round seemed to incite the Germans in and around Bunker 4. They began to pour machine gun and rifle fire down on Bunker 3 and the half-tracks.

It was a pointless effort, though, at least as long as the GIs were protected by the half-tracks and the bunker's unyielding walls.

"Hold your fire," Sean told his men. "Let 'em waste their ammo. We're gonna need ours when we make our move outta here."

The volley of smoke rounds arrived. "Well, it ain't perfect," Sean said as he watched the wind billow the smoke toward Bunker 4, "but it's *close enough for government work.*"

Grabbing the walkie-talkie, he called for the infantrymen in the tunnel to start moving. Joining forces with the lead half-track, that vehicle and the men on foot around it made a slow bee-line toward the perimeter wire. They expected German fire as they neared the fortified trench on the fort's southern boundary.

To their relief, they received none. The trench appeared empty.

Sean took a look at the smoke screen. "It's holding up pretty good," he said. "I figure we got about two minutes before it blows away. In the meantime, the Krauts can't see us for shit."

He ordered the next wave of GIs—the engineers, the men from the first floor, and the *gun-wagon* half-track—to get moving.

The Germans might not have been able to see the GIs, but they knew they were beyond that smoke *somewhere*. So they kept firing blindly.

One lucky, sweeping burst from a machine gun took down three men. They were lifted onto the bed of the gun wagon as the exodus continued.

Sean and his men on the top floor prepared to make their exit. He took one last look at the smoke screen and then told his radioman, "Tell them cannon-cockers to *repeat*...if you can."

The radioman keyed the mic, began to speak, and then stopped. There was no point in continuing. The battery was dead again. A shake of his head was all the info Sean needed.

"GET MOVING, RIGHT FUCKING NOW," Sean ordered, and fifteen men were barreling down the staircases before he'd finished the sentence.

As they neared the doorway that marked the line

between protection and vulnerability—perhaps life and death—Sean added, "Don't bunch up, you guys. Let's not give 'em a compact target."

To a man, they had never felt their grasp on life so tenuous as the moment they began that hundred yard run to the wire.

But they were making it. The bullets that whizzed past never found their mark until—just yards from the wire—Sean heard a *CLUNK* and the radioman running beside him tumbled forward to the ground as if pushed by a giant hand. Without breaking stride, Sean dragged him through the opening in the wire and behind the safety of a tree.

The radioman screamed the whole way. When he got behind the tree, he began to struggle with the harness strapping the radio to his back. "Help me, Sarge!" he wailed. "It's burning like a son of a bitch."

It was only then Sean realized the radio set on the man's back was sizzling. A bullet had pierced the radio's case and ignited its dead battery. He wasn't shot. The back of his field jacket was on fire.

Within seconds, the radio was discarded and the fire extinguished.

Sean heard a sound he'd never expected: the putter of a small engine. It took him a few seconds to realize the sound was coming from directly above them.

He looked up to see an L-4 observation plane pass slowly overhead, just above the treetops.

As the sound of the L-4's little engine faded, he could hear another sound from the sky, this one the deep rumble of multiple engines. But he couldn't see the high-flying aircraft through the clouds.

✦✦✦✦

Major Kidd—*Rocket Man*—had the feeling that something was very wrong: *There are still GIs on Driant. And we're only a couple of minutes away from this "special air ops." I've got to put this thing on hold, whatever the hell it is.*

He called the Air Liaison at 5th Division HQ and reported what he'd just seen.

The reply: "Negative. All friendlies clear. Mission is a *go*."

Orbiting the southern boundary of the fort, he could see two tanks—obviously Shermans—near Bunker 3. From his vantage point, they looked perfectly serviceable, *maybe with their crews still on board.*

But in the diminished light from a darkening sky, he couldn't tell those tanks were charred, burned-out hulks.

Both were from Sean's platoon. One of them had been his *Lucky 7*.

The Air Liaison said, "Repeat, mission is a *go*. Clear the area."

✦✦✦✦

Orbiting at 8,000 feet, Colonel Pruitt was wondering how long he'd be able to see Fort Driant through the thickening cloud deck below him.

Jimmy Tuttle, flying *Blue Two* on the opposite side of the orbit, told himself, *This is going to be an abort, any second now. I can feel it.*

They'd both heard what *Rocket Man* had reported. The possibility of accidentally incinerating GIs with napalm gave them both a sick feeling in their stomachs.

But it wasn't their call anymore. At this point, they had no choice but to execute their part of the mission.

Tommy was growing more confident by the minute that *Bucket* was actually going to work. The baby was handling like a big, compliant truck, without any unsettling quirks.

More docile than the Culver, even. Just so she stalls clean.

The television reception was flawless.

But then he'd heard *Rocket Man's* report of GIs still on Driant…

Plus Division HQ's insistence the mission was a *go*.

And that confidence suddenly felt like a mortal sin.

The ship's radio operator had crawled down to the nose and pulled Dandridge up to the cockpit, where he regained consciousness. Wanting to do something—anything—to alleviate Dandridge's suffering, he put him on oxygen. That seemed to help, but the stricken sergeant complained of a monumental headache. In a pained whisper, he described it: "It feels like someone's trying to split my head open with a wedge."

"We can't fly any higher," Lieutenant Wheatley had said as they leveled off at 5,000 feet. "I think the altitude's killing him, and it'll take less time to get him back on the ground once we're done up here."

Five thousand feet put them in the lowest deck of scattered clouds and afforded poor visibility of the ground. Tommy triggered the smoke pod beneath the baby's tail. The white line it painted across the sky in her wake helped. But not much.

The damn clouds are white, too.

"Get her below this cloud deck," Tommy told Wheatley, "or I won't be able to see the baby at all."

He really wanted the mothership—and the baby—to be higher for the attack. But that was out of the question now.

I'd better stall her right on the money, he told himself, *because as low as she's going to be, I might not have enough sky to get her on target.*

There was still the hope that the napalm would make ground visibility not much of an issue. All he'd have to do was aim for the bright light. He gave the signal for Colonel Pruitt to make his run.

They'd find out in a few moments just how bright that light would be. Pruitt's dive had begun.

"I'm lined up dead on a gun battery," Pruitt reported. "I don't know which one, though. But those three circles in a rectangle are pretty hard to miss. Releasing...NOW."

As he pulled out of the dive, Pruitt asked, "Looks like I'm right on the money. Do you want that second load, too?"

"Negative," Tommy replied. "I've got the fire in sight."

There'd be no time for Tuttle to deliver his napalm, anyway. The baby was on course, only seconds away from the start of her own dive to target. Waiting for Tuttle would mean putting her through a gradual, time-wasting full circle before having to line her up all over again.

Her final plunge had to begin now.

Tommy was suddenly so consumed with the improvised technique of diving the baby that he forgot, for a moment, *Rocket Man's* report of GIs still on Driant…

And that one of those GIs just might be his brother.

The baby was less than a mile from the fort. The camera in her nose was providing a clear view of the napalm fire.

Tommy had been slowing the baby gradually for the last few minutes. It was time to begin the stall maneuver.

Throttle back all the way…hold the elevators up. Airspeed dropping…down to 105, coming up on 100…

The baby seemed to hang in mid-air for a few seconds. Then her nose dropped suddenly, like the chop of an ax.

She'd stalled. Now it was time to guide her fall.

Pretty clean…wing drop wasn't too bad. I've got them back level already and on course. Got to get those flames up to the top of the screen…

There we go. Right where I want that target picture.

Holy cow…look at that airspeed pick up. She's one heavy bird.

Okay…little bit of down elevator to keep her from going long…

That's good.

Fifteen hundred feet and going down like a brick.

Man, she does take her sweet time responding, doesn't she?

Can't let her get ahead of me.

As she flashed through one thousand feet, the monitor showed objects on the ground, outside the napalm flames. Familiar shapes he'd seen from the air so many times before:

On, no. Are they Shermans?

Please, Sean…not you.

Then, like a movie from Hell, the flames filled the video screen. Before the next beat of Tommy's racing heart, the screen's image cut to *snow*, the thousands of dancing dots in varying shades of gray that indicated loss of signal.

The baby was down.

Tommy pulled his face from the monitor's hood to look out the plexiglass nose. There was just enough of a break in the clouds to see the fireball and the rapidly expanding shock wave spreading in all directions.

But it all looked so disappointing. Hardly the cataclysmic eruption he'd hoped for.

Even the buffeting as that shock wave reached up to the mothership several seconds later felt like little more than mild turbulence.

And then, as they turned back to A-90, the clouds—like curtains closing—concealed everything from their view.

Chapter Thirty-Two

There was no time for relaxing on the mothership. They were barreling the thirty air miles back to A-90 at low level, trying to beat the squall line moving quickly to meet them from the opposite direction. Colonel Pruitt and Jimmy Tuttle were still airborne, too, looking to beat that same storm front home. But the mothership had landing priority. She had a casualty on board: Sergeant Dandridge.

I should've made sure he didn't fly, Tommy thought. *Dammit, I even helped him. If he's got bleeding on his brain, he's in big trouble.*

If he dies, it's at least partly my fault.

And Sean...

Did I just kill my own brother, too?

No...I'm being crazy. There's got to be hundreds of Shermans in this part of France right now.

I mean, what are the odds?

But odds be damned. What if I did?

Major Kidd was thanking his lucky stars he'd been airborne at 1,000 feet and a mile south of Fort Driant when the Fortress fell. The shock waves of the ensuing explosions rocked his L-4 like a barrel in a storm-tossed sea. At one point, she was nearly inverted. No sooner had he gotten her upright, she sank rapidly, as if a giant hand was pushing her down. She was brushing the treetops before Kidd could get her climbing again.

Had she been any lower when that thing crashed, it

would've shoved her right into the ground, for sure. And she's just been through a lot more aerobatics than she's built for. Better take it real easy.

But as long as he could still fly, he was responsible for providing the BDA, and *Almighty Four-One* was giving him the *all clear* to start it. Gingerly, he turned his battered little machine back toward Driant. All the while, he asked himself, *What the hell did I just see? Did a bomber just crash? Maybe it got shot down? Or was it some kind of flying bomb?*

He started high—1,500 feet—to get a wide view and—hopefully—be a little less of an easy, slow-moving target for gunners on the ground. But near as he could tell, no one was shooting at him. In fact, the fort looked deserted, as it usually did except when you could see the tracers being hurled up at you. But there was something definitely out of order with the four main gun batteries.

To begin with, the battery that stood just south of the fort's center was nothing but a deep, smoking crater, littered with the twisted, charred, and unrecognizable remnants of what had once been an aircraft.

The other three batteries, once lined up across the center of the fort's expanse as neatly as a game of dominos, were now askew and smoldering, as if some sore loser had upset the playing table and then torched it. Their steel-domed turrets, each containing one cannon of 100 or 150-mm caliber, were smoking and displaced atop their concrete bunkers, each in its own peculiar way. Some were split open; others were tilted at odd angles, a few with their guns protruding like broken limbs.

The concrete bunkers that housed those three batteries were still standing, but each had obviously suffered catastrophic internal explosions. Kidd could plainly see giant cracks in their structure, even from high above. Large chunks of their thick concrete roofs and walls had been blown out; those chunks now littered the ground all around the batteries.

The other bunkers and the central fort's blockhouse appeared scorched, with black scars like chalk smudges on the walls above the gun ports. Flames still licked from a few of the openings.

The only structure that looked perfectly intact was the one they called the Moselle Battery, a three-turret bunker surrounded by its own barbed wire outside the fort proper's perimeter, some seventy-five yards from its southeast corner. It had always seemed like some military architect's afterthought, separated from the main fort as it was. The battery was buttoned-up, each gun pulled into a turret which was retracted into the concrete refuge of the bunker, like it always was when not actually firing. If there was anybody inside that bunker, Kidd couldn't tell.

By his second orbit of the fort, he'd seen enough. He radioed his report to 3rd Army HQ. His assessment: With the exception of the Moselle Battery, Fort Driant appeared dead.

Kidd could see the storm coming, too. He wouldn't dare try to penetrate it in his fragile craft, especially not after the beating she'd just taken. But he knew he'd never make it back to A-90, either. A small grass airstrip beside a field hospital a few miles to the southwest would be the port he'd seek to ride out this storm.

The winds were blustery and it was already raining

hard as the mothership touched down on A-90, its landing roll using up almost all of the slick pavement. Lieutenant Wheatley got her clear of the runway quickly so Colonel Pruitt and Jimmy Tuttle could land while they still had enough forward visibility to do it. The ambulance, with the flight surgeon on board, was waiting as the mothership, brakes squealing, shuddered to a stop on the taxiway.

Sergeant Dandridge was lifted off the ship on a stretcher and hurried to the ambulance. Tommy was one of the stretcher bearers. The doctor did a quick and gentle examination of Dandridge's head and eyes and then asked Tommy, "Has this man had any seizures or vomiting, Lieutenant?"

"No, sir. Just loss of consciousness and a splitting headache."

"And I'm told he received a head injury in a vehicle accident last night?"

"Yes, sir, that's correct."

The doctor shook his head in dismay as he muttered, "What the hell was this young man doing up in an airplane?" Turning to Dandridge, he said, "You're in good hands now, son. Just relax. We'll get you fixed up."

Then he motioned for Tommy to get out of the ambulance. His voice soft and fatherly, the doctor said, "I've got it from here, Half. You can check back on him later. Now scoot."

✮✮✮✮

General Patton wasted no time getting troops back on the burned-out shell of Fort Driant. Even the pouring rain was to be no deterrent, he ordered. "The Hun has been dealt a killing blow," his commanders were told. "Let's seize the advantage and move on to Metz without delay, gentlemen."

The first order of business was to neutralize Driant's Moselle Battery. A company of 5th Division infantry undertook this task, surrounding its perimeter. The company commander pondered how on earth he'd actually take this bunker without the cooperation of the Germans inside—if there really *were* any inside.

Or maybe we need another mysterious blow like the one that just leveled the main fort, he told himself.

The company first sergeant had an idea: "Why don't we just knock on that li'l ol' door, Captain?" He pointed to the formidable steel door on the back side of the bunker, large enough to roll carts full of ammunition inside.

One look at the captain's face and it was obvious he had no intention of sauntering up to the door.

The first sergeant smiled and said, "Oh, I don't mean *in person*, Captain. I was thinking maybe a three-round burst from that thirty cal over there, right off the door. I'll bet it sounds just like someone knocking real hard if you're on the other side."

That was the best idea the captain had heard lately. And definitely the safest.

As ordered, the machine gunner bounced a three-round burst off the door.

But there was no response from inside the bunker.

"Give it another try," the first sergeant told the gunner, who quickly complied.

The echo of those last three shots was still ringing as the GIs heard a muted *clank*, like a heavy metal bolt being disengaged. The door cracked open just enough for a white flag to be thrust outside.

"You don't think it's some kind of trick, do you?" the captain asked.

"Let's find out, sir." Then the first sergeant bellowed, "SOLDATEN, RAUS!"

It took a few minutes before the door creaked fully open. They came out slowly, hands up, a soldier with the white flag leading the way. There were twelve in all; a few were older men, haggard and stooped from the weight of war; the rest were terrified teenagers, some of whom looked no older than fourteen. Their ill-fitting uniforms, getting steadily soaked by the rain, made them look even more pathetic and harmless.

"These sure ain't the same bunch of lunatics we run into before in this place," the first sergeant said. "They sure don't look like no *supermen* to me."

"Just twelve men in a three-gun battery?" the captain wondered. "You'd think they'd need twice as many to keep these things firing."

"Well, sir," the first sergeant said, "I guess things are tough all over now. It ain't like the handful of replacements we been getting are the cream of the crop, neither. But let's check inside all the same."

A squad went into the bunker. Minutes later, they emerged. "All clear," the squad leader reported.

The infantrymen and engineers—two battalions' worth—who swarmed over Fort Driant had much the same to report: *All clear.* Most of the Germans they found were dead. Those in and around the gun batteries were charred to a crisp. In the tunnels, they found corpses without visible wounds: "Killed by concussion," an engineer colonel concluded.

There were some survivors, mostly in the main fort's observation posts and the outlying barracks. They were still stunned by the tremendous explosions that had struck them like mighty fists. They cowered in corners, the thought of actually fighting the Americans who were suddenly all around them the furthest thing from their minds.

There was no need for them to offer the word *kamerad.* Their eyes were unmistakably pleading surrender.

As best as the Americans could tell, there had been less than two hundred German troops manning Fort Driant. But there would never be an accurate count. Too many men had been turned to ash.

An infantry colonel was having trouble understanding the devastation all around him. "One stinking airplane did all this?" he asked.

The engineers already had a hypothesis for what had happened to Fort Driant. It didn't take much, they explained, to understand the demolition of the battery into which the airplane crashed. A hurtling aircraft full of explosives and gasoline was apparently more than enough to shatter the structure and its guns. But how did the fort's other fortified structures—some hundreds of yards away from the impact—suffer the devastation they were now recording?

The engineer colonel used diagrams of the fort—the same diagrams the GIs had used in yesterday's attack—to illustrate his conclusion on what had just happened.

"It's obvious the airplane that crashed into the fort

must have been loaded full of bombs and fuel. Our hearts go out to any crewman who might have been on board, of course. The fact that it struck the fort so perfectly, though, has to be the most incredible piece of luck that ever befell the US Army. But once it did crash and blow the bunker it hit to smithereens, initial indications are that the ammunition in the bunker—a huge supply, it seems—detonated immediately. The combined explosive forces were channeled through these underground tunnels like a high-pressure hose spewing incredibly hot gases. Even those steel doors didn't prove much of an impediment to its brute force. Those gases torched everything flammable and shattered everything breakable. Within seconds, it set off the ammunition in the other batteries, too, cooking their crewmen. The only people we're finding alive are the ones who apparently weren't underground at the time of impact."

An infantry colonel asked, "So you're saying we got pulled back at the last minute to make way for some big bombing raid, and one very unlucky crew turned it into an unbelievable break for us?"

"Do you have a better theory, Bob?" the engineer asked.

"It's just that usually when there's a big air raid coming, we can hear them miles off. A formation of heavy bombers is about as quiet as a battalion of tanks. But nobody heard a damn thing. Hell, we don't even know if that wreckage is an American plane or not. It could be British. It could be German, too."

"Regardless, it seems like someone just did us a big favor. Are you complaining, Bob?"

"Hell, no, I'm not complaining…not about getting

rid of Fort Driant, anyway. But if whatever the hell just happened here was part of some high-level secret plan, I sure as hell don't like being left in the dark about it."

Heavy rain or not, Patton was going to get to Fort Driant and savor his victory in person. His jeep pulled through the towering and wide-open iron gates of the fort's main entrance just after 1600 hours. Within minutes, he was posing for Army photographers as they snapped picture after picture of him in raincoat and steel helmet atop a shattered gun turret, their cameras beneath makeshift tarps to keep them dry.

Convening his senior commanders in the shadow of the main fort's observation tower, he said, "It's time you gentlemen found out what exactly just happened here. We've unleashed a new kind of weapon, one of amazing killing power, as you can see."

Patton went on to explain the details of *Operation Bucket* and its mother, *Operation Aphrodite*. He concluded with, "I expect you all to keep the information I've just given you under your hats, gentlemen. We just might want to use one of these new-fangled flying bombs again in the near future. It wouldn't do if some casual talk tipped off the Krauts to what we had in store. After all, they're still just big, vulnerable airplanes...and they can be knocked down very easily if you know they're coming."

At A-90, Major Staunton and his men were packing

their gear, loading what they could fit into the mothership, leaving the rest for the C-47 cargo plane that would arrive and take them all back to England once the weather cleared again. The mood that hung over the men of *Operation Bucket* was like the sad but merciful relief one feels when a long-suffering loved one has finally passed away. Tommy Moon couldn't understand all this gloom, so he asked Staunton to explain.

"It's very simple, Lieutenant," Staunton began. "Despite the fact that we're the only Aphrodite mission that's ever succeeded, it looks like we're getting the rug pulled out from under us anyway."

"Why, sir?" He could sense the major bristling at his insistence, but he didn't care. He had to know.

"Again, Lieutenant, it's simple: while we were succeeding brilliantly, two other Aphrodite missions were being attempted against U-boat pens in the North Sea. Both failed miserably to reach their targets. Shot out of the sky, crashed into the sea. I've just been told that General Spaatz is on the verge of standing down the whole project. Apparently, one success out of fourteen tries, no matter how brilliant that success, no matter how much we've learned achieving it, is not sufficient to sustain the project."

"Gee, that's too bad, sir."

"Yes, it is, Lieutenant." Then Staunton's irritation melted as he extended his hand to Tommy. "I do want to thank you, though, for the great help you've been. Sergeant Dandridge thanks you, too. He'll be fine, the doctor says. Just needs some rest...and no flying for a while. I'd like to say there'll be medals all around for what we've accomplished, but I can't guarantee anything. Once you've fallen out of favor, the rewards are slow in coming, I'm afraid."

"No problem, sir. I'm not in it for the medals."

"Nonsense, Lieutenant Moon. Everybody wants that recognition."

He didn't bother to disagree with the major. As they shook hands, Tommy was more sure than ever that those who had never been in combat could never fully understand the motivations of those who fought. You didn't fight for the brass or the medals they doled out. You fought for your buddies...

And your brother, too.

"By the way," Staunton said as Tommy was leaving, "every one Aphrodite mission counts as five on your service record. I'll see to it that you get credit for those five."

"Thanks, sir, but that doesn't matter very much around here. I can usually log five missions every couple of days. Weather permitting, of course."

Tommy drove back to his squadron's ramp and parked beside *Eclipse of the Hun II*, his P-47. Sergeant McNulty was working in her cockpit, the canopy closed to keep out the steady rain. That also caused the canopy to fog up; he didn't slide it back to have a look outside until he heard footsteps on the wing.

"Did the colonel take good care of her?" Tommy asked.

"The old man did her just fine," McNulty replied as he climbed out and quickly slid the canopy shut again. "Let's get in the vehicle and out of this damn rain."

Under the canvas roof of the jeep, McNulty asked, "You been in Operations lately, sir?"

"No. Why?"

Eyes downcast, he replied, "You just better go in

and hear it for yourself, Lieutenant."

At the operations shack, Tommy was handed a standard message form. It read:

To: Moon, Thomas P, 1LT, 301st FS, XIX TAC
Subject: Next of Kin Advisory

Moon, Sean J, T/SGT is listed as missing in action,
effective 13 October 44, 1530 hours.

Signed,
Abrams, LTC
CO, 37th Tank Bn

Chapter Thirty-Three

Colonel Pruitt knew one thing for certain: there'd be no point trying to talk Tommy Moon out of the wild goose chase he was proposing. Third Army was moving—and moving quickly—all across its front, capitalizing on the sudden removal of its prime obstacle, Fort Driant. *He has a snowball's chance in hell of even finding his brother's unit, let alone one man. It's chaos out there, no doubt, just like it always is when things start to happen really fast.*

But Tommy was dead set on finding Sean. Or at least finding out what happened to him.

If I tell him no, Pruitt thought, *he's upset enough to go AWOL.*

"I've got to know what the story is, sir," Tommy said, his voice a reflection of the torment within him. "If I had anything to do with it, I'll—"

The colonel cut him off. "Come on, Tommy...you've got to get thoughts like that out of your head once and for all. Like you said, *what are the odds?*"

"I've still got to know, sir. We won't be flying for a couple of days, anyway. Please...give me leave and let me take care of this."

Pruitt tore the leave slip he'd already signed out of the book and handed it over.

"Of course you can go, Lieutenant. I'll give you seventy-two hours. But I'll need you to check in via landline once a day. I don't want to have to declare you as MIA, too."

"And this leave doesn't start until first light tomorrow, sir?"

"Sure. That's fine with me."

Tommy stuffed the leave slip into his shirt pocket. "Thank you, sir. I really appreciate it." Then he made straight for the door.

"I'm serious, Half," Pruitt called after him. "Seventy-two hours."

Forty-eight hours later, Tommy still hadn't located the 37th Tank Battalion, much less his brother. He'd been back and forth along the roads between Nancy and Metz, sleeping rough for just a few hours, scrounging water and coffee from support units not on the move. He'd only eaten twice, more snacks than meals, both times at small cafes in villages whose names he couldn't remember.

The continuing rain had cast a slick, gray pallor over everything and everyone. Twice the jeep had become mired in roadside muck as he was forced to make way for GI convoys under instructions to stop for nothing. The first time, some cooperative civilians helped push the jeep out. The second time, he had to dig it out all by himself, using his GI blanket as a traction pad beneath the wheels. He'd never be able to use the sodden, filthy blanket to sleep in again. But that was the least of his problems.

In the late morning of his third—and final—day of leave, he blundered into a roadblock manned by 4th Armored Division MPs outside St. Nicholas, a town southeast of Nancy. "Sure, Lieutenant, we know where Thirty-Seventh Tank is," an MP corporal said after Tommy told his story. Pointing east over his shoulder, he added, "It's about ten miles that-a-way." As Tommy dropped the jeep into gear and gunned her engine, the corporal added, "But hang on a minute, sir...we can't let you pass. No unauthorized traffic allowed." As soon as he said that, a column of deuce-and-a-halfs blew past, the MPs eagerly waving them through. Each truck was loaded to the frames of its cargo tarp with supplies. On their fronts and sides were large chalk markings indicating their convoy serial number.

"If my lieutenant wasn't watching, sir, I'd let you slip on by," the MP told Tommy. "But I've been on his shit list long enough, if you know what I mean."

"That's okay, Corporal, I'll figure something out."

"I'm sure you will, Lieutenant. And I sure hope you find your brother, too."

Tommy remembered a transportation battalion marshalling yard he'd passed near Nancy. *Maybe all I've got to do is get over there and hitch a ride with one of those convoys.*

He'd worry about how to get back later.

At the marshalling yard, an old master sergeant listened to Tommy's story—and his request for a ride-along.

"I can do you one better, Lieutenant," the sergeant said. "Maybe *two* better. You don't want to lose these wheels of yours. You'll never see them again if you leave them here, I guaran-damn-tee it. So how's about I get you marked up with one of these serial numbers?" He waved a fat stick of white chalk in the air. "Then you'll be part of the convoy and them sumbitching MPs will have to let you through, no questions asked."

"Sounds good to me, Sergeant," Tommy replied. "But what did you mean by *two better*?"

"You say your name's *Moon*, sir?"

"Yeah, it is."

"Well, there's a bunch of tankers got shanghaied into driving trucks for us a couple days back. One of them's a real big tech sergeant. A New York fella just like yourself. Don't exactly recall, but his name just might've been Moon."

"Where is he right now, Sarge?"

The sergeant thumbed through the papers on his clipboard and then shook his head. "Don't rightly know, sir. But he's got to be somewhere east, between here and Dieuze. That's where we been running today."

It had been a long, tiring afternoon of driving, looking into the cab of every truck that passed in the opposite direction. At least the rain had stopped, if only for a while.

Just outside the town of Dieuze was another marshalling yard, with tenders lined up to refuel the glut of GI vehicles blanketing the roads. Deuce-and-a-halfs by the dozens were offloading supplies and troops and then tanking up for their next run.

There he was, directing trucks to the gas line like a Times Square traffic cop. Even though Sean's back was toward him, Tommy would've known his brother even without the tanker's clothing that set him apart from the rest of the fatigue-clad, olive drab GIs.

He would've known his brother in the dark.

Tommy walked up behind him and called out, "Hey, Sergeant...you look pretty good for someone who's missing in action."

Sean turned, the smile of recognition already on his face.

"What the fuck you doing here, Half? And what's this *missing in action* shit?"

He showed his brother the next of kin notification. Sean's face first registered true surprise and then real anger.

"What the fuck's wrong with these assholes?" he said, pounding his fist on a truck's fender. "Some fucking major gathered up us guys who came off Driant and put us to work with these truckers temporary-like, until our units could pick us up. And they were supposed to notify our units we were upright and breathing, too. Stupid sons of bitches."

He balled up the notification and threw it on the ground. "*Ol' Abe*—I mean Colonel Abrams—he didn't sign that, neither. He'd know better and wait a bit. That was his shithead of an adjutant who did it, I'm sure. Or some knucklehead admin sergeant."

Then he straightened up like he'd just gotten an electric shock. "Dammit! They didn't send one of these things to Mom, too, did they? I'll fucking kill 'em..."

A clog of trucks were trying to jockey past each other to be next at the gas nozzle. None of them were winning, just blowing their shrill horns in frustration, causing a traffic jam while the nozzle sat idle and precious time was wasted.

"Hang on, Half," Sean said as he stormed off to straighten out the mess. "Meet me over at the ready shack in a couple of minutes."

As Tommy started walking that way, he could hear Sean bellowing, "NEXT ONE OF YOU NUMBNUTZES WHO LEANS ON HIS FUCKING HORN'S GONNA NEED IT SURGICALLY REMOVED FROM HIS ASS."

★★★★

"So you were at Fort Driant?" Tommy asked as they settled onto stools with cups of coffee. "When?"

"Two days and a night, right up to when that fucking B-17 fell on it and blew it to shit. We just barely got our asses out of there in time."

Tommy fell silent for a few moments, trying to figure out the right way to break his news. Finally, he decided to say it this way:

"I did that, you know." It wasn't meant to sound apologetic, but somehow it did.

Confused, Sean replied, "Did what? You didn't shoot it down or nothing, did you?"

"No, no. I was...I was the pilot. Well, not exactly. I was the remote controller."

"Wait a minute," his brother said, looking very skeptical. "What do you mean, *remote controller*? Is this all part of that *big thing* you volunteered for, you idiot?"

Tommy explained the whole business of *Operation Bucket*. When he was done, Sean asked, "So when're you gonna do it again? That was the greatest thing since sliced bread. Just give us a little more warning next time."

"Don't think there'll be a next time, Sean. Looks like the Air Force pulled the plug on the whole deal."

Sean leaned back, shaking his head. "Ain't that

always the damn way?"

"So what're you going to do now?" Tommy asked.

"They'll come get us in a day or two, as soon as there're some replacement tanks to go fetch. I sure as hell hope the next batch has that seventy-six millimeter gun. Getting real tired of watching my rounds bounce off stuff. What about you?"

"Back to the jugs," Tommy replied. "I've got an idea, though. See if you can get leave around Christmas. You must have enough time coming to you. I know I do, even after I just burned these three days looking for you. Maybe we can get together in Paris. Or maybe Berlin."

Sean looked at him like he was out of his mind. "We ain't gonna be in no Berlin by Christmas, Half. No fucking way." Then he smiled, adding, "But Paris sounds good. I'd like that. I'd like that a lot. Maybe you can bring along them French girls, too?"

Chapter Thirty-Four

November 1944 was brutally cold, and they were told the worst of the winter weather was yet to come. Between the freezing rain, sleet, and abundant snowfall, good flying days had been few and far between. The relentless chill had brought progress on the ground to a halt, as well. The Allied armies were knocking on the German West Wall all along the front, from southern Holland to the Swiss border. But there were still many swift and wide rivers, snow-glazed mountains, and bewildering forests to cross before they would reach Berlin. Perhaps too many.

It was on a rare sunny day that a note was waiting for Tommy Moon when he returned from the day's mission. It said simply:

Back in Toul for a few days. Meet me tonight, if you can. Same place.
S.

He laughed as he rolled her words *if you can* over in his head.

I'm pretty damn sure I'll find a way.

It seemed almost as cold on the evening streets of Toul as the cockpit of his jug at altitude. His flying boots crunching on the snow-packed sidewalk, Tommy made his way to the front door of the boarding house. He was surprised when Sylvie greeted him with her coat buttoned up and snow boots on.

"Let's go eat first," she said, "I'm famished."

She waited a moment for his dismay to peak. Then she threw the coat open to reveal she was wearing absolutely nothing underneath.

"Only kidding," she said, and then pulled him to the bed.

The lovemaking was quick but wonderful, leaving weeks of loneliness and apprehension shattered in its wake.

Later, as they settled down to supper at a café just a short walk from the boarding house, Tommy asked, "How long are you going to be in Toul?"

"A few days." Then she smiled wickedly and added, "Just long enough for you to get tired of me."

"Not likely, *mademoiselle*."

He saw the frown come over her face.

"So it's still *madame*?" he asked.

She nodded sadly. "Annulment takes time, Tommy. So much time."

They fell quiet as the waiter brought ersatz coffee and sweets. When they were ready for their second cup, she asked, "So where have you been flying?"

"Actually, we've been flying pretty deep into southern Germany. Practically to Czechoslovakia. Nobody in the squadron—or Third Army—is very happy about that, either."

"Why? Are the *Boche* resisting strongly there?"

"Yeah, but that's not the reason. We want to be going more northeast—toward Berlin. We've got orders not to bomb those Kraut airfields in southern Germany, just strafe them. I guess they figure we're going to be moving in there real soon, and they want them in as good a shape as possible for immediate use."

"I don't understand," she replied. "Is that a bad thing?"

"It's bad because we always thought the Allies coming up through Italy would take care of southern Germany, plus Austria and Czechoslovakia, too. Now it looks like Third Army and Nineteenth TAC—in other words, *us*—are going to be the ones to do it. That means the prize of Berlin goes to someone else."

Sylvie stifled a laugh. "I didn't realize the Allied armies were in a competition. I thought you just wanted to finish the job as quickly as possible and then go home. But you're wrong about Italy. The Allied armies there now will never be able to come north and assist you."

"What makes you say that, Syl?"

"The Alps, Tommy. The Allies will never dislodge the *Boche* from those mountains. Trapping them— cutting them off from Germany—is your only hope."

Looking skeptical, Tommy said, "And how do you know so much about what's going on in Italy?"

"I was there for a while, Tommy."

"Weren't you in the south of France all this time?"

"I was for most of it. But I'm a courier. There were dispatches to be carried. I was available, so…"

"But Italy, Syl? What business does the Underground have there?"

"We're not the Underground anymore, Tommy. We're very much *above* ground now."

"But there aren't even any French forces in Italy," he said.

She gave him that smile she saved for when she had secrets. "Oh, really? How would you know, Tommy?"

"Okay, you've got me on that one. I surrender."

She took no joy in her small victory because there was more to tell him.

"I learned something in Italy," she said. "Something I find very frightening. You may find yourself face to face with it very soon."

"Really? What's that, Syl?"

"I was introduced to several Yugoslav partisans who were negotiating for arms from the British. They tell some incredible stories."

"You mean a Yugoslav resistance, like your *Underground*?"

"Exactly. They've been fighting the Germans for almost as long as we here in France have, you know. But now they find themselves with a new enemy, one that calls itself a liberator, yet it murders, rapes, and loots those it liberates with a savagery that makes the *Boche* look almost civilized."

"Who the hell are you talking about, Syl? What kind of *liberator* does stuff like that?"

A world-weary look came over her face, one that made her look so much older than her twenty-two years.

Then, in a whisper, she answered his question:

"The Russians, Tommy. Our allies, the Russians."

* * *

More Novels by William Peter Grasso

Moon Above, Moon Below
Moon Brothers WWII Adventure Series

France, August 1944. In this alternate history WW2 adventure, American and British forces struggle to trap and destroy the still-potent German armies defending Normandy. But the Allies face another formidable obstacle of their own making: a seething rivalry between generals leads to a high-level disregard for orders that puts the entire campaign in the Falaise Pocket at risk of devastating failure—or spectacular success. That campaign unfolds through the eyes of two American brothers—one an idealistic pilot, the other a fatalistic tanker—as they plunge headlong into the confusion and indiscriminant slaughter of war.

Operation Fishwrapper
Jock Miles WW2 Adventure Series
Book 5

June 1944: A recon flight is shot down over the
Japanese-held island of Biak, soon to be the next jump in
MacArthur's leapfrogging across New Guinea. Major
Jock Miles, US Army—the crashed plane's intelligence
officer—must lead the handful of survivors to safety. It's
a tall order for a man barely recovered from a near-
crippling leg wound. Gaining the grudging help of a
Dutch planter who has evaded the Japanese since the
war began, Jock discovers just how little MacArthur's
staff knows about the terrain and defenses of the island
they're about to invade.

The American invasion of Biak promptly bogs down,
and the GIs rename the debacle *Operation Fishwrapper*,
a joking reference to their worthless maps. The infantry
battalion Jock once led quickly suffers the back-to-back
deaths of two commanders, so he steps into the job once
again, ignoring the growing difficulties with his leg.

When his Aussie wife Jillian tracks down the refugee mapmaker who can refine those *fishwrappers* into something of military value, the tide of battle finally turns in favor of the Americans. But for Jock, the victory imparts a life-changing blow.

Operation Blind Spot
Jock Miles WW2 Adventure Series
Book 4

After surviving a deadly plane crash, Jock Miles is handed a new mission: neutralize a mountaintop observation post on Japanese-held Manus Island so MacArthur's invasion fleet en route to Hollandia, New Guinea, can arrive undetected. Jock's team seizes and holds the observation post with the help of a clever deception. But when they learn of a POW camp deep in the island's treacherous jungle, it opens old wounds for Jock and his men: the disappearance—and presumed death—of Jillian Forbes at Buna a year before. There's only one risky way to find out if she's a prisoner there…and doing so puts their entire mission in serious jeopardy.

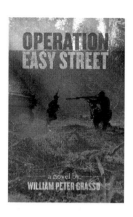

Operation Easy Street
Jock Miles WW2 Adventure Series
Book 3

Port Moresby was bad. Buna was worse.

The WW2 alternative history adventure of Jock Miles
continues as MacArthur orders American and Australian
forces to seize Buna in Papua New Guinea. Once again,
the Allied high command underestimates the Japanese
defenders, plunging Jock and his men into a battle
they're not equipped to win. Worse, jungle diseases,
treacherous terrain, and the tactical fantasies of deluded
generals become adversaries every bit as deadly as the
Japanese. Sick, exhausted, and outgunned, Jock's
battalion is ordered to spearhead an amphibious assault
against the well-entrenched enemy. It's a suicide
mission—but with ingenious help from an unexpected
source, there might be a way to avoid the certain
slaughter and take Buna. For Jock, though, victory
comes at a dreadful price.

Operation Long Jump
Jock Miles WW2 Adventure Series
Book 2

Alternative history takes center stage as Operation Long Jump, the second book in the Jock Miles World War 2 adventure series, plunges us into the horrors of combat in the rainforests of Papua New Guinea. As a prelude to the Allied invasion, Jock Miles and his men seize the Japanese observation post on the mountain overlooking Port Moresby. The main invasion that follows quickly degenerates to a bloody stalemate, as the inexperienced, demoralized, and poorly led GIs struggle against the stubborn enemy.

Seeking a way to crack the impenetrable Japanese defenses, infantry officer Jock finds himself in a new role—aerial observer. He's teamed with rookie pilot John Worth, in a prequel to his role as hero of Grasso's East Wind Returns. Together, they struggle to expose the Japanese defenses—while highly exposed themselves—in their slow and vulnerable spotter plane.

The enemy is not the only thing troubling Jock: his Australian lover, Jillian Forbes, has found a new and dangerous way to contribute to the war effort.

Long Walk to the Sun
Jock Miles WW2 Adventure Series
Book 1

In this alternate history adventure set in WW2's early
days, a crippled US military struggles to defend
vulnerable Australia against the unstoppable Japanese
forces. When a Japanese regiment lands on Australia's
desolate and undefended Cape York Peninsula, Jock
Miles, a US Army captain disgraced despite heroic
actions at Pearl Harbor, is ordered to locate the enemy's
elusive command post.

Conceived in politics rather than sound tactics, the futile
mission is a "show of faith" by the American war
leaders meant to do little more than bolster their flagging
Australian ally. For Jock Miles and the men of his patrol,
it's a death sentence: their enemy is superior in men,
material, firepower, and combat experience. Even if the
Japanese don't kill them, the vast distances they must
cover on foot in the treacherous natural realm of Cape
York just might. When Jock joins forces with Jillian

Forbes, an indomitable woman with her own checkered past who refused to evacuate in the face of the Japanese threat, the dim prospects of the Allied war effort begin to brighten in surprising ways.

Unpunished

Congressman. Presidential candidate. Murderer. Leonard
Pilcher is all of these things.

As an American pilot interned in Sweden during WWII,
he kills one of his own crewmen and gets away with it.
Two people have witnessed the murder—American
airman Joe Gelardi and his secret Swedish lover, Pola
Nilsson-MacLeish—but they cannot speak out without
paying a devastating price. Tormented by their guilt and
separated by a vast ocean after the war, Joe and Pola
maintain the silence that haunts them both...until 1960,
when Congressman Pilcher's campaign for his party's
nomination for president gains momentum. As he dons
the guise of war hero, one female reporter, anxious to
break into the "boy's club" of TV news, fights to
uncover the truth against the far-reaching power of the
Pilcher family's wealth, power that can do any wrong it
chooses—even kill—and remain unpunished. Just as the
nomination seems within Pilcher's grasp, Pola reappears
to enlist Joe's help in finally exposing Pilcher for the
criminal he really is. As the passion of their wartime

romance rekindles, they must struggle to bring Pilcher down before becoming his next victims.

East Wind Returns

A young but veteran photo recon pilot in WWII finds the fate of the greatest invasion in history--and the life of the nurse he loves--resting perilously on his shoulders.

"East Wind Returns" is a story of World War II set in July-November 1945 which explores a very different road to that conflict's historic conclusion. The American war leaders grapple with a crippling setback: Their secret atomic bomb does not work. The invasion of Japan seems the only option to bring the war to a close. When those leaders suppress intelligence of a Japanese atomic weapon poised against the invasion forces, it falls to photo reconnaissance pilot John Worth to find the Japanese device. Political intrigue is mixed with passionate romance and exciting aerial action--the terror of enemy fighters, anti-aircraft fire, mechanical malfunctions, deadly weather, and the Kamikaze. When shot down by friendly fire over southern Japan during the American invasion, Worth leads the desperate mission that seeks to deactivate the device.

Printed in Great Britain
by Amazon

78945520R00233